*Malinda stared at him, stunned,
shocked back to herself by his words.*

೦ᄍᄍᄵ

This wasn't supposed to happen—he couldn't be sending her away. She had offered herself to him; she had conquered him—he was hers. He wouldn't dare. "No," she said, grabbing his hair in her fist to pull his mouth back down to hers.

He kissed her sweetly, but only for a moment, then caught her wrist in a grip of iron. "Yes," he said, his expression as empty as his tone. "Let me go—"

"Let me go!" she cried, scrambling back, her eyes on fire with rage, as wild as the burning he felt. "You bastard!"

"Malinda, stop it." She had moved off the bed, out of his reach, and he made himself be still. "You'll wake your parents—"

"And why shouldn't I?" she demanded. He had let her think she was taming him, but it was all a lie, a trap, a way to get back at her for frightening him, to put her down again. "What do you want?" she all but screamed, senseless with frustrated fury.

"You kissed me, remember?" he said, his face a mask again, a mask she wanted to rip to bloody shreds. She couldn't answer; nothing would save her now, restore her pride. He was right: she had kissed him, not once but twice. She must be losing her mind. He must be some sort of enchanter, a better magician than she could ever hope to be. . . .

Also by Jayel Wylie

A Falcon's Heart

Available From Pocket Books

THIS
DANGEROUS
MAGIC

JAYEL
WYLIE

SONNET BOOKS

New York   London   Toronto   Sydney   Singapore

This book is a work of fiction. Names, characters, places and
incidents are products of the author's imagination or are used
fictitiously. Any resemblance to actual events or locales or
persons, living or dead, is entirely coincidental.

An *Original* Publication of POCKET BOOKS

 A Sonnet Book published by
POCKET BOOKS, a division of Simon & Schuster, Inc.
1230 Avenue of the Americas, New York, NY 10020

ISBN: 0-7434-1840-9

First Sonnet Books printing September 2002

10 9 8 7 6 5 4 3 2 1

SONNET BOOKS and colophon are trademarks of
Simon & Schuster, Inc.

For information regarding special discounts for bulk purchases,
please contact Simon & Schuster Special Sales at 1-800-456-6798
or business @simonandschuster.com

Front cover illustration by Brian Bailey

Printed in the U.S.A.

Acknowledgments

೧ාක්ම

Many and eternal thanks to my editor, Lauren McKenna, who has played the most amazing of faery godmothers to this story since the moment of its conception with her insight, creativity, and patience, and to my agent, Timothy Seldes, whose kind support and brilliant judgment are gifts I will always cherish and pray I will never lose. Kudos and kisses and credit untold to my first (and second and third) draft readers, Mama, Sarah, Rachel, Petey, and Isabel, all of whom I adore and drive insane in equal measure. Thanks as ever to Marcia Addison, M.L.I.S., for her excellent research into everything I've ever asked.

Genealogy Chart

(broken line denotes nonmarital relation and/or illegitimacy)

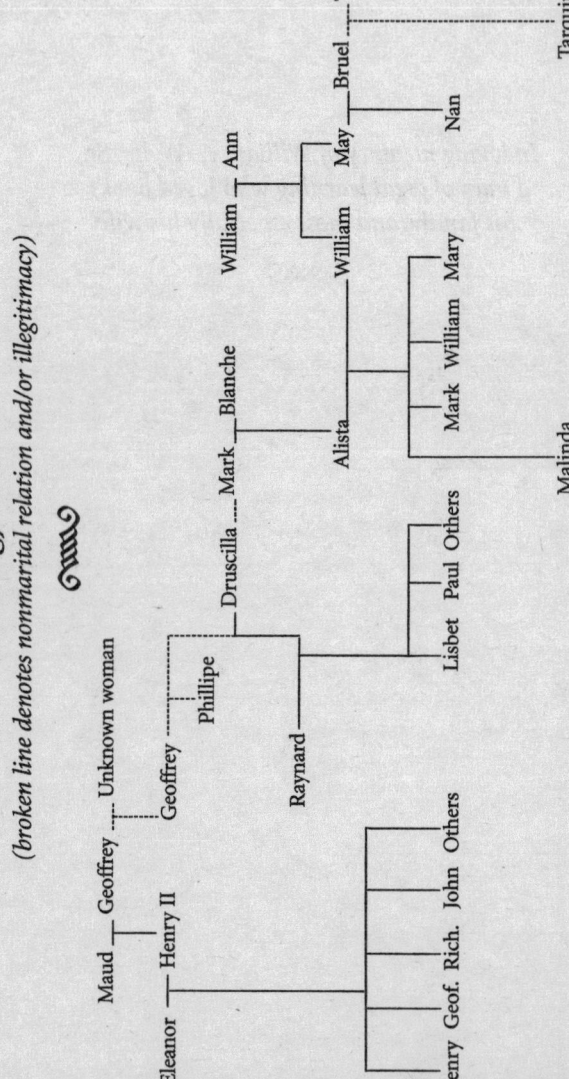

Prologue

Falconskeep Castle
1138

Blanche climbed the stairs of her tower, her blond hair torn free of its braids by the wind as she emerged at the top. A falcon waited on a splintered perch, fixing her with golden eyes as she approached. "Is he found, my friend?" she asked lightly, shivering with hope and the chill in the wind. This messenger was the last of a dozen sent out over the past week, and all the others had failed . . . "Did you find my love?"

The bird of prey allowed her to untie the tiny scroll from its leg, barely shifting away from her touch, but as soon as she began to unroll the message, her heart sank, knowing what she would find. *Dearest husband, when will you come home?* was written there in her own script, her own words returned untouched. A single sob escaped her as she let the paper fall, and the falcon shrieked once as if in sympathy before taking flight again.

"Never mind," she said, steeling herself against tears that wouldn't help. "I have other ways."

As if in answer, a child's laugh swept up to her from the courtyard far below, and she smiled, looking down. Alista was playing with the Italian priest, Brother Paolo, and leading him a merry chase from what her mother could see—blind man's bluff, perhaps? The young man had been in residence at Falconskeep for most of the little girl's life, and she adored him with good reason. He was gentle as a maid, but he was strong, too, in heart as much as body. He would gladly die to protect Alista and her mother as well, and Blanche cherished him for his love. But he wasn't Mark. He was not her husband; he was not her love. Mark was far from Falconskeep, fighting for his king, and had been these three years past. Alista had been barely toddling when he had gone; she didn't remember her father's face. But Blanche remembered . . . his face . . . his arms . . . his kiss. The tears she despised slipped down her cheeks, stinging her skin as the wind swept them away. She couldn't reach him, not even her falcons could find him, not for many months past. And something was coming, some disaster. She could feel it in the wind.

Watching Alista run, a tiny creature on the ground, she made her decision. Hurrying down the stairs, her feet flying faster and faster, she knew what she must do. Without pausing to speak to anyone, she left the castle and ran down the stairs that led to the beach and then on to the cliffs beyond.

Picking her way carefully among the slippery rocks, she found the crevice she sought, a tiny crack that an unschooled eye would never notice. Glancing back to make sure she wasn't watched, she slipped quickly inside, the walls closing in before opening out into a passage that dropped off steeply ahead, plunging her almost immediately into darkness. She hadn't visited these caverns since before Alista was born, but she found her way easily in the dark, the cool currents of air like the breath of the spirit she sought. She stopped for a moment and closed her eyes, one hand on the glass-sleek wall. She had to be calm. Such magic as she intended was dangerous even in peaceful meditation; in a panic it would almost surely be fatal. She must forget her fears, forget everything but the will to know; only then could she succeed. Taking another deep breath, she opened her eyes, and the darkness seemed to melt into a tender light her faery eyes could see, lighting her way ahead. Her hand went unconsciously to the pendant she wore, a heart-shaped stone that glowed in her palm with this same warmth and light. The heart had been carved from the rock of these caverns, a gift from the spirit of water and earth that made her refuge here, the spirit Blanche of Falconskeep now sought. Perhaps the heartstone would keep her safe if her own powers could not.

The passage opened suddenly into a chamber of silver-gray rock, the light brighter now, dancing pale from a thousand bumps and impressions in the walls worn smooth and bright as gems. The source of the light was here, glowing up from a pool that lapped the edges of the chamber and fell off at its center into impossible depths no human or faery had ever explored. "*Sister*," a woman's voice sighed in the faery tongue as Blanche approached the pool, and the surface of the water rose and shuddered as if in pleasure.

"Sister," Blanche replied, feeling a dangerous content-ment of her own surge through her as she knelt at the water's edge. Written in faery script around the pool was the truth of her falcon race, the tale of how the queen of the wind had taken human form as a gift from this spirit and founded Falconskeep. Other words were carved into the walls in all the languages her foremothers had spoken, a living record of enchantment. Blanche had spent many hours before she was married transcribing these words into a book to keep them close at hand, a book she still cherished more than any object other than the heartstone, but she had barely begun to read all that was here to be learned. No doubt the very charm she now sought was here somewhere, if she'd only had time to find it. But she knew her time had run out.

"Sister, I need your help," she said, dipping her hands into the icy water. "I need your magic."

"*What power is left that you do not already possess?*" the spirit laughed at her, and she felt a phantom hand brush past her own, mimicking human touch.

"The power to see far," Blanche answered. "I need you to show me my love."

Another swell rose on the surface, but the voice turned cold. "*You know his face.*" The spirit hated Mark as she hated all men, knowing him as the force that had driven her underground so many centuries ago. "*You have his child.*"

"He is far away, and I fear for him," Blanche pressed, her heart beginning to race with desperation, her illusory calm dissolved. "Show him to me; let me see he is safe. Show me when he will return—"

"*I cannot,*" the spirit interrupted, almost angry now. "*My eyes are not like yours.*"

"Then take my eyes," Blanche insisted, the water now rising to her waist as she stood. "Help me; make me see."

The surface of the water boiled, but the voice was silent. This was the magic she had promised her own mother she would never attempt, the game that brought death to the foolish and vain, the sorceress greedy for power. The spirit was a creature of eternity, trapped forever in her waters and rocks while the world above moved on. A human woman saw the ways of the world, understood the passage of time, but her body was trapped in her place, her reality. The Falconskeep sorceress was human and faery in one, a faery spirit in a fragile human shell. With the spirit's greater magic, she could see through time and space, far beyond her human eyes. She could join her soul to the more ancient power, see past the constricts of her narrow mortal life, but her mortal body could not contain such power for long. It could tear her brain apart and drive her mad; it could rupture her heart in her breast. Blanche knew these things, knew the terrible peril of what she asked. But fear and love would not let her turn away.

"Please," she almost whispered. "I cannot live unless I know he will return." The light in the pool had shrunk and sunk until it was no more than a glowing orb in the bottomless depths, distant as the moon above. The spirit loved the sorceress, had loved the faery women who had come before her and lost them to their greed in just this way. She would not willingly risk such a tragedy again. "Please," Blanche repeated, kneeling deeper to let her tears fall into the water. "Only this one thing, and I will let you go." The glow began to expand again, to rise through the water toward her. "One question," she promised as her fingers touched the light. "Show me when Mark will come home."

The icy cold of the water seemed to flow into her blood, flow through her until she could no longer feel where her body ended and the water began. She opened her eyes and saw the gates of Falconskeep Castle, the portcullis rising, an army on the road. Mark was coming through the gates—this was the future, and he was alive. But no one came to meet him. He strode through the courtyard alone, his face distorted with rage or grief. Where was she? Why did she not come out to greet him? Why was her castle deserted?

"No," she said, her voice now the voice of the spirit. "Show me myself . . . What brings such pain to my house?"

The vision changed, not Falconskeep any more but a tiny inner chamber, richly appointed, but hot—the fire was too hot. A woman she didn't recognize was standing near—a queen; her crown was set on a table at her side, and on another table lay Blanche's book, the book of Falconskeep magic. Blanche seemed to be with her; she felt furious and afraid, but she was separate, too, as if she were two women at once. She wanted to take her book, but she couldn't move; someone or something held her fast. She could see a mirror across the room, a long fall of golden hair in its reflection, a woman's angry face wavering in the light of torches held by men all around her and the light of the fire in the hearth. Was she this woman? She struggled in the grip of the men who held her, and the reflection moved as well—then suddenly the book was falling into the flames, flung there by this strange queen. "No!" Blanche screamed, and the reflection shattered as the flames leapt up, and she was falling, falling back through her vision, back into herself, back into the present.

She kept falling back into the water as the spirit left her, her head sinking below the surface. She was so tired, and she had learned nothing. Sinking deeper, she could feel the water swirling around her, the spirit's touch, loving-frantic, as she tried to lift her to the surface. *"Alista,"* she said, drawing the name from the future and Blanche's own mind, reminding her of her child.

Blanche made herself swim, made her aching limbs start to move. The pool had swollen as she had forced the spirit to her will until now it nearly filled the chamber and there was nowhere left to stand. The despair of her vision dragged on her heart as the current dragged her down again, making her want to surrender, but she couldn't. She had to save Alista; she had to save her magic. The vision could not come true. Opening her eyes, she saw the spirit's glow pointing her to a tiny door set into the rock, a door she knew led to a well—a well that opened inside her own castle. She made herself swim toward it, her lungs bursting, screaming for air. By the time she reached it, her fingers were numb and she couldn't think, couldn't work out the logic of the latch. She had to risk losing the door again to kick to the surface, and all the while her limbs felt heavier and heavier, her mind more addled with exhaustion and pain. Breathing in a few quick gasps, she dove again, trusting her instinct more than sight to take her back to the door. This time she opened it easily, and the current rushed through, dragging her through the opening barely wider than her shoulders.

The water was low in the well, and she was nearly washed down the shaft in the rush and lost for good and all. But somehow she caught hold of the lever that opened the door from inside the well, and though her weight twisted it back against the wall, somehow it held. She leaned her head back from the rushing water, breathing in more sweet air, trying to find the strength to pull herself up. Finally she could move, and her fingers found a crevice in the rock, and another, and another. Using the last of her failing strength, she pulled herself over the side, collapsing on the floor of a room beneath her tower.

The next thing she knew was a voice. "My lady!" Gwyneth, Alista's faery nursemaid, was running toward her down the stairs. She tried to answer her, but no words would come, and when she tried to raise her head, her body refused to obey. "Never mind," Gwyneth was saying as she wrapped a cloak around her, but Blanche could hear the faery woman was near tears. "You will be fine."

"No," Blanche whispered, so softly she doubted Gwyneth could hear. "No, I will not."

1

❦

Montferrand, France
Christmas, 1172

To all appearances, the Christmas court of King Henry II was another triumph of his glorious, twenty-some-odd-year reign. At his side remained his queen, Eleanor of Aquitaine, Christendom's great beauty still, and ranged around them were their children, a brood to make the angels weep in envy. The oldest and heir to the throne was Henry, already crowned "the Young King" these two years past and married somewhat longer to Margaret, daughter of the King of France. The next two sons were betrothed to princesses of their own and already made dukes: Richard of Aquitaine and Geoffrey of Brittany, at least for the moment—Henry had a jovial habit of switching his land-gifts around when it suited his fancy. The youngest royal, John, was rather famously ill-tempered and held no lands at all, but he was only four years old, so 'twas assumed he would mend on both counts. Even the daughters, Matilda and Eleanor, seemed perfect, having inherited a great deal of their mother's famous beauty and very little of her infamous wit.

All in all, the family made a magnificent picture for the nobles gathered in this hall to admire them as they feasted.

If the Queen was known to despise her husband as much as she adored him these days, 'twas no great matter—they'd been married more than twenty years, after all, and Henry's roving eye remained a great portion of his charm. And if the princes were known to all bear certain grudges against their king and one another, that was to be expected as well—they were barely more than children; their father would keep them in line. Henry had kept peace in his reign longer than any English king before him by sheer force of his great will. Surely he could control his own family. So the nobles assured themselves that Christmas night as they toasted their God and their king.

Malinda Brinlaw harbored no doubts at all; to her, the night was perfect. Sitting with her parents and cousin, Nan, at a table at the foot of the dais, she felt perfectly at ease, perfectly at home, and she drank in every detail, the royal glamour entirely untarnished to her eyes. The King was splendid and mildly terrifying, just as a king ought to be; the princes and princesses were too beautiful to be real. And Queen Eleanor was her idol, perfect in every way. Malinda knew every romantic detail of her astounding history, how she had once been queen of France, how she had come to marry Henry when he was no more than a duke's young son and had come to see him crowned king of England, how she ruled her own court of love and chivalry and changed the face of the world at her whim. To Malinda, Eleanor had achieved all that a woman could hope, and she fervently longed to know her. She adored her for her pride, her beauty, even her famous temper. Her fondest wish was to become a lady-in-waiting, to dwell in her shadow, to breathe the rarefied air of her fanciful court. Unfortunately, her parents did not share her hero worship; indeed, her father made no secret that he considered the Queen something of a twit. As one of Henry's favorite nobles, Will Brinlaw could have seen his daughter well placed in the royal orbit long ago, and Nan, his niece, as well, but such honors did not impress him, and his wife, Alista, concurred. But Malinda was determined. She had never in her life been denied anything for long; she didn't expect to be now.

"Aren't they beautiful?" her best friend, Lisbet, whispered in her ear, returning from a dance to sit beside her. "Which one will you have, Malinda?"

"Which what?" she laughed, turning to her friend.

"When you marry," Lisbet laughed with her. "Now that you're finally at court, it's time to decide which of the princes you will choose."

"Henry is already married," Malinda pointed out, taking a sweet from the tray piled high before them, "and Richard and Geoffrey are both betrothed to girls with crowns." She took a bite and savored the way it melted on her tongue, finer than anything she'd ever tasted at home.

"Figs and apples for their crowns," Lisbet scoffed, taking the rest and popping it into her mouth. "You have more beauty in one of your toes than the both of them taken together, and you can do magic besides." She licked her fingers with kittenish satisfaction. "You can pick whichever one you please, and the poor boy will be undone."

Malinda smiled, embarrassed, but pleased nonetheless. "We aren't supposed to mention magic, remember?" she scolded softly, giving Lisbet a poke that made her snicker. She looked back at the dais, pretending to peruse its wares. "Too bad Henry is the oldest and the prettiest besides," she sighed. "Richard is almost as nice, but he seems too serious—he hardly ever smiles."

"Perhaps he's shy," Lisbet offered.

"Perhaps, but still . . . he may just be ill-tempered." She tapped her chin in thought. "And Geoffrey is really too young—"

"Not for a prince, he isn't," Lisbet grinned. "Bewitch him now, and you can bend him to whatever shape you like."

"There is that," Malinda laughed, enjoying the sheer silliness of the game. "No, I can't choose," she sighed. "You pick yours, and I'll take whatever's left."

"An admirable plan," Nan teased. "Just don't tell my uncle."

"No, don't," Will Brinlaw retorted, catching only the end of the conversation. "Whatever it is, I'd rather not know."

"Be careful," warned Malinda's mother, who had heard all. "Your words may haunt you later." Lady Alista was as well-known for her candor as her beauty, and she rarely spared her husband, dearly as she loved him still. "Soon we'll all be keeping secrets from you."

"And how will that be new?" he grumbled.

"Nan has trusted you with all her heart," Alista pointed out, casually taking a sweet of her own. "She came to you in all good faith—"

"Not this again," Will cut her off in mid-sentence. "Not tonight."

"If not tonight, then when?" Nan demanded. "I'm growing older by the second."

"I'd hardly call you a crone just yet," her uncle answered with the faintest trace of a smile.

"You might not and neither would I, but what of the rest of the world?" Alista chided gently. "Twenty-four is well past the age when most women marry, love."

"And Guy de Lancey is even older," Lisbet offered helpfully from her seat beside Malinda. "Keep putting him off, and he might find someone else."

"No, he could not, so if that's what you're waiting for, Uncle, you may as well stop," Nan said, her cheeks beginning to flush, angry not at Lisbet but Will. "Guy loves me; he could never be married to anyone else, no matter what you may believe, and I love him."

"But why, in heaven's name?" Will asked. "I have no doubt de Lancey will wait for you until time ends given the slightest encouragement, but why would you want him? The man is as dull as a plank."

"Not really," Nan insisted. "He's shy, but not with me."

"Besides, sweet, when I met you, you were rather dull yourself," Alista pointed out without the slightest hint of a smile to betray she was teasing. "And you turned out all right." Malinda giggled into her napkin—the war was already won.

"Be that as it may," Will said dryly, his expression saying he knew he was beaten as well.

"Mama, look there," Malinda interrupted, her attention taken by a pair of knights coming across the hall as quickly as courtesy would allow. "It's Mark!"

"And Phillipe!" Lisbet added, jumping up.

"Finally," Alista said, getting up herself.

Malinda's younger brother, Mark, and Lisbet's older half-brother, Phillipe, had been knighted the summer before after three years of service as squires, and they had served in the King's personal guard ever since. All told, they hadn't been home in forever, and everyone was most eager to see them, particularly their sisters, but they had been in a hunting party when the family arrived the day before. Now apparently they were back at last. "Merry Christmas," Phillipe said, sweeping Lisbet up in a hug.

"To you, too," Lisbet laughed as he swung her around. "We've missed you so much."

"Both of you," Malinda agreed as Mark embraced their father and kissed their mother's cheek. "Just look at you, monster—you're huge!"

"Only compared to you," Mark teased, kissing her as well.

In truth, he hadn't just grown since they'd seen him last summer; he was transformed. Phillipe seemed mostly unchanged—a bit thinner, perhaps, but as handsome as ever, a golden-haired idol. But Mark looked like a different person—specifically, a younger version of his father. The gawky crane of a boy was gone, replaced by the perfect picture of a knight-at-arms, from noble brow to battered armor. "Look at him, Papa," Malinda said. "He's nearly as tall as you."

"And thin as a twig," Alista added. "And Phillipe as well—you could snap in a breeze, both of you. Don't they feed you at all?"

"Nothing like at home," Mark admitted, hugging her again.

"You are too thin," she insisted as he drew back.

"'Tis all the exercise he gets chasing wenches," Phillipe laughed. "Runs the fat right off him."

"And what is your excuse?" Mark retorted with a blush that made him look more his old self.

"I lose mine running from them," Phillipe replied without hesitation.

"I believe it," Lisbet chided him.

"Oh, I do not," Alista said with a mischievous gleam. "All we've heard since we arrived is what models of decorum you two have become. Would you prove your friends untruthful?"

"Not for our lives, Mama," Mark promised.

"We've just lost our heads at seeing you all again," Phillipe agreed, putting an arm around Lisbet's shoulders and kissing the top of her head.

Malinda, meanwhile, had been watching her father and Nan. Will had continued to speak to her softly, and Nan had been listening with barely concealed impatience, obviously ready to protest. But suddenly she let out a shriek and threw her arms around her uncle's neck. "Thank you!" she repeated in a joyful chant punctuated with kisses. "Thank you, thank you, thank you!"

"You thank me now," Will grumbled, hugging her back just the same. "A year from now when you're wretched, 'twill all be my fault."

"A year from now I shall be delirious with joy," Nan promised.

"And that, husband, will be your fault as well," Alista agreed, taking his hand with a smile. "Nan, where is your beloved now?"

Will frowned. "How would she know—?"

"On duty as guardsman," Nan answered at once. "He asked to be allowed to stay away from the hall tonight for fear . . ." Her voice trailed off, and she shrugged. "He didn't want a quarrel."

"We must send someone to fetch him," Alista decided.

"You should go," Phillipe suggested to Mark.

"Aye, indeed," Mark grinned. "Welcome him to the family."

"You'd better behave yourself," Lisbet warned.

"Oh, he will," Malinda said. "And Phillipe as well. They know Nan can still thrash them if they don't."

"And will, without hesitation," Nan agreed, a dangerous glint in her eye. As the eldest of the Brinlaw brood, she was accustomed to ruling with an iron fist when necessary.

"I shall greet him as a cousin, Cousin," Mark promised.

"And swear yourself his servant," Phillipe suggested.

"Of course," Mark agreed. "Unless he should fall into the moat." Before Nan could react, he was gone, running across the hall as his father and Phillipe laughed and the women fumed.

"Don't you dare," Alista called, giving Will a healthy swat.

"Don't worry, Nana," Malinda said. "He's only teasing."

"The swine," Lisbet agreed.

"Aye, lady," Phillipe promised, kissing Nan's hand. "If de Lancey is your choice, you know we will give him all love." He turned to Malinda. "Will you dance?"

"No," Malinda protested as he took her arm. "We can't leave Lisbet—"

"I left you, goosey," Lisbet scolded. She glanced over at Malinda's father and grinned. "Don't you want Richard to see you?" she asked softly. "Or was it Geoffrey?"

"Neither," Malinda laughed, allowing herself to be led toward the dancers. "My heart is set on little John."

The space at the center of the hall was crowded with other dancers, but Phillipe led her easily through the throng. "You're looking well, by the way," he said as he swung her into the dance.

"I thank you, sir," she said, making a deep curtsey. Another girl danced close by and cast a frankly admiring stare at her partner as she passed. "Not so well as you, it seems," she laughed. "How is it you're still so handsome?"

"God's grace and a sturdy helmet," he smiled. "Don't be

too impressed—fresh meat is always welcome." He nodded toward a group of knights gathered near the musicians. "See for yourself." All of them were staring at Malinda, making no effort to mask their interest. One of them was actually pointing!

"Cheeky, I call that," she said, blushing and a bit horri-fied.

"You're supposed to be flattered." Phillipe grinned. "Hasn't anyone ever told you? You're a peach."

"Even so," she said, pleased at the compliment in spite of his teasing tone. The closest thing she had to an older brother, Phillipe was as dear a friend to Malinda as his sister, Lisbet, and she had missed him horribly. No doubt the gossips watching would think they were sweethearts, she thought with an inward snicker. So let them. She would take it as a compliment. "In my father's hall, the men have better manners."

"In your father's hall, the men all know your father," he pointed out with a laugh. "Speaking of that, catch me up, daisy. What's all the news from Brinlaw and Bruel?"

"At Bruel, your mother and Raynard are well, as are the rest of the children," she said before another man swept her away for a moment. "But nothing ever happens at Brinlaw," she finished as she met him again.

"Poor daisy," he sighed, only half teasing. "Blooming alone in the wild."

"Not all alone," she pointed out. "Lisbet is blooming with me."

On the dais, Queen Eleanor watched the pretty creature dancing with Geoffrey d'Anjou's bastard. She was too old to be a newcomer—twenty perhaps? Her body was ripe, a woman's shape instead of a girl's, and she moved with con-fidence, her eyes fixed on her partner's handsome face with no attempt at feigning modesty. The way she tossed those golden curls—beautiful. Her eyes were wide but not the fashionable blue—green, Eleanor saw as they passed closer to the dais, with long, dark lashes—harlot's eyes, she decided, feeling sick. A beautiful young woman she had never seen before, dancing among the nobles in a fine, expensive gown. This was Henry's latest mistress, planted in her husband's hall specifically to torture the queen with envy. Now that she looked, everything about the chit seemed made for tupping, even her mouth, full, sensuous lips and little white teeth that showed when she laughed, a throaty, woman's laugh that ended with the slightest flourish of a giggle, the best of both, well-practiced, no doubt. The Queen glanced down the royal table in dreadful resignation—yes, damn his eyes, Henry was watching her, too.

Back at the Brinlaw table, watching Mark return with Guy, Alista noticed Henry's look as well. "Will," she said softly, touching her husband's arm. "Mind the King."

Will looked at the dais, then out at the dancers, and his smile turned to a scowl. Henry could barely be trusted when sober these days; drunk, he was dangerous indeed. He had known Malinda since she was a baby, but that wouldn't stop him if she should strike his fancy now, and neither would his lifelong friendship with her father. "Nan, go get your cousin," he ordered.

"Wait," Alista said. "It's all right. Mark has gone."

Malinda passed through another figure of the dance to find Mark glaring at her. "Thanks a lot," he grumbled, taking her hand rather roughly from Phillipe's. "I turn my back for five minutes, and you make my sister a spectacle." His tone was light but only with an obvious effort, and his face was serious.

"You think I would not protect her?" Phillipe answered, his smile more natural but with an edge nonetheless.

"Come and speak to Guy," Mark answered, tucking his sister's arm through his and leading her away with Phillipe following behind.

Eleanor saw the object of her jealousy return to her parents and almost laughed out loud with relief. Brinlaw's daughter—of course. She even looked like him a bit; Eleanor thought she had admired that mouth somewhere before. She was well aware how much Brinlaw disliked her and how much he loved her husband. But he was far too much the paragon of virtue to let his daughter play the whore, even for his king. Still, it was strange the girl had never been to court. She would be twenty, or nearly, and she wasn't betrothed to anyone—with two brothers already and a mother still capable of breeding, her dowry wouldn't be much. But there was something else, some stigma on the family . . . they were whispered over, particularly among the older knights. Brinlaw himself was much admired, and the boy was well liked enough among his peers, but still, there was something she couldn't quite remember.

"Malinda, you and Lisbet go to bed," Will ordered as soon as his daughter was within his reach, subtle as ever.

"Papa, no!" Malinda protested, barely crediting her ears. The dancing was barely begun; they hadn't seen the boys in months; Nan had only this moment become engaged. He couldn't mean to pack them off upstairs like naughty children.

"Malinda, do as your father asks, please," Alista said in a more gentle tone that still left no room for debate. "And pray look in on Baby Will on your way."

"Am I a baby as well?" Malinda retorted as sharply as she dared. She still couldn't believe they were serious, and could see no reason why she and Lisbet shouldn't be allowed to stay. No one was suggesting Mark should retire, and he was younger than either of them.

"That remains to be seen," Will answered, his eyes and expression stern enough to silence a stronger creature than his daughter. "Go, Malinda. Now."

"We will, my lord," Lisbet promised, giving her friend a warning pinch. "Good night, my lady."

"Good night," Malinda grumbled, kissing each parent with as good a grace as she could muster.

"Good night, my loves," Alista said, giving her daughter an extra comforting squeeze. "Sleep well."

"I'm not sleepy," Malinda muttered as they embraced, still hoping against hope.

"You will be," Alista promised. "Now go."

Lisbet took her hand and dragged her away before she could make matters worse. "I don't know why you bother," she said as they made their way through the crowd. "You have the dearest parents in the world, but they aren't going to ever change their minds about anything just because you say so."

"Yes, and that's so wrong," Malinda complained. A pair of dashing would-be courtiers smiled and bowed as they approached, but the girls crushed them with a pair of withering looks. "I'm a woman old enough to marry and have been for years now, yet this is the first time I've kept Christmas at Queen Eleanor's court, the first time I've dined with the King at all, and my father on the privy council, thank you very much. It's ridiculous. Why should they keep me locked up at Brinlaw? Why shouldn't I have some say in where I go and what I do there?"

"Because you're too pretty and too clever, with very little common sense," Lisbet said, never one to mince words with her friends. "You get into all manner of scrapes at home; just imagine what could happen here at court."

"Thank you kindly, vixen," Malinda retorted, wide-eyed. "'Tis such a comfort to have you on my side."

"I am on your side, piglet," Lisbet shot back with a smile. "I think your parents mean to keep you safe is all."

"I hate being safe," Malinda muttered, turning away.

Back at the royal dais, Eleanor called her favorite minstrel. "Gaston!" He looked up from crooning at her daughter-in-law and hurried to her side. "The Brinlaw girl," she asked in an undertone before he could speak. "What is her name again?"

"Malinda, Majesty," he answered.

"Malinda," she repeated, musing. Brinlaw and his wife had obviously dismissed their daughter from the hall, and she just as obviously had not cared to be dismissed. Surely a queen outranked a father . . .

"Will there be anything else?" Gaston asked, eager to go back to his lute.

"Yes," she said, a plan forming in her mind. Henry would tup any pretty thing that would have him; after so many years of marriage, she had given up trying to make him stop. But if the baggage in his bed were loyal to the Queen, she could prove very helpful indeed. Besides, Brinlaw was an ass; he deserved a bit of humiliation. Mistress Malinda had stopped at the arch and turned back as if she felt Eleanor's eyes, and the Queen smiled and raised her cup in salute. "Bring her back," she said. "Malinda Brinlaw—tell her the Queen wishes to see her."

Gaston's eyes widened, but he was far too wise to

protest. "As my queen commands," he said, making his deepest bow before hurrying away through the throng.

"I told you she would notice you," Lisbet said, hot on Malinda's heels as they hurried up the stairs.

"I can't believe it," Malinda said, still stunned. The Queen had been looking at her, had raised her cup as if to say farewell.

"Why not?" Lisbet demanded. "Just think, Malinda—if she asks for you especially as lady-in-waiting, your father can't very well say no."

"You must not know my father," Malinda joked with a grimace as she drew a tiny velvet purse from the folds of her skirt.

"Still . . ." Lisbet saw what she was doing and laughed. "Malinda, no! You can't!"

"And why not?" she asked, glancing back down to make certain they weren't being followed.

"Because you promised your mother," Lisbet protested, following her to a curtained alcove at the top of the stairs.

"My mother thinks I'm an idiot," she retorted.

"Malinda, she doesn't." She watched her friend take out her components, the bits of rubbish she could make work miracles. "You lucky thing—will you at least promise to be careful?"

"Of course I will." Malinda smiled. "I promise I only want one more look around. I'll be up in half a moment."

"You had better be," Lisbet warned, giving her a hug. "I'll look in on the monster, and if you aren't in our room when I get there, I'll be very cross."

"Stop, you're scaring me," Malinda teased. With a final squeeze, she let her go. "I'll see you in a bit."

As soon as Lisbet was gone, she ducked out of sight

behind the tapestry just as a minstrel was rounding the corner from the stairs. He passed on by—obviously he hadn't seen her. Clutching her spellworks tightly in her fist, she murmured the incantation that would make her clothes vanish as her body faded as well. Being her mother's daughter, she was half faery, and one of her talents was the ability to cloak herself in magic that made her blend in perfectly with her surroundings so that she appeared to vanish into thin air. But her clothing wasn't subject to this supernatural phenomenon. As a child, she would simply strip naked and hide her clothes before striking out on invisible adventures, much to her parents' dismay. But once Mark was old enough to know what she was doing and steal her clothes for a prank, she had been forced to learn more discretion. That was when she had stolen her mother's conjuring book and learned to vanish her clothes as well. Faery magic happened for her almost without thought; conjuring was harder and required components—that was why she needed her little bag of spellworks. For this particular spell, all she needed was a bit of glass worn smooth in the rushing brook at Brinlaw and a smear of ash from silk burned in oak.

She heard a man clear his throat and flattened herself against the wall just as the tapestry was drawn back. It was the minstrel she had escaped before who stepped into the alcove, and she held her breath. He froze, confused, and she had to bite the inside of her cheek to keep from laughing, he looked so surprised. He looked around again with a sigh. "God's mutton," he muttered, turning on his heel, snatching the tapestry back as he went, obviously annoyed. Malinda let out her breath in a rush, weak for a moment with relief. If he had brushed against her, she might well have been very embarrassed. Her clothes were vanished with a conjurer's spell that would hold even if she were touched, but her body, under a faery glamour, might well have reappeared.

She knew other spells as well, though nothing too complicated—she always had to be able to memorize the directions quickly so she could slip the book back into its place in her mother's trunk before Alista missed it. Her mother had no objection to her using her faery powers, so long as she was careful not to startle strangers or use it for mischief, but she would have punished her for conjuring without permission, even now, old as she was. "Conjuring is dangerous," she had warned Malinda at least a thousand times. "I don't dare try it myself; I can't in good conscience let you." Malinda always said she understood, of course, and she did, sort of. Conjuring was dangerous, particularly the spells that required the calling of powerful spirits. But privately she still considered it marvelously convenient.

Taking a last deep breath, she decided the coast was clear and slipped back down the stairs into the hall. From a corner near the archway, she thought about how best to proceed and waited to get her bearings. Being inside the faery glamour was like being an entirely different creature. She felt lighter, less aware of her own senses, more attuned to the world around her. In this state, if she concentrated, she could touch a wall and feel what the mason who built it had felt as he set the stones. She could witness scenes of great emotion that had passed in a place centuries ago as readily as she saw the people moving around her now. Her mother had always hated this part of their faery gift; 'twas the main reason she so rarely used her powers. Sometimes when the magic was on her, the past would invade a faery's consciousness whether she willed it or not. But even so, Malinda loved it; she loved everything she could do. She was endlessly curious, eager to learn anything her magic could teach her, trivial or profound. As a child, she had told her mother as much, insisted she would be the greatest sorceress their family had ever known. As she had grown older, she had seen the concern in her parents' eyes and learned to keep silent or at least pretend to be careful. But inside, she was fearless.

She made her way carefully around the edge of the room, pausing near her parents' table. Guy and Nan were obviously being congratulated—nothing unusual was happening at all. She could see no reason why she and Lisbet shouldn't have been allowed to stay. "So when will you marry?" Phillipe was saying as he refilled everyone's cup.

"As soon as possible," Guy answered, one arm around Nan's waist, a slight flush on his cheeks.

"But not before the spring," Nan said. "We have to wait for Tarquin."

Will and Alista exchanged a look. "Love, it's been ten years and more," Alista began.

"He will come home for my wedding," Nan said with a stubborn set to her chin. "He will give me away. He promised."

"Then he must surely come," Guy said, kissing the top of her head.

"May God will it so," Alista agreed, but she didn't sound very hopeful.

"In any case, we will wait until the spring," Will said, taking Alista's hand.

Malinda turned away to continue her circuit of the hall. Tarquin FitzBruel was Nan's half-brother, and she loved him so . . . Malinda barely remembered him herself, but her parents had loved him, too. Nan was an heiress, a noble.

Her father, Bruel, had been a knight, in name, anyway, and her mother was Will Brinlaw's sister. When Bruel died in a drunken tumble down the stairs, Nan was left an orphan. Her mother had died somehow when she was still an infant, and Malinda thought it must have been something bad because her father wouldn't discuss it. At any rate, Nan was only four years old, and the only one left to care for her at Bruel Castle was Tarquin, her father's bastard with a local peasant woman. No more than ten himself, he had stolen a horse from the stables and spirited the child away, riding the length of England in the dead of winter to find Nan's uncle and deliver her to safety with him.

Both children had stayed at Brinlaw Castle. Nan said she barely remembered any other home. Tarquin had served as Will's squire and been educated as a nobleman's son. Malinda had a vague recollection of him as a rather shy boy who seemed able to do anything from fix a broken doll to break a balky horse no one else dared touch. She had still been a toddler when he was old enough to go to war with her father every spring, so her memories after that were even less clear. She knew he had been a good soldier and had heard it whispered he had been offered the privilege of knighthood in spite of his bastard birth, just like Phillipe. But he had never been knighted. When she was eight years old and Tarquin was eighteen, the castle priest, Brother Paolo, had decided to return to his own family in Florence, Italy, and Tarquin had offered to escort him.

That had been more than ten years ago, and Tarquin had never returned. Brother Paolo had written her parents of their safe arrival in Florence, and Alista and Nan had both received a few letters from Tarquin himself at first. But no one had heard a word from him in years. Malinda knew her parents had all but given up on ever seeing him again. Her mother lit candles for him in church nearly every day. But Nan was apparently still convinced he would come home.

A page boy darted past her, so close she felt a breeze, and she backed against the wall, her heart in her throat. She looked back at her family, still deep in happy conversation, and suddenly the joy had gone out of her prank. What was the fun in watching a celebration if she couldn't participate? And what if she were caught? Suddenly she felt as much like a child as her parents believed her to be, spying on grown-ups. With a last frustrated look, she headed back for the stairs.

"Majesty, I beg your patience," Gaston was saying, returning to his queen in frustrated disgrace. "I cannot find the girl to save me."

Eleanor had all but forgotten the minstrel's mission, he had been gone so long. "She ran from you that fast?" she asked, arching a brow.

"I haven't even seen her!" he protested, horribly vexed. He explained how he had followed both maidens to the staircase but found only one at the top. "I've searched up and down and can find no trace of her," he finished. "'Tis as if she disappeared."

"'Tis as if you've drunk more wine than shows, more like," the Queen chided him with a smile, but in truth, she was intrigued. She looked back at Alista Brinlaw, still so lovely after three children and twenty years of marriage. Something was wrong with the women of that family, with Lady Alista, and she suddenly remembered what it was. 'Twas said she was a witch.

2

North Africa, the Mediterranean Sea
Christmas, 1172

The sea was so still, the ship was barely rocking in its moorings, the bow bumping and scraping against the dock in a regular lullaby. But Tarquin couldn't seem to fall asleep. A lamp was lit beside his makeshift berth, and he took it to the beam where he marked off the days. As he ran his fingertips over the splintery wood to count the slashes cut there, the queer sadness that was keeping him awake grew stronger, the last trace of a feeling he had thought was dead long since. "Christmas," he murmured aloud. "It's Christmas."

The woman still lying among the cushions looked over at him, a question in her ebony eyes, but she didn't say anything. "It's nothing," he promised her in Arabic, going back to the berth. She slipped a honey-brown arm around his waist as he put out the light, but he pushed her gently away—he had only let her stay so long already to keep her from wandering the docks. "Go to sleep."

At Brinlaw, would anyone still be awake? he wondered as he stared into the sultry dark. Most of the village would have feasted inside the castle walls after Mass had been said this morning, but by now they would have all gone home and left the family alone. In his mind, he could see them gathered in the solar, the children still the toddling tykes they had been when he left, his own Nan barely more so. But that wasn't right. The children he had known would be grown now, and Nan would be a young lady—an heiress. Bruel Castle would be hers by now. Will Brinlaw himself would be fifty, nearly an old man—impossible to imagine. And his wife . . . The perfume of the little prostitute in his bed was suddenly sickening in its sweetness, and he rolled away from her, shifting a cushion between them. In his mind, Alista would always be young.

He reached for a nearby bottle the way a child might reach for a favorite toy. Since he had taken the ship and come to the Mediterranean, he had heard no news from England, had lived in a different world, and he had imagined this was what he wanted, the closest thing to happiness he could find. But tonight some sentimental madness was making him remember home, making it hard to remember why he had so needed to be free. He hadn't intended to stay away forever, had he? He had just wanted to escape. Too old and experienced a fighter to be a squire any longer, he had felt the future pressing in on him like a torturer's vault, the thought of knighthood like a fist clenched around his throat, cutting off the air.

There was no sane reason he should have felt so. Will had even offered him his own parcel of land, had offered to use his influence with King Henry to have him granted permission to build a castle of his own. But as much as he should have wanted these things, castle and knighthood and royal favor, he couldn't. The very idea made him literally tremble with fear. He loved his home, his family, his guardian—in Tarquin's mind, Will Brinlaw would always be the best knight in the world, the best a man could be. But he knew he wasn't like Will and would never be, would never belong in his world. No matter how long he lived in peace and love at Brinlaw, he never forgot Bruel Castle, never forgot his own parents, never forgot that this was the blood that flowed in his veins, a gentrified savage and a whore.

As a child, he had still felt hope. Alista told him he had a noble soul that had nothing to do with his birth; Will treated him like a son. He had learned the rules of chivalry, learned to believe a man should only fight for God and right and king, to protect the weak and serve the good. But in battle, all his good lessons were forgotten. He fought well, but he fought out of rage, for survival, just like always, and it wasn't just in battle that he felt the evil in him. Even at home, where he was safe and should have been able to be good without even trying, his worst instincts ruled him, made him feel and do things no true knight could ever have felt or done. And no one seemed to notice. That was worst of all, the truth that when he knew it made him desperate to flee. As long as he said the right things, killed the right men, kept his secret sins secret, no one could tell he was bad, not even Will, his idol, the hero he trusted to protect him from the past.

He had been nearly eighteen when he had finally known he was hopeless. It was summer, but for once there was no war—they were home at Brinlaw with no one to fight. He had been restless, but that was natural; all the soldiers were, and the ones who had no wives and children spent their days in the fields or with the horses, and at night they went to a tavern in the village, Tarquin among them. One of the serving girls had paid him special notice, tried to convince him to walk out alone with her some night. He never had, had teased her for her lack of ambition, but he had liked her; she was sweet. Then one night, she wasn't in the tavern, and the man who kept it had told him she had married. He had been happy for her and had thought of her no more the rest of the summer. But when the fall harvest came, he went to the village to the fair, and he saw her. Her face, so pretty a month before, was swollen out of shape, one eye bruised black. When she saw him, her mouth fell open in dismay, and he saw at least one of her teeth was gone. "Who did this?" he demanded, grabbing her by the arm before she could run away.

"No one," she answered, her good eye dull with fear. "I did it to myself."

"My lord?" The husband wasn't tall, but he looked strong, with a laborer's neck and shoulders. His fists would be like hams, one blow enough to cover one whole side of her face. "Has my wife offended you?"

He barely remembered what had happened next; it was all a blur of rage and blood. He seemed to say he was no man's lord; he remembered the feel of the first blow, the wet crack of shattered bone. But though it must have gone on for some long time, it seemed to be over in a moment. The man had fought back; Tarquin had been bruised and sore for days. But he didn't remember being struck at all. Everything was scarlet fog, with a dead man lying at his feet when he emerged on the other side.

"'Tis no great matter," the village reeve had said, giving Tarquin a drink in his neat little cottage as though 'twas the murderer who'd been hurt and needed comfort. "The man will hardly be missed."

"Where is my lord, Brinlaw?" Tarquin said, staring at the floor, shaking as if in a fever. "Who has gone to fetch him?"

"No one," the reeve promised in a confiding, friendly tone. "No one will trouble him with this—'tis only one peasant, after all."

Tarquin just stared at him, too sick to speak. He had done murder in the village square; was he not to be punished? "Here, Sir Knight," the reeve's wife said, setting a basin of water on the table before him.

"I'm not a knight," Tarquin snapped, looking up at her.

"No," she hastened to agree, stepping back as if from a dragon.

"Take this," the reeve said, taking the towel she held and offering it to Tarquin. "Wash yourself—you can't go home like that."

Tarquin looked down, saw the dead man's blood splattered on his tunic, his hands coated sticky red. Looking into the basin, he saw it on his face as well, his father's face, his mother's evil eyes. His heart screamed out, but no one seemed to hear . . .

"It's all right, boy," the reeve continued, a kindly uncle soothing a difficult child. "Lord Brinlaw will never know."

And so he had not. If Tarquin had told Will himself, then faced the consequences of what he had done, he might have had hope for salvation. If he had been a man who could confess such evil and pay its price, he might have been worth saving. But he couldn't do it. He couldn't look into his guardians' eyes when they knew what little good their love for him had wrought. He knew they could never understand. Alista would blame herself, would think she hadn't loved him hard enough, but Will would be even worse because he knew what it was to be a man, knew the right and wrong of such a crime. Will knew what it was to be angry, but he had never known the rage that had no meaning, that burned in his blood like a hunger that could never be sated, that had no true object but its own delight. Will knew what it was to kill, but he had never taken joy in killing, had never craved the power that came from taking another man's life. Will knew what it was to love as deeply as any human creature who ever lived, but his love was tempered with reason and charity; he had never run mad with a passion to possess at any cost, had never feared he must destroy the very object of his desire, had never felt an unreasoning compulsion for revenge that could not be denied. Will had known Tarquin's father and hated him as he would a beast too cruel to live. If he knew what Tarquin had done, saw what Tarquin really was, he would hate him just the same. At age eighteen, Tarquin feared no physical pain man could devise, not even the loss of his life. In battle, he was fearless. But he couldn't bear Will's hate. So he kept silent, and all his hopes for a soul were lost. In that moment, he had known his evil mother had been right, that he was what she had promised he would be, what she had conjured to make him, no matter what Alista might believe. He had known he was a demon. Tortured by this knowledge, he had withdrawn more and more from those he loved, and when Brother Paolo announced he was going home to Florence, he had seen his escape. He had begged permission to escort the priest as protector, and he had never stopped to look back. Not until tonight.

Drunken laughter drifted down from the deck like the ghosts of his father's hall come to haunt him. His sailors served him as his father's knights had served, not out of loyalty and love but out of fear and greed.

It was to be expected; he had hardly come by his position as their captain by virtue or nobility. "What will you have?" the old man who had owned the ship before him had asked, so grateful to this young Englishman who had saved his precious cargo from pirates.

Tarquin had looked at the silks and spices, the casks of wine and oil and seen nothing but trash he couldn't use or carry. "The ship," he had decided, a challenge in his eyes he knew the old man was too weak and frightened to meet. "I will take your ship." The man drew back in horror, and Tarquin once again saw his reflection, this time in a stranger's eyes. By then he was a man indeed, a giant—he stood a good head and shoulders taller than most men, and ten years of almost constant battle had given him the broad, thick shoulders of a wolf. His once-red hair had darkened to a deep, mahogany brown streaked with glints of copper, and he wore it long, carelessly braided back, and kept a scruffy, three-day beard, being too lazy to shave and too vain to let it grow. But while all of this had made the old man shudder, what had clearly frightened him most were Tarquin's eyes. They were pale gold ringed in black, an animal's eyes, the only feature he had inherited from his mother. Witch's eyes, she had always called them, and those were the only times she had smiled on him in approval, seeing proof of her success.

The old merchant had looked into those eyes and surrendered his ship without a whimper, and most of his crew had stayed on. Once again, the devil had smiled on Tarquin. He had been a passenger on his way to nowhere, and now he had an occupation and a home.

Before taking the ship, he had been a mercenary, a bodyguard for hire for the weaker and more squeamish men on their way to fight for God in Jerusalem. Before that he had been a Crusader himself, a sort of last grasp at grace. "I have to try something," he had told Brother Paolo, standing in the courtyard of the ancient monk's new home in Florence, itching to be gone. "I have to be good for something."

"You are better than you know," Brother Paolo had said, looking on him with mild brown eyes that could see no evil. "Go home, Tarquin, I beg you. Pray for your destiny there."

But Tarquin had gone to Jerusalem to let God use him as He would. But God wasn't there, at least not so far as he could see, and the men who were there offered gold sooner than they did salvation. In the East, he had become his true self, the demon he couldn't escape, and he had learned to revel in it. He couldn't be what Alista wanted, so he would stay away from her. If he was halfway around the world, what he did couldn't hurt her or Nan. Let Brinlaw and his kin think Tarquin was dead; the boy they had loved had never lived, not really. He would be alone, but he would be himself, and the ones he loved would be safe.

It was a good plan, and it worked for years. Whenever he had doubts, he let his temper fly, let the demon hold sway, and he was soothed, knowing he'd made the right choice. As a mercenary, he had few friends, mostly men as bad as he was, and once he had the ship, his crew learned to read his moods and anticipated his rages the same way they looked for storms at sea. They suffered his temper for the sake of the gold he brought them—if you had a cargo that must get through at all costs with no questions asked, the only choice was the *Falcon*. Just mind not to anger the captain.

The noise from the deck swelled again, more loudly this time. From the sound of it, every sailor on the ship was in on the joke, whatever it was. Scowling darkly, Tarquin got up and climbed the ladder, the girl mewling once in protest before turning back to the wall.

The crew was gathered in a knot at the stern around the place where the cargo was chained. Tarquin grabbed the first man he reached by the scruff of the neck and sent him sprawling, announcing his presence with the sailor's yelp of alarm. The rest of the crew, some half a dozen men, turned around at once, and all laughter died as soon as they saw their captain's eyes. The storm had come, and it was a bad'un. Every man tried to find a safe place to look without attracting attention to himself.

In front of the crew sat the cargo, a large group of men in chains, slaves hand-picked by the agent of a Spanish nobleman. Their leader, an aged creature with a white beard and a bent back, was the only man who didn't seem the least bit intimidated by Tarquin—he looked up at him unperturbed, a scattering of polished bones before him on the deck. Tarquin's scowl deepened, and the man smiled.

"He's a soothsayer," the first mate explained with a cough. "He was telling our fortunes with these." He bent and scooped up the bones and held them out to Tarquin.

"Your whole fortune in these?" Tarquin asked as he took them, becoming more amused than annoyed. The first mate was at least twenty years older than he was, yet he looked like a scolded child. "There must not be much to tell," he said, closing his fingers to hide the bones in his fist.

The crew laughed again, turning back to their tasks or their pallets. The squall had passed over them after all; best to move off while they still had the chance. "I hope they paid you for your trouble," Tarquin said, dropping the bones back into the soothsayer's lap as they were left alone.

The slave smiled, his eyes taking Tarquin's measure. "What of you?" he asked. "Your future can hold wonders, Captain. Set us free, and I see great joy for you."

"And the man who has paid me to deliver you to Spain?" Tarquin asked. "Will he bless me as well?" He shook his head as he turned away. "Save your speech, old man."

"Your contract means more than your soul?" Tarquin turned back with a scowl, but he didn't answer, and the slave was still smiling. "So you don't believe a man can see far," he said.

"I believe a man's fortune is chaos," Tarquin answered, torn between wanting to end this and a perverse desire to hear what the man would say next. "No man can see it all until he lives it."

"You are wise for a criminal," the slave said, his smiling mask fading somewhat into a more human face, his eyes coming to life.

Tarquin almost smiled. "You're no seer if you think so," he said, ready now to walk away in earnest.

"I do see," the man insisted, standing up. He was well made in spite of his age, and even with his bent back, he was tall, as tall as Tarquin himself. Standing, unsmiling, he suddenly looked able to snap his chains like so many twigs. "You fear the future," he said, his dark eyes gleaming in the moonlight. "More even than you fear the past." His hand came up suddenly, and Tarquin flinched, his own hand on his knife. But the man only held a tiny glass bottle.

"A magician's trick," Tarquin said, annoyed at himself.

"Magic," the slave corrected. "It will show you your future."

"Mine and every man's," Tarquin answered as he took the bottle and examined the dark brown liquid through the glass. "Poison brings death," he said, handing it back. "Every man's destiny."

"Not poison," the slave said, an urgency in his tone that could mean just as easily that he was a liar as that he told the truth.

"Then why give it to me—?"

"Because you are not this criminal, as you believe. You are not this man." He grabbed Tarquin's wrist in a painful grip, and a charge of anger raced between them. Tarquin wanted to strike back, strike him dead. "Take this, Captain," he said, putting the bottle back into his hand. "See what you may become."

Tarquin held the bottle up to the lamp, tilted it to let the amber potion flow back and forth, thick as syrup. He had tasted such magic before—oblivion distilled. Every charlatan in Africa offered as much. As a boy in England, he had seen real magic, black and white and all the shades in between; he knew it didn't come in a bottle. Magic was born in the blood. The old man meant to poison him. He held the bottle back out to him. "You first."

The old man smiled again, his teeth startlingly white in the darkness. "As you will," he said. "We will go together . . . for a price." He took the bottle. "I will be your guide; we will drink together. If we both wake up with a headache and no wisdom, you will take us to Spain. If we both find death, your men will murder mine." He met Tarquin's eyes with his own, no longer smiling. "But if I can show you the truth, you will set us free."

Tarquin's eyes narrowed. The truth shall set you free . . . a joke, another of God's great jests. Every chain on his soul was forged from truth, the truth of who he was, what he must become. What could this magician show him that would melt those chains away? Death? He looked behind the old man to the other slaves for whose lives he bargained. They were listening, absolutely still, but they didn't seem afraid. Perhaps they considered death a better fate than bondage. Perhaps he felt the same. "How will you show me?" he asked.

"Come," the magician said, settling back down on the deck, and Tarquin did the same. His first mate hovered nearby, curious, but Tarquin fixed him with a glare, and he quickly took himself away. "Take out that knife you love so much," the slave ordered. He peeled back the bottle's waxy seal, and the heady smell of cinnamon filled the air, strong and sweet. "We must be brothers if I am to walk with you between worlds." He held out his hand, the palm hard and thickly lined. Pausing only a moment, Tarquin cut a shallow gash in the old man's flesh, saw him barely flinch. He let a few drops of his blood fall into the open bottle. "You as well."

Wiping the blade first on his sleeve, Tarquin cut his own palm, took the bottle and let his blood drip in. He handed the bottle back, and the old man swirled it, mixing the blood into the potion. "You drink first," Tarquin said.

The magician smiled. "Of course." He turned the bottle up and took a drink. Tarquin watched him for a long moment, saw his eyes go soft, the pupils contract in spite of the dark. "Your darkness is strong, my brother," he said, and tears slid down his cheeks. "Let us find the light."

Tarquin took the bottle and lifted it to his lips, the smell of cinnamon overwhelming his senses. Such a scent could mask any poison, sweeten the taste of death. Even death could be sweet . . . Was death what he sought? He had thought of it before, flung himself barely armed into the thickest chaos of battle, stood alone in contemplation on high cliffs, imagining the fall, braced against the rail on the deck of his ship during violent storms when all his crew cowered and clung like rats below. But death had never found him. Perhaps this time it would. Perhaps the old man's potion was magical indeed. He tilted the bottle back, let the spice fill his mouth, tasted the blood—his blood—and he was lost. His eyes were blind; the rush of the sea filled his ears. He heard the bottle shatter as if from far away, but he felt no sensation of falling, knew nothing but sweet oblivion and the taste of bitter blood.

When he opened his eyes again, the sun had leapt back up to the horizon and was setting into the sea. The ship was gone; he was standing on solid ground with the old man beside him, his white beard blowing in the gentle breeze. "Where are we, my brother?"

Tarquin breathed in the sea air—the air had changed as well, grown fresher. They were on an open beach, the beach where he had fallen in love with the sea, the beach at Falconskeep . . . But that was impossible. "Nowhere," he said, "I don't know . . ." A child laughed, and his head snapped around. A tiny girl was playing in the breakers, chasing the foam. "Nan," Tarquin said, his heart clenched like a fist. Falconskeep . . . he had returned to Falconskeep.

"She remembers your promise," the old man said. "She fears you have forgotten."

"Promise me you will come back," an older Nan said, holding his hands in the garden at Brinlaw. This was real, a real moment in his past, the other fading away. "For my wedding, Tarquin—promise you will give me away."

"I promise," Tarquin answered, speaking aloud, the boy and man in one. The Brinlaw vision faded, and the sun had disappeared into the sea, the sky stained purple and red, the phantom beach once more.

"She needs you," the old man said. "You have to go home."

"No." A shadow had fallen, spilled across the sand, a shape of dread. He was losing the sense of where he was, how he had come to be there, what was real and what was not. The wind was stinging his face, and he smelled smoke. Fires were lit all along the shoreline in the distance, sparks rising orange in the black of night. A terrible fury took hold of him for no reason, hatred for the creatures who had lit the fires and waited for him in their light. "There . . ."

"No," the old man answered, catching hold of his arm. "That is not our place—we are not welcome there."

"I am welcome." The rage was rising inside him, rage born of fear, but he couldn't stop. He moved faster, running down the beach. He heard the cry of falcons, always falcons in this place, but there were people, too, reaching out to him as he drew near their fires. They were pale, paler than he had ever been, paler than anyone he had ever seen, white skin glowing blue and gold in the dark of the shadows and dancing light of the flames. They smiled as he reached them, spoke to him as he walked among them, but he couldn't understand their words. They tried to hold him back, and he hated them. The fires were theirs, but they had stolen something from him. He heard the old man calling, fear in his voice, but he didn't care, and he didn't look back. The thing that was stolen was a woman, and he was looking for her, desperate with love, desperate with hate for these shining creatures who tried to keep her from him. They were smiling and beautiful; they wanted her for themselves. A woman touched his arm, entreated him to join her in the dance, but she wasn't the one he sought. "Leave me!" He was two people again, the Tarquin of the ship and this other man he didn't know, a creature not yet born, desperate and afraid. He shouted something else, a name forgotten as soon as he spoke it but desperately important, the key to everything.

"Tarquin, wait!" the old man called, closer now. "Come back, or you are lost!"

"I am lost," Tarquin said, turning back toward the raging sea. "I have always been lost . . . My love is lost." The dancers were moving on, shining fingers trailing along his shoulders, and then he saw her, standing in the surf.

She was not like the others; she was human, with long, golden hair curled and matted down her back. This Tarquin knew her as his heart, and he called out her name again, but the Tarquin of the ship couldn't hold the word, had never seen her before. She turned to him as he approached, her hair falling loose around her face, a beautiful face, sweet but cunning, too, a woman, not a child. But she was so delicate, so pale, as pale as the faeries at the fire. Her eyes sparked as if she knew him, but she didn't speak, and as he came closer, she retreated farther into the surf. "Come back," he said, his voice rough with rage and desperation. "Come back to me." He spoke her name again as if he knew it, held out his hand to her. She frowned, and tears spilled down her cheeks—was he the reason she was so afraid? What had he done to hurt her? She held up her hand as if to ward him off—her nails were broken and bloodied to the quick, and a bruise was fading on her cheek. Had he done this? How could he have done this? *I'm sorry!* the real Tarquin wanted to shout, but the man in the dream wouldn't say it.

"Come with me," she said, so softly the words were almost lost in the crash of the surf. "Come and take me home."

"Tarquin!" Nan's voice again, Baby Nan, the ray of light behind him in the past. Turning, he saw her, a tiny child again, far away down the beach, holding out her arms to him. "No leave me!" she screamed. "Please come back!" The old man stood beside her, straight and tall, holding out his hand as well. Tarquin turned his back on them, turned back to his love. But she was fading; everything was fading, the screams of the falcons dying away on the wind . . .

He opened his eyes, choking on the stench of the ship, his face pressed flat against the wooden deck, and he could feel the sun on his back. It was morning; he must have slept. The wind had picked up; he could hear the creak of the sails. Rolling onto his back, he saw the falcon unfurled in the brilliance of the dawn.

"So we live." The old man was sitting on the deck as before, his back bent over again. "Do you remember what you saw?"

"My sister, Nan," Tarquin answered, his tongue dry and thick in his mouth. "She is at Bruel." How did he know this? He hadn't seen . . . but he knew it just the same. Nan was at Bruel, the place where they were born, and she wanted him to come to her.

"Your home," the old man said.

"No." He made himself sit up, his stomach rolling like the waves. Parts of the vision were already fading; something vital was being lost, the most important thing. "My father's home. Her home now, if she lives." Nan would be grown now, not a child; she would have come into her inheritance. Bruel Castle would belong to her and to her husband . . . He had promised to give her away.

"She lives," the old man said. "She needs you. She was the one who found you in your dream."

"Yes." Nan had found him. Nan was at Bruel, but there was something else, someone else he had found in a different place, a place he'd thought he loved. He tried to focus his mind on that part of the vision, but it was like trying to capture a dream.

"You should go back to this Nan," the old man persisted. "Go home."

"Come with me," a voice spoke in his mind, a woman's voice. *"Come and take me home."*

"What else?" he asked the old man, grabbing his shackled wrist. "What else did we see?"

For a moment, Tarquin thought he wouldn't answer. "Strange magic," he said at last. "Power I could not touch. Listen to me, brother. If it will leave you, let it go."

"Tell me," Tarquin persisted. "Help me remember."

"I couldn't see," the magician said. "Strange lights, and the screams of birds . . . You left me, and I couldn't see where you had gone."

For a moment, rage flared up inside him, made him want to strangle the life from the man. But he could see he didn't lie. "So have I seen the truth?" he asked, getting up. "This dream you couldn't see and I can't remember?"

"You know you have," the magician answered, returning his bitter smile in kind. "The future is chaos, remember?"

Tarquin kicked the guard who was snoozing at the rail. "Give me the keys."

"Captain?" He handed them over, obviously at a loss.

"They'll need provisions. Go get them." He began to unlock the chains, ignoring the sailor's gaping shock until he turned and went to do as he was told.

"So you are a man of your word," the old man said, the last to be unchained.

"No," Tarquin answered. "Not usually."

The soothsayer smiled. "So already you are a new man." He held up his wrists, scarred but free, as the rest of his party gathered what little they had, talking excitedly among themselves. "Don't fear what you have seen, my brother," he said. "Your destiny will find you, whether you fear it or not. Better to face it, live your chaos through."

Tarquin shook his head with a wry smile of his own. He had promised Nan; she was haunting his dreams to hold him to his promise. And something else as well . . . He was afraid, afraid of his vision, afraid of himself. But he felt almost happy, alive in a way he had not in years. Like these other slaves, he was going home.

3

The summons came at dawn, and Malinda told no one, not even Lisbet. She put on her favorite gown, bright red with gold-embroidered trim, and tucked her hair under a filmy gold veil. She wiped the early-morning frost from her silver mirror and examined her reflection for defects with a ruthless eye. Nothing she could fix, alas. Her nose was too wide—a perfectly nice nose for her father, but too assertive for a woman. How she longed to have her mother's feminine little button! But it couldn't be helped. She had her father's mouth as well, too full for delicacy, but her teeth were small and even, and a fetching dimple appeared at one corner when she smiled. Her skin was smooth—faery skin, Lisbet's mother called it. Alista had never taken much notice of her own beauty, much less her daughter's, but Druscilla, her mother's best friend since before Malinda was born, was an expert. If only Auntie Dru were here now, she could have transformed her into a princess, or at least a lady-in-waiting, without breaking a sweat. But that couldn't be helped, either.

Her best features were her eyes, she decided. Her

mother's eyes were so brown they looked black, and her father's were dark blue, but somehow Malinda's were green with flecks of gold, tilted slightly upward at the corners to give her a kittenish look no matter what her expression might be. In Malinda's opinion, her eyes were her true self.

She batted her eyelashes at herself, then winked once for luck. She would need it.

Even at this hour, Queen Eleanor's anteroom was buzzing with activity. Malinda started in just as a page weighed down with empty dishes was darting out, and he managed a semblance of a bow as he passed, but otherwise no one paid her any mind at all. Two clerks were busily scribbling in the beams of light coming through the windows, and three young women about Malinda's age were cooing like children over a basket of spaniel puppies on the rug before the fire. Several men were obviously waiting with petitions—a pair of mud-spattered knights who looked asleep on their feet, a pair of velvet-clad courtiers chatting briskly in Italian, a bishop by himself looking monstrously vexed. Meanwhile a steady stream of servants and nobles passed back and forth through a studded door set deep in an alcove—the door to the Queen's private rooms, Malinda surmised. She looked around for someone to whom she could present her summons, but everyone seemed busy, and no one seemed to be in charge. She was just about to approach the girls when the door opened again, and Eleanor herself emerged, trailed by another clerk, two more ladies, and a trio of knights in royal livery, one of whom was Malinda's own brother, Mark. His eyes widened at the sight of his sister, and Malinda couldn't resist a wicked wink as she sank into a curtsey, the rest of the company assembled making obeisance as well.

"My Lady Malinda, thank heavens," Eleanor said as she swept past, handing a heavy scroll over her shoulder to the clerk, who scrambled to take it. "Come along, chérie."

"Your Majesty, I must insist—" the bishop began, but Mark and the other guards blocked his path to the queen.

"Later, Your Eminence," Eleanor sighed wearily, waving her clerk toward the Italians. "Ambassadors, please leave your letters with Denis, and he will see that they reach my husband's attention. Politics makes my head ache just now." A tiny smile at Malinda belied her words—as if Eleanor of Aquitaine could ever lose interest in intrigue. "Sir Roger, mon Dieu—you and your friend look exhausted!" The knights perked up, rising from their knees in a clumsy-weary scramble that made Malinda bite the inside of her cheek to keep from laughing. *How she keeps them hopping,* she thought, admiring her idol even more. Her own mother commanded absolute authority at Brinlaw, second only to her husband, but no one ever tripped over himself to obey her, except maybe her husband. "Unless you bring word of invasion, I pray you, take your ease," Eleanor continued to the knights. "I will send for you later, and you may make your report then."

Sir Roger looked a bit confused, but relieved even so. "As my queen commands," he said, making another bow.

The girls who had been playing with the puppies had fallen in with the other ladies behind the Queen, and Malinda joined them, feeling rather like minnow caught in the tide. One of the others gave her an encouraging smile. "That's a very pretty dress," she said in a confiding murmur.

"Thank you," Malinda murmured back.

"Yes," Eleanor agreed, turning suddenly to look at her as

if no other matters concerned her in the slightest. "A very pretty dress indeed. But where is your mother, my lady?"

"Forgive me, Majesty," Malinda stammered, confused. "Your summons didn't mention—"

"No, it did not mention Lady Alista," Eleanor agreed, her smile deepening. "But I wonder at your courage, Malinda. Most maidens would not have dared to come alone."

"My sister's daring is the stuff of legend, Majesty," Mark said, his own smile not so warm.

"Then I shall love her all the better," Eleanor said, holding out her hand. "What a pretty thing you are," she went on as Malinda took it. "Come, let us walk alone."

"As you say, Majesty, of course," Malinda agreed, feeling rather dizzy. Last night she had gone to sleep a country nobody, now she was to have a private audience? It hardly seemed possible. She glanced back at Mark and found him scowling, looking so much like Papa, 'twas almost comical. No doubt he would have quite a tale to tell her parents and would not stint on details. Resisting the urge to stick out her tongue at him, she followed the Queen out into the gallery.

"So how do you like my husband's court?" Eleanor asked pleasantly when they were virtually alone—even the gallery had its share of people dashing back and forth.

"Very much, since Your Majesty is here," Malinda answered boldly.

"You do not care for the King?" Eleanor asked. "Don't you find him handsome? Most maidens do, I'm told."

"King Henry is magnificent, of course," Malinda said, privately thinking Henry far too old for such considerations but not wishing to cause offense. "But . . ." She tried to think of an artful way to put her thoughts into words, but she couldn't. "He is my father's friend," she said at last, opting for plain truth. "At his court, I am always a child."

"And you do not wish to be?" Eleanor said, watching her closely from behind her lowered lashes.

"Wishing has nothing to do with it; I'm not." In her heart, she had always believed if anyone could understand her restlessness, 'twould be Queen Eleanor, and she couldn't stop herself from telling all. "I'm not a child—I'm nearly twenty! I've never had a single real suitor, never met a single creature whose suit I'd care to hear. I never see anyone, never get to do anything but try not to upset Mama, and I feel . . ." She was almost ready to cry, and she had to stop, brutally embarrassed.

"You feel as if the whole world is a wonderful secret, and you're being shut out," Eleanor finished for her, her eyes and expression serious for the first time. "You have all these gifts—you truly are quite beautiful, Malinda—and it's all going to waste, or so it seems to you. And when you let yourself think of it, you know that if you don't break free soon, you'll run mad." She smiled. "And whenever you try to explain, the people who should understand are either frightened or angry and tell you to keep your peace and pray God for the wisdom to be grateful for what you have."

"Yes," Malinda answered, stunned. Just hearing the words was like a weight coming off her heart, as though this woman had peered into the book of her soul and read it off to her. "You do know—"

"Of course I do, chérie," the queen laughed. "'Tis the story of my life." She patted Malinda's cheek, ignoring the noblewoman with an amazing coiffure who was making a curtsey astonishing to behold nearby. "You spoke of having suitors," she continued, walking on. "Is love the extent of your ambition?"

Malinda thought immediately of her magic, her irresistible urge to know all it could teach her, to know herself as a sorceress. She longed to blurt this out as well, but caution and loyalty won out—her mother would be horrified. "For the moment," she said shyly, lowering her gaze to the floor. "I haven't really thought much of anything else."

Eleanor laughed again. "'Tis natural," she admitted. "At your age, neither had I. Very well, then." She stopped again. "If it's suitors you wish, then you shall have them—or one really marvelous one, at any rate. Better than your dreams, I assure you." Malinda frowned, and she laughed. "Don't look so worried, chérie—you'll like him, I promise." She touched her chin, turned her face from side to side, considering it. "You might well find yourself a princess," she mused.

Before Malinda could answer, the door they'd left opened again, and Mark came rushing toward them. "Forgive me, Majesty," he said. "The King has asked to see you."

"A pretty courtesy," Eleanor said lightly as she let Malinda go. "It seems that I am summoned." She smiled. "Be happy, chérie. I command it."

Malinda expected Mark to go with the Queen, but he stayed with her instead. "You should have brought Mama with you," he said when Eleanor was gone.

"Why do you say that?" she said peevishly, annoyed by his tone.

"She could have kept that woman's hooks out of you," he answered, taking her arm and propelling her back in the direction of the family quarters. "What does she want from you, anyway?" He frowned. "She didn't ask you about your sorcery, did she?" he demanded, turning on her. "You didn't—"

"Of course I did not." She was accustomed to a completely different Mark, an awkward boy who adored her, trusted her opinion on every subject, thought she could do no wrong. Who was this condescending stranger? "What is the matter with you? Why are you treating me this way?"

"Am I treating you in a particular way?" he asked, his manner softening somewhat. "I hadn't noticed." He stopped, seeming to remember himself. "Forgive me, please," he began again. "It's this place . . . You have no idea, Malinda." For the first time, she saw that he wasn't being hateful; he was genuinely upset. "Mama says you want to be a lady-in-waiting, but you don't, I swear," he went on. "You think it's grand here and interesting, but it's just . . . You'll be happier at home."

"Mark, what has happened?" she demanded. "Who has hurt you?"

"No one," he scowled. "It's not . . . Everyone lies here; nothing is what you think it is, and when they do tell you the truth, you'd rather not know."

"What truth?" she pressed more gently, the look in his eyes breaking her heart. She wanted to hold his hand and make him tell her all his secret hurts as she had when they were at home together, but he was a man now and wouldn't confide so easily.

"They lied, Malinda," he said, turning Mama's black eyes on her from Papa's face. "I think they thought they were doing it for us, for Phillipe, but . . ." He stopped, seeming to remember himself, his face going pale. "Never mind," he said, trying to turn away.

"I do mind." She touched his cheek, made him look at her. "Tell me. What about Phillipe?"

"Nothing," he insisted. "Come on. Mama will be wondering what's become of you."

"Mark—"

"Malinda, I can't!" His voice broke with anguish, but his expression went blank in an instant. "I shouldn't have said anything," he went on, turning away, and when she tried to touch him again, he pushed her away. "It's nothing, I promise."

"I don't believe you," she retorted, hurt for herself now as well as him. "And I don't understand why you can't just tell me what's bothering you."

"What's bothering me is you, so desperate to get away from home, to follow behind Eleanor like a lapdog," he said. "If you have half the brains you pretend to have, you'll run back to Brinlaw as fast as you can and forget all about court, find some nice plank-face, like Nan, and be happy."

For a moment, she couldn't even speak, she was so angry. "That was a horrible thing to say, about me as much as Nan," she said at last.

"Is it?" he demanded. "If you get what you want, if you get to stay at court, I'll ask you again in a month if you still feel the same." He put his hands on her shoulders, bitterness replaced by pleading. "Listen to Mama and Papa; believe what they tell you," he begged, and she didn't doubt for a moment he meant it. "Let them take care of you."

"Let who take care of whom?" Lisbet said, coming around the corner. "There you are, goose. I've been looking everywhere for you, and so has your mother." She seemed suddenly to notice the looks on their faces. "What's wrong?"

"Nothing," Mark said, letting Malinda go. "I have to go back to the Queen."

"Mark, wait!" Malinda called, taking a step after him.

"I can't," he called back, never slowing down.

"Duty calls, I suppose," Lisbet sighed. "So what is it? Did you quarrel?"

"Not exactly," Malinda answered. She knew she should race after Mark, make him tell her what he meant, why he was so adamant that she should go home to Brinlaw. But she didn't want to know. She wanted to be happy with her success with Eleanor, to imagine how blissful she was going to be at court. Be happy, Eleanor had ordered. She wanted to obey. "He's just annoyed with me," she explained to Lisbet. "I went by myself to see the Queen."

"You lie!" Lisbet cried, grabbing her arm. "You didn't!"

"She summoned me first thing this morning, and I went," Malinda answered, feeling better already. "She was splendid—"

"Did she say you will be a lady-in-waiting?" Lisbet interrupted.

"Not in so many words, no," Malinda admitted, frowning slightly as she tried to remember exactly what the Queen had said. It had all seemed so clear at the time, but now it was hard to be sure what, if anything, had been decided. If only King Henry hadn't summoned his wife at just the wrong moment, everything would have been settled, she was certain, and surely Eleanor meant to continue their talk, put the wheels in motion, as it were. "I think she meant to," Malinda went on. "She told me to be happy, not to worry about it anymore." Her smile grew more impish. "She said I might end up a princess."

"I knew it!" Lisbet shrieked, drawing the full attention

of the page boys who had been glancing at them every few moments. "You're going to marry Richard!"

"Lisbet, don't be ridiculous, and do be quiet," Malinda scolded, yanking her friend into their room and slamming the door behind her.

"It isn't ridiculous," Lisbet insisted with a knowing smile.

"Of course it is," Malinda answered, trying hard not to smile back. "Richard is already betrothed to Alice of France—"

"Who is already King Henry's mistress," Lisbet finished. "Everyone says so. Phillipe told me at breakfast."

"Really?" Malinda said with a pleasant little thrill of horror. Alice had been a fosterling at Henry's court since she was a child. Could he really be—?

"Really, Lisbet, I'm surprised at you," Nan said, coming in from the next room with a stack of folded clothes. "Repeating such gossip. I can't believe Phillipe would tell you such a thing."

"Just because it's awful doesn't mean it isn't true," Lisbet quite reasonably pointed out.

"Yes, but it doesn't mean it is true, either," Nan scolded as Alista came in as well with Baby Will trailing behind her.

"What is true?" Alista said, putting more clothes into a hamper. "Malinda, thank heavens, are you packed?"

"Packed?" Malinda echoed, confused.

"That's what I was going to tell you," Lisbet said. "We're leaving as soon as your father says good-bye to the King."

"Look, Malinda," Baby Will said, holding up a wooden top in one hand and the untied cord in the other. "Mark made it for me. Isn't it nice?"

"It's lovely, Willie," Malinda agreed, taking it and tying

the cord back on with clever fingers. At five years old, Willie was like his sister's pet, much cherished but often ignored. "Mama, I can't leave yet. I was summoned by the Queen."

"That's where she was," Lisbet explained.

"Yes, I know," Alista answered. She wasn't frowning, didn't seem angry, but she didn't seem pleased, either.

"Look how it spins!" Willie cried joyfully, squatting over his toy. "Look, Malinda!"

"I see it," Malinda answered without looking, watching her mother instead. "I think she liked me, Mama."

"Why shouldn't she like you?" Alista answered. "You're an extremely likeable woman."

"Yes, but she's the Queen," Lisbet pointed out.

"Yes," Alista agreed with a smile, exchanging a look with Nan.

"Come on, Willie," Nan said. "You, Lisbet, and I will find Phillipe and show him your top."

"I know he's seen it," Willie complained.

"But perhaps Guy hasn't," Lisbet said. "Don't you want to say good-bye?"

"I suppose," Willie grumbled, allowing himself to be led. "Isn't Malinda coming?"

"Not this time, love," Nan said, ushering them out.

"You knew I was with the Queen?" Malinda asked as soon as they had gone.

"I thought you might be," Alista answered. "Henry told your father that she wants you to stay on at court as a lady-in-waiting."

So the wheels had already been in motion when she had been summoned . . . "And what did Papa say?"

Alista took both her hands in her own. "He said no, sweeting," she began.

"No?" Malinda said weakly, unable to say anything else for a moment. She had never been disappointed in her life, not seriously, not about anything important, and this was the most important opportunity of her life. They couldn't seriously mean to deny her, not when she had so rarely been denied anything else. "He couldn't," she insisted, shaking her head.

"He had good reason," Alista answered. "Malinda, you don't belong here—"

"How do you know?" she exploded, breaking free of her mother's grasp. "Just because you have always hated being at court, being away from home, you assume I will hate it, too, but I don't. I love it here. I love being among strangers, never knowing whom I might meet or what might happen. Mama, please—"

"Malinda, listen to me—"

"Why can't you listen to me?" Malinda cut her off, too upset to be dutiful, desperate to make her understand. "Sometimes I lie awake at night and think about what will happen the next day, and do you know what? I'm always right—I always know every single thing that will happen."

Alista was actually smiling. "That isn't entirely a bad thing."

"Maybe not for you—"

"Malinda, I'm sorry you're bored at home, I truly am." She looked away as if loath to say what she must. "But I won't let you risk burning just to amuse yourself."

Malinda felt her face go pale, but she wasn't ready to back down. "I hardly think—"

"What if you had been caught last night?" Alista cut her off, her voice calm but real worry in her eyes. "What if your concentration had been broken or someone had touched you?"

Malinda could occasionally be a sneak, but she was never a liar. "How did you know?"

"Willie said he didn't see you last night, only Lisbet," Alista explained. "I knew you must have come back into the hall."

"I only wanted to see—"

"And if you had been caught, you could have put all of us in danger, yourself most of all," Alista interrupted before she could explain how careful she had been. "Since Becket's murder, even Henry himself is whispered about for consorting with the devil. What do you think would happen to a silly girl practicing witchcraft in his castle?"

"It isn't witchcraft—"

"You and I know that, but—"

"And I am not a silly girl!" She faced her mother, furious, openly defiant for the first time in her life. She knew Alista loved her and wanted only what was best, but this was ridiculous; she would not be treated like a child another moment, not without a fight. "In case you haven't noticed, I am a full year older than you were when I was born!"

"In years, yes, you are older," Alista answered, obviously unmoved. "But in judgment, I sometimes think you must be younger than Willie. A woman would never have worked a fragile spell in the midst of a royal banquet just to 'see,' not after being specifically forbidden again and again—"

"So to prove myself a woman, I must do as I am told?" Malinda scoffed.

"Nay, love," Alista said with a bitter laugh. "To prove

yourself a woman, you must do what you know is right without being told."

"And what is right is obviously whatever you and Papa want," Malinda fumed.

"For pity, Malinda," Alista sighed.

"Forgive me, Mama, but it all seems so unfair—"

"It is unfair!" Alista retorted with such sudden fury her daughter was shocked silent. Mama almost never lost her temper, but when she did, it was an amazing sight. "It's unfair that Henry is such an ass that he has turned the entire Church against himself and his kingdom. It's unfair that because of this and because of some mystic curse I never asked for, I have to be afraid not only for myself but for my child. It's unfair that after twenty years spent protecting this child, this daughter, the darling of my soul, teaching her who she is and how to be safe even so, this same child should then defy me and treat me as if she thinks me an idiot."

"But it isn't a curse, Mama," Malinda insisted, chagrined but not convinced. "It's a gift—"

"Do you think the bishop would think so?" Alista retorted. She stopped, the fury in her eyes dying back to weariness again. "If you had been caught, you would have been charged as a consort of Satan—"

"Ridiculous —"

"Of course ridiculous, but true, even so," Alista went on. "People are afraid, darling, even the King. They're calling Thomas à Becket a saint. They're saying his death has brought God's wrath down on the entire realm. When those knights murdered him, whether Henry knew what they intended or not . . . England feels cursed, and the priests like it that way, believing it will get them what they want. Any gesture they can make to feed this frenzy, they will, and Henry will not bother even to try to stop them."

"I don't see what any of this has to do with us," Malinda grumbled. "It isn't as if we're practicing black magic—"

"At Brinlaw, people know us for what we are, and we are safe," Alista continued. "But at court, if you were caught working any kind of magic at all, black or white or purple, you would never be allowed to explain, and even if you did, no one would believe you. A woman who can make herself vanish is a witch, and therefore a devil. Any talk of faeries is a lot of English peasant nonsense."

"I'm sorry, Mama," Malinda said, genuinely contrite. "I didn't realize—"

"If you had been caught last night, your father could probably have saved you, somehow. He could have convinced Henry to intercede on your behalf," Alista said. "But what if he weren't here? What if you were caught at such mischief as a lady-in-waiting with your father far away at Brinlaw? You would be charged, tortured, and burned before we ever heard tell of it."

"I wouldn't let them," Malinda insisted. "If they tried to take me prisoner, I would let myself turn into a falcon and fly away." This was the ultimate secret of the Falconskeep line. One woman in every generation was born with this power, inherited from the first lady of Falconskeep, a faery in falcon's shape who had turned into a woman for the love of a human man. With her human body had come the heartstone, a heart-shaped pendant she wore around her neck and passed on to her daughter and so on to every female descendant. So long as the Falconskeep lady wore the heartstone, she would remain a woman, her faery spirit bound to an earthly form. But if she took it off, her spirit could fly free as a falcon. Alista's mother, Blanche, had proven this power was still real after a hundred generations, taking flight from her deathbed in the presence of her daughter when Alista was a little girl of four. As soon as she was old enough to understand, Alista had told Malinda how this had happened and why, and she had told her that she herself had nearly been transformed herself on two different occasions, once almost by accident before the heartstone came into her possession and again in circumstances she had never explained. But she had made certain Malinda understood this power, had made it the first lesson in her magical education.

Now she turned pale as death, her dark eyes wide, to hear Malinda speak of it so blithely. "Then you would be lost to us even so," she said, struggling to keep her voice even. "And your father would likely be punished in your place. At the very least his lands would be forfeit."

"I would never let that happen, Mama, truly," Malinda promised, regretting her hasty words. "I won't use a single spell, not even faery magic. I know I've been reckless, and I speak before I think, but I can be careful. I know I can." She sank to her knees at her mother's feet, clasping Alista's hands as she had as a child. "Please, speak to Papa. Tell him you know I'll be safe," she entreated. "If you say I'll be all right—"

"But, sweeting, I can't," Alista said sadly. She pulled a hand free to cradle her daughter's chin. "I don't know you will be safe, no matter how sincerely you try to be careful. Your magic is so much a part of you in a way even I don't understand—"

"You don't trust me." Malinda got up and backed away, her temper closing her off from everything but her own thwarted desires.

"I don't trust your powers," Alista said. "And your father doesn't trust Eleanor. Even if your magic wasn't a consideration, I don't know that he . . ." She let her words trail off unfinished.

"What?" Malinda demanded, whirling around. "What does he think the Queen means to do, feed me to a dragon?"

"In a manner of speaking," Alista muttered with a bitter smile.

"What does that mean?" Malinda cried, half mad with frustration. "Why can't you just tell me the truth, all of it, without trying to protect me from my own life? It's my life, Mama, not yours, not Papa's—"

"Is that so, in faith?" Alista demanded. "Yes, my darling, you are a woman, a very beautiful woman, and don't think Eleanor hasn't noticed. Henry has, I promise—I saw him, and so did your father."

"So what?" Malinda said with a sullen shrug. "King Henry notices all kinds of girls."

"And most of them find themselves in his bed, usually sooner rather than later," Alista shot back bluntly. "Then when he tires of them, he marries them off to whatever noble toady will have them, usually with a royal bastard on the way. Is that the sort of excitement you crave, the marvelous diversion you're missing at Brinlaw?"

"That would never happen to me," Malinda insisted. In truth, she was rather appalled, but she refused to admit it. Mama was just trying to scare her into obedience—stay close to home, little children; the woods are full of wolves.

"And why not?" Alista asked. "Because you are so wise?"

"Because I wouldn't allow it."

Alista opened her mouth to say more then closed it

again, shaking her head instead. "Enough," she said at last, going back to packing. "You're going home with us, and that's the end of it. If that makes you unhappy—"

"I can sew it in a pillow and ride it back to Brinlaw because it makes no difference at all," Malinda finished for her. Lisbet was right; she might as well have kept her peace for all the good it would ever do to argue. To her parents, she would always be a child, a fragile, stupid creature good for nothing but to be protected until her designated plank-face turned up to take her off their hands, just as Mark suggested. *Not me,* she swore in her silent heart. *Never, ever, ever.* "So I suppose I may as well go pack."

"Yes," Alista answered tartly without looking up. "I rather imagine you should."

4
෨෴෬

Tarquin put into port on Corsica as the sun sank behind him. Getting clear of Russadir had been something of an adventure—the Spaniard whose slaves he'd set free had been predictably annoyed and wealthy enough to cause trouble. But once they had returned his money and eluded the other mercenaries sent to sink the *Falcon,* the voyage had gone well. He had even managed to pick up a more profitable cargo to satisfy his crew, leaving it at its destination on Cyprus two days before. But he couldn't sail to Bruel. At some point he would have to leave the ship, and for that he needed Davyd.

Once the ship was safely secured at anchor, he made his way through the narrow village streets. Davyd was the nearest thing to a partner he had found since leaving England, a Muslim Arab he had met in a caliph's prison during his soldiering days. Tarquin had beaten some poor sod senseless in a drunken rage and been locked up while the authorities worked out who he was; Davyd had seduced the caliph's daughter. Both of them had been in rather desperate straits. Together they had managed to escape the caliph's justice, and this had made them friends. They had even hired on together occasionally for disputes that didn't involve the name of the Almighty. But when Tarquin had taken a ship, Davyd had declined his invitation to join him at sea, smitten by then by another noble lady who couldn't leave her husband. By now Tarquin figured that liaison would have come to naught, like all the others, so it seemed likely that Davyd was home. His mother kept a house on Corsica, bought with her son's ill-gotten gains, and even if Davyd wasn't there, she would almost certainly know where to find him.

"FitzBruel!" The shout came from the roof of the house. Looking up, he saw the man he sought, a tall figure with waist-length, jet-black hair. "Allah save us, you live!"

"No thanks to Allah!" Tarquin shouted back, smiling and squinting into the dying sunlight.

They met in the courtyard as Davyd's mother set out the evening meal. "My friend," Davyd smiled, white teeth dazzling against his dark face and beard.

"And mine," Tarquin agreed, embracing him.

"I call it God's grace that you are here," Davyd said as they parted. "Have you come to hire on with the Frenchmen?"

"What Frenchmen?"

"Then you have not heard." He motioned Tarquin to a chair. "A small group of French knights have just come to the island looking for soldiers for hire." He filled two glasses, and Tarquin drank. "They say they need an army."

"Crusaders?" Tarquin asked, confused. Corsica was Islam; why would Frenchmen come there to recruit?

"I'm thinking not," Davyd said, black eyes twinkling over his glass. "They're up to mischief, no question, or they would use their own troops. And the pay is suspiciously good, particularly for captains who speak French and English as well as Arabic." He grinned. "We could make a fortune."

"Another fortune, you mean," Tarquin answered. Unlike most mercenaries who spent their wages on wine and wenches almost before they were earned, Davyd was notorious for accumulating wealth. "I suppose this means you will have no interest in helping me."

"Perhaps we can help each other," Davyd said. "What is it you need?"

"Another pair of hands I can trust." He nodded thanks to Davyd's mother as she set a tray of food between them. "I'm going home, my friend, to England."

"Wonderful news!" Davyd knew nothing specific about Tarquin's reasons for staying away from his home, but he knew they were not happy ones, that there were people in England he missed. "What has convinced you?"

"I made my sister a promise," Tarquin answered. For a moment he considered telling Davyd everything, all about his vision, but he wasn't really sure what he would say. Nan was the most obvious thing, the one element of the dream that had always been clear in his mind: she was at Bruel; she needed him; he had promised—this was all reason enough for him to face his fears. But other details from his "destiny" had begun to come back to him since he left Russadir, images that inspired fierce and painful emotions that made no sense—an open beach, pale figures at a fire. A woman's face . . . he was haunted the most by a woman's face; wide, green eyes . . . Something about her was familiar, but try as he might, he couldn't think where he had seen her before. But he knew her, this woman from his dream; he longed for her; he dreaded her. She was joy and pain together, fear and elation—she was his, the mirror of all that was good and evil in his heart, his sin and his salvation. She was part of his need to go home. "And other reasons, too," he finished. "It's time, I guess."

"Long past time," Davyd agreed, watching his friend with interest. Ordinarily Tarquin was stone-faced as a pagan god and as subtle as an axe, but now he spoke in riddles, and a dozen emotions passed over his face between one word and the next. If Davyd hadn't known him so well, he would have thought he was in love. "So what do you need me to do?"

"Go with me," Tarquin said bluntly. "Sail with me to England; drop me off; take my ship. Meet me before another winter comes in case I want to leave again."

"That is quite a favor," Davyd said. "What would I get from this, besides the pleasure of serving a friend?"

"A ship," Tarquin answered with a smile, tearing off a bit of his own. "If I decide to stay in England, the *Falcon* is yours. And if I don't, you will have whatever profit you make from it in the meantime."

"That could please me," Davyd said. "But what of these Frenchmen? I'm to meet with them tonight to negotiate a price—a difficult business with my bad French and their idiotic Arabic." He tore off a chunk of bread. "Now if I had someone to translate, tell me later what they said to one another when they thought I could not understand, that would be a great help."

"So what do you propose?" Tarquin asked.

"Come with me tonight," Davyd answered. "Help me discover what they truly mean to do, if their gold is worth the trouble. If it is, I will thank you and help you find

another, better man to keep your ship. If it is not, if they
mean great harm or think to cheat me, I will sail with you
myself."

Tarquin could find no fault with this. In Davyd's place,
he would have said the same. "Agreed," he said, offering his
hand. "And I thank you."

The meeting was conducted in a silken battle tent on the
beach, Tarquin, Davyd, and three French knights, one very
old, one very young, and one in the middle who did most
of the talking. This man and Davyd negotiated the details
of their contract in a patois of Arabic and French, with
Davyd pretending not to understand any details that didn't
suit him. Tarquin sat back and listened in silence, his face
utterly impassive, not so much pretending not to understand as giving no indication that he did. Even with his
deep sailor's tan, he couldn't pass for an Arab, but he did
look as if he might be an Italian or Spaniard. But the oldest
knight looked at him as if he knew him, his sharp black
eyes alive with interest, his thin lips twisted in a knowing
smile in the midst of his dirty beard. Tarquin stared back
until he finally looked away.

The young one looked at Tarquin, too, his eyes darting
away when Tarquin looked directly at him. He was dressed
better than the other two, his leather armor studded with
silver. But it didn't seem to fit very well, or at least he didn't
appear terribly comfortable wearing it. He kept gnawing at
his nails, then snatching his hand away from his mouth as
if remembering he wasn't supposed to fidget. He suddenly
drew his dagger, and Tarquin froze, wary. The boy gave
him a sheepish little smile, then began to play with the
weapon, balancing the point on the arm of his chair and

twirling it round and round. Tarquin almost smiled back. Alista used to do that and had ruined half the chairs at Brinlaw.

"You speak of an army, as if your enemy were very great," Davyd was saying. "Will our forces—"

"He is a demon," the boy suddenly spoke in a nobleman's French far removed from the commoner's tongue his companion used to address them. His eyes were still focused on the twirling blade, the flashes of firelight it cast dancing over his puffy-smooth cheek. "His granddam was a terrible serpent, and his uncle was born with the face of a pig."

The middle-aged knight turned to him with a wary smile. "Oui, my lord, 'tis true," he said carefully as if he were the boy's servant. "But he himself is only a man—"

"No!" The young one looked up, and Tarquin saw madness burning in his eyes. "He is chosen of Satan to be king—his blood taints God's lands, and soon it will be too late! Do you not know he has many sons? I have seen it!" Davyd glanced over at Tarquin, one corner of his mouth turned up in the hint of a smile, and the boy lunged to his feet. "The blood of the unrighteous!" he shouted into Davyd's face.

"My lord, please," the servant-knight said, though the old man was actually smiling. "These men mean to help us."

"Heathens," the boy muttered, his face dark with contempt, but he allowed himself to be put back into his chair.

"Is there a problem?" Davyd asked mildly, careful not to look at Tarquin again. He had understood very little of the young one's ravings, but he had heard enough to think perhaps sailing to England might be the better choice. The plotting of fanatics rarely turned out well.

"Your part in our enterprise will be quite small," the servant-knight answered with a scowl. "No more than a single battle." He dropped a heavy bag on the table. "If you survive, you'll be rich."

"And if we don't, it won't matter," Davyd agreed with a genial grin. He picked up the bag and peered inside, then looked over at Tarquin. "What do you think?" he asked in rapid Arabic, a nomad's dialect far removed from the simplified version the Frenchman could barely twist his tongue around.

"You do what you will, but I can't," Tarquin answered him in kind. "The boy is mad, but I know what he meant—he speaks of my king." The rumors of Henry's demonic heritage had been told since before he was crowned king of England, and having had some dealings with his kin, Tarquin could almost believe them. But he still couldn't participate in a conspiracy against him.

"I didn't know you had a king," Davyd said.

"I don't," Tarquin admitted. "But my patron does, and he will fight for him."

"Ah," Davyd nodded. One of the few details of Tarquin's past he knew was that his friend had once served a man he still loved. He had refused jobs before for this reason, and Davyd respected his loyalty even if he didn't understand it. "You will forgive us, messieurs," he went on, reverting back to halting French. "We cannot help you."

"Like father, like son," the old man suddenly spoke, his twisted grin growing wider. "I knew I saw Bruel in your face; now I see him in your actions."

The servant-knight looked from Davyd to Tarquin, and even the boy looked up. "You know this brute?"

"I knew his father," the old man said. "Gaston Bruel. I

served him once when my luck had run sour, and this one was no more than a pup."

In an instant, every nerve in Tarquin's body came to life. This man had been at Bruel Castle when his father had fallen down the stairs and died. This so-called knight had been among the ones casting lots to marry Tarquin's half-sister, Nan, a baby barely four years old but Bruel's only legitimate heir.

"The heir was a girl," the old man continued, echoing his thoughts. "The pup was a bastard—Bruel would have drowned him if he hadn't been afraid of the devil. His mother was the village witch; not even the other peasants would touch him." He smiled again. "Or do I mistake your face?"

"No," Tarquin answered, his own voice hollow and distant in his ears. He had stolen Nan from them, spirited her away to her dead mother's brother, William of Brinlaw, and he'd never let himself think again of the pack of curs they'd left behind. Will's friend, Raynard, had gone back and taken possession of Bruel Castle on Nan's behalf, scattering the scoundrel garrison to the winds. But here was one of them turning up on the far side of the world like a nightmare that wouldn't die. "You don't mistake me," Tarquin said aloud, cold as death. His hand itched for the feel of his sword, but he wouldn't reach for it, wouldn't kill again for no more cause than ridding the world of this old villain. Let the rheumatism take him and hell after.

"A spy," the boy-knight suddenly said, staring at Tarquin with eyes wide with fear. "One of Henry's minions." He stood so quickly, his chair fell over. "I cast thee out," he said, holding up his dagger, the shaft and quillons making a cross. "To you, O devil, begone! *Tu autem effugare, diabole!*"

"My lord, stop it," the servant-knight said, shrinking from the boy as if he feared to touch him.

"His mother was a witch," the young man insisted. Tarquin stood up, and the youth stumbled back a step, his expression wild with horror. "He said it."

"He lies," Tarquin said in the same nobleman's French, his tone almost kind. In truth, he felt no animosity toward the poor creature. The boy had a madman's sight; he spoke no more than truth. Why should he be punished for that?

The boy lunged forward, a wild strike with the dagger that Tarquin easily avoided, but Davyd stood up, even so. "He was joking," Tarquin went on in the same even tone.

"Oui, my lord," the old man agreed, but he was still smiling, watching them all with avid fascination.

"There, you see?" the servant-knight soothed, but Tarquin saw a threat in his eyes. The boy had said Henry's name aloud; Tarquin and Davyd knew too much. Tarquin glanced at Davyd, saw he understood as well.

"Truly?" the boy asked the old man, still trembling. "You do not know him?"

"Of course he does not," the servant-knight soothed, putting a hand on the boy's shoulder. "How could he?"

Davyd was becoming more and more confused. Tarquin seemed calm enough, but he knew that light that burned in his eyes, had seen the killing madness take him before. Something the old man had said had brought it out, not the boy, but what? "What is it?" he asked in Arabic, his hand going to his sword under his long coat.

"Nothing," Tarquin answered, his eyes on the servant-knight, the most likely threat. They had seen no one else coming in, but others could be hiding in the rocks outside. His berserker madness might yet serve them well.

"Then you are blind!" the boy suddenly screamed, lunging for Tarquin in earnest. "In the name of Christ, you die!" He fell full weight on Tarquin, the fiery brazier scattering sparks around their feet as Tarquin fell backwards with the boy still lunging over him. He only meant to push him back, to deflect the arc of the cross-shaped dagger plunging toward his face, but when his right arm came up to shove him aside, the boy thrashed and twisted to his left, impaling himself on Tarquin's own dagger. He screamed again, this time in pain, tears streaming down his cheeks, but he still kept coming, still striking, slashing at Tarquin's arms as he chanted more Latin gibberish, impossible to understand in the midst of his sobs. Still trying to save him, Tarquin grabbed his greasy black hair in his fist and landed a heavy punch to his jaw. The boy's eyes rolled back in his head as he fell, his face still twisted in a teeth-baring grimace.

Tarquin rolled free of him, rose to his feet, and drew his sword in a single motion. The servant-knight was coming toward him, sword drawn, and Tarquin struck, a slashing blow across the face that opened the flesh to the bone. The demon had him now; he was invincible, fearless in fury. A howl of pain, then another flash of the victim's sword, upward toward his belly, and he dodged, twisted away easily, struck back again, a stab where the shoulder met the arm, the sword point glancing off chain mail but the edge of the blade making contact, cleaving the arm away. Another, better scream, and the servant-knight fell, pleading mercy, praying God, and Tarquin killed him, slashing the blade across his throat.

A sound pierced the scarlet fog. Laughter—the old man was laughing. Tarquin felt a snap, the last fiber of his reason letting go. He lunged for the old man bare-handed, his sword falling away. He felt the brittle bones of the aged shoulders crackle like twigs, saw the rheumy eyes roll back, but he didn't let go. He made a fist, felt pain in his own shoulder as he hit him again and again, seeing his father's face.

"Tarquin, enough!" Davyd was grabbing at his arms, pinning them back, as strong as Tarquin himself. "Let him be!" Tarquin turned on him, his eyes wild, and the old man fell to the ground. "It's all right," Davyd said, suppressing a shudder at the look of madness in Tarquin's eyes. In that moment, he could almost believe the dead boy had been right. He let Tarquin go, then put a hand on his friend's shoulder as he turned away, the passion seeming to drain from his body as the expression drained from his face. "Sweet Allah," he muttered, turning his face away.

Tarquin shook his head, unable to speak, barely able to see, but he could hear, gasping sobs amidst the roar of his own blood. He felt something touch his ankle, looked down, and saw the boy crawling toward him, slow and clumsy, grabbing at his boot. The rage drained away like blood from a wound as he saw the madman's eyes, entreating mercy, blazing hate.

He dropped to his knee, fighting back the nausea that always came when the demon had gone, willing himself upright. "Be still," he ordered in French, slashing the straps on the boy's padded shirt. He peeled back the leather and almost swooned at the sight and stench of what he found underneath. The boy was wearing the hair shirt of a penitent, and it was crawling with vermin and causing the flesh underneath to crack and fester. Worse was the burn, a cross-shaped wound in his breast just over his heart that looked to have been made and remade many times over with a red-hot blade and never allowed to heal. The deep puncture Tarquin's dagger had made in his stomach seemed clean and kind by comparison. "My father's mark, demon," the boy rasped, a strange smile on his face. "He makes my murders righteous." Tarquin looked away, sickened as much by these words as the horror of the wound that inspired them.

"Holy Father, save him," Tarquin muttered in his native English, barely aware he spoke the words as he held the torn leather over the wound and pressed, not wanting to touch him but wanting less to watch him die, this innocent monster he had killed. "Save him, in Christ's sweet name . . ."

The boy smiled, his eyes focused for a moment on Tarquin's face. "Can a demon pray?" he mused. "Or have I saved you?" He raised his hand and made the sign of the cross. "In nomine Patris, et Filii . . ." The words trailed off as his hand fell and his eyes glazed over, dead.

"The son is nothing." The old man's voice was hollow and weak, the rasping words of a ghost. "But this father he spoke of . . ." One eye was still whole and alive, focused on Tarquin's face. "The father will hunt you the rest of your days, son of Bruel," he swore, barely louder than a whisper. "He'll mount your head on a pike."

Let him, Tarquin thought, sitting down hard on the ground. He looked down at his hands, covered in blood, powerful arms bloodied as well from the pointless stabs the boy's dagger had made in his flesh. The boy lay beside him, split open like a butchered animal; the old man had fallen silent, gasping and wheezing for breath. Tarquin heard his mother gasping for air, felt her grip on his wrist growing weaker and weaker . . . Twenty years and more, and he still felt her, was half-surprised not to see her lying on the floor in front of him between the old man and the boy.

Davyd watched his friend, mystified by his behavior, the obvious pain on his face. Why should this killing so touch him when so many others had not? "Come on," he said at last, taking hold of Tarquin's arm. "Let's leave this place."

I can't, Tarquin thought but couldn't say. *I am my father's son.*

5

◉⁓◉

Bruel Castle, England
May, 1173

Malinda was out of the castle at sunrise, over the drawbridge and into the woods, outrunning the safety of home. The family had been at Bruel for more than a month, waiting for Guy de Lancey to come and marry Nan, but so far he hadn't appeared. The wedding had been planned for April the first Sunday after Easter, but Guy was with the King, and the King was at war. The three eldest princes had rebelled just after the start of the new year, and they were giving their father rather more trouble than he had expected. Mark and Phillipe had turned up Easter Sunday as planned, but they hadn't seen Guy or the King in weeks, so they couldn't tell when they might arrive. All anyone could do was wait. Nan was beside herself with worry, but in truth, Malinda was just bored. Since Christmas, she had felt cut off from her family, out of sorts with the world. Nothing seemed to make her happy; everything she did seemed wrong. Even Lisbet had begun to lose patience with her moods. Her father had actually threatened to send her to a nunnery for her own protection after she suggested to Nan she might be better off if

Guy were in fact to fall in battle. In short, she had become a witch indeed. She didn't want to be—inside, she cringed to hear the words that came out of her mouth. But she couldn't seem to stop herself. And since they had come to Bruel, she had been even worse.

She untied her mantle as she entered a clearing, the new sun already hot. At Brinlaw, she knew every tree for miles, but these woods were less familiar. Growing up, they had rarely been at Bruel—her father hated it. Even Lisbet and Phillipe thought of Brinlaw as home. But Nan had decided she must be married at her own manor, and her uncle had finally agreed. Malinda rather liked it here, with the thicker woods and the salt smell of the marsh. But with all the wedding preparations, this was the first real chance she'd had to explore.

Her pet goshawk, Rufus, swooped down to skim the pale green grass, searching for breakfast. Like her mother, she had always been able to charm any bird of prey; 'twas part of her faery heritage. But Rufus was her favorite. He had chosen her as mistress of his own accord when he was barely more than a fledgling. She called to him now, and he abandoned the hunt to settle on her fist, cocking his head to one side as if to see her face more clearly. "Thanks, sweet soldier," she murmured, stroking his crested head. His feathers were a soft, pale brown tipped in reddish gold, and either eye was ringed in stripes of white. "Pretty thing," she crooned. "You still love me anyway."

The lethal little beak opened, and he made a clicking sound in his throat, the same sound he would use to beguile his prey. Winking at her once more, he took flight, and she laughed, feeling almost herself again. It could be worse, she thought, the tall grass tickling her outstretched palms as she walked deeper into the clearing. She could be like poor Queen Eleanor, locked away from the world. Mark and Phillipe had been stationed at Falaise as part of her guard, and they said she still kept her court of chivalry just the same, but Malinda thought it must be very empty and sad. What was the point of chivalry, after all, if the knights who purported to adore you were actually your jailers?

The remains of a tiny cottage stood at the edge of the next copse of trees, and she stopped, puzzled. What was one peasant cottage doing so far from the castle? The thatch roof was gone, but the stones didn't seem so old— no older than the other houses in the village. She moved closer, and a hot wind swept out of the doorway to engulf her, as if she'd opened up a fiery furnace. "Rufus?" she said softly, though the bird had flown out of sight. "Did you feel that?"

She let herself fade invisible as she passed through the doorway, barely aware she had done it, dissolving into the past. For a moment, the smell of smoke was overwhelming, made her cover her nose and mouth with her hand, then suddenly it was gone, replaced by the smell of drying herbs. She walked over to the fireplace, put a hand on the rough stone mantel, and suddenly she was falling forward . . . No, someone else was falling, falling through her, another spirit falling through her own transparent form. She opened her mouth to scream, and another woman's voice came out. A woman with fire-red hair fell against the hearth at her feet; there was a horrible sound as her head made contact with the stone. A fire was burning; a pot was on the fire; the room was dark but for the firelight—

"Witch!" Whirling around, Malinda tried to scream

again. A man was coming toward her, a giant, his face scratched down one cheek, his features contorted with rage. He moved through Malinda just as the woman had, both of them swearing murder in roars and screams. He grabbed the woman, then hit her again in the face with his fist. Malinda felt sick, hearing the crack of shattered bone, and she wanted to run away, but she felt frozen to the spot. *Not real,* she promised herself, trying to back away, bumping into a wooden bed that had been a pile of shattered kindling a few moments before. *Just a vision . . . The past—it's already happened; it's done.* But no vision had ever captured her so completely, held her so fast. Usually she could see, but only as shadows; this nighttime cottage looked real. She couldn't escape it, couldn't look away. The man was beating the woman to death. Her struggles meant nothing; he meant for her to die. "I will be free," he kept repeating, a guttural chant in time to the rhythm of his blows, and still she fought him tooth and nail, shrieking words Malinda couldn't understand, singsong gibberish like her own faery language run mad.

Suddenly another phantom passed through her, smaller, but more intense—a child, and her heart broke to feel him. She tried to catch him, hold him fast, but he was running, running at the man, a thick stick of firewood clutched tightly in both hands. He struck the man hard across the back, made him stagger, but the brute was too big, the boy too small. He held on to his stick with all his might even as the man wrenched it away. Malinda heard the child's wrist snap. "No!" she screamed as the man grabbed the child by the throat, lifting him off his feet. "Help him!" But the woman just watched, half crouched by the hearth, her eyes pale gold ringed in black. The child made no sound, but his legs kicked madly, one hand tearing at the man's grip around his throat, but it was no use—his lips were turning blue. "Let him go!" Malinda screamed again, grabbing for the man, but in this world, she was the ghost; she had no solid form. "Stop it," she wept, sinking to the floor as the boy stopped struggling, his eyes rolling back as he fainted. "I'm sorry," she wept as the man flung the seemingly lifeless little body to the floor. She saw his eyes open slowly, eyes like the woman's, pale gold ringed in black, watched him, weeping, as he watched his mother die. Malinda closed her eyes, unable to bear to see more, and she smelled the smoke again, felt flames singeing her skin. Opening her eyes, she saw the room engulfed in fire, saw the child staring through her to the body burning on the floor before the hearth, a flaming torch in his hand. "Run!" Malinda shouted as the flames danced all around him, cutting off his escape. "Run away!"

The boy looked up as if he'd heard her, his eyes changing focus as if he saw her face. "Run away," she repeated. "Run away and be safe." His mouth opened, his eyes opened wide, but no words came, only tears. After a moment, he turned and ran for the door, his form fading to transparency as he passed the threshold, the flames fading away as well, and the corpse, and all, leaving the empty ruin open to the sun.

Malinda looked down, saw her empty sleeves, willed herself solid again. Outside, she could hear Rufus crying out in triumph—he must have caught a mouse. She climbed back to her feet, her legs trembling beneath her. What a *vision* . . . She would have to remember not to come back here. As if she could ever forget . . . Suddenly she was running, desperate to escape, her mantle falling forgotten behind her.

Tarquin had awakened from restless sleep to the sound of distant screams—a woman screaming. *"Let him go!"* she cried as he rolled over on the dew-damp ground, closing his eyelids more tightly against the bright morning light. He was still dreaming, he thought, throwing his arm across his eyes. *"Run!"* the voice screamed, tearing into his doze again. *"Run away!"*

He sat up, blinking, his head spinning but his senses alert. Birds were singing; the wind was whispering in the new-made leaves. No human sound . . . He stood up and walked over to his horse, which stood grazing peacefully nearby. He must have still been dreaming.

Davyd had left him in a tiny cove in a village near Southampton three days before, promising to return there on the last day of November. Tarquin had ridden the rest of the way on horseback, arriving within sight of Bruel Castle just after sundown the evening before. He had watched the twilight fade behind the battlements from the shelter of the forest, unable to make himself go in. The Brinlaw pennant flew above the tallest tower, the golden dragon catching the last of the light. Will Brinlaw and his family were here, just as Tarquin had known they would be. But the flickering lights in the windows were too familiar. Looking up at them, all he could remember was his father's hall, his own dear vision of hell.

By full dark, he had decided to wait until the morning to go inside. One more night of freedom—surely his destiny could not begrudge him that. He wanted to see Nan and Alista, but now that the moment was at hand, he was afraid. Once he saw them, he couldn't change his mind.

He had made camp in a thicket, a familiar haunt from childhood. The brush was so thick that even from the path no one could tell he was there or even see his horse. Home was not far—Tabby's cottage was no more than a short sprint away.

Now he found himself gazing down the path through the tangled branches and heard the sound of footsteps running toward him, small and light. He knew he had heard something before. He waited silently, half expecting to see his own ghost. He stepped through the screen of undergrowth just as a woman came running down the path.

The man appeared out of nowhere, so suddenly Malinda stumbled and nearly fell. She caught herself, started to speak, but the words dried up in her throat. It was her vision come after her, the same man from the cottage, only more terrifying. He had grown even bigger, not just tall but massive, towering over her, blocking the path, and his appearance was even more savage, his hair longer, his clothing more rough.

But no, this was not the same man at all . . . The face was similar, yes, but as her heart settled down a bit, she could see that the features were finer, almost delicate, the cheekbones more pronounced. His long hair was brighter, dark brown streaked with red, and thicker, as lush as her own, tied and braided back in clumps that made him look like some Viking warrior in an ancient tale. He was dressed like a warrior, too, in stained leather armor, and he wore both a sword and a dagger. No, this was not the same man, but she still had reason to fear. The brute in her vision hadn't known she was there; this man did. He was looking right at her with pale gold eyes ringed in black, the same eyes as the child.

"Holy Christ," Tarquin breathed. It was her. All the details of the vision he had lost came back, sharp as a blade. *"Come with me,"* those lips had spoken. *"Come and take me home."* Green eyes fixed on his face, filled with fear and fascination, golden hair loose and tangled . . . she was just the same.

"Who are you?" Malinda demanded, the sound of his voice giving her courage. In truth, he looked almost as frightened as she felt. "What are you doing here?" Rufus swooped down from a branch behind her and settled on her shoulder.

Whoever she was, she was real; she had a voice. "Why did you scream?" he asked her, remembering the sound that had awakened him, remembering the beach. Everything was all mixed up, his vision and his dreams and the reality of this moment in which she didn't seem to know him at all. "Who is with you?"

"No one," Malinda said before she thought, wanting the words back as soon as they were spoken. He was probably some Saxon bandit hiding out in the forest, and here she was telling him she was all alone. "What do you want?" she asked coldly, covering fear with haughtiness.

"You," Tarquin answered automatically, and something like the familiar rage gathered around him, only made more intense by desire. She had called to him, now she wanted to treat him like the lowest of the low. His own vision meant to turn him away. He felt drunk, unable to think clearly looking into those eyes. "I came here for you."

Malinda gasped, her heart skipping a beat. As a nobleman's daughter, she had heard often enough about the perils of strange men in the forest, particularly men who looked like this one. But she would never have expected a rapist to be quite so blunt or quite so verbal. If he meant to ravish her, why would he waste time saying so? But if that wasn't what he meant, what did he mean? "No," she answered, taking a step backward. "Leave me alone."

"I can't." He had to touch her, just to be certain she was real. "*Come with me,*" she had ordered in his dream, and he had abandoned his every hope of peace to obey . . . "I won't hurt you," he promised, moving closer, and it was true. He didn't want to hurt her, couldn't bear it; in his dream, he had seen a bruise on her cheek and been miserable at the thought that he had been the one who caused it. But he had to touch her, tame her as she had tamed the hawk on her shoulder.

Run, Malinda's brain was screaming just as she had screamed at the ghost of the child. Rufus took flight as if he heard, but her body refused to move. She felt captured, frozen, as the man's eyes turned soft. "*I came here for you . . .*" If he touched her, she would be lost.

He touched her cheek, felt her tremble, heard her breath come short, but still she didn't run. Wide green eyes gazed up into his. "Are you real?" he murmured, tracing the shape of her jaw. "Are you mine?"

"No," she answered, a puff of ragged breath. "I am my own."

Slowly he bent to kiss her, unable to resist, and still she didn't fight him, surrender in her eyes. His eyes closed first as his breath mingled with hers.

Yes, Malinda thought, her senses alive with him. He smelled of the wild forest, the scent coming stronger as he came closer. She would taste his soul in his breath, warm and sweet, a tender flame, and suddenly she ached for him, burned to be consumed. "No!" she cried aloud as his mouth brushed hers, pushing him away, stumbling backwards when he didn't budge. He was magic—she would be lost. Rufus dove at him, screaming, and she ran, branches tearing at her hair and clawing her skin. She could hear his footsteps behind her at first, and she ran faster, her lungs burning in her chest.

"Malinda!" Mark's voice was so welcome and so unexpected, Malinda could barely believe she'd heard it until she crashed into his arms. "What are you— What's wrong?" he demanded, catching her before she fell.

"I—there's a man," she stammered. "He was . . . I don't know who he is or where he came from, but he's back there." She turned, half expecting to see her supernatural seducer bearing down on her. For such he must be; no ordinary man could have confused her so, made her so afraid and so excited all at once. "I saw him, Mark, I swear."

"I believe you," her brother promised, drawing his sword. "Go back to the house—"

"No!" She grabbed his arm, though she was uncertain why. She should want his protection, should want Mark to cut down this brigand where he stood for touching her. But she couldn't picture it, couldn't imagine Mark, knight that he was, being able to hurt him. "Please, let's just go home."

"Don't be ridiculous," he scoffed. "Was he truly as frightening as all that?" In truth, Mark was quite concerned. Malinda was hardly the type to go to pieces just because she'd seen a stranger. "Did he hurt you?" he demanded.

"No," she promised. "I was just startled—Mark!" He

had started back the way she had come so fast she had to run to keep up.

"Where is he?" he asked, stopping where the forest reached out to all but block the path.

"Just there." She looked around, even more confused. "I was walking—running, actually, and he just sort of appeared."

"Why were you running?" Mark asked.

"I saw something," she explained. Mark knew all about her powers, or at least all she knew herself. "A vision, something I think must have happened in the past. It upset me, and I was running away, and this man just appeared— Why are you smiling?"

"No reason," he said, feeling much relieved. "The villagers all say these woods are haunted. Maybe they're right."

"You think I saw a ghost?"

"Do you?"

"No . . . I don't know." She looked around again, but there was no sign of the man she had seen. Could she have imagined it? *"I came here for you."* She touched her mouth, still burning from his near-kiss. Her mother's book spoke of spirits that haunted the ancient places, demons and the souls of the old ones long dead . . . She herself was descended from a faery race. Perhaps the creature she had seen had been called by her own magic. She thought of his eyes again, the same as the child she had watched be nearly murdered . . .

"Malinda?" Mark pressed.

"I don't know," she repeated, shaking her head. "Whatever it was, it's gone now." She looked at Mark. "What are you doing here?"

"Looking for you," he answered. "We've had word from de Lancey—he and King Henry should be here by dinner tomorrow." He touched her arm. "Are you sure you're all right?"

"Yes," she promised. "Let's just go home." She suddenly realized her hawk was nowhere in sight. "Rufus!" She turned in a circle, looking up into the trees. "Rufus, come here!" she called in faery-speak.

"You probably frightened him, tearing through the woods that way," Mark said. "He'll come back."

The hawk had flown at the man she had seen; that's how she had escaped. "Rufus!" she called again, a note of desperation in her voice.

From his hiding place, Tarquin reached out and stroked the hawk's soft breast. He was lying flat on his belly in the densest part of the thicket, watching the two beautiful nobles decide he was a ghost. The boy could be no one but Brinlaw's son—seeing him was like seeing Will as he had been when Tarquin was a child. The hawk had settled on a branch just beside his hand and was watching as well, seemingly content. Once Malinda had escaped, the hawk had apparently been willing to be friends . . . *Malinda?*

"Malinda, come on," Mark said. "He's probably chasing a rabbit. You know he'll come home soon."

She looked ready to cry, but she nodded. "I hope so," she answered, letting him lead her away.

Malinda Brinlaw . . . Tarquin rolled onto his back and stared up at the sun-dappled leaves. He remembered a willful little girl whose hair always seemed to be in knots, stamping her foot and demanding her own way . . . Will Brinlaw's firstborn child. "I don't like you," she had told him on the day he left Brinlaw Castle, little fists planted on her hips. "You made my mama and my cousin cry." Alista's daughter, the faery heir of Falconskeep—the beach in his vision had been the beach at Falconskeep, a place he hadn't seen since before Malinda was born. Malinda . . . he smiled grimly, a joke at his own expense. The vision he had chased all the way from Russadir wasn't his at all, nor would she ever be. "*I am my own,*" she had said in the moment he had touched her. But that was wrong, too—she belonged to Brinlaw. If she hadn't escaped him . . . But she had escaped; they both had.

He sat up, and the hawk fluttered his wings as if ready to follow wherever he might go. "Rufus," he said, holding out his fist, and the bird came to him as if he'd been trained to his hand. Alista had charmed falcons; her daughter was likely the same. He stroked the creature's throat. Malinda's pet . . . He would keep his promise to Nan, see her again once more, then he would go. He didn't dare do anything else. If he stayed near Malinda . . . He pushed the thought from his mind. One short visit, then he would be gone for good. Her good as well as his own.

By the time Malinda and Mark made it home, the castle was in an uproar, preparing for the wedding and the King. At her brother's insistence, Malinda gave a sketchy account of her encounter with the stranger, leaving out her vision and the kiss. Will and Phillipe were both concerned at first, but Raynard was convinced it was some farmer poaching deer, and he soon had them convinced as well. Alista and Dru scolded Malinda for not being more careful. Lisbet took Mark's joke to heart and decided it must surely have been a ghost. But ultimately, no one seemed to care much. Will insisted that Mark and Phillipe must accompany Nan,

Malinda, and Lisbet on their expedition to pick berries for King Henry's tarts; otherwise, the preparations went on as before with very little change.

"So, was he handsome?" Lisbet asked, swinging her basket as they skirted the edge of the pond.

"Who?" Malinda asked. Willie was carrying her basket and emptying it almost as quickly as she filled it up, but she barely noticed. On the one hand, she hadn't wanted to tell her family about her fright in the first place. On the other, since she'd been forced to tell, they might have been a bit more excited—she could have been killed or worse, after all. So she was feeling more than usually cross—not to mention all the queer feelings the encounter itself had inspired.

"Your ghost," Lisbet teased, leaning far over the water's edge to reach a particularly juicy-looking cluster of berries.

"No," Malinda answered. "He was dirty and rude." Watching her friend lean over even further, she was possessed by an irresistible demon . . .

"You filthy cow!" Lisbet sputtered as she surfaced, her hair and gown streaming muddy water.

"Malinda!" Nan cried, appalled, as Malinda shrieked with laughter.

"Me next!" Willie yelled, headed for the pond.

"No, you don't," Mark warned, catching him.

"No, Willie, not you," Lisbet said, stalking toward Malinda with obvious intent.

"Lisbet, don't you dare," Phillipe warned, putting himself between his dripping sister and her giggling friend.

"And why not?" Malinda demanded, grabbing one of his arms as Lisbet grabbed the other.

"No!" Nan cried as all three tumbled into the water, the

poor knight dragged under, armor and all, by a pair of wicked water nymphs bent on his destruction.

"Well done!" Lisbet crowed, catching Malinda's hand and lifting it in triumph as they emerged victorious, waist deep in the pond.

"Very ladylike," Phillipe grumbled as he dragged himself toward the shore, armor creaking. "What would Queen Eleanor say?"

"Oh, posh for Eleanor," Nan said, laughing in spite of herself.

"Amen," Lisbet said. "I hate being a lady all the time."

"You aren't a lady even half the time," Mark retorted, helping his friend climb out on the slippery bank and nearly getting himself dunked in the process.

"Even half is too much," Lisbet answered airily, sinking out of sight up to her chin.

"I want to swim," Willie protested, trying to wriggle out of Nan's grip.

"We aren't swimming, Willie, truly," Malinda promised. In truth, she felt better, the childish prank clearing her head a bit.

"Malinda, look," Lisbet said, giving her arm a tug. "Is that him?"

Coming toward them across the meadow was a man dressed like a brigand, leading a horse in the fringed tack of an Arabian. Even from such a distance, Malinda could see he was clean-shaven, cleaner altogether, but he was still the same man she had encountered in the woods. The man who had tried to kiss her . . .

"Tarquin!" Nan shrieked, sprinting toward the stranger. Before anyone could think how to stop her, she had flung herself into his arms.

Tarquin laughed as he swung his half-sister off her feet, returning her hug in kind. "I knew you'd come back," she said, kissing him again and again. "I knew it."

"Pardon, mam'selle, but have we met?" he teased, squeezing her close. He hadn't realized just how dearly he had missed her. She was all grown up, so beautiful, and she still loved him—for a moment, he almost forgot what he was. "It's all right," he promised, a kiss against her ear.

"God save us, it is Tarquin," Phillipe laughed as Malinda and Lisbet came out of the pond. "Daisy, is that the man you saw?"

"No," Malinda lied, trying hard not to blush. He couldn't be Tarquin. Tarquin was Nan's brother—nobody special. Nothing to do with her at all, no one to frighten her, certainly. *"I came here for you,"* he had said, the words echoing inside her head as she watched him hug her cousin.

"You remember Phillipe," Nan was saying, leading him by the hand. "And Mark was barely walking when you left."

"Yes," Tarquin agreed. Geoffrey d'Anjou's bastard looked just like him—always had, even as a child—and up close Mark was even more a copy of his father. A pretty creature, sopping wet, with Druscilla's tempting figure and Raynard's wicked smile—Lisbet, he remembered—and a stocky little boy with Alista's black curls. And of course Malinda . . .

"We were all babies," Lisbet laughed, coming forward to kiss him. "Welcome home, Tarquin."

"That's Lisbet, of course," Nan went on. "And don't you remember Malinda?"

"Malinda . . . yes, of course," he answered, meeting his faery-dream's eyes.

"Maybe he remembers me too well," Malinda said

lightly. He was staring at her, daring her to tell them all what he had done. *Would he deny it?* she wondered. Suddenly she was very aware of how wet she was, her gown clammy and clinging.

"You were rather a monster," Phillipe teased, putting an arm around her shoulders. Phillipe had been rather distant since he and Mark had come home, lost in his own thoughts, but he now seemed to sense his friend's discomfort and was quick to offer his support even as he teased her with a charming smile for Tarquin on his face. "I warn you, Tarquin, she's actually gotten worse."

"I'll remember that," Tarquin said, making himself smile, making his eyes tear free of her gaze. *Could this boy be her lover? Would Brinlaw allow such a thing?* The demon inside him snarled fury at the very idea, made him almost forget Nan, still cleaving to his side.

The scream of a hawk broke into his thoughts as Rufus swooped down among them. "Rufus!" Malinda cried, relieved, putting out her hand. But rather than coming to her, the bird flew to Tarquin, settling on the saddle of his horse. "Rufus!" she repeated, shocked and appalled.

"That is my sister's hawk," Willie informed Tarquin, only being helpful.

Tarquin looked at Malinda. For some reason, she was soaked as well, and there was no mistaking the fury burning in her eyes. She was magnificent; it tore his heart apart just to see her. She was still clinging to this Phillipe, still sheltered under his arm, and suddenly he couldn't bear it, had to hurt her as she hurt him. "Oh, I don't think so," he said aloud. "He belongs to me."

Malinda's eyes widened. *Liar!* she wanted to scream. How dare he? Was trying to ravish her not enough? Now he must steal from her as well? This was too much; she couldn't keep silent. "Does he in faith?" she demanded, all but laughing at the sheer absurdity of his claim. "How strange, when he belongs to me."

"Strange indeed," Tarquin answered, calmly meeting her eyes with his own as he stroked the goshawk's breast. "Since he seems to know you not."

"That is strange," Lisbet agreed.

"Rufus," Malinda began, losing patience, then she stopped, her face flushed hot but her temper still in her control. Nan was still looking up at her brother as if the whole world had suddenly bloomed, as if her happiness were finally complete. "It's all right, Willie," she began again with her sweetest, deadliest smile. "If Rufus wants to be with Tarquin, I don't mind."

"I'm pleased to hear it, my lady," Tarquin answered with a deadly smile of his own.

"So am I," Mark said, mystified. If his sister had a prize possession, it was the hawk, and she was rarely so eager to share. "Come on, let's go tell Papa and Mama Tarquin has come home."

Bruel Castle's hall was still swarming with activity, with nobles and servants in an equal state of frenzy preparing to greet the King. But Will and Alista might as well have been alone in all the world for all they noticed, so engrossed were they in speaking to each other, as always a circle of two. "At least now we know that Guy is all right," Alista said, handing back Henry's letter.

"Yes, at least that," Will agreed. A tiny frown of worry had appeared between his dear one's brows, and he kissed it softly. "It will be all right."

"Yes," she agreed with a sigh, leaning for a moment against her husband's chest, willfully oblivious to their audience of retainers. She sometimes thought Will had spent more time with Henry since their marriage than with her, but it couldn't be helped. If the King was making war in earnest, he would have Will Brinlaw with him or be damned. And Will Brinlaw would have her.

"Willie can come with us," Will said, continuing her thoughts as easily as if they were his own.

"Yes," she repeated, reluctantly letting him go. "But what about Malinda?"

Before he could answer, a sudden commotion of barking hounds and shouting children spilled into the hall. "Lady Alista, look!" Lisbet cried. "Look who has finally come home."

Tarquin was carrying Baby Will in one arm, but as soon as he walked into the hall, he forgot the child was there, lost in the memory of being a child himself. The last time he'd been in this room, all the fireplaces had been lit, belching black smoke from their soot-encrusted depths, and the floor was slimy with rotten rushes and filth. The walls were bare and black with dirt, the one tapestry that hung behind his father's chair a threadbare emblem of a wolf. "*Stop looking at me!*" his father had roared, unreasoning fear in his drunken eyes as he flung his rusted shield at his bastard. Nan was cowering on the floor behind Tarquin, shivering in the chill the fires never seemed to keep at bay.

"It's very different, isn't it?" Nan said softly, standing at his elbow.

He looked down at her, shocked to find a grown woman instead of a frightened child. Looking around again, he saw a single merry blaze in a hearth swept clean, fresh rushes, rich tapestries, the homey bustle of servants and knights-at-arms. "Yes," he answered, hugging her close with his free arm, Willie's arms now draped around his neck. "Very different."

"Tarquin!" Suddenly he was swept up in a woman's embrace—Druscilla, as flirtatious as ever. "Mon Dieu, you're tremendous," she teased. "And so fierce—it frightens me to look at you."

"Mama, stop it," Lisbet protested, taking Baby Will from him. "You're embarrassing him."

"He's not embarrassed," Alista said, coming to join them. "He's stunned."

Tarquin just looked at her, unable for the moment to speak. He had loved her with a kind of blind fury from the first moment he saw her, had sworn in his heart to never love another. When he'd known what he was, known that he was lost for good, Alista had been the one he most needed to protect, the love he most feared to destroy. Looking at her now, he found her as beautiful as ever, and he loved her just as dearly, but to his shock he found his love had changed. Meeting her eyes was no longer a kind of torture—it was coming home, an illusion, certainly, but a kind one nonetheless.

"Your timing is perfect," Alista was saying now, smiling in sweet contrast to the tears in her eyes. "But Nan never doubted you would come in time." She hugged him close, and suddenly he could move, and he squeezed her so hard he knew he must be hurting her, but he couldn't stop.

"I'm getting married," Nan explained.

"Against my better judgment," Will Brinlaw said. He embraced Tarquin as well, Alista sheltered for a moment between them.

"Married?" Tarquin echoed, confused. He had promised to come home for Nan's wedding; his vision had come just in time—but that was madness.

"I wanted to tell you," Nan was saying. "I tried to wait until you came home." She grinned, the wicked little girl of old. "And so, you see, I have."

"Sweet Christ!" Raynard swore, coming in from outside. "The prodigal hath returned." He embraced Tarquin as well, then drew back to arm's length to look at him. "So how did you like the world?" he asked.

"As well as anything, I suppose," Tarquin answered.

"I hope you didn't come home looking for quiet," the castellan laughed, clapping him on the cheek. "Will, another messenger has come. The King is encamped, but he will definitely be here tomorrow."

"You picked quite a day to come home, mon cher," Druscilla teased Tarquin with a smile.

"He picked the perfect day," Alista insisted, hugging him again.

Tarquin looked over Alista's shoulder at Malinda. She was watching him, her face impassive, her green eyes cold. Before anyone could say more, she turned and walked out of the hall.

6

The hall had pretty well emptied out. Tarquin was sitting near the fire, picking at the trencher of food Druscilla had insisted he have while Nan sat beside him and reread her letter from Guy. "So who is this person, anyway?" he asked her.

She smiled, knowing exactly who he meant. "Guy de Lancey, and he's wonderful," she said. "I can't wait for you to meet him."

"Are you sure about that?" he teased.

"Yes, quite." He sounded almost the same as always, and she could still see the handsome boy he had been under the routier's wildness, but there was no denying he had changed. He had never been exactly lighthearted, never been much of a talker, but now he was too quiet, too sunk in his own thoughts, and they didn't seem to be happy ones. *Where have you been?* she longed to ask him. *What could have happened to you?* But she was afraid to know. "Once you get to know him, I know you'll be friends. You'll just have to give one another time—he's almost as shy as you are." She touched his hand on the table. "Assuming you have time, I mean." His hand closed around hers, and she breathed an inward sigh of relief. "You've been gone so long," she went on, choosing her words with care, almost afraid to say anything. "Have you come home to stay?" He looked away, and her heart skipped a beat. "Tarquin?"

"I don't know," he finally answered. He didn't want to hurt her, but he couldn't lie to her either. And he couldn't stay here, not at his father's castle, not even at Brinlaw. As much as he loved Nan and her aunt and uncle, he didn't belong here any more, never had really, but now even less. The only real connection he had ever had was Nan, and she was about to be married, to start a family of her own here at her own castle, a place where he would never live again. And besides, her husband would hardly want her brigand half-brother hanging about, no matter how much time they spent learning to be friends. So Bruel was out of the question. And Brinlaw . . . Brinlaw had Malinda, and Malinda he could not have. The soothsayer had called their shared vision Tarquin's destiny . . . more like a cruel joke, God's jesting vengeance on a son of the devil.

Nan watched emotions flicker across her half-brother's face, the tiniest changes in his eyes. "Why did you come back if not to stay?" she pressed. "Why did you stay away?" She paused, knowing the injustice of what she meant to ask, but she couldn't stop herself. "Don't you love me anymore?"

He looked at her, obviously stricken, and she threw her arms around him, wishing she could take it back. "Of course I do," he promised as she clung to him. "Always . . ."

"I know," she admitted. "It's just that I've missed you so much."

"And I've missed you," he said. He kissed her hair before

pulling back, and she smiled at him through her tears. "I'm not going anywhere right now," he promised, unable to deny her. Magic, destiny, loyalty, and whatever else be damned, she was his little sister, and he couldn't hurt her, not yet. "Not until after your wedding at least."

"You promise?" she pressed.

He smiled. "I promise."

Will had come back into the hall and seen the last of this exchange from across the room. *Always the same,* he thought with an inward sigh. The first time he had seen Nan and her brother, she had been doing the same thing, begging him to stay with her while all the while he was desperate to be free. They had been children then, and Will and Alista had both thought Tarquin needed to stay, would outgrow his restlessness. Will still thought he should stay, though he understood the restlessness better, seeing him as a man. "He looks well," Raynard said, as usual reading his thoughts. "Though I never thought he'd be so tall as that—he's as big as you are."

"I thought he might be," Will smiled, but his eyes were still sad. "His father was a coward, but he wasn't a weakling."

"And Tarquin favors him?" Raynard said. Will had once been old Bruel's squire, had abandoned his post to escape him. His sister had been Bruel's wife; she had hanged herself to escape.

"Only in looks," Will answered. "I'm just not certain he knows that."

"Then we have to convince him," Raynard said. Will looked at him, their eyes meeting in perfect understanding, and the castellan grinned. "I think he's the answer to your problem."

*   *   *

That night at dinner, Tarquin was struck anew by how much everything had changed, how far he had come from the boy who once almost belonged here. When he and Nan were children at Brinlaw, they had been casual as commoners with their guardians, calling Will and Alista by their Christian names and joining into the conversation as readily as any noble knight when only the family was present. But Mark and Malinda were quite formal with their parents, calling them "my lady" and "my lord" as often as "Mama" and "Papa" and waiting on them more like retainers than children. Everyone apparently had his or her place at the table, and though the talk was easy, everyone's manners were impeccable, even Willie's. He sat at his mother's left and nodded drowsily over his cup, but he was a perfect little lord. Tarquin thought of Alista and Brother Paolo arguing philosophy so loudly the plates rattled, Nan perched on Will's lap to share his bowl, Raynard helping Tarquin sneak scraps to the dogs under the table. More often than not, Alista would have been wearing breeches, and Will would have brought his letters to the table to consult with her on his replies. In that world, he had felt safe and welcome. Now Will and Alista were grand as royalty, their household noble and perfect, and he felt like a barbarian come to raid the castle.

"Forgive me, Tarquin, but where have you been?" Mark asked as the next course of food was passed. "Brother Paolo said you went on the Crusade; have you been there all this while?"

"No," Tarquin answered. He wasn't quite sure how he should go on. How could he explain the life he had led since he left them without killing them all with the shock? "I was in Jerusalem a little more than a year."

"Did you like it?" Will asked, glancing at his wife.

"Not a bit, just as you told me I would not," Tarquin said. "I did well enough, I guess, but it's pointless—neither side will ever win."

"You mean we should give up Our Lord's Holy Land?" Phillipe asked, appalled.

"It's holy to the Turks as well," Tarquin pointed out. "And the Arabs. Why should they give it up?"

"Because ours is the True Faith," Phillipe answered, looking around at the others as if he couldn't believe his ears.

"So we believe, and we may be right," Tarquin answered, warming to the argument in spite of himself. "But they're the ones who live there."

"And so they may continue, if they will be converted," Mark said.

"And how will we convert them?" Tarquin asked. "By putting their children to the sword?"

"It doesn't seem the most efficient method, does it?" Alista interrupted, taking Will's hand under the table. Her husband had gone crusading once himself when he was young and single, and he had come to much the same conclusion as Tarquin. But he had enough discretion to keep his opinions to himself. "Enough of crusading, Tarquin— where have you been since?"

Speechless with shock, Malinda watched her mother smooth things over. Never in her life had she heard anyone say the things Tarquin was saying. He questioned the truth of the Church, spoke of Arabs and Turks as though they were perfectly nice people, no more to be despised than the French. Mark and Phillipe were gaping at him as though he had sprouted horns. But she found she didn't think him horrible at all, at least not for his words. He looked better than he had that afternoon—he'd obviously had a bath, the unkempt beard was gone completely, and even his hair had been cut. He was wearing clean, normal clothes, and his manners at table were as fine as any knight's. But even so, he barely looked civilized, a wild animal only pretending to be tamed. His eyes were still the same, and his words were like his eyes, savage and shocking and completely his own. "Yes, where?" she asked, bringing those eyes back to her. "Did you go back to Florence?"

Tarquin looked at her, surprised. She sounded almost civil. Since they had come back to the castle, Malinda had avoided him like the wages of sin, which in a sense he supposed he was and for which he could hardly blame her. But now she addressed him as if he might be a human creature after all. "Only briefly," he answered her. "I haven't stayed anywhere for very long. After I left the Holy Land, I hired on to fight for many different men, and I went where they sent me, wherever I could find work."

"My boy," Raynard grinned. He had been a mercenary himself when he and Will Brinlaw had met.

"Never say so," Druscilla scolded. "Tarquin, I am surprised at you."

"As am I," Nan agreed. "What would Brother Paolo say?"

"Nothing good," Tarquin admitted. It was strange; he was being scolded for professional murder as one would scold a pie thief. But that really wasn't so strange at all; it was the same old problem. They loved him, thought they knew him, and the boy they knew could never be truly evil; he must have just lost his way. A bit of scolding, a little extra attention, a few more prayers before breakfast, and he was bound to come back to the righteous. He looked over at Mark and Phillipe, the perfect products of this system, and he felt almost sick with envy. What would he not give to be like them, even Dru's boy with his Angevin blood? They knew what was expected, and they did it, pure in spirit, perfect in rest. No demons haunted their sleep, nor would they ever, be they old as he or Brinlaw or ancient Brother Paolo, no doubt sleeping the sleep of the innocent in Florence right now. Malinda had run to her brother's arms for protection from him in the woods, and Phillipe had put his arm around her at the pond, protecting her again . . . This was what she needed, the kind of lover she must have. Never him . . .

"Leave him alone," Raynard said.

"Yes, Mama, for pity," Lisbet laughed. "Tell us all the places you've been, Tarquin."

"All of them?" he laughed. "How much time do you have?" A squire refilled his cup, and he gave the boy a brusque nod, unaccustomed to such service after so long without it. "Italy was the most grand," he went on. "Florence truly is beautiful, Alista, just as Brother Paolo described it. But there are so many people—not even London comes close, not even Paris." He trailed his knife down the tabletop, mentally drawing a map. "In Africa a man can breathe, especially in the desert."

"You liked the desert?" Raynard laughed, looking over at Will.

"I loved it," Tarquin answered. "There are cities there, too, beautiful cities like Alexandria—"

"Alexander the Great," Willie mumbled, half asleep.

"Exactly," Tarquin said with a smile. "All the buildings are so white, it hurts your eyes to look at them, and the light there is so clean ... Greece is the same, only more so, simple and beautiful. We think of England as ancient, but you feel history there. You walk on the streets, and you can't help but think of all the men who must have walked there before ..." He let his voice trail off, embarrassed. "It's hot," he finished.

"That much I remember," Will agreed. "But I never traveled so far. You must have spent half your time on ships."

"More than half," Tarquin replied, nodding. "Especially the last few years. I have a ship of my own—the *Falcon*. I have a falcon worked on the sails."

"Should I be flattered?" Alista smiled.

"Yea, lady, you should," he answered, smiling back. "'Tis in your honor."

"Where is this ship now?" Malinda asked, studiously polite.

"I know not," Tarquin answered, surprised again to be addressed, even in such a tone. She had the bearing of a princess, with the thin sheen of untouchable elegance her mother had never perfected, beautiful as she was. He thought again of his vision, the raw feeling in the vision-woman's eyes. What kind of evil spirit could have shown him such a lie? "I have lent it to a friend."

"So you mean to go back to it," Malinda asked, glancing over at Nan.

"He hasn't decided yet," Nan answered for him before he could speak.

"Nothing is decided yet," Will said. "Once Henry makes his wishes known, we will make our plans, and so will Tarquin."

"Will you go with His Majesty to war?" Malinda asked,

turning her attention to her father and tempering her attitude accordingly.

"If he asks me, yes," Will answered. "Of course."

A new trouble nagged at her mind. "Will Mama go with you?" she asked. "May I?"

"You will stay in England," Will said, his expression like stone as he met his daughter's eyes. Until this moment, Tarquin hadn't realized just how much they looked alike.

"As you say, love, nothing is decided," Alista said, laying a hand on her husband's arm. "No need to quarrel now."

"No," Malinda agreed, looking down at her plate. "No need." Looking up, she found Tarquin watching her again, and she wanted to fling her spoon at him or sink under the table. He had sailed around the world; she couldn't get out of the house. She tried to imagine Alexandria, what it must be like to walk down those ancient streets and look on those pure white houses, or to be on a ship, sailing the Mediterranean under a falcon sail. But she couldn't even imagine it. Everything about Tarquin seemed to mock her, make her feel what a pitiful, miniature life she had to lead. *"I came here for you,"* he had said. Why? To make her miserable?

"Poor Willie is breaking his neck," Dru suddenly laughed. The smallest Brinlaw had fallen asleep at last, his curly head propped precariously against the side of his mother's chair.

"Wake up, sweeting," Alista urged, trying to straighten him up, but he was limp as a sodden rag. "Willie," she laughed, giving him a gentle shake.

"I'll take him," Tarquin offered, getting up.

"No, I'll do it," Mark said quickly.

"Please let me," Tarquin said. He took the child up from his mother, and Willie flopped gratefully to his shoulder, already snoring. "Someone just tell me where to put him down."

"I'll show you," Malinda said, getting up.

Alista looked at her daughter, trying in vain to read her expression. Lisbet looked a bit put out, but Malinda seemed innocent as a lamb. "Put him in our room," she said. "We should all be upstairs soon—the morning will be here before we know it."

"Speak for yourself, love," Will sighed as he got up. "Raynard and I still have to divide the garrison." He put a hand on Mark's shoulder. "Come and help us, sirrah."

"Of course," Mark said, hastening to obey.

Malinda led Tarquin up the stairs. "In here," she said, opening the door to the smaller room where her parents would sleep during King Henry's visit. She watched as he lay Willie on the cot at the foot of the bed and crouched down to tuck the blankets around him. "I want my goshawk back."

"Shh," Tarquin said. "You'll wake him."

"I couldn't wake him with a gong," she retorted. "Where is Rufus?"

"I hate that name." He looked up at her and couldn't help but smile. Perhaps he had misjudged her at the table. All the haughty ice had melted, leaving a most attractive fury in its place. "I think I'll have to change it."

Malinda wanted to hit him hard enough to smack that smirk through the back of his head. But that would not be the act of a lady. "Give him back," she ordered through gritted teeth instead.

"I didn't take him," he protested. "He came to me—"

"You bewitched him—"

"Hardly." He straightened up, towering over her again. "That's your talent, not mine."

"As if you knew anything about it," she scoffed. "Why did you try to kiss me?"

His expression changed, every trace of humor gone. "I didn't," he said, turning away.

"I beg your pardon?" She followed him out into the hall. "You did, most certainly."

"No." He stopped, fixing her with those haunted, haunting eyes. "You dreamed it. And so did I." Before she could form a reply to this madness, he walked away, leaving her to fume.

Will Brinlaw didn't make it back inside until well after midnight, and he wasn't able to talk to his wife until they were in bed and the rest of the castle was quiet. In the dark, he told her his plan. He couldn't see her face, but as soon as he finished, he could feel her doubtful smile. "Are you sure that's wise?" she said, rising up on her elbow.

"Why not?" he grumbled, annoyed. He had found the perfect solution to what had seemed an insurmountable problem, so naturally his wife had to find something wrong with it. "Tarquin grew up around you; he's been to Falconskeep. He'll know what's at stake."

"That's true," Alista admitted. "But . . . don't you think you might be shutting the fox in to guard the chickens?"

Now it was his turn to sit up. "Since when don't you trust Tarquin?"

"I trust him completely, of course." She pushed him back down on the pillows and snuggled down on his shoulder. "But in case you haven't noticed, our daughter is not a child."

"As if I could not notice," Will muttered, twisting a lock of her hair around his finger. "But Tarquin is her cousin—"

"No, he is not," Alista demurred before he could finish. "Nan is her cousin, and Tarquin is Nan's half-brother, but Malinda and Tarquin are no blood kin at all. Your sister was Nan's mother but not Tarquin's."

Will contemplated this for a moment, but try as he might, he couldn't find a hole in her argument. "You seem to have given this matter a great deal of thought."

"I haven't, actually. It's only now occurring to me." She rolled over to look at him, her own eyes more useful in the dark. "If you ask Tarquin to stay and tell him to watch over Malinda while we're gone, I have no doubt he will lay down his life to do it," she went on. "I just want you to know what you're asking."

"And I want you to stop creating problems where they don't exist," he retorted, drawing her back down into his arms. "Tarquin needs to know I trust him, that we all do, and I need someone at Brinlaw that Malinda can't order around or manipulate. The last I heard she had set her cap for Prince Richard; I hardly think she's about to succumb to the charms of a bastard routier, no matter how dearly we all may love him. And Tarquin will act with honor, whether he knows it or not. He won't betray our trust." He heard her draw breath to argue some more, and he kissed her before she could. "When the time comes, Malinda will choose the right man," he promised when the kiss was broken. "She is her mother's daughter."

Alista smiled to herself. "Aye, she is," she said with a resigned little sigh. "That's what I'm afraid of."

*   *   *

Malinda was in the room she was sharing with Lisbet, getting ready for bed, when she heard the cry of a hawk outside the window. "Rufus!" She ran and opened the shutter, and the hawk circled toward her as she leaned out, hand outstretched. But at the last moment, he wheeled away, climbing higher as he turned. For a moment, she lost him in the dark, then she saw the outline of his beating wings like a shadow against the light of an open window in the tower opposite—Tarquin's room. "Damnation!" she swore, not caring who heard her as she slammed the shutter closed.

"It's only a hawk," Lisbet said, watching her own reflection as she braided her hair for bed. "It isn't as if you'll never find another."

"Lisbet!" Malinda scolded, astonished. "Fine friend you are, taking Tarquin's side."

"I wasn't aware sides had officially been drawn," Lisbet said, putting down her brush to face her.

"Well, they have," she retorted, making a face. At dinner, she had found herself almost liking Nan's brother, almost forgetting the man who had frightened her in the woods, but he had fixed that quickly enough as soon as they were alone. He wasn't some mysterious spirit—he was a mean-spirited clod, and she was determined to put him out of her mind.

"Tarquin really took him?" Lisbet asked. "I mean, he had him, obviously, but how could he have taken him from you?"

"He just . . . I don't know how he did it. He just did," Malinda grumbled.

"All right, he did," Lisbet said quickly. "And that makes me angry, too, for your sake. Still . . ." She blushed and smiled a wicked smile. "Don't you think he's rather . . . interesting?"

"Sort of, I suppose, but . . . oh." She blushed a bit herself. "Good Lord, no!" *Are you sure?* a chorus of wicked little imps whispered in her mind. But that was just silly—she wanted someone noble and kind like Papa, not some half-mad criminal rogue. She had thought about it. If she was being completely honest, she could even admit that for a moment in the forest she had almost wanted—no, she had definitely wanted his kiss, had fairly burned for it. But that was only a moment, a tiny spark, quickly burned out, definitely over and done. It certainly didn't mean that she wanted him to kiss her again, that she thought Tarquin was "interesting," as Lisbet put it.

"He's awfully handsome," Lisbet teased. "And Rufus is only a hawk."

"Rufus is mine," Malinda answered softly, more to herself than to her friend, "and I am going to have him back."

7

CRITICAL

Tarquin closed his shutter, the goshawk perched on his fist. The bird had flown to the window and out an hour ago, and he had assumed it was gone for good, but apparently it had returned, easily finding its way. "Your lady is not pleased," Tarquin said, taking Rufus to the perch Alista had kindly provided and smiling a little at the thought. Brinlaw's daughter was out of his reach in every possible way, but at least he had her pet.

He built up the fire in the tiny hearth more for light than warmth. The room was cozy, well appointed, everything he could have wished, certainly better than he ought to have expected with the royal entourage on its way. But as in the hall, he couldn't forget he was in his father's house, a castle full of ghosts. He threw off his borrowed clothes and fell across the bed—when had he last slept in a proper bed? The puzzle soothed him as he considered it . . . Brother Paolo's house in Florence had offered him a room much like this one, but surely that couldn't have been the last . . . Davyd had taken him to an Arab bawdy house where the couches were certainly soft, but they couldn't properly have been called beds . . . The widow who had said she loved him in Alexandria had owned a bed, but he'd never exactly slept in it . . . He drifted off to an uneasy sleep on these musings, the ghosts of his past held for the moment at bay.

Malinda lay in bed listening to the gentle rhythm of Lisbet's breathing, trying to decide what to do. She rolled to her side toward the window. She had opened the shutter again before coming to bed, hoping Rufus might return. Now the moon was rising, a crimson sliver on the face of the dark, another mocking grin. Which Tarquin was real? His manner was like his appearance, savage one minute and civilized the next. But what was he like when there was no one there to see, no one to frighten or impress? A thought struck her, and she sat up with a start. She had promised her mother no more magic, 'twas true, at least when they were away from Brinlaw, but her mother would never know. One peek, and she would come back, and she could steal back Rufus as well. She smiled as she thought of it, carefully climbing out of bed. She would take back what was hers, and who knows? She might give Tarquin a bit of a fright in the bargain. *Serves him right,* she thought as she unlaced her shift. He thought he was so clever, so daring. He frightened her in the forest, stole her prize possession, and thought she could do nothing about it. He believed he had her beaten because she wouldn't hurt Nan by telling, and he was right, as far as that went. But she wasn't so helpless as he thought. She was a sorceress. Letting her shift fall to the floor, she slowly faded from view.

The corridors were deserted; everyone except the guards outside had long since retired for the night. She could hear her parents talking in hushed tones as she passed their door, and she stopped for a moment, considering. But she quickly decided to move on—eavesdropping on her parents had lost its charm long ago.

She found the door to Tarquin's room unlatched—a stroke of luck. She slipped inside, holding her breath as the leather hinge creaked and came to rest. But the man on the bed didn't stir. His fire was still banked high, and she paused for a moment by the hearth, letting the warmth soak into her faery-chilled flesh as orange light wavered along the outline of her invisible form. Then she turned to the bed.

Tarquin was sleeping. He was lying on his side, the blankets pooled at his waist, one arm laid out along the pillow beside him. She moved closer to see his face. *"He's awfully handsome,"* Lisbet had said. He wasn't handsome; he was beautiful. Streaks of gold gleamed in his hair, and she found herself longing to touch it, to brush it back from his brow and feel its texture between her fingers. It was the same instinct that drew her toward falcons, made her want to charm them from the sky . . . *Rufus.*

She looked around the dimly lit room, found a pair of bright eyes gazing back at her from the corner. "There you are," she whispered. "Come here, right now." But the hawk just blinked at her, keeping his perch. She moved closer, and he took off with a whir of wings. "Rufus!" she complained, still in a whisper quiet as thought, as he settled at the head of the bed, just out of easy reach. "I ought to leave you here." She held out her hand, but the hawk backed away, sidestepping along the headboard. She knew he could see her, could sense her presence even if he wouldn't obey. He wasn't afraid; he was being obstinate. Just like a man, Druscilla would say.

She looked down at Tarquin, still sleeping, oblivious. He

must have been very tired . . . Imagine traveling so far. His lashes looked dark, but they were tipped in gold like his hair, longer than any man's ought to be. His brow drew up in a frown for a moment, as if he didn't like his dreams, and she held her breath, every nerve drawn taut. Even asleep, he still seemed dangerous, a predator ready to strike. He had tried to kiss her, and she had almost let him . . . What else might he have done if she hadn't run away? For the first time, she let herself imagine it . . . the soft brush of breath she had felt deepening into a real kiss, those powerful hands on her skin, molding her to his will. Her breath came short as she passed a hand just over his chest, tracing his shape in the air, almost touching the fine, golden down that looked so soft on his stomach, barely visible in the fire's light. If she touched him, the spell might break . . . but it might not. The glamour was an illusion, her mother said, but she had never been caught. Besides, he was asleep . . . She bent closer, close enough to feel his breath on her mouth. Malinda was intrigued . . . One kiss could hardly hurt. Bending closer still, both hands braced on the pillow on either side of his head, she touched her mouth to his.

Tarquin came awake in an instant, his dream shattering around him, and felt the faery spring back out of reach like the dream as his knife flashed up by reflex. "Where are you?" he asked the empty air, still wary, his heart pounding painfully in his chest. When he was a child and Alista had first begun to learn the mechanics of her magic, she had gone invisible for practice once with Tarquin, Nan, and Druscilla looking on. Alista had touched him while he couldn't see her, the lightest brush of her hand across his hair, and the sensation had nearly made him faint, like someone reaching inside him and touching his soul. This kiss had been the same, only more so, and he still trembled with it, his dream forgotten. "I know you're here," he went on, the knife still held before him. "Did I hurt you?"

"No." The voice was female, defiant, a tiny bit fearful— Malinda. "Did I hurt you?"

He smiled in spite of himself. "No," he answered, letting the knife fall. "Unless making my heart stop counts." He heard a rustle near the foot of the bed and focused his attention there. "Show yourself, Malinda."

"I can't." The voice had moved to the window, and he turned again, disoriented. "I'm not wearing anything."

Tarquin made his expression go blank. Just because he couldn't see her didn't mean she wasn't watching him. What could she be thinking? What had he done to make her want to drive him mad? Could Alista's child be so cruel? "Put something on, then," he ordered, trying to sound older, wiser, in charge, and utterly unaffected by the image of this enchantress bending naked over his bed to kiss him as he slept.

The shirt he'd been wearing when he arrived had been washed and hung to dry on a rack beside the fire. As he watched, unable to look away, the shirt picked itself up, shook itself out, rose up, and finally came to rest in the intoxicating shape of a woman. "You're not dressed, either," she pointed out as he felt her settle at the foot of the bed. He looked down, appalled, but the bedclothes were still safely in place, covering his lower half. When he looked up again, she was there, perched like a cat at his feet, her face turned ever so slightly away.

Malinda gritted her teeth and willed herself to stop trembling. For a moment she had thought he really had killed her, he had drawn that knife with such speed. "I didn't mean to startle you," she ventured, making her eyes meet his.

"What *did* you mean?" He sounded as furious as he looked, and she was secretly pleased. At least she'd gotten his attention, shaken him up a bit. "Do your parents know you wander the castle naked in the middle of the night?"

"My parents have nothing to do with it," she retorted. "I came to get Rufus."

"And what would they say if they knew you were here?" he demanded. He looked so strong—she couldn't have circled his arm with both her hands. *He didn't need a knife*, she thought, *he could have snapped me in half like a twig*. She clenched her fists, still shaking like a rabbit. Why had she kissed him? How could she have been so stupid? Now all she could do was bluster her way through on courage, and be a great deal more brave than she felt.

"What would they say if they knew you tried to kiss me in the woods?" she countered, setting her little jaw. "I've always done magic, gone invisible, and my parents know it perfectly well. My mother is the one who showed me how to do it when I was still a little girl."

"An age ago, in faith," he said, sarcasm fairly dripping from each word.

"It was a long time ago," she insisted, stung. "I'm not a child."

"You'd never know it by the way you behave," he shot back. Swallowed by his shirt, with her legs tucked under her and her hair a tousle of gold on her shoulders, she looked anything but childish, and he had to look away. "Playing with magic to retrieve your toys, wandering the forest without an escort—I would think Will and Alista's daughter would have more sense."

"Will and Alista's daughter can bloody well think for herself," she answered, fear forgotten as she lost her temper indeed.

"Not that I've seen—"

"You haven't seen much," she cut him off.

"No," he agreed, taking a deep breath, trying to back off. This was wrong; the last thing he should be doing was picking fights with this woman. He should send her off to bed if he had to throw her out bodily into the hall. "So your mother doesn't mind—"

"My mother thinks I'm a child, just as you do," Malinda cut him off again. "She only taught me so I wouldn't accidentally hurt myself." She had to calm down, stop arguing. If he told her parents what she had done, she'd never escape the castle again. But he made her so angry, she couldn't help herself. "She hates magic," she finished, scowling as she looked away.

"So do I," he answered. "Particularly when it's being practiced on me. And your father?"

"The same as Mama in everything," she answered, still peevish. He knew her parents as well as she did; she may as well tell him the truth. "If Mama breathes in a puff of smoke, Brinlaw sneezes."

He almost smiled in spite of himself, she sounded so cross. "'Twas not always so," he promised, remembering. When he had first come to Brinlaw, Will and Alista had been unable to agree on anything, had barely been able to pass a civil word between them. That had changed dramatically in the space of a very few months, but he was glad to see the change had stuck. Still, it seemed strange that their child could know them so little. "They used to disagree on everything just on principle."

"I don't believe it," she retorted. "They're like one person—you can't imagine. She even goes to war with him."

"Since when?" he asked, surprised. When he was Will's squire, they had left Alista at home, a sorrow for them both.

"Since he almost died in a battle." She settled back against the bedpost, trying to feel easy, as if it were perfectly natural for them to be talking this way, half naked in the middle of the night while the rest of the castle was asleep. *Nan's brother,* she told herself sternly. *Tarquin is only Nan's brother.* "I was fourteen, and Mark was twelve. Papa and Raynard had gone with King Henry to put down a rebellion in Wales. A Welsh bowman shot Papa with an arrow just here." She touched a spot at the base of her throat just beside her collarbone, and Tarquin flinched. A man so shot could drown in his own blood before a surgeon could reach him. "Raynard brought him home to die, and Mama nearly died herself. She used her book to conjure every cure she could find—she had never practiced such strong magic before, nor has she since." She shivered. "We thought they both would die."

Tarquin flung the blanket down to her. "You must have been afraid."

"Terrified, all of us, Mark especially. He worships Papa, thinks he's the best knight who ever lived." She wrapped the blanket around her, then noticed he was smiling. "What?"

"So do I," Tarquin admitted.

"Oh." Her plan was working; she was starting to relax, and he seemed almost friendly. "Anyway, obviously he didn't die. He got better, and so did Mama, once she knew he was safe. But she said that was it, that if he insisted on going off to fight, he would have to take her with him. She said she was afraid he would die with her far away, and he must have been, too, because he agreed. Baby Will was born the next year on a campaign in France."

"And you and Mark stayed at Brinlaw?" Tarquin asked. She was calmer now, less angry, almost friendly. She thought he was safe, that she was safe with him; she had decided he wasn't a threat. The demon inside him smiled, feeling its prey come closer, and he closed his eyes, trying to push it back.

"I did," she answered. "Auntie Dru and Lisbet came and spent the summer with me, and I learned to be chatelaine. But Mark and Phillipe both left to foster as squires that year. This spring is the longest they've been home since." She looked up at him, a question in her eyes that made him shiver. "And now you're home as well."

"For now," he agreed, unwilling to say more.

"I barely remember you," she admitted. She hadn't moved any closer, hadn't changed expression, hadn't done anything at all that he could see. But the demon was more aware of her, smelled her skin, saw the glimmers of gold in her wide, green eyes, and he wanted her. She seemed to be willing him to her—but that was insane, more tricks of his mind, his nature. She might be half faery, but she was still an innocent maid. Any will that drove him to ruin her was his own, not hers. "Do you remember me at all?"

"I remember a little girl," he answered. "I didn't recognize you."

"You didn't?" Malinda asked. "But you said—"

"I know what I said," he cut her off. "But I didn't know who you were."

"So you didn't mean it." Suddenly he wouldn't meet her eyes; suddenly it was Tarquin who seemed afraid. A strange feeling of power crept over her, made her move closer.

"No," he said, shaking his head.

"Tarquin, why did you come home?" she pressed. "You were free. You had the world, your ship. Why come back here?"

"I came for Nan's wedding." He made himself meet her eyes, but he couldn't hold her gaze, not without losing control. "I promised her before I left that I would come back and give her away."

"But how did you know she was about to be married?" Malinda persisted. This was exactly like taming a falcon, a lethal, savage creature enchanted to her will. Would he hurt her? Would he be hers? She touched his cheek, her hand moving of its own accord. "Why did you come back now?"

He caught her hand, pushed it away. She was fearless; she didn't know what she touched. "Malinda . . ."

"No," she said softly, an enchantress' sigh. "Please, don't push me away." Before he could answer, she kissed him, framing his face with her hands, and she felt his surrender as a tremor that passed through them both, felt it in his arms as he crushed her close, tasted it on his tongue as her lips parted to let him inside. He was hers . . .

She was his . . . He felt her body rise to meet him, strong arms around his neck as he fed on her mouth, tasted her, smelled her, the scent of flowers in her hair, the sweet musk of her skin. He raised his head, broke the kiss, and she smiled, her eyes open, full of wicked innocence. She was not Alista, sweetness and light. She was herself: a willful, dangerous thing, as lethal in her way as he was himself, as quick to court destruction. She started to speak, and he kissed her again, harder this time, bruising her mouth with his.

Mine, Malinda thought, languid and tingling at once. Being kissed was like being invisible, a surrender more powerful than will. She felt as if she were dissolving, but instead of disappearing she was becoming something new, a creature like nothing she had ever known. She was only half herself; the other half was him, this tantalizing other. He pressed her back against the bed, and she let him, fear dawning but distant. He was hers; she could bend him to her will.

She surrendered, and he was lost. The demon fire that ruled him cared only for her kisses, the rose-petal softness of her skin. He could take her, break her beneath him, and the last frayed shreds of his soul would be lost. And the demon wouldn't care . . .

"Malinda." His voice barely sounded like his own. She rose up to kiss him again, but he stopped her with a hand to her mouth, the demon howling in fury inside him. "You can't be here," he told her, blood roaring in his ears. "You have to go away."

Malinda stared at him, stunned, shocked back to herself by his words. This wasn't supposed to happen—he couldn't be sending her away. She had offered herself to him; she had conquered him—he was hers. He wouldn't dare. "No," she said, grabbing his hair in her fist to pull his mouth back down to hers.

He kissed her sweetly, but only for a moment, then caught her wrist in a grip of iron. "Yes," he said, his expression as empty as his tone. "Let me go—"

"Let me go!" she cried, scrambling back, her eyes on fire with rage, as wild as the burning he felt. "You bastard!"

"Malinda, stop it." She had moved off the bed, out of his reach, and he made himself be still. "You'll wake your parents—"

"And why shouldn't I?" she demanded. He had let her think she was taming him, but it was all a lie, a trap, a way to get back at her for frightening him, to put her down again. "What do you want?" she all but screamed, senseless with frustrated fury.

"You kissed me, remember?" he said, his face a mask again, a mask she wanted to rip to bloody shreds. She couldn't answer; nothing she could say would save her now, restore her pride. He was right; she had kissed him, not once but twice. She must be losing her mind. He must be some sort of enchanter, a better magician than she could ever hope to be.

"Why?" she repeated more softly, a catch in her throat. "Why are you doing this? Why do you hate me?"

"Go to bed," he ordered, the pain in her eyes like a knife twisting inside him. "Don't make me tell your father."

She opened her mouth to answer, but no words would come. She was breathless, as if she'd been struck. Rufus cried out instead, and she looked at him. "Come," she said, holding out her arm, willing the hawk to her, and he obeyed, flying to her hand. Turning without letting her eyes touch Tarquin, she left, her head held high. She would tame him. She would make him pay.

Tarquin watched her go, breathing hard, an animal entranced. She was a goddess, a creature of magic and light, and his kiss was an abomination, an offense against heaven itself. He closed his eyes, feeling his blood pulsing in the dark, the madness rising in him, the fury that drove him on. But this time he would resist it. If the demon tore his soul to shreds, he would still resist. Malinda would be safe.

8

Tarquin rode out over the drawbridge at dawn, mindless of the soldiers haphazardly assembled there. The King had been sighted; Guy de Lancey was on his way; Nan would marry as soon as the King had been fed, and Tarquin would be beside her. But he had to make another visit first.

He had expected the stone-pile ruin of the cottage to seem smaller now that he was grown, but the sight of it still gave him a shock. If the roof had still been thatched and the door timbers still standing, he would have had to stoop to go inside. It looked like something from a tale of dwarves, a bitter fairy tale. Leaving his horse to graze clover in the tiny, overgrown patch of yard, he walked to the doorway, braced his hands in the frame, and leaned in. To anyone inside, he would have seemed to blot out the sun. He had been inside once, sitting before the hearth in springtime, with the door standing open to the day. He had still been young enough to wear an infant's gown, a peasant brat with bare, dusty feet who was playing with a stick of kindling, pretending 'twas a man. The sun had suddenly gone out, and he had turned, afraid. A man had leaned in the doorway just as Tarquin leaned now—his father, Sir Gaston Bruel. Thinking back, he couldn't remember any time when he had seen Bruel before that moment, but he had started to cry, fearing him instinctively. His mother had told him to go outside, but he was afraid to pass by the giant in the doorway, and the giant refused to move. The toddler had danced in the middle of the room, howling, while Tabby beat his bare legs with a switch until finally the noble knight tired of the spectacle. "Come here, you," he'd said, snatching Tarquin off his feet and holding him in front of his face, bathing him in breath that stank of wine. "You're barely more than a bite yet," he'd grinned, his face still almost handsome then, only the eyes puffy and dead. "I'll let you grow a bit." And just when Tarquin had thought he must either faint or fight, the knight had flung him out the door like a cat. Rolling over once in the grass, he'd heard Bruel still laughing, and he'd scrambled to his feet and run into the forest as far and as fast as he could, stopping only when he literally collapsed, his bare feet cut to ribbons. He'd hidden there the rest of the day and all through the night, shivering and sobbing in fits and starts, cursing Bruel in between with every oath he'd ever heard. But in the morning when the sun came up, he'd made his way home again—where else was he to go? She was his mother; he had no one else.

He had found her sitting alone in the dooryard, crushing something green and fragrant between her fingers and tossing the pulp into a jar of water. "Never mind, Tarquin," she had said as he came into the tiny clearing, barely glancing up. "You will avenge us both when you are grown." He hadn't come closer, and she looked up and smiled. "Come and kiss me."

"I'll not." Was that the first time he had come home so, or later? He couldn't be sure. That time was all mixed up in his mind, all the years of his so-called innocence blended into one.

"Oh, aye." Her eyes had narrowed, making his blood run cold. "You will, little demon, for 'tis I who brought you up." She had held out a hand, fingers stained green from her simple, and he had run to her at last, buried his face in her neck and sobbed. She had let him cling to her only for a moment before she pushed him away. "Go into the house."

He stepped back through the cottage door a man—the giant and the child in one. The old beams would have barely cleared his head; the herbs that Tabby had always hung to dry from them would have brushed his cheek where he stood. The stone chimney was still intact, but grass had grown up from the dirt floor, and a blackthorn bloomed where Tabby's bed had stood . . .

Long ago, he had touched a torch to the straw-stuffed mattress, trying not to see her eyes as she stared up at him, blind and cold, her face swollen, her throat still purple from Bruel's deadly grip. The hanging herbs were next, and they sparkled as they caught, a final explosion that caught the thatch above. He had meant to stay among the flames, to let them burn him up as well, but at the last moment he had run. Someone had called to him; he had heard a voice . . .

"Tarquin." Will Brinlaw bent down to step through the doorway. "I didn't want to startle you," he explained.

Tarquin wiped away the tears he hadn't realized were

running down his face until he heard another living voice, but he didn't try to hide them. "It's all right."

Will nodded, looking around the tiny, ruined room. "Alista knew what this place was," he said. "We wanted to be with you if you ever came back." He picked up a bit of blackened wood as if it interested him, giving Tarquin another moment. "We talked about it a lot when you were a boy."

"Really?" Tarquin asked, surprised. Brinlaw seemed out of place, his whole stature and manner putting everything around him into weird perspective, and the idea of his and his lady's giving this hellhole a moment's thought seemed weird and wrong as well.

"I was away at war the first time she saw it, and you were with me as squire," Will answered. "She wrote and told me about it, asked if I thought we should make you come here when we returned, make you face it so you could forget." He flung the bit of wood away. "But I wasn't sure, and you never mentioned it. It seemed cruel to bring it up. If you had said you wanted—"

"I didn't," Tarquin said quickly.

Will smiled, but his eyes were sad. "We just wanted you to be happy," he said with a sigh. "But we both knew you wouldn't forget. When you stayed away so long, Alista thought . . ." He let the words trail off undone. "It doesn't matter," he finished after a moment. "You're home now."

"Will, I can't stay here." Suddenly the ruined walls seemed to be closing in around him, so much he had to get out or suffocate.

"Here at Bruel?" Will asked, following him into the yard. His horse was grazing peaceably beside Tarquin's. "Or here in England?"

"I don't belong here," Tarquin tried to explain. "Nan is about to be married—"

"She has missed you—"

"Do you think I don't know that?" Unable to meet the older man's eyes, he looked away into the lightening forest. The sun was just crawling over the tops of the trees, a red, accusing eye. "Do you think I haven't missed her?" he asked more quietly. "All of you?"

"No." Will was almost smiling. He still didn't understand. "I don't."

"But nothing has changed." He hadn't been able to explain eleven years ago, before he had fully become what he was, but he had known he didn't belong, had known Will couldn't see it. Now, when it should be obvious, he still couldn't see, and Tarquin still couldn't explain. How could he unless he told him everything, all the things that would make his mentor despise him? But maybe that was the answer. Maybe he should just tell him the truth—*I'm a monster, a murderer, a coward just like my father, and guess what I want more than anything else I've ever known? Your precious daughter.* That should settle any conflicts Brinlaw might still harbor about letting him just disappear. But he couldn't do it, couldn't make himself say the words. He could leave and be alone forever, but he couldn't reveal his true self. Even now, he needed to know that somewhere in the world, someone still thought well of him, someone still loved him, even if everything they loved was a lie.

"Everything has changed," Will answered, hearing only what he said. "You're a man now, and I need you." Tarquin was shaking his head, preparing to protest. "I am in earnest, Tarquin," Will cut him off before he could speak, knowing time was short and his audience stubborn. "Will you hear me?"

After a moment, Tarquin nodded. "Of course."

"I have to go to France, and Alista says she will go with me," Will began. "In truth, I would be loath to leave her even if she would allow it." He saw a flash of understanding in the younger man's eyes and felt encouraged. This boy had been with them almost from the beginning; in some ways he was closer to Brinlaw and his love than their own children, no matter how long he might have stayed away. "Raynard has agreed to stay on at Bruel until Nan's husband has decided where he means to live—he is his father's heir, and their manor is in France—but someone has to stay at Brinlaw to watch over Malinda. Will you do it?" Tarquin's face went blank as stone, even his eyes closing off, shutting Will out of his thoughts. When he was a child, this trick had always given Will a frisson of dread, and he liked it no better now. "Tarquin?"

"No," he said. "Take her with you—"

"I don't dare," Will said bluntly. In truth he was surprised. He had expected a token protest, but not flat refusal. "She's a sorceress, much more so than Alista, and she doesn't . . . it isn't in her to be careful. Not to mention she's of age and unmarried." He scowled, angry just remembering. "Henry's battle camp is no place for a maid." His eyes met Tarquin's. "So we have to leave her at Brinlaw. But she'll be no safer there with no one to curb her wilder instincts. Ranulf, the castellan, is entirely in her thrall and would take the castle down stone by stone if she wished it."

"She's not a child, Will," Tarquin pointed out. "Don't you trust her?"

"I trust her heart completely. I trust her virtue more than I trust my own," Will answered. "I just don't trust her judgment."

Tarquin's first instinct was to defend Malinda. Alista had been younger when she'd been left in full charge of Brinlaw Castle with Nan and Tarquin besides. But after last night, he knew better than Will how dearly she needed protection. After last night, he knew he was the last man on earth who could be trusted to protect her. She'd be safer in King Henry's own tent. "So leave her brother in charge," he suggested, genuinely trying to be helpful.

"Mark is sworn to Henry," Will said, shaking his head. "And Malinda could run him in circles, too, I suspect. There is no one else, Tarquin. It has to be you."

"No," Tarquin insisted. "Not me."

"Tarquin, please." The word came hard to him; it always had, and Tarquin looked at him, unable to stop himself. "I understand better than you know how much you want to be gone," Will went on. "But I have no choice. For all of us, I'm asking you to stay."

"Will, you don't hear me," he said. "I am not the man you want. You don't know what I—"

"You have a temper, yes," Will finished. "You always did, as I recall, even as a child. Poor Tom the stable boy barely lived to see manhood."

"No," Tarquin said, shaking his head. "You have a temper, Will. I have a kind of madness. You can't imagine—"

"Think you not?" Will laughed. "You were a child when you first knew me. There was much you didn't see." He put a hand on the younger man's shoulder. "I trust you, Tarquin, as much as any man I've ever known. For my sake, will you not try to trust yourself?"

Tarquin felt as if he were being ripped in half. Will thought he understood, but he did not. He thought he had plumbed the depths of Tarquin's evil when he had scolded him for thrashing a stable boy, and nothing Tarquin could tell him would change his mind. At least, nothing he could bear to say. Will didn't have it in his nature to truly understand. But Will had taken him in when he had nothing. The peasant bastard of a man he hated above all others had become his ward, then his squire, as if he were born to it, as if he had deserved it. He had given Tarquin a home when he would have starved or frozen to death without it. He had cared for him, treated him like his own son, tried to give him a life with meaning and purpose and honor. How could he refuse him? *I'll make a mess of it,* he wanted to protest. *I'll hurt her, destroy everything, make you curse the day you ever saw me.* But he couldn't. He was a coward. "As you will, my lord," he said aloud. "If you truly want me, I can hardly say no."

The second Will Brinlaw was searching for someone to help him tie his shoes. He had done pretty well with his clothes, he thought, donning his best tunic with no help at all, but his good shoes had complicated laces, and after a few fruitless attempts to make them come out right, he knew he was licked. He had tied the laces together, slung them over his shoulder like freshly dressed rabbits, tugged on his muddy riding boots, and tramped off in search of assistance, but there was no one to help. Everyone was gone or too busy—he couldn't find his mother or sister at all. Lady Dru was in the kitchen, but she hadn't even heard him when he asked for help; she'd just shoved a fish in his hands and sent him out the door, thinking he must be hungry. So now he had knotted shoes and a fish he didn't want. Mark and Phillipe were with the rest of the knights somewhere. He had thought his father might be in the main hall, but as soon as he got there, some page ran in and shouted, "The king comes!" and everyone ran out into the courtyard. Now all he could do was loiter by the dais and try to think what to try next.

"Nice fish," a voice said from behind him. Whirling around, he found Tarquin towering over him, and he grinned, rescued at last. Unless Tarquin was busy, too . . .

"It isn't, really," he explained, looking down at his forlorn and now rather cold bit of breakfast. "I don't even like fish." He looked back up with a hopeful smile. "Do you want it?"

"Not really," Tarquin said, smiling back. Last night Willie had heard his brother and Phillipe marveling at how rough and bad Tarquin seemed, and he supposed he did look rather fierce, but when he smiled he seemed nice as could be. He took the fish with a solemn wink and tossed it with a flourish to one of Raynard's dogs, a massive wolfhound who could swallow it whole without worrying about the bones. "But the dog seems to like it," he said, taking out a handkerchief and wiping Willie's hands clean. "Better?" Willie nodded. "Can I ask you something else?" Willie nodded again. "Why aren't you wearing those shoes?"

That settled it: Tarquin was a genius and a saint besides. "Because I can't tie them," he explained. "I've been trying and trying to find somebody . . ."

"Here, let me see what I can do." He set the child up on the table and tugged off his boots, then took the shoes. "You tied this knot all by yourself?"

"Yes," Willie answered, bracing to be scolded. In his travels, the knot had worked itself pretty tight.

"Good job." He untied it quick as anything and didn't swear once. "I could have used you on my ship."

"You have a ship?" Willie asked, fascinated.

"He does," Malinda said, coming through the door behind the dais. She looked beautiful in her best dress, so pretty it made Willie feel happy just to look at her, and from the way Tarquin was staring, he must have felt the same. "He told us last night, but you were already sleeping."

Tarquin took his eyes away from her with an effort and concentrated on Willie's shoelaces. "She's right," he said. "You dropped off like a stone before dessert."

"I never!" Willie protested, indignant.

"Oh yes, you did," Malinda said, pushing his messy curls into something resembling order. "Tarquin had to carry you up to bed." She looked at Tarquin, an ill-tempered gleam in her eye. "I'm rather surprised to see you—I thought he might not give you back."

"Your sister was with you, too, in case I should want to abduct you," Tarquin said. "You weren't in any real danger."

Willie glanced back and forth between them, confused. They sounded angry. Malinda always sounded that way when someone hurt her feelings, and that someone usually lived to rue the day. But what could Tarquin have done? "The King is here," he volunteered to his sister.

"Yes, I know," she answered. "And Guy as well."

"De Lancey?" Tarquin said, looking up. "Where?"

"Outside with his troops, I believe," she answered. He looked almost interested—perhaps he really did care for Nan. And Willie—he was being perfectly nice to him.

Maybe Malinda was the only one he wanted to see humiliated. She had lain awake most of the night trying to work out the logic of his actions, the logic of her actions toward him, but it was hopeless. Nothing either of them had done or said since the moment they met had made the slightest bit of sense. Only one thing was certain—somehow she would pay him back in kind. She would make him burn in vain as she had, make him want her and then push him away. The pain he would feel would be a thousand times more sore than hers, his thwarted desire a thousand times more sharp. She was a sorceress; she could do it. "Nan's already getting dressed for the wedding," she continued. "But Guy seems to be taking his time."

"I'll go get him," Willie offered, jumping down from the table, well shod at last.

"No," Tarquin said, mussing the boy's hair again. "Let me."

Less than an hour after King Henry's arrival, the fields around Bruel had been transformed into a bustling, crescent-shaped city of tents. The King was famous for traveling with his entire government packed up and carried around him; now that he was at war, his entourage had swollen even bigger. A single castle had no hope of containing it, especially a small fortress like Bruel. Many of the knights and virtually all of their foot soldiers were reduced to camping outside the castle walls, and even then they were crowded.

Tarquin had no trouble moving through the rush. Anyone who noticed him at all assumed he was one of Brinlaw's knights or perhaps a mercenary captain. He grabbed one of the younger soldiers, running past carrying a basket of bread. "Guy de Lancey," he said. "Where is he?"

The young man blinked, rather stunned by the

stranger's size and the look of grim intent on his face. Alas for poor de Lancey, he thought privately. "Far west end with his captain," he answered. "Do you—"

"Thanks," Tarquin nodded, walking away.

In truth, he was rather surprised at the size of the royal force. He had been so wrapped up in his own concerns, he hadn't thought much about Henry's war. But seeing these troops assembled, his mind returned to his odd disaster in Corsica and the boy he had killed. Discontent with Henry's reign was nothing new, particularly among the continental nobles, and the only link between that dead boy and the boys now making war on their father was probably his own bad luck that made him privy to both. But the coincidence preyed on his mind nonetheless.

Turning the corner into the westernmost corridor of tents, he saw a young knight in dazzling chain mail standing among the muddier rabble, looking rather out of place but obviously in charge. Brinlaw and his son had both described Guy de Lancey to him as having the personality of a block of oak; watching this young nobleman consult with his captain, Tarquin was pretty well certain he had found him. As he drew closer, the knight took off his helmet and pushed back his chain mail hood in a gesture that bespoke annoyance, but his face was as mild as a lamb's and nearly as expressive. *"Give him a chance,"* Nan had ordered. Determined to do as she asked, he went to greet her intended. "Sir Guy!"

The young man turned his head. "Yes?" he said, looking Tarquin up and down as he came forward, his face still betraying no emotion whatsoever.

"I'm Tarquin FitzBruel," he said, extending his hand. "Why are you—"

Before he could finish, the knight had caught him in an awkward but apparently heartfelt embrace. "Mon frère," he pronounced, kissing a startled Tarquin on both cheeks. "You have come home at last." He stepped back, a smile bringing his handsome face to life. "You cannot know how glad I am to see you."

"Really?" Tarquin asked, now completely confused. "Why?"

"My love would not marry without you," Guy explained. "I had begun to think I would have to abduct her and have her drugged to bring her to the altar." From a man more naturally merry, this would have obviously been a joke, but with de Lancey, 'twas impossible to be sure. "But you have come in time," he finished with another smile.

"But you have not," Tarquin said, remembering his quest. "My sister is waiting for you at the castle; she means to be married today. What are you doing out here?"

"Last-minute details," Guy answered with a sigh. "When I go in to see my love at last, I intend to stay—no interruptions until we leave for France. That needs planning—"

"But surely your captain can manage now," Tarquin finished with a friendly smile barely edged in warning. "Besides, we have to talk." He took Guy's arm and began steering him toward the castle.

"Of course," Guy nodded, his voice a little flustered but agreeable enough. He walked with Tarquin through the camp without a backward glance.

"My sister says I must give her to you," Tarquin said. He stopped on the bridge to the castle moat and leaned against the stone railing. "She says she loves you."

"I love her as my soul," Guy answered, a sudden light in

his eyes underscoring his words. "You need have no fear for that."

"Oh, I don't," Tarquin said with an easy smile. "But will your love endure? Will you always feel the same?"

"I swear it," Guy answered at once.

"Be careful," Tarquin warned. "Do not be forsworn—"

"I will not." At last the knight was beginning to look angry, and Tarquin was encouraged. "Nan is all my joy. How could my soul change?"

"You might be surprised." He looked back at the castle, the same squat, brown towers as when he was a child for all the changes made inside. "Has Nan told you anything about her mother?"

Guy looked at the castle as well, as if to see what Tarquin saw. "Some," he allowed. "What will you tell me of her?"

"Our father was well pleased with her at first," Tarquin answered. "She was beautiful, like Nan, and full of grace— a far sweeter bride than he deserved or could ever have expected. He made a great fuss over her, swore his love to the stars." Tarquin's own mother had lived in great peril in those days. If she hadn't threatened him with witchery, Bruel would likely have had her moved off his lands altogether. "But this great love he spoke of didn't last the winter," he continued. "By spring, he despised her, made her life hell because she saw him for what he was. By the time winter came again, all of her beauty and grace were gone, crushed out of her. Another winter came, and another, and another, and she knew nothing would ever change, that no one would ever come to help. So she killed herself— hanged herself in the empty church." He looked at Guy, saw in his eyes that he had heard at least some of this before. Nan trusted him; that spoke well for him.

"Sanctuary," he finished. "By the time her brother knew what was happening, it was too late; she was gone."

"I am not your father," Guy said. "Nan may not always have a happy life, but her sorrows will never come from me, and I will give my life to mend them."

"Yes, you will, one way or another," Tarquin answered, no trace of humor in his tone, no sign to indicate a threat. He spoke the simple truth alone. "Nan is all my joy as well, and if she feels pain, I will know it, wherever I am." He fixed the knight with his witch's eyes. "And whoever brings this pain will hear from me."

Guy didn't smile, but he didn't flinch either. "Then she shall be safe indeed," he promised, holding out his hand.

Tarquin smiled. "Aye, she will," he said, drawing Guy into an embrace much as the knight had drawn him. "Come, brother. They need us in church."

9

Malinda watched Druscilla and her mother make Nan ready for her wedding with a careful smile and a heavy heart. Nan was so happy; she wouldn't spoil that for the world and all its stars. But she couldn't share her joy. Everything was changing—Nan was becoming a wife; her parents and brothers were going off to war. Only Malinda was being left behind. The only one who had wanted change was the one whose life would remain just the same. And Tarquin . . . she wouldn't even think about Tarquin, not now, not with Nan's wedding only a few minutes away. She would just have to talk to her father alone, away from her mother's influence, and convince him to take her away . . .

As if on cue, a heavy knock came at the door. "Nan!" Tarquin's voice called. "Aren't you ready yet?"

Lisbet ran to open the door. "She's perfect," she said, flashing Tarquin a dazzling smile as he and Will came in. "Come and see."

Nan rose as he approached her, and Tarquin found he could barely breathe. "Do I look all right?" she teased with a smile.

"Yes," he nodded, no better words coming to mind. In truth, she looked very much like her mother had looked the first time he had seen her, a kind of angel, too fine for the brutal world. Glancing over at Brinlaw, he could see he felt the same. "De Lancey is at the church," he said, finding his voice. "I took him there myself."

"Did you scare him to death?" she laughed.

"Not to death," he admitted, smiling back. "He seems to be all you say." He took her hand, still marveling. She was so grown up, so calm . . . "He even says he loves you, though why I can't imagine."

"Tarquin!" Alista scolded, pretending to be shocked.

"No doubt he is blinded," Nan said, unperturbed. "He'll wake up soon enough."

"He promises me not," Tarquin answered, leaning down to kiss her cheek.

"The King and his people are on their way to the church," Will said, hiding his own emotions in the bluster of a general on the move. "The main street is probably blocked, but you can ride in from the back. Nan can show you—"

"Will, don't be ridiculous," Alista protested. "Nan must go in a coach—"

"No," Nan said quickly. "Tarquin and I will ride."

"But your dress—" Druscilla protested.

"Are we having a wedding or not?" Raynard demanded, coming in.

"Yes," Nan said, taking Tarquin's arm. "Go tell them we're on our way."

Malinda watched her father hang back as everyone else filed out. Her mother stopped and smiled at him, but she went on out with Nan. "She'll be fine, Papa," Malinda said, taking his hand. "She's happy."

"Yes," Will agreed, smiling down at her for a moment. "May she remain so." He drew her close for a moment in a hug, surprising her and touching her heart. When she was a little girl, her father had been very demonstrative with her when he was home. Her mother had joked 'twas a miracle Malinda ever learned to walk at all, so rarely did her feet touch the ground. But since she had grown up, their relationship had become more formal, their interactions more distant. She had become a whirlwind he had to control; he had become an obstacle she had to avoid. Only the love underneath remained unchanged, and for a moment it was easy to feel it. "Come," he said, letting her go. "We'll join your mother in her coach."

"Wait a moment, Papa, please." Another such moment might not come; she had to ask him now. "I know this is the wrong time, Nan's time, and I promise I won't argue, no matter what you say, but please . . ." She took his hand again. "Will you take me with you to France?"

For a moment, he didn't say anything, glanced at the door as if he were hoping her mother would reappear and answer for him. Then he drew her close again. "I cannot, Malinda," he said. "You wouldn't be safe; there's no way I could keep you safe." He drew back, and she started to speak. "You promised not to argue, remember?" he pointed out with a wry half smile. "The war isn't going well. There's no telling where we might be or how we might be living." He touched her chin, preventing her from turning away. "Or with whom," he continued. "You'll be safe at Brinlaw. I wish I could leave Willie with you there as well, or that Lisbet could stay to keep you company. But her father wants her home, and I can't say I blame him—I want my daughter home as well."

"What if the princes' armies come to Brinlaw?" she

pointed out, not arguing, really, just mentioning a possibility he might not have considered. "I have never held off a siege."

"No," he agreed with a smile. "But Tarquin has. I think that between you both you'll manage."

"Tarquin?" She couldn't have heard him right. "Tarquin will be at Brinlaw?"

"Yes, he has agreed to stay and act as castellan until your mother and I return." He took her arm and steered her toward the hall. "Now come, before Nan thinks we aren't coming at all." She didn't move, and he stopped. "Malinda?"

She was so shocked, she felt frozen. Tarquin as castellan at Brinlaw? For a split second, she thought of telling her father everything—the forest, Rufus, last night. If she truly wanted vengeance, that would certainly bring it. Surely her father wouldn't leave Tarquin to guard her virtue if he knew what he had done . . . what she had done. That was the problem. She couldn't report all of Tarquin's transgressions without confessing a few of her own, and those few were damning indeed. If Brinlaw knew how she had behaved, he might still slap Tarquin in irons, but she would be locked up as well and for a much more lengthy sentence. She'd never see even what little freedom she had ever again. "Yes," she said aloud, conjuring the smile she'd worn all morning. "Let's go."

Tarquin and Nan had reined in their mounts at the top of a rise overlooking Bruel Village to watch the others go into the church just below. Will's monument to his sister was a cathedral in miniature, the pure white stones so new they gleamed in the noonday sun. "It's beautiful," Tarquin said, rather stunned. The old village church had been another thatch-roof cottage distinguished only by a wooden cross on top, and even that had been a virtual ruin by their father's reign as lord. But this one, while small, was as fine as anything in any town in England.

"Isn't it?" Nan said. "My uncle had the old one taken down to the ground and all the pieces burned and all the ashes buried." Most of the village was still gathered in the churchyard after their glimpse of the King, and as Brinlaw and his family appeared, they broke out in cheers. "It's odd, isn't it?" she mused. "The way things change."

"Yes." Some of these same peasants had thrown rocks at him when he was a child, making the sign against the devil whenever he passed, and they had called Nan a "poor, godless mite" and made the sign of the cross whenever her name was mentioned. "Come, let's show them how pretty you look."

"Wait," she said, her mare taking a dancing step back.

He stopped. "You aren't afraid?" She smiled. "You haven't changed your mind?"

"No and no," she answered. "I just wanted a moment to thank you."

"For what?" he frowned, embarrassed. "De Lancey is waiting—"

"For keeping your promise," she cut him off. "For being here to give me away." Her eyes turned serious. "But mostly for saving me." He started to protest, but she shook her head, and he kept silent. "Every happiness I have, you gave me when you took me away from here to Brinlaw," she continued, reaching out to take his hand. "When will you believe how good you are, how good you've always been?"

He lifted her hand to his lips. As if he could have been anything but good to her, loving her as he did. "I saved myself more than you," he said, letting her go.

"Did you?" She looked away for a moment, as if choosing her words with care. "As I recall it, we both—"

"No." He held her hand more tightly for a moment, then let it go completely, remembering. "You were innocent."

"And you . . . he would have . . ." She stopped, gazing off down the hill to the church, letting the words die unfinished. She knew he was right, that the sins of that night were his alone to bear, no matter how dearly she loved him. "Guy is taking me to France," she said at last. "He wants me to be close enough that he can see me a little. Only heaven knows how long this rebellion will last. His father is a sweet old man; I'll be glad to stay with him." Her eyes met his. "You could come with us."

He smiled. "I can't." She started to argue, but he cut her off. "I already promised Brinlaw I would stay and watch over Malinda."

Her eyes widened, but she smiled, obviously relieved. "Alas for you," she laughed. "Routier or not, I'm not sure you're up to that."

"Nor am I," he agreed with a wry face. Someone below had spotted them, and fresh cheers broke out—Nan's people celebrating her joy, just as she deserved. Too little too late, as far as he was concerned. He thought again of the night they had left here, a pair of urchins with nothing but rags and a stolen horse between them. How many in this cheering throng would have offered those children so much as a molded crust? The memory made him feel sick, hearing them now. But as she would always be, Nan was a better soul than he—she smiled and waved, returning their love in kind, the past forgiven and hopefully forgotten. "You look beautiful," he said, poor words for the feeling they expressed.

She turned her smile on him again, and he saw sweet tears in her eyes. "Thanks, brother," she said. "Now take me to my lord."

Malinda found herself standing between Lisbet and Phillipe in the front corner of the church, with Mark on Lisbet's other side and her parents on the other side of him with Baby Will between them. The King stood just behind Guy in his father's place, a rare honor that pointed up Brinlaw's status as a royal favorite as much as de Lancey's. The church was full to bursting with noble knights on their way to fight, and the King's own pet bishop was presiding. The village priest was reduced to blithering ecstasy at his superior's grandeur and trembled at his elbow, ready to assist. All that was required was the bride. Malinda turned to look back at the door and gasped along with the rest of the assembly as Nan and Tarquin appeared. "Isn't she beautiful?" Lisbet breathed as they came up the aisle.

"Yes," Malinda whispered back, her own troubles forgotten for the moment. Nan had always been lovely; Guy had always been handsome. But in this moment, they were transformed. Tarquin put Nan's hand into Guy's, and her breath caught in her throat again, tears welling in her eyes. They looked so happy, so completely at peace. *What must it be like to be so certain?* she thought with an inward sigh. Her gaze strayed to Tarquin as he stepped back, their eyes meeting for less than a moment before she looked away. For a moment last night, when they had kissed, she had almost thought . . . but that was madness. When she looked up again, her eyes were dry, and he was watching Nan and Guy, frowning slightly as if in concentration. Was he sad to see Nan marry? As Guy spoke his vows, his eyes never left Nan's face, and his voice, usually something of a drone, shook with emotion. Nan smiled as if to encourage him all through his speech, and when she was asked if she accepted his troth, her response was strong and clear.

"I will," she said, and the whole church smiled as one, from the King himself down to Baby Will. The bishop finished his Latin chant, and the village priest stepped forward, his throat working frantically with shyness.

"By authority of England and Holy Mother Church, I pronounce ye to be wed," he stammered, translating the gist of the Mass into words all could easily understand. Guy swept up his bride in a heartfelt embrace, and his friends shouted their approval as he kissed her.

"Lovely," Phillipe pronounced as the crowd began to disperse.

"Wasn't it?" Lisbet sighed. Will and Alista had moved forward to congratulate the newlyweds, but Mark turned toward the others.

"De Lancey looked almost alive," he agreed, offering Lisbet his arm. "Mam'selle, may I take you in to banquet?"

"Why not?" she said, taking his arm. "Are you two coming?" she asked Phillipe and Malinda.

"Of course," Phillipe answered.

"In a moment," Malinda interrupted. "Go along with the others, Phillipe; I want to speak to Nan."

"Don't tarry," he ordered. "I will have your first dance."

"First and second," she promised, accepting his kiss on the cheek.

"Don't make promises you can't keep," Lisbet laughed as they walked away.

Alista was giving Tarquin a hug as Malinda approached.

"Nearly half an hour in church for you, and not a single stroke of lightning," she teased.

"God was busy blessing Nan," he said, hugging her back. "He'll deal with me later."

"No doubt," Nan said, letting go of Guy's hand just long enough to hug her brother as well.

"Is Tarquin married, too?" Malinda said lightly as she joined them. "Why are we congratulating him?" As soon as Nan let him go, she hugged Tarquin as well in the same sisterly fashion, and he made himself hug her back instead of pushing her away. Her body pressed against his for just a moment longer than necessary, and he felt dizzy, momentarily blinded and everyone else forgotten.

"Or perhaps you all just pity him," she said, stepping back out of his reach. "I hear he's to be left alone with me."

"He'll manage, I think," Nan said, tugging a lock of Malinda's hair in gentle reproof. Her little cousin's powers of flirtation were as legendary as her temper, and she didn't care to see them practiced on Tarquin.

"What's this?" Alista said, looking confused.

"Papa told me," Malinda explained. Will was busy talking to Henry and didn't notice his wife's sudden glare, or else his blood might have run cold. "I'm to stay at Brinlaw while the rest of you go to France, even Nan, thank you very much, and for his own injury added to my insult, poor Tarquin has been stuck with the task of watching over me." Her words were sharp, but her tone was playful, and she cut her eyes at Tarquin. "And Brinlaw Castle," she finished with a cryptic little smile.

Alista looked from her husband to her daughter. The two of them looked very much alike in spite of their different coloring, and their characters even more so. The will of

Will lived on ... "I'm glad to see you so resigned," she said. "I didn't realize the matter was settled, much less that your father had told you."

"It was just before the wedding," Malinda explained. "Do you object, my lady?"

Alista smiled. "Of course not," she said. "Now come—Druscilla will need us in the hall."

"Yes, Mama," Malinda said, the picture of obedience. But as she walked away, she caught Tarquin's eye behind her mother's back, and her look was anything but meek. In truth, she looked as if she would have liked to stab him in the heart.

"I do pity you a little," Nan said softly as they left, speaking for Tarquin's ears alone. "Malinda made it very clear she didn't wish to stay at home, and she's quite accustomed to having her way. She'll hold a grudge against you if she feels she has been wronged." She paused, making sure Will was still attending his own conversation with the King. "Has she?"

Guy had taken her hand again, was obviously ready to leave, and besides, what could he tell her? "No," Tarquin promised. "Not by me."

The atmosphere at the wedding banquet grew steadily more festive as the afternoon gave way to evening, as if everyone had suddenly realized that tomorrow they would leave again for war. The hall at Bruel Castle had rarely seen such an assembly, noble knights and ladies fair all dancing and laughing and wooing, trying to fit a lifetime into a single night. And in the midst of this merry chaos, no maiden was more besieged by swains than Malinda. Everywhere she turned, she found another charming smile, another extravagant compliment, another plea to dance, until she felt quite dizzy. But try as she might, she couldn't seem to enjoy it. A week ago she would have, immensely—her own little version of court. But Tarquin had spoiled everything. He wasn't charming; he wasn't complimentary; he certainly wouldn't dance. Even now she could see him, standing to one side with Raynard, looking as if he thought them all a lot of silly fools. *Just wait, you,* she thought, smiling at the young knight who'd just brought her a drink. *Someday the fool will be you.*

"My lady?" The knight who had brought her drink touched her arm. "Will you dance?"

She turned toward the sea of dancers, and her eyes found Tarquin again, watching her from the other side of the room with a strange light in his eyes, one corner of his mouth turned up as if he were about to smile. "Yes," she said, gifting the knight with her prettiest smile as she set the drink aside and took his arm. "I will."

Tarquin watched another noble knight take possession of Malinda, and his heart clenched hard with envy, another wild emotion suppressed but for a tiny twitch at the corner of his mouth. In his vision, she had danced alone, a wild faery at the edge of a magical sea, waiting only for him. Here in reality, she danced with one after another of her own noble kind, pure-blooded lambs on their way to the slaughter. How many of these clean-hearted blockheads would fall on the green fields of France, their eyes still wide with shock at the bloody truth of all their chivalrous vows? But one of them would survive to claim her, would make her his wife. And there Tarquin would be, guarding the gate at Brinlaw, waiting to turn her over as he was bid, protector of a treasure he himself could never touch.

"Good night," he said to Raynard, leaving before he heard an answer.

Malinda had let the knight lead her to the dancers, turning her back on Tarquin. But as she turned in the dance, she saw him leaving the hall, and something in his face made her pause and lose her place in the figure. "Forgive me," she said to her partner. "I can't . . ." Leaving the dancers behind, she hurried toward the door.

The courtyard was as crowded as the hall with revelers not quite noble enough to take their ease in the royal presence. Tarquin stopped at the head of the steps and closed his eyes, trying to hold on to control, but it was useless. Jealous rage throbbed through him like a supernatural pulse, rage against Malinda for dancing out of his reach, more rage against himself for wanting to touch her at all.

"Move off, can't you?" a voice complained in a drunken slur as someone jostled him aside, nearly sending him sprawling down the steps. He found his balance and grabbed the man before his eyes were open, slammed him against the wall as soon as he saw his face.

"Move yourself," he snarled, the shock in his victim's bloodshot eyes a balm on his raging heart. This was nobody; he could pound him to pulp, and no one would care in the slightest. He raised his fist, barely hearing the rasp of metal against leather as the knight drew his sword—

"Fair evening, Cuz," Phillipe said pleasantly, drawing his own sword against Tarquin's attacker as Mark grabbed Tarquin's arm from the other side. Phillipe knocked the other knight's blade aside, barely sparing him a glance. "Have you dined?"

"He meant to murder me!" the other knight cried, waving his blade in an unsteady arc for punctuation.

"He's right," Tarquin said, his lip curled in a madman's contempt. "I did."

"On our patron's doorstep?" Phillipe asked mildly, strengthening his grip. "At darling Nana's wedding? Surely not." He turned his eyes on the other knight for the first time as if he'd only just noticed he was there. "You must need killing indeed."

"I barely spoke to him!" the knight protested, fear making him sober up fast. He really was a nobody, the son of a tradesman who'd been knighted some years past for providing King Henry cheap silk for the sails of his ship. This was his first war, and he'd been rather enjoying himself. But while he didn't know Tarquin from Adam, he recognized Brinlaw's son and old Brinlaw's bastard. And even if they had been nobodies, they had one another, and he had no friends here at all, or none worth speaking of if it came to a fight. In short, he was wishing he had stayed in the barracks and helped his squire polish up the armor. But who was this thug who had attacked him? Why did they defend him?

"Come," Mark urged Tarquin, giving his arm a tug. "Let's go back inside. Whatever he said, you are avenged."

Tarquin looked at him, just like the blockheads he had so disdained, and his rage redirected itself for a moment. The difference was, this one he loved, try as he might to escape it. He was Will's son, part of the little circle of Tarquin's misanthropic duty. He couldn't hurt him, couldn't let his evil touch him, no matter what he might want. And the boy was right in any case; he couldn't dis-

honor Will by brawling on his doorstep—or Guy de
Lancey's, or whoever the hell had charge of this cursed
place. Far from this place among strangers, he could have
let the fury have him, let the demon run its course, but
here he could not.

"He didn't say anything," he said, glancing back at his
half-forgotten victim. Observed calmly, he looked almost
comical, a scared, stodgy little drunk waving a sword as he
might a fishing pole. "My mistake," Tarquin muttered,
turning to walk away.

"Tarquin, wait." Phillipe clattered down the steps
behind him while Mark spoke quietly with the other
knight. "Will you not tell me what's wrong?" he asked,
catching up.

A sickly lump of disgust was forming in Tarquin's
stomach, the aftereffects of the rage, but he almost smiled.
When this boy was a child, he had watched him like a
hawk for signs of treachery, some trace of the evil father in
the face of the innocent son. Even yesterday, he had
looked on him with suspicion, seeing him not as a part of
his idolized family but as a threat to them. But while
Phillipe was Geoffrey's twin in looks, his nature was
apparently his own. Like Malinda and her brothers and
Lisbet, he had grown up in love, innocent of evil and hurt.
"Nothing is wrong, Phillipe," he promised. "All is right in
the world."

A strange, sad smile crossed the handsome face. "Aye,
Cuz," he answered. "Like you, I wish that were true."
Turning away with a final wave, he went back inside to
Mark. For a long moment, Tarquin watched them. He
could go back inside, rejoin the circle in the brightly lit
hall, pretend to be one of them again. Except for Malinda.

He couldn't watch Malinda and pretend. Turning away, he disappeared into the dark.

From the shadows of the arch, Malinda watched Tarquin go, mystified and frightened. His eyes . . . his expression had never changed, even when he raised his fist, but his eyes were alive with a feeling she couldn't understand but tingled to touch. Fury, yes, but hurt as well, and something else, something she had seen before, and her heart beat faster, remembering. "The boy," she said softly, the vision reborn in her mind, the cottage burning all around her and the child who had set it aflame. "Of course . . . the boy was Tarquin."

"Milady?" a voice spoke beside her. She looked up, expecting to find the young knight who had asked her to dance, but this man was older, in his late thirties at least, and from his clothing seemed far more wealthy than the usual knight-errant. "Are you well?" he pressed.

"Yes," she said, forcing herself back into the now. This man's face was familiar—he was one of Henry's advisors. She had been introduced to him that morning, but she couldn't quite remember his name.

"Robert Farrars," he supplied with a smile. "Are you quite certain you're all right, Lady Malinda?"

Tarquin was gone, disappeared into the night, and this man was a friend of the King, an associate of her father. "Positive," she answered. His smile made him seem younger, belying the strands of silver in his hair. "Thank you for your concern, Lord Farrars."

"Not at all." He looked out at the crowded courtyard. "Isn't that your brother?"

"And my cousins, yes," she answered. Mark and Phillipe were still talking to each other, arguing, from their faces.

"I know Sir Phillipe," Farrars nodded. "But the other cousin—who is he?"

"Only half a cousin, really—my cousin's brother," she said, forcing herself to be polite. "Tarquin FitzBruel."

"FitzBruel," he mused. "Perhaps I have heard of him, too . . . Has he any name?"

"None but his own," she answered. "Or did you mean a title?"

"Forgive me, my lady," Farrars said, his smile turning contrite. "I did not mean to speak ill of your kinsman. And you must think me horribly inquisitive, a perfect old granny." He pursed his lips in imitation of a disapproving crone, and she laughed in spite of herself. Most men his age would have sooner died outside God's love than made such a face, and she found herself rather liking him in spite of her own worries. "Please let me beg your pardon."

"Of course," she said with a more genuine smile of her own. She offered her hand, and he kissed it in courtly fashion. "In truth, I should thank you for your concern."

"Not at all." He offered his arm. "Will you allow me to escort you in?"

She looked back at the crowded hall. Druscilla had joined her husband and was watching Malinda, a knowing smile on her still-pretty face. Everyone thought she was having the time of her life. "No, my lord, but thank you," she said. "I'm rather tired; I think I will retire."

"Then I will say good night." He held out his hand again, and she took it.

"Good night, Lord Farrars," she said with a tiny curtsey.

"Robert, if you please," he said. "So we'll be friends when next we meet."

"Robert, then," she answered. "Good night."

"Good night," he said, winking at her as he bowed. "May all your dreams be sweet."

"Yours as well," she answered automatically.

"Oh, I believe they will," he replied with a smile that made her laugh again.

"Please, my lord," she scolded. "Good night."

10

As the banquet began to wind down, Will Brinlaw looked up to find his oldest son standing over him, followed closely by his friend, Phillipe. "Forgive me, Papa," Mark said, glancing over at Alista and Nan, still engrossed in talk of their own. "May we speak with you in private?"

Mark was not likely to disturb the dais table for trifles, and even Phillipe looked anxious. "Of course," he said. Nodding to Henry, he led them to the solar.

"Forgive me," Mark began as soon as the door was closed.

"I already have, Mark, I promise," Will said, laying a hand on his shoulder. When had he become such an object of reverential terror to his children? Not for the first time that day, he felt a wistful pang for the days when they were all as young as Willie, with baby desires easily granted and baby problems easily solved. "What troubles you?"

"Tarquin," Mark said bluntly. "Are you sure he's the best choice to stay at Brinlaw with Malinda?"

"I am," Will answered. "Why should I not be? What has

Tarquin done?" His imagination fairly reeled with possibilities, but he wouldn't panic just yet.

"Nothing of consequence, my lord," Phillipe insisted. "A minor disagreement—"

"The argument was minor, yes, but Tarquin's reaction was not," Mark cut him off. "A knight accidentally bumped into him in the courtyard, and Tarquin went after him as if to murder him with his bare hands. Papa, the man had a sword. If Phillipe and I hadn't stepped in, I shudder to think what might have happened."

"The man was a piss-poor swordsman and drunk besides," Phillipe argued. "At worst, he would have dropped his sword on Tarquin's foot on his way to the ground after being punched in the face."

"And how is that a comfort?" Mark demanded. "Tarquin was ready to kill that poor sot—he admitted as much—and for what?"

"Perhaps you and Phillipe only witnessed the end of the quarrel," Will suggested. Secretly, he was relieved the problem was no more serious than this, but he was worried, even so.

"So I thought as well," Mark said. "So I questioned the knight, and Captain Raynard, who was with Tarquin just before he left the hall, and other men in the courtyard. No one knew anything, saw anything to suggest a quarrel between Tarquin and this man beyond a misstep on the stairs. The knight himself swore on his honor that he didn't even know who Tarquin was."

"His honor," Phillipe scoffed. "That and a penny will buy you an apple at the fair. So he didn't know Tarquin— all the more reason to believe this quarrel was nothing."

"The quarrel was nothing," Mark repeated, his jaw stubbornly set. "Tarquin's temper is not. Forgive me, Papa; I know how dearly you love him, as do we all. But is this the man in whose hands you will place the safety of Brinlaw and, more importantly, of my sister?"

"Yes," Will answered. Mark looked shocked, and he shook his head. "I have known Tarquin since he was a child, and yes, his temper has always been his most dangerous foe," he said with a wry smile. "I don't doubt for a moment that this quarrel happened just as you describe it, that he attacked this knight with little or no provocation and with genuine deadly intent, though I do suspect he would have stopped short of murder."

"Then how——?" Mark began.

"Because I also have no doubt that he would be just as impetuous, just as deadly, if he had to fight for Brinlaw," Will went on. "He is as fierce in love as in everything else, and he does love us well. Brinlaw is his home; he loves it as we do."

"Then why——?" Mark stopped, thinking better of his words. "That well may be, my lord," he began again. "But surely someone else——"

"There is no one else," Will cut him off.

"How can you say that?" Mark demanded, feelings getting the better of his duty. He glanced over at Phillipe and stopped, a crimson blush coloring his face. "Forgive me," he mumbled, looking away.

"I will not, for you've done nothing that needs forgiving," Will said, brusque with love. "Phillipe, will you excuse us?"

Phillipe nodded. "Yes, my lord."

"You can speak your mind to me, Mark," Will said when he had gone. "You wonder why I would say Tarquin is my only choice when you, my son, are as good a man as he and a knight besides."

Mark stared at the flickering flame of a torch mounted on the wall. "Yes."

"You have every right to ask me this—in your place, I would," Will said. He sat down on one of the cushioned benches and motioned for Mark to join him. "Your knighthood, your worthiness—these are the very reasons why you must not stay at Brinlaw," he said when Mark had taken a nearby chair. "This war means far more than land or money, though even Henry himself refuses to see it. The war will end. The King and his sons will reconcile. None of them has a choice. They are his heirs; he is their sovereign. Even if they win, they will not dare depose him, for that would leave them with no kingdom to inherit. Eleanor is well-loved in her homeland, but Aquitaine is hardly big enough to bear a queen and three kings. And English lords have had enough French puppets. Without a single, powerful sovereign, they would rebel."

"So what?" Mark said. "War for war's sake is hardly new."

"It isn't," Will agreed. "But in such a war, what matters isn't the outcome but the fight itself. When it's over, whoever wins will count their spoils not in land but in men, and how each noble knight is seen in war will determine his status in peace."

"And you believe King Henry will win."

"I know he will," Will answered with a tiny smile with very little joy in it. "But even if I didn't, I wouldn't let you stay at Brinlaw. No matter who wins, you must be seen as a man who will fight for his sovereign's interests if so called. Better you should join the Young King or Richard than stay at home—that would look as if you didn't care who won, that your only concern is your own castle."

"And so you fight, Papa, even though you really don't care who wins," Mark said, understanding.

"Exactly—and for that reason, so must you," Will replied. "Tarquin has no such concerns. Try as I might, he refuses to be anything but his own man, to have anything to lose but his freedom."

"Sounds rather appealing to me," Mark grumbled.

"Doesn't it?" Will grinned. "But you, alas, have a name. You're my son, and Brinlaw will be yours, if it remains mine to give." He held out his hand, scarred long since from his own battles to keep this legacy intact. "Will you take it?"

Mark clasped his father's hand in a grip of iron, for a moment unable to speak. "Yes, Papa," he managed at last. "I will."

Malinda sat on the side of her bed, one shoe off and one on, trembling all over. She had come upstairs more than an hour before, feeling perfectly well, intending to go to bed at once and put the day behind her. But somewhere between closing the door and getting undressed, her thoughts had taken hold and put her in this trance, the same cycle repeating in an endless loop inside her head. The boy she had seen in her vision at the cottage had been Tarquin, the child he had been. The man in the vision must therefore have been his father, Bruel, Nan's father, too—the high-born brute who had done something horrible to Malinda's aunt. What had he done? After her vision, she could believe him capable of anything. The boy Tarquin had watched his mother's murder, but he had escaped. He had heard Malinda's voice calling out to him across time to run away, to save himself from the flames . . . Was that possible? If she could see the past, could she not touch it as well? Otherwise, what was the point? But if that were true, if she had reached back before her own birth to speak to Tarquin, she had known him before she was even born. But no. He had known her.

She had run away from the cottage into the forest, and she had found Tarquin, a man. She had been afraid, but he had known her. *"I came here for you,"* he had said, reaching out to touch her, reaching through her fear. But she hadn't known him; she had run away. But later she had kissed him, drawn to him by some power beyond her control, and he had kissed her back, and when the kiss was broken, when the power was thwarted, she was lost, furious, twisted all out of her usual frame. Everything else—Nan's promise, Papa's duty—these were no more than distractions, minor threads against a larger pattern of Tarquin's soul woven to her own. Tonight in the courtyard, she had seen the boy again, lost and furious, helpless to resist, and she had seen the man, deadly in his fury, desperate to destroy, to be free of something he couldn't understand. And still she had been drawn to him, wanted to touch him, rescue him somehow, and still she had been afraid. No one else had seen him as she had, no one else understood. No one else had seen the forge where he had been made, beaten like a lethal blade in fire.

A knock came on the door. "Malinda?" It was her mother's voice.

"I'm here, Mama." She put her shoe back on as Alista came in.

"Lisbet said you had gone," she said. She carried a bundle wrapped in silk. "She also said you were a bit out of sorts."

"I was," Malinda admitted. "I am."

Alista smiled. "I thought you might be." She sat down on the bed. "So I brought you a present." She put the bundle into Malinda's lap.

"What is this?" Malinda asked, though she knew already. She had stolen it a hundred times. Under the wrappings was the Falconskeep book.

"I want you to have it," Alista said, watching her unwrap it. "The power is already yours. Perhaps this will show you better how to use it. But whatever you do will be your choice. The book is yours."

Malinda touched the cover, the faery script worked deep into the leather, undamaged by time. She had wanted it so long, bristled at being denied its use. But now that it was being offered to her, she was afraid, not only of the book but of her mother's reasons for giving it up, changing her mind at last. "Why?" she had to ask.

"Because you are a woman, not a child," Alista answered. "Because it is your right. But I would ask that you take an obligation with it." She took the heartstone from around her own neck and put it around Malinda's.

"Mama, no." She touched the silver-pink pendant, still warm as her mother's living flesh. "I can't—these things are yours—"

"No more than they are yours," Alista cut her off with a smile. "You are a faery of Falconskeep as much as I am, and a great deal more gifted at sorcery. You need these things, both of them—the book to show you the way you have already chosen, the heartstone to keep you safe." She touched Malinda's hair. "You look very like my mother," she mused. "Have I ever told you that?"

"Not really," Malinda admitted. "Brother Paolo used to

say I had her eyes, but you never mentioned it. I thought maybe you had forgotten how she looked."

"I do forget sometimes," Alista said. She pulled Malinda's hair free of the chain, settled the pendant more smoothly against her daughter's chest. "But she comes to me in dreams sometimes, even now, and Brother Paolo was right. You do have her eyes." She smiled. "She wasn't afraid of magic, either."

Malinda looked down at the heartstone, remembering the story. Her grandmother had taken it off and given it to Brother Paolo to be hidden away. While he was gone, with Alista watching, a tiny child unable to understand, she had transformed into a falcon, cheating death with magic. Without the heartstone, she was free to fly away. "I'll never take it off," Malinda promised. "But what if you need it, or the book?"

"Your father will protect me better than they could," Alista said. "He always has."

"I know." She thought of Nan at the church, so certain and serene, her smile like Mama's now. No confusion, no fear, no madness that tore their hearts apart. But had it always been so? "Mama, may I ask you something rather silly?"

"Of course," Alista laughed.

"You've always told me my love would be destined, that because of who I am, there would be one man in all the world whom I would love," Malinda said, trying to keep the words from falling over themselves in her rush to have them out. "You said it has always been that way for us, that it was the same for you and Papa."

"Yes," Alista nodded.

"But was it always? Did you always love Papa, from the first time you saw him?"

"Not at all," Alista admitted with a laugh. "I had only just met him when we married. And then when I did know him, I was even more unhappy—I hated him."

"Mama, you did not!"

"Oh yes, my love, I did," Alista said. "I even tried to murder him once, and I ran away . . . but all that time, I loved him, too." She smiled. "That must sound very silly."

"Actually, no, it doesn't," Malinda said. "So how did you finally know?"

"That I loved him?" She chewed her lip, a girlish gesture that made her seem as young as Malinda herself. "It's hard to say exactly. I know I didn't want to admit it. Then for a long time after I did, at least to myself, I thought he didn't love me. It seems ridiculous now, but at the time . . ." She let her voice trail off. "In any case, you needn't worry. Whoever your destined love might be, he will find you. And no matter what you do or he does or what barriers the world might put between you, you'll be together in the end."

Malinda shivered, remembering Tarquin's eyes. "That's rather scary, when you think of it."

"Very," Alista agreed with a laugh. "But is it any more scary than the rest of your magic?"

Yes, Malinda thought but didn't say. "I suppose not."

"Get some sleep." Alista got up, and Malinda followed. "Only heaven can tell when the King will decide to leave, maybe first thing in the morning." She picked up the heartstone. "So you promise never to take this off?"

"I swear." Suddenly the thought that her parents were leaving so soon was too awful to be borne. They were at war; it might be years before they came home, before she would see them again. A terrible chill passed through her, making her hug her mother as tightly as she could. "I'm sorry, Mama. I've been horrible, I know."

"You haven't, no such thing," Alista scolded, hugging her back. She drew back to look into her eyes. "Just promise you'll be careful."

"I will," Malinda promised, hugging her again. She wasn't virtuous or wise, and she was beginning to believe destiny had dealt her a dangerous fate to meet. But she would be as careful as her fortunes would allow. "I won't fail you, Mama."

By full sun the next day, King Henry's troops and entourage were packed and ready to move, with a smaller train prepared to head for Brinlaw. "You'll have about a dozen men, all under your command," Will was telling Tarquin in the midst of the bustling courtyard.

"Even the knights?" Tarquin asked with a wry grin.

"Especially the knights," Will answered, grinning back. "There are only four of them and not a one over sixteen— they'll be glad enough to have someone to follow. But the others are seasoned fighters. You shouldn't have any trouble, but if you do, you'll be well prepared." He handed over a small, rolled scroll. "The present castellan at Brinlaw should recognize you, but just in case, here's my official letter."

Tarquin took it with a heavy heart. This was wrong; he was wrong to accept it. "Will, are you sure—?"

"Yes." He looked up as another knight approached from the castle's main door. "Well met, Lord Farrars."

"Fine day, Lord Brinlaw," the other man answered with a smile as pleasant as his words. "His Majesty asks if you are ready to depart."

"Nearly, yes," Will answered. "But since when has your station sunk to herald, my lord?"

"You know as well as I," Farrars laughed. "But who is this? Another of your sons?"

"My niece's brother, Tarquin FitzBruel," Will answered. "Lord Robert Farrars, Tarquin."

"My lord," Tarquin nodded.

"Tarquin," Farrars nodded back. "I think I know you by reputation."

"Then you must think ill of me indeed," Tarquin answered, pleasant but wary.

"Quite the opposite, I assure you," Farrars laughed. "Brinlaw, are you taking this young brigand to France? Rather mean to the Baby King and his brothers, don't you think?"

"Tarquin is going to Brinlaw to act as castellan," Will explained.

"Very good," Farrars said. "A fine choice, I'm sure."

"I'll do my best," Tarquin said. Something about the man seemed familiar, but he couldn't place him. Will seemed to know him well enough, but he had introduced him as a stranger, so he wouldn't have encountered him as Will's squire. On Crusade, perhaps? But no, Farrars wore no pilgrim's cross. Of course, neither did he.

"I will tell King Henry we await his pleasure," Farrars said, making a bow to Will. "Until we meet again, Tarquin," he said with a smile before he turned away.

Malinda could hear Lisbet and her mother arguing as she came up the hall to Lisbet's room, but when she knocked, the raised voices abruptly stopped. "Come on in," Lisbet said, opening the door. "Tell my mother to make Papa let me go with you to Brinlaw."

"Can't she, please, Druscilla?" Malinda said. How else could she bear being left behind?

"I'm sorry, darlings, but his mind is quite made up," Dru smiled with a sigh. "By the way, Malinda, I saw you made quite a conquest last night." Malinda looked at her, uncomprehending. "Robert Farrars?"

"Oh," Malinda said dismissively. "I'd hardly call him a conquest."

"I don't know why not," Dru said. "He's quite eligible, you know, and in the market from what I hear. And handsome. There's a great deal to be said for a man who's already grown when you acquire him."

"Mother, really," Lisbet scolded.

"He doesn't have a wife already?" Malinda asked.

"She died in childbirth when they were both very young," Dru explained. "He had two sons, about the same ages as Phillipe and Mark, but both of them were killed on Crusade within a year."

"How horrible," Lisbet said. "Poor man."

"Yes, indeed," Dru agreed. "But he is still young, and his estates are said to be exceptional. Not to mention that he is a favorite of the King. Some noble maid will be very lucky to have him."

"No doubt," Malinda agreed, shooting a glance at Lisbet, who rolled her eyes in sympathy.

"Hullo!" Willie called, coming in from the hall. "We're leaving. Papa says you must all come and say goodbye."

Malinda and Lisbet ran out into the courtyard with Baby Will hot on their heels. Brinlaw was at the front of the caravan with the King, but his wife was just outside with

Tarquin and Raynard. "So soon?" Malinda complained, hugging her mother.

"Henry will be gone at once or die in the attempt," Alista sighed. "He says we must make Southampton by Friday, or the war's already lost."

Will joined them with Mark and Phillipe behind him. "Has anyone seen de Lancey or Nan?" he asked as his youngest son climbed him like a tree.

"Not since breakfast," Alista answered. "Are they not coming with us?"

"Here they come," Tarquin said as Nan emerged from the tower door, her veil fluttering out of her reach in the breeze as she tried to get it fastened. Guy stopped her on the steps and pinned it for her.

"Whenever you're ready," Will called, sounding cross, but he was smiling.

"Pray pardon," Guy mumbled as they reached the others. "We had some trouble getting Nan packed."

"Getting me dressed, more like," Nan laughed, making her new husband blush. "Is everyone else already here?"

"As a matter of fact," her uncle said, pretending to scowl.

"Don't tease them, Will," Alista ordered. "They're here now, and we're ready."

Wait! Malinda wanted to cry. Everything was moving too fast. Her mother was saying a final word to Druscilla; Lisbet was kissing Phillipe. In a moment, they would be gone, and she didn't know what to do. The whole world was turning upside down, and she couldn't stop it.

"Malinda," Willie said, tugging on her hand. She knelt down to his reach, and he hugged her tight. "I wish you could come with us," he said, uncharacteristically tearful.

"I do, too, monster," she said, kissing his cheek. "But I will see you soon."

"Do you promise?" he persisted, drawing back to look at her. "When we come home, do you promise you'll be there?"

"Of course I promise," she said. "Where else would I be?" He looked so frightened suddenly, not like Willie at all.

"We'll all be home before we know it," Mark said. He offered Malinda his hand to help her up. "Now go and tell Mama we must go."

"Will they let you stay with Papa?" Malinda asked when the child was gone. There was so much she had meant to say to Mark while they were together, so many questions she had promised herself she must ask, but it had all seemed so hard, and she had gotten so turned around in the past few days, and now there was no time. He seemed happier than he had at Christmas in spite of the war, but she still didn't know what had troubled him. Had it simply gone away? Or was he just hiding it better?

"Who knows?" he shrugged. "It doesn't matter, really." He glanced over his shoulder at Tarquin, who was saying good-bye to Nan and Guy. "Promise you'll stay out of trouble."

"At Brinlaw?" she laughed. "Yes, idiot, I promise."

"I'm serious, Malinda." He touched a lock of hair that had fallen free of her veil. "Tarquin isn't Papa or Raynard; he won't know how to handle your mischief."

"Mischief?" she echoed, arching a brow.

"Don't be offended—you know what I mean," he frowned. "He's supposed to keep you safe, and you hate that, but you have to promise me you'll let him."

"All my brothers want promises," she said lightly, but in truth she felt a chill. Mark's words were priggish and insulting, but she saw real concern in his eyes.

"Malinda, please," he said. "Promise you'll keep out of his way."

"Fine," she said, patting his cheek as she had when he was still her baby brother. "I promise."

Henry's trumpeters sounded a blast, and in the field below, the troops began to move, a great snake twisting down the road. "I know I've forgotten something," Nan fretted, giving Tarquin a final hug.

"We'll buy a new one, whatever it is," Guy promised, leading her to the coach.

Malinda found herself being passed from one rough hug to another as Mark and Phillipe rushed off to join their own troops. "Be careful!" she called as they ran for the road.

"Write soon!" Lisbet added.

"We will!" Phillipe answered, running backward for a moment to wave, a foolish trick that would have sent another knight rolling head over heels. "You too, daisy!"

"I promise!" Malinda called back.

"Come on," Will said, taking Alista's hand. He touched Malinda's cheek. "Are we forgiven?"

"Of course." She threw herself into his arms, fighting back tears. She was a woman grown, not a child who could cry at being left behind. "Just come home soon."

As Alista watched them, a terrible foreboding passed over her heart. She had kissed her own father good-bye once just this way, and she had never seen him again. *We're not going,* she almost said aloud. But that was foolishness. She looked over at Tarquin, saw him watching them as well, his handsome face the same mask of stone it always became when he was struck by some powerful feeling. She should speak to him, make him talk to her. But there was no time . . .

"Safe journey, Mama," Malinda said.

"You, too," Alista answered. She felt as if a piece of her heart were being torn from her, and crying wouldn't help. "We'll see you soon, my love."

Tarquin watched Malinda fight her tears until the caravan was gone. She was so beautiful and trying so hard to be brave that a fierce feeling of protectiveness for her washed over him. "It will be all right," he promised.

She turned her eyes on him, cold as emerald ice. "Yes, it will," she said, her tone as cold as her eyes. "I don't understand you. I don't know what you want. I certainly don't know what you said to my father to get yourself named castellan. But you needn't think for one moment that I come with the castle. You have no power over me, and I will not be ruled."

"You think I want to try?" he demanded, hot fury meeting her cold. "You think I asked to be left in charge of a castle and a spoiled brat besides? Why would I do that? Believe me, Malinda, given my choice, I would be back at sea, not at Brinlaw. I hate castles, and—" He broke off. For once in his life, something penetrated his anger before it took control—the sudden hurt in her eyes.

"And you hate me?" she finished, barely a question.

"No," he said brusquely, his anger fading. "Of course not. But I didn't ask for this. Your father asked me to watch over you and Brinlaw, and I couldn't refuse him."

"But you would have if you could," she pressed, her tone still clipped and sharp.

"Yes." He looked away, unable to face those eyes. "I don't blame you for mistrusting me. I don't belong here. I certainly shouldn't be the one protecting you. But we're stuck." Lisbet was only a few steps away with her parents, and he saw her notice them. "So I'll make you a pact," he said. "You try not to do anything too dangerous or foolhardy, and I will leave you alone." A blush rose in her cheeks. "I'm afraid that's the best I can do."

What do *you want?* Malinda wondered. One moment he kissed her; the next he pushed her away. She knew they were connected somehow, and that frightened her to death. Surely she had more reason to be afraid than he did. Yet he was the one who wanted to run away, who wanted to leave her alone. "Then I suppose it will have to suffice," she said crisply, turning and walking inside.

Over the next few days as they made the journey to Brinlaw, Tarquin had ever more reason to regret his decision, loyalty to Brinlaw be damned. Malinda had always been resentful of authority, but to Tarquin she was positively rude. If he suggested the women ride in the litter along certain desolate stretches of road to protect them from being seen by bandits, Malinda developed motion sickness and would ride her horse. If Tarquin suggested they all ride to make up some time before nightfall, Malinda felt sleepy and insisted the litter be opened so she could take a nap. The young knights who traveled with them found themselves in quite a quandary. They feared and respected Tarquin, but Malinda they adored, and her insolent attitude only underscored the fact that they were technically taking orders from an inferior. Meanwhile, the foot soldiers all thought Lady Malinda would profit tremendously from a good spanking and had begun to set wagers as to when Tarquin would give it to her.

On their third afternoon away from Bruel, Malinda had ridden a short distance ahead of the main caravan with two of the knights to fly her goshawk in an open meadow against Tarquin's specific request. "I dare say Sir Harold and Sir Bruce can protect me from any murderers hiding in the grass," she had laughed as she rode away.

"It isn't you," promised Sir Arthur, the youngest of the Brinlaw knights, riding up beside Tarquin.

"It is me," Tarquin said with a grim little smile, watching the goshawk fly back to Malinda's fist, the bird of prey as docile as a pigeon. No doubt she would have him just as tame given half the chance. She had already rendered him incapable of looking at or even thinking of anything else but her. Every mocking smile, every cutting remark, every toss of those golden curls was another shiny little hook in his soul, binding him closer and driving him mad. What's more, he was certain she knew it. She felt he had wronged her, humiliated her, and she was punishing him for it, and he could hardly blame her. But she should realize he had no choice—she was being a child, a wicked, magical child inside a woman's form. *Just get her safely home,* he told himself again, the chant that kept him sane.

"It's getting dark," Arthur said, the look in the new castellan's eyes giving him a chill.

"It is," Tarquin agreed, looking up at the sky. Clouds were gathering, but the sun was setting, too. "We should make camp before it rains."

"I'll go tell my lady." He rode across the field as the caravan stopped and broke apart to make camp. "We're stopping," he announced.

"Already?" Malinda complained, stroking Rufus's throat to calm him after the hunt.

"It's going to rain," Arthur explained.

"Oh, bollocks," Harold scoffed. "Come, my lady. If your father's man is so timid, we will escort you on, and the rest can catch up in the morning."

"I don't know," Bruce said doubtfully, looking up at the darkening sky.

"I think that's a marvelous idea," Malinda said. "A bit of rain might be refreshing in any case." She looked at Harold with her sweetest, most fetching smile. "I'm sure I'll be quite safe."

"On my life, my lady," Harold answered with a catch in his throat.

"Fine," Arthur said with a devilish grin. "Go and tell the captain, Sir Harold."

This brought the knight back to earth right quickly, just as his friend had suspected. "Then again, those clouds do seem rather dark," he said, blushing scarlet.

"Aye," Bruce agreed with a grin. "Very dark indeed."

"Cowards," Malinda laughed. "I'm ashamed of both of you." Wheeling her horse around, she galloped back toward the camp.

11

Malinda sat in her tent listening to the rain outside and feeling perfectly wretched. She hated being such a nasty little horror; she knew very well what the men-at-arms were saying, and she agreed with them completely. But she couldn't seem to stop. It wasn't that she wanted the knights' attention—quite the opposite. Compared to Tarquin, Sir Bruce and Sir Harold seemed like fawning little boys to her. She didn't want them; she wanted Tarquin, wanted him more sorely with every day that passed. But he didn't feel the same. He went out of his way to ignore her. So she went out of her way to make his life as difficult as possible.

Her maid brought her something to eat, and she smiled at her. "Thanks, Hildy. You had better go and rest yourself."

"Thanks, my lady." She lit extra candles beside Malinda's cot and set the magic book out on a little table—a new ritual begun on this journey. Like most of the servants at Falconskeep, Hildy knew about her mistress's magic, at least enough to know the book was for study. "No doubt the captain will want to make an early start after this rain."

"No doubt." Malinda watched her turn down the blankets, then smiled and nodded again as she left her alone in the tent. She missed Lisbet. If only she had come . . . But no. Lisbet would scold her for the way she was behaving; her sharp little eyes would see the truth, and she would make Malinda explain her whole heart. And Malinda didn't want to explain, not even to herself.

She thought about the first moment she had seen Tarquin in the woods, the terrifying hunger in his eyes. She had thought he was a spirit come to steal away her life or at least a brigand who meant to steal her virtue. But he was more complicated than that and far more dangerous. He was the frightened, angry boy who ran from the burning cottage in her vision. He was the thug who had meant to murder a stranger for nothing at her cousin's wedding. He was the forbidden lover who set her blood on fire with his kisses. He was her father's trusted castellan who sent her back to bed like a naughty child. She couldn't marry him; she couldn't even make love to him. He was her father's servant, horribly unsuitable, and besides, he frightened her half to death. But she wanted him, and she would not be denied. He would burn for her as she burned for him, and he would know how it felt to be rejected. She might be childish to want this; she might be the spoiled brat he had called her, but she didn't care. She would make him hers before she let him go. She would be the one to decide. The power to choose would be hers and hers alone.

The rain stopped after midnight, the clouds drifting apart to reveal a full, high moon. She pulled her gown back on over her shift and slipped barefoot into the sultry night.

Most of the men were sleeping as well, tent flaps tied down against the weather. The two on watch nodded as she passed, and she smiled—no doubt they thought she was mad. "Is everything all right, my lady?" one of them asked. "Can we get you anything?"

She saw Tarquin standing at the edge of the circle of light from the campfires, a tall shadow under an ancient oak. "No, thank you," she answered. "Everything is fine."

Tarquin's back was turned to the camp, but he felt more than heard her approach, her little feet almost silent on the grass. "I'm not invisible this time," she said, laying a hand on his arm. "And I'm dressed."

He looked down and almost smiled. "Nearly, anyway," he answered. "You never gave my shirt back, by the way."

"Nor will I ever." He looked away, even the half smile gone. "I wanted to apologize," she pressed on, refusing to be daunted. "I know I've been rather difficult." He didn't answer. "I am sorry," she finished in a teasing tone that sounded anything but.

"Are you?" He turned to face her, his back against the tree, his arms crossed over his chest. "I didn't notice you were being much different, but I don't know you well." She looked like a faery princess from some ancient tale, the mist rising from the wet, warm ground enhancing the illusion. "You should be asleep," he said, looking away.

"So should you." The woods were full of sound, birds and crickets celebrating the end of the rain. Standing under the canopy of glistening leaves, they might have been alone in all the world. "I should have brought Rufus," she mused, looking up.

"Why call him Rufus?" he asked. "Why not Hannibal or Buzzy or Jack?"

"I don't know," she laughed. "Rufus just seemed to be his name."

"You sound like Nan," he smiled. "She used to have three different dogs named Virgil, all at the same time."

"Yes, I know," she said. "As a matter of fact, unless he's met with some misfortune in the past month or so, one of the Virgils is waiting for us at home."

"You can't be serious—"

"Oh yes." She reached up and touched a branch, sending a shiver of raindrops falling over them both. "Nan wept to leave him, but he couldn't make the trip to Bruel anymore, much less France. He's old as Methuseleh, for a dog at least, half blind, smells atrocious. But she loves him just the same."

"Nan has that gift," Tarquin answered. "Loving creatures no one else could."

"Like you, I suppose you mean."

"Yes."

"And my mother? Is she gifted this way as well?"

"Yes."

"I see." She wanted to reach out and touch him, whether he willed it or not, and not just to torment him. She thought of the child she had seen, the same look in his eyes. She thought of the brush of his lips in the woods before she had run and again in his room at Bruel when she had kissed him first, and all her careful plans for vengeance dissolved into an instinct far more profound. "Why don't you want me?" she heard herself say aloud.

Tarquin just stared at her, unable to form an answer. She sounded so tender, so genuinely hurt. *I do,* he longed to answer, to take her into his arms and kiss her fears away. For a single, heady moment, he let himself imagine what might be if she were only his. He thought of her first kiss, innocent and fearless. She had known him—but no, she had not. She knew the lie her parents knew, the mask he kept so carefully intact. Only once had she caught a glimpse of his true self, in the woods at Bruel. All unknowing, he had touched her, and she had run away. "Why do you care?" he said aloud.

"I . . . I don't," she stammered, her own mask falling into place—the careless brat again—but it was hopeless. He had already seen the truth. She tried to think of something else to say, something callous and hurtful to rebuild her defenses, but before she could speak, he was kissing her, and she was lost.

He hadn't meant to touch her, had reached for her with hands that barely seemed his own, but as he tasted her mouth, he let himself feel the desperate truth of his desire, just for a moment, dying for her sweet breath. He traced the curve of her throat, the line of her jaw, skin as soft as silk, bones fragile as a bird's . . . the falcon faery.

Malinda's knees felt weak, the earth falling away beneath her. He didn't hold her, only kissed her, leaving her free but luring her still—her own tricks turned against her. She broke the kiss, lips still parted as she backed away, her eyes now locked with his, a more abstracted touch. He didn't try to stop her or reach for her again, but he didn't look away. The mask dissolved, and raw feeling made her heart ache. The boy from the cottage, the man from the wood—he was both, here in this moment, and she wanted him like nothing she had ever known. "Tarquin," she began, reaching out, but he stopped her, catching her wrists in a grip so strong it made her gasp. She thought he would push her away, and she braced for the hurt and anger she would feel. But he just held her there, his eyes locked with hers, a long moment that seemed to last forever. "Tarquin?" she whispered again, barely finding breath to speak. His eyes closed, and in a sudden, graceful movement that made her gasp again, he bent his face to her hands, kissed each palm as he sank to his knees before her. A tremor raced through her, made her sway on her feet as he pressed his face to her stomach. No one had ever touched her so before; she had never even imagined such a thing. His hot breath burned her skin through her gown, and she had to lean back against the tree to keep from falling, her hands braced on his shoulders. He nuzzled her hip, climbed back to his feet as he kissed his way upward again, his arms around her waist. The guardsmen were close enough to hear them; she should be afraid. He wanted her; he couldn't deny it now. She should punish him, push him away. But she couldn't. He raised his head to look at her, and she framed his face in her hands, drunk on the desire in his eyes.

A small sound like a lute string badly plucked broke the silence, made her look away, confused. Tarquin lunged for her, knocked her to the ground as the arrow streaked past his shoulder to bury itself in the thick bark of the tree. Suddenly the air was full of sounds, screams of guardsmen in the camp, shouts of triumph and alarm. "Stay low," Tarquin ordered as he grabbed Malinda's wrist, keeping her close as he ran.

Malinda stumbled, struggling to keep up. In less than an instant, they had fallen into war. She couldn't wrap her mind around it, couldn't seem to catch up and react. Luckily, Tarquin could. "Stay together!" he shouted to her father's men—his men. They obeyed at once, guardsmen already bleeding and knights stumbling out of their tents, half-dressed with swords upraised. Men in leather and rags were pouring out of the darkness, scattering the fires, firing more arrows. Bandits? But they seemed so sure in their course, so well-prepared—the camp was completely surrounded. A brigand lunged for her, and Tarquin snatched her back, his sword slicing upward, and the man fell in a splatter of hot blood.

Don't scream, she chanted to herself, trying to stay calm. *Don't scream, don't scream, don't scream.* Another man came at Tarquin from behind, and she did cry out, but he was turning around before the sound was made. The man's arms were raised with his sword, and Tarquin drove a fist into his face. Blood gushed from his mouth and nose, and Malinda heard a sickening crumple of bone. The man fell forward to his knees, clutching at Malinda's skirt, and Tarquin kicked him away to plunge the sword two-handed through his chest, pinning him to the ground.

"Hildy," she shouted, trying to make him hear her over the din. "I have to—"

"You!" Tarquin grabbed Sir Bruce. "Take her and find her maid. Get them out of here."

"No!" Malinda cried.

"Do it," Tarquin ordered, grabbing her again to put her hand into the knight's.

"Yes," Bruce promised him, dragging her away.

Her tent had been cut down but was otherwise untouched, and a lump of life was moving frantically under the fallen canvas. "Hildy!" she cried, breaking free of Bruce to reach her. A dagger suddenly ripped through the fabric, and the maid emerged, looking terrified. "Are you all right?"

"I think so," Hildy stammered, struggling to stand up, her arms full of Malinda's possessions. "My lady, what is happening?"

"I don't know," Malinda admitted. "It just started all of a sudden."

"My lady, come on," Bruce urged. "We have to find you someplace safe—"

"Like where?" Malinda asked. The battle still raged all around them, but she noticed something odd. By all rights, she and her maid should have been besieged on every side. If these were the bandits they appeared to be, the two women would be their most profitable prize. But now that she was away from Tarquin, no one but Bruce seemed interested in her at all. Tarquin . . . She looked back, focusing her attention on the battle. *Look at the details,* her father's voice urged inside her head. *Find the key.*

The attack was a circle, which made sense—so was the camp. Some of the brigands had pressed in more deeply as soldiers had fallen, but the center was still almost clear— no one was breaking formation. At the center stood Tarquin, fighting on every side. Tarquin was the key—the brigands were here for him. He was fighting two at once, making her heart pound with fear, but he didn't seem overly concerned. His sword swung around in an easy arc, like a scythe through stems of wheat. One man's torso fell at his feet, his head flying backward, rolling away in the dark. "Tarquin!" she screamed, shocked and frightened.

Tarquin didn't hear her, didn't hear anything. A rider was bearing down on him, crouched low in the saddle, and he feinted the second brigand back, kicked his feet out from under him as he staggered. He whirled around and grabbed the horse's bridle as the great head loomed over his shoulder, yanked it off balance with all his strength as he rolled aside, his shoulder giving way with an ominous pop.

"Do something," Malinda muttered, watching in horror. "We have to do something."

"Here." Hildy put her book in her hands, one of the objects she'd retrieved from the fallen tent. "Will this help?"

"I don't know." She could turn herself invisible, but she couldn't sneak up on a dozen or more men at once. She could turn Tarquin invisible if she could stop the battle long enough to find the spell and work it, but that didn't seem likely, either. She clutched the book to her breast, frantically trying to think, and clouds began to gather, distant thunder drawing close.

Tarquin rolled onto his back, saw the horse's hooves come down on his second opponent, crushing him into the mud. But the rider was still coming, tearing frantically at the reins to bring the horse around. Tarquin climbed into a crouch and ducked behind him, drawing his dagger, and as the horse turned, he drove the blade deep into the rider's leg, making him shriek in pain. Tarquin grabbed his leg to drag him from the saddle, and the man raised his crossbow, firing wild. The bolt streaked by, tearing a shallow gash in Tarquin's shoulder as the rider came off his horse, the two of them falling, rolling in the mud, rain spattering around them.

A flash of lightning lit the sky as the rain began. "Perfect," Bruce said sarcastically. "Just what we need."

"Yes," Malinda agreed, focused completely on Tarquin. Something strange was happening, and she was the cause. She felt the power coursing through her, pulsing like her blood. Tarquin was back on his feet, bodies piling up around him and more still coming, dark shapes in the rain. A tremor passed through her, a teeth-chattering chill, and lightning flashed again, and thunder crashed like the earth splitting apart.

Tarquin's ears were ringing; he was slowing down. The muscle in one shoulder was torn from grabbing the horse, the arm all but useless, and the scratch from the crossbow's bolt was beginning to burn. Another brigand was coming toward him, this one tall as he was and thicker in the neck and arms. He looked like a bull standing upright. "We ain't going to kill ye," he grinned, the first coherent words Tarquin had heard since the attack began, echoing crazily inside his reeling head. "Somebody else wants that." The bull was circling, both of them with swords half raised. Tarquin lunged, but he was clumsy. The other man's fist found his jaw, snapped his head back, made him stagger and sway on his feet. Malinda . . . where was Malinda? He tried to look, and the bull hit him again, the hilt of his sword smashing into the side of his head. He stumbled, feet tangled in a fallen corpse, and he was falling, saw the other man's sword go up in a flash of blinding light, ready to cleave him in two.

Hildy grabbed Malinda's arm as Tarquin fell, but the sorceress was calm. "Come," she said in faery speech, lifting her face into the wind, the words formed in her blood. "Come now." The brigand raised his sword, hilt up again instead of blade but lethal nonetheless, and she shouted the words again, a roar above the storm. "Come now!"

Lightning struck the brigand's sword with a deafening roar, a flash of white-blue flame exploding in every direction, and the stench of burning flesh as he froze and tilted, falling slow as a new-cut tree. Hildy screamed as Tarquin scrambled back out of the way, then staggered to his feet as the brigand hit the ground. The man's eyes were open, his lips still moving in shock as flames licked over his face. Then it was done.

The other brigands froze in shock of their own, the guardsmen staring as well—all staring at Tarquin in fear. Then the brigands were running, sprinting back into the woods. "Wait!" Tarquin yelled to one of the knights, grabbing his arm as he moved to give chase. "Let them go." Brinlaw's troops were already outnumbered, and in the woods, the brigands would have an even better advantage. They could pick them off one by one from the safety of the trees.

"What did you do?" Bruce demanded of Malinda, too shocked to be polite. He had seen it: the girl had called down lightning from the sky. "How—?"

"I didn't do anything," Malinda answered in her usual tone. She felt sick, the ground beneath her no more solid than the air, but she couldn't let it show. This poor knight was already looking at her as though she might be Hecate new-sprung from hell. "I'm perfectly all right."

Tarquin came staggering toward them. "Go help the others," he told Sir Bruce. "Find out who's hurt and who's dead."

"Do you think they'll be back?" Hildy asked.

"I don't think so." He still felt woozy, as if he'd drunk too much or been drugged. In fact, the feeling was getting worse. "That lightning strike seemed to scare them off pretty well."

"I shouldn't wonder," Bruce muttered, glancing once more at Malinda before going off to do as he was told.

"Are you all right?" Tarquin asked. "Both of you?"

"We seem to be," Hildy answered.

"We're fine," Malinda agreed. "But you're not." His forehead was bloodied from a cut hidden somewhere under his hair, and from the glaze in his eyes, she could tell he could barely stay on his feet. "Come here and sit."

Tarquin wanted to argue, but his legs dissolved beneath him, and he sat down hard on the ground right where he was. "Tell them to take down the rest of the tents," he told Hildy. "We'll move out at the first show of light."

"It's all right," Malinda promised, opening his shirt. "I can fix it."

"Yes, Captain," Hildy said, going after Sir Bruce.

"What exactly are you doing?" Tarquin asked as she ripped open his shirt even further.

"You've been poisoned." The tiny scratch where his neck and shoulder joined was already starting to fester. "We should check the others. I can fix it, but only if we catch it in time, before it gets a good hold on the blood."

He watched her probe the wound, her brow knit in concentration, her touch delicate but sure. "You seem pretty calm."

"Only seem, I promise," she smiled. "As soon as we're safely home at Brinlaw, I intend to have hysterics."

"Thanks for the warning." She lifted the hem of her gown to retrieve a small velvet bag tied around her thigh. "What is that?" he asked, making conversation so he wouldn't notice her leg or the way the rain was turning the rest of her white linen gown transparent against her skin.

"Magic," she retorted. "You'll just have to trust me and bear it." She took out a small bundle of dried leaves tied together with bright red thread and held it in her open palm to be wet down in the rain. "Actually, it's a perfectly ordinary healing simple; I can just make it work faster." She squeezed the leaves, rubbing them between her fingers to soften the thick fibers. "So you really think we're safe?"

"For tonight, at least." His head felt heavy, and keeping his eyelids open was becoming a struggle. "But first thing in the morning, we have to move, and we can't stop until we're at Brinlaw."

"Home," she corrected. "Why can't you ever just say home?" She pressed the dense, green compress to the wound, felt a tingle underneath her fingertips. "Do you feel that?"

"Yes." His entire arm was tingling as if he had ice crystals in his veins, but the thick, sleepy feeling was beginning to go away. "It isn't my home."

"Of course it is. You lived there most of your life." She could feel the poison rising out, and a thin stream of green-white fluid began to run down the muscle of his arm, disgusting but harmless. Whatever the poison was, it wasn't meant to be fatal; it gave up and let go too easily. "But I forgot; you are the wind."

"Something like that," he smiled. In truth, he was surprised at her, smitten all over again by an entirely new Malinda. Neither the mystic faery nor the willful brat, this new version was an adult, capable and calm. She wasn't weeping in terror or raving in fury after the attack; she was doing what had to be done. "You shouldn't worry about me," he told her.

"Oh, but I must." She wiped away the poison with the torn edge of his shirt, singing a bit of faery spell under her breath to seal the blood against infection. "I'm conjuring over you; you're mine now."

Something in her tone reminded him unmistakably of what they'd been doing when the attack began, the kiss under the oak. As his perceptions came clearer again, so did his memory—another reason to feel drunk. "Malinda, don't say that," he began.

"Hush, please," she scolded lightly. "I'm trying to concentrate." He was going to tell her again that she couldn't have him, that their kisses were a mistake, and she didn't want to hear it.

"It isn't that I don't want you," he pressed on. "How could I not? How could you not know how much I do?"

"Maybe because you keep telling me you don't," she suggested. The poisoned scratch seemed clean now, and she began to examine him for other wounds—a nasty scrape behind his ear, for one. "The rain seems to have stopped."

"You're beautiful, and you know it bloody well," he retorted, flinching as she probed the knot on his head. "But even if your father were not the dearest friend I've ever known, even if he hadn't charged me with your protection, you'd still be noble; I'd still be a routier. You could no more be with me—"

"And who decides that? You? My father?" she demanded. Never mind that she had thought the same thing little more than an hour ago. Everything had changed. Couldn't he see that? For days—weeks!—she had been trying to make him talk about the way he felt, all the reasons why he kissed her one minute and pushed her away the next. Now, when half the guardsmen were wounded or worse and the entire camp was in chaos and they might be attacked any moment, he wanted to explain. Her nerves were shattered, and she was having to defend her own position, to try and make him understand her truth when she wasn't even sure what it was. She didn't really want to marry him, did she? And if she didn't, what did she want? To dishonor her father's name by taking him as a lover? Surely not, but . . . she couldn't work it out, not now, not when everything was so confused. It wasn't fair; she wasn't ready, but he was giving her no choice. "What about me, Tarquin?" she continued, stepping back to look him in the face. "Don't I get a say?"

"Not really, no," he answered. "You don't understand. You think you know me, that you know what you want, what you're doing—"

"Of course I know, and I never said what I want," Malinda protested, even more incensed. He acted as if she had asked him to marry her already and he was turning her down, as if she were some desperate, lovesick harridan clinging around his ankles, refusing to be shaken off. She tried to find the bitterness she had felt before, the anger that had made her long to seduce him and turn him away, but somehow it was gone, replaced by a new frustration, something even more hurtful and strange.

"You don't know," Tarquin answered. "You don't know the first thing about me, who I am or where I came from. You think you do—"

"I do!" she insisted. "I saw you." She hadn't intended to tell him her vision while matters between them were still so confused; she wasn't sure she meant to ever tell him about it at all. But maybe that was what he needed to hear to make him trust her, to make him stop trying so hard to protect her. And she knew she wanted him to stop treating her like a child, no matter what else she might feel. "That first day in the woods at Bruel when I was so afraid, it wasn't you who frightened me; it was your father."

Tarquin had been headed toward a clear and lucid point, a final say that would put the whole matter of their impossible attraction to rest for good and all. Now he was confused and horrified all over again. "What are you—?"

"I saw a vision," Malinda explained, the words coming out in a rush. "At your mother's old cottage." A name rose to the top of her mind. "Tabby's cottage," she continued. "I saw them, your mother and father, fighting . . ." The look in his eyes was horrible, rage and hurt and shocked disbelief. The boy who'd fought the evil giant looked out at her from inside the man who'd slain half a dozen brigands by himself. "I saw him murder her," she went on, putting a hand on his arm. "And I saw you . . . I saw you try to stop him, and I saw him hurt you, and I hated him. I wanted to kill him as much as you did."

"Stop it," Tarquin growled.

"I saw you set the cottage on fire," she persisted. "I was afraid for you. I called out to you to run, to save yourself, and you heard me. I saw your eyes. I know you heard me—"

"I said stop!" He caught her by the shoulders, bruising hard. He wanted to shake her, strike her, anything to make her stop talking. She had seen it—everything he kept so carefully hidden, all the pain and madness he fought so hard to keep inside. He felt as if his heart were torn apart, as if someone had ripped a doorway into his soul and peered in at the demon inside. And this thief, this destroyer was not a priest, not an enemy to be destroyed, but Malinda, his own pure hope, his perfect faery treasure.

"Somehow we're connected, you and I," Malinda said. He was hurting her, but she didn't care. Suddenly, reaching him, making him understand, was all that mattered. "I don't understand it myself, but I know it's true, and my father, my nobility—none of that matters. Your past doesn't matter. All that means anything is what we want. We get to decide, you and I together—"

"No!" He shook her so hard his own torn shoulder flashed with pain, hard enough to make her stop talking, her green eyes wide with fear. "I have already decided," he went on more softly as he let her go. "Whatever we may want, whatever you may have seen, we are not connected. We can't be. We won't be, ever." She started to protest, and he caught her face between his hands, every muscle alive with the effort of not crushing her delicate skull. "You know what I am, Malinda," he said. "Everything you saw, everything you hated, that was me."

"No," she whispered, closing her eyes against him, tears running down her cheeks.

"Yes." He wanted to pull her close, to kiss away her tears, to pretend to be what her innocence willed him to be. But he could not; he would not. After all his crimes, all he had left to give her was the truth. "Every evil you've ever imagined, every black deed ever told, I have done it and more, and nothing you can say can wash that away. It's in my blood; I can't escape it. But you can." He pressed his mouth to her brow for a moment, felt her clutch his shirt, felt her tears stain his own cheek. "You will." He let her go. "If you have any feeling for me at all, let me do this. Let me keep you safe."

He believed every word he was saying, Malinda realized. He was wrong, but he believed it. "And if I say no?" she asked.

"Then I am damned in truth." He touched her cheek, now smeared with the blood from his hands. "You can't say no, Malinda. This time, the choice is mine." Before she could answer, he had walked away.

Hildy came back, watching Tarquin go. "How bad is it?" Malinda asked her, standing up, trying not to think of what had just been said, to just get through the next moment.

"Bad," the maid answered. "Three of the guardsmen are dead, and Sir Harold may not live to see the morning."

"I'll see to him," Malinda said. "Pack up what you can salvage. I'll be back to help as soon as I can."

Tarquin, meanwhile, surveyed the damage to his force, a thousand aches and agonies springing to life as his strength and awareness returned. All told, about a dozen brigands had been killed. They had outnumbered the Brinlaw faction, but they'd suffered many more losses, so he supposed that meant Brinlaw had won. All that remained of the outlaws' wounded was the man who had come at Tarquin on a horse. He was bleeding badly from a wound in his stomach, and his leg where Tarquin had stabbed him was useless. Sir Bruce was bending over him, lashing his hands to a short, thick pole, but it was a pointless precaution. This man was almost dead.

Tarquin squatted beside him to look into his eyes. "Who are you?" he asked mildly.

"You killed me," the brigand snarled back, pale and sleek with sweat under the blood on his face. "Get spat."

Tarquin lifted the gore-soaked rag Bruce had laid over the gaping wound. "I can cut your throat now," he answered. "Or I can leave you for the wolves." The brigand's eyes widened until white showed all around. "Who are you?"

"Nobody," the man promised. "Hired on . . ." He stopped, grimacing in pain, and Tarquin pressed the rag back in place to give him some relief. "To capture you, just you."

"Hired by whom?" This man was a routier just as he was himself; this could just as easily have been he with his guts falling out. "Where were you supposed to deliver me?"

"God's truth . . . I don't know," he answered. "Only the captain . . ." He looked over at his half-cooked comrade lying on the ground nearby. "They said you were a demon."

Tarquin's eyes narrowed, but in truth, he was satisfied. "Thanks," he answered, putting a hand over the brigand's eyes. With a single stroke, he slashed his throat, releasing him from his pain.

"Holy Christ!" Sir Bruce was staring at him, shocked, angry, mostly looking young, younger than Tarquin himself had ever been. "We could have saved him—"

"No," Tarquin promised, suddenly feeling very tired. "We could not."

"Then a priest—"

"A priest couldn't have saved him either." He stood up, wiping his hands on his shirt. Nearby, another pair of knights were digging a trench in the mud. "What is this?" he asked.

One of the boys looked up, his blond hair standing up in rain-wet spikes, his blue eyes rimmed in red. "For the dead, Captain," he explained.

"Leave it," Tarquin ordered. "Our dead will come with us."

"You mean just leave them to . . . ?" All three were staring at him, eyes wide.

"Their friends will bury them or not," Tarquin answered. "We have no time. Help the guardsmen pack up." They hesitated, obviously conflicted. The rules of chivalry expressly demanded the fallen be tucked out of sight and prayed over. Otherwise, their deaths could be construed as sin, a stain on their murderer's honor. But these boys weren't stupid, either. They knew they had to move, that they'd never survive a second attack like the first. "It's all right," Tarquin promised. "Think of Lady Malinda and her maid."

That did it—the safety of noble ladies far outweighed respect for the dead. "Yes, Captain," the blond one answered for all.

Coming back from stitching Sir Harold's wounds, Malinda watched Tarquin take the noble knights in hand, saw the relief on their faces when he told them what to do. He was a natural leader, whether he liked it or not. He was brave and strong. His father had been a nobleman, no matter how horrible he was. He could be a knight . . . but no. She thought of his face as he spoke of the desert and the sea, the shining cities of the East. He was like a falcon; he needed to be free. He could never be a noble knight, never be content to be shut up in a castle, mediating the disputes of his peasantry and making war at the pleasure of the King.

"I don't care," she said softly to no one in particular, her heart pounding in her chest. Hildy was packing and didn't need her help. Everyone else was busy. She might as well have been alone. She sat down on a fallen log, her knees suddenly too weak to hold her. "I love him," she whispered, the words like a shiver in the air. "He is my destined love." She remembered the way he looked as he moved close to kiss her, the longing in his eyes, the tender burning of his touch. She had known she wanted him; she had known they were connected. She had called down the lightning to save him. Remembering the way the magic had felt as it coursed through her, she could hear her mother's voice. *"No matter what barriers the world might put between you, you'll be together in the end."* But it wasn't the world that was trying to keep them apart; it was Tarquin himself. But it didn't matter. "You will be tied, beloved," she whispered, touching the heartstone at her throat. "I will make it happen. I am a sorceress."

By first light, they were ready. Sir Harold was tucked away in the ladies' litter, heavily dosed with herbs from Malinda's bag to make him sleep in spite of the pain. The rest were able to ride. "Brinlaw is no more than a day and a night away," Tarquin promised as they prepared to set out. Malinda looked pale, but he thought she could make it—her green eyes were determined. Hildy was riding pillion on Sir Bruce's horse, already dozing with her head on his shoulder. The foot soldiers would take turns on Hildy's and Harold's horses; those who didn't know how to ride could be led. In short, his little band was as well prepared as he could make them. He had briefly considered sending them on without him, trying to track down whoever was trying to capture him, but he quickly abandoned the thought. In one way, if he really was the only target, they might be safer. But if he wasn't, if the dying man had lied and they were attacked again, they would need him. He had promised Brinlaw to take care of his daughter. Time enough to track down his enemies when she was safely behind castle walls.

"I want to ride with you," Malinda ordered, watching this brigand, who swore he cared for nothing and no one, shoulder the weight of the world. He looked down at her, and she put a hand on his arm, a silent plea in contrast to her tone, which was imperious and sharp. "Someone else can use my horse." She hurt in a way she never had before, her heart shattered to bits, and her mind was racing. She was so exhausted, she felt physically numb, but she couldn't have slept even on a featherbed under an eiderdown quilt. Her body was tired, but her feelings were wide awake. She loved him; he had to love her back.

He looked for a moment as if he meant to argue, then he nodded. "All right." He caught her around the waist and lifted her onto the saddle, then climbed on behind her.

She turned her face to his shoulder, savored the sweet ache she felt in the circle of his arms as he took up the reins. *Just you wait, beloved,* she thought as they started to move. *Just wait till I get you home.*

12

ᏊꙊꙊꙊꙍ

M alinda finished writing her miniature note at her father's great table in the solar. "I suppose that will have to do, Rufus," she sighed, setting her pen aside. "'Safe at Brinlaw. Wish you were here. M.'"

They had been home for almost a week, routine settling over everyone like dust. Even Tarquin seemed almost at ease, taking up the duties of castellan with efficiency if little enthusiasm. But Malinda refused to fall back into her old patterns, refused to give up and be the same discontented girl she'd been when she left for Nan's wedding. She couldn't have been, even if she had wanted to be. Everything about her had changed, inside and out. She loved Tarquin; she was convinced he could love her in return, that he did, if he would only admit it. With every day that passed, she felt more certain, her fears giving way easily in the face of destiny. Here at Brinlaw, she was certain she could convince him as well, put his fears away just as completely. At Brinlaw, they were safe—no ghosts, no kings, no parents, no priests, no outside world at all. At Brinlaw, he would learn to let go of all that kept them apart and take the heart she offered him in exchange. All she needed was time—and perhaps a little witchcraft. Her book was full of spells designed to find and entice one's beloved; if necessary, she need only choose the right one.

"Come here, then," she said, holding out her hand. The goshawk flew to her from his perch by the window. "Thank you," she said softly as she tied a tiny leather case to his leg with her message inside. On the rare occasions in the past when she and her best friend had been parted, Rufus had often carried messages back and forth between Brinlaw and Bruel; she had every confidence he could find his way again. "Be careful," she instructed him as she carried him back to the window on her fist. "Fly straight to Bruel and straight home." She leaned out and launched the bird into the air. "Safe journey, Rufus!"

"Where is he going?" Tarquin's voice asked from behind her. Turning, she found him in the doorway.

"To Bruel," Malinda explained. "I sent a message to Lisbet to let her know we got here safely."

Tarquin nodded, not really surprised. He had seen Arab warriors use such messengers in the desert, and their birds weren't nearly so well trained as Rufus. "Why Lisbet?" he asked. "Why not your parents?"

"Because I don't know where they are," she explained. "And Rufus has never traveled so far as that. I'm not sure he could find his way home." She noticed he was dressed in traveling clothes himself, the stained leather armor he'd been wearing when she first saw him in the woods at Bruel. "Are you going hunting?"

"In a manner of speaking." He had been dreading this conversation for days now, had put it off as long as he could. But the trail was already cold; he couldn't wait any longer. "I have to find out who sent those men to capture me," he said.

"You're leaving?" Malinda was appalled. This would ruin everything. "But you said yourself it could be anyone, that you've made hundreds of enemies as a routier."

"Very few of whom would have the resources to launch that kind of attack," he said. He thought again of the conspirators on Corsica, the boy he had killed. *"The boy is nothing,"* the old man had said. *"But the father . . ."* The more he thought about it, the more convinced he was that the man who'd sent mercenaries after him on the road was this father or someone connected to him. Whoever had been behind the rebellion being plotted in the Mediterranean would have plenty of money to hire a band of brigands to hunt him down. And if he was that determined, he wouldn't just give up now. "Men were killed, Malinda," he went on. "You could have been hurt."

"But I wasn't, because you were there to protect me," Malinda pointed out. "We're safe here, all of us. If you go out looking for them—"

"I can't stay here forever—"

"I don't know why not." She stopped, remembering his voice as he described his ship, the sea, the streets of Alexandria. "Actually, I do know, and I don't expect you to stay forever," she admitted. "But why can't you wait until Papa is here to help you sort this out?"

"It isn't Brinlaw's problem," he said with a stubborn set to his jaw.

"How can you be so sure?" she asked. "What if those men were actually hired by someone who wants to hurt our family, someone who wants to get you out of the way so he can lay siege to Brinlaw?" Her arguments were sound, but in truth, she barely heard them, much less thought them through. All she could think was that he meant to leave her, and she couldn't let him do it. "You promised my father to keep me safe—"

"You are safe." She seemed to be making sense, he had to admit, but was that his own sound reason talking or something else, the same old madness that made him want to follow her around like that poor, besotted hawk, made the very idea of leaving her seem impossible?

"For now, yes," she was saying. "But if you aren't here, how will you know? If all my father wanted was someone to deliver me safely to Brinlaw, he could have done it himself."

"He wasn't afraid of anyone from the outside coming in to harm you," Tarquin said. "He was worried what you might do to hurt yourself."

"Yes, and he was quite right," Malinda answered, teasing and threatening at the same time. "I've got no more judgment than a newborn fawn, and I'm always getting into scrapes—ask anyone. Left to my own devices, I could turn this castle upside down in half a day. I'll have the knights at one another's throats just by innocently dropping a glove, conjure up a dragon to burn the whole place to the ground while just trying to boil water." She smiled, a dangerous glint in her eyes. "If you leave me, I can almost guarantee it," she finished. "And then what would my father say?"

Tarquin just stared at her, aghast. From what he'd already seen, he had no doubt she could and would do exactly what she described, without the slightest hesitation, just for spite. Once again she had him, trussed and seasoned, ready for the oven. "I don't want to go," he began, fighting back with candor.

"Then don't," she cut him off, refusing to give ground.

"Do as you promised. Stay here and protect me and Brinlaw. Then when Papa comes back, if this enemy of yours is still out there, you can find him together."

"If I don't go now, he'll find me," he answered. She was winning her battle; her green eyes sparkled with triumph, but he could see fear there as well. He couldn't leave her alone to be afraid. "But you're right," he finished. "I promised." She smiled, and he had to look away. What kind of insanity could make her happy at the prospect of being with him? "I will stay."

"I should hope so," she said primly. He couldn't even look at her . . . how could she bear it? *I will fix it,* she promised herself.

"But only until Will and Alista return," he said. "Then I'm leaving, and I won't be coming back."

"Never, ever, ever. Yes, I know," she retorted. He was wrong, but it still hurt to hear him say it. But telling him so wouldn't help her cause and would embarrass her to boot. "I'll sing you to the road and fling roses in your path. But until they come home, you will stay."

"Yes," he promised. "Until then."

Will Brinlaw stared at his sovereign, unable to credit his ears. "Harry, are you ill? Have you lost your mind?"

"Will," Alista scolded, putting a hand on his arm. "What he means, Majesty, is why have you reached this decision?"

After almost five months, the war was still not going well, at least not for King Henry. While he had lost no significant battles, he hadn't won any, either. Nor had he managed to capture even one of his errant sons. Geoffrey, always a crafty little rotter, was apparently a wizard at escaping the field just before his troops surrendered. The Young King, Henry, had

French Louis's protection—any time the battle turned against him, he merely ducked over the border. And Richard simply didn't lose any battles; if he couldn't win, he withdrew to attack again another day. With this strategy, he had managed to take possession of great chunks of his father's kingdom, sometimes for weeks at a time before a larger force came after him and he had to disappear again. In short, Henry had realized that he wasn't going to have the crushing victory a warrior of his skills and experience might reasonably have expected over a trio of teenagers. He had even tried to make peace, inviting his sons to negotiate at the ancient tree in the village of Gisors where such contracts were traditionally signed. But the treaty had failed as miserably as the war. Someone on one side—no one could agree who or which—had taken offense at something someone on the other side muttered under his breath, and someone else had ended up stabbed in the throat. Peace was ripped asunder, as was the sacred tradition of the Gisors oak. Now winter was fast approaching, and Henry was positioning his pieces for the months of slow, sporadic fighting. And Lord Brinlaw objected to where he intended to move his Queen.

"As long as Eleanor is on the continent, Richard has a rallying point," Henry pointed out. "She's too close—close enough to help him. For all I know, she's the brilliant strategist behind his great success."

"You have her under lock and key," Will answered. "Your man reads all her letters. None do see her but your own—"

"My own men?" Henry finished with a laugh. "I wouldn't trust a single man I know to keep faith where Eleanor is concerned." He glanced at Alista and had the decency to grimace as though he might have been embarrassed. "You and your own son excepted."

"Then you are right to send her to Britain," Alista agreed. "But why Brinlaw?"

"Because no one would suspect I would, not even Geoffrey," Henry said. "It's isolated—"

"So is Scotland," Will grumbled.

"Good Lord, Will, she hardly deserves such punishment as that," Henry laughed. "She only committed high treason." His friend looked unconvinced, and he frowned. "It must be Brinlaw. None of my sons have ever been there; Eleanor has never been there. Farrars will transport her there, and your Tarquin will help him hold off any siege that might come. I can trust them, as I trust you."

"No doubt," Alista agreed. "But I still don't see why you can't choose somewhere else."

Now it was Will's turn to be the diplomat. "You've truly thought this through?" he asked the King, sending his wife a weary warning with his eyes. "You are convinced this is the best course?"

"I have," Henry answered. "I do."

Will took Alista's hand. "Then Brinlaw will be pleased to serve."

The King's messenger found Brinlaw's entire household in the fields when he arrived, every noble, soldier, and peasant assisting with the harvest. "Lady Malinda?" he asked one of the women gleaning behind the wagons.

"Over there," the woman answered, pointing toward the trees.

Malinda was helping set out a huge picnic at the edge of the largest field. Rain had begun to threaten the horizon; any wheat not taken in before it fell would be ruined. To stay fed through the winter, everyone would work straight through the day and into the night, the overlord's daughter included. "My lady!" the herald called, unsure which woman he wanted. All of them were dressed the same, or nearly so, and many looked quite fetching in their kerchiefs. "Lady Malinda!"

"Yes, what is it?" Malinda asked, wiping her hands on her apron. She took the scroll he offered, her heart beating faster with alarm as she recognized his livery. All the news they'd had from France so far was bad. But the message wasn't about Papa or the war at all. Eleanor was coming. She was to be housed at Brinlaw, with Lord Robert Farrars charged with her protection. The protection of the manor itself would be left in the hands of Tarquin FitzBruel, as per Lord Brinlaw's instruction. "How long?" she asked the herald, keeping her manner calm.

"A day, maybe two, but no more than that," he answered. "Lord Farrars asked me to tell you to make no great fuss, that the Queen's visit should be kept as quiet as possible."

"Of course," she nodded. "So they could be here tomorrow?"

"Very likely," he said.

"Very good," she lied. One more night? Only one more night, and everyone busy with the harvest? It wasn't fair—she'd been working up to something all summer, and now she was supposed to finish her quest in one night? "Do you have letters from my parents?"

"No, my lady. 'Twas thought best not to give them to a man alone, things being as they are. But I believe Lord Farrars—"

"Good," she cut him off. "Our hospitality today is a bit haphazard, I'm afraid, but I'm sure we can find you something to eat. Mary, will you please see to this man's comfort?" With a nod to acknowledge the herald's final bow, she went off to find Tarquin.

She found him standing in one of the wagons, catching the great sheaves as they were tossed up and stacking them for transport. "Guess what," Malinda said, climbing one of the great wheels like a ladder to reach him. "Or rather, guess who's coming."

Tarquin stopped, wiping the sweat from his brow. "John the Baptist," he guessed, too busy to be amused.

"Tarquin, that's blasphemy," she scolded. "And wrong. It's Eleanor." He had stripped out of his shirt hours ago, and she found herself fascinated by the rivulets of sweat running down his chest and the way the light glistened on the soft, gold hair. "Queen Eleanor," she said, forcing herself to focus on the matter at hand.

"Coming here?" Tarquin asked, appalled. "Why?"

"The King doesn't really say," she said, handing over the scroll.

He read the King's message with an increasing sense of doom. Queen Eleanor and someone named Robert Farrars—wasn't that the one he'd met just before they left Bruel? An entire noble assembly descending like locusts to turn quiet Brinlaw into a royal court. After three months, he had almost gotten comfortable again, almost found a kind of peace. Being castellan gave him plenty to do all day, and at night he avoided the hall and kept out of Malinda's way. But now everything was changing. "This Farrars—do you know him?" he asked aloud.

"Yes, a little. I'll be glad to see him," Malinda agreed. "And the Queen."

"Good for you." Lisbet had mentioned something at Bruel about Malinda's wanting to be a lady-in-waiting more than anything else in the world. This must seem like her dream come true. "Perhaps you'll feel safe enough with them here to let me go find the man who wants to see me dead."

Malinda was startled and hurt. He hadn't mentioned leaving in weeks. She'd taken that as progress, thought he'd given up on the idea entirely. But apparently she had been wrong, and now she only had one more night. "Perhaps," she answered. "Or maybe once you see what things are like, you won't want to leave."

"Not likely," he grumbled, going back to work.

As the sun began to set, Malinda sat on the stone floor of the highest tower bedroom, her magic book open before her. For months she had studied these pages, committed each lover's enchantment to memory, but still she was afraid. Tarquin loved her; every day she felt it more, not by magic but by the way his eyes lingered on her face, the sound of his voice when he spoke to her without remembering to be gruff. He tried to stay away from her, she knew—with every two steps toward her, he took a step away. But still, he was coming, slowly but surely. Given enough time, she knew she could win him with only herself. But now there was no time. Tomorrow Queen Eleanor would be here; the castle would be crawling with strangers. All the progress they'd made would be lost. Tarquin would withdraw again, remember who she was and all the reasons why he couldn't have her, why he didn't want to be hers. Already he was talking again about leaving—with another of Henry's lords here to watch over her, he would have an excuse. She would lose him forever if she waited. Afraid or not, she had to bind him to her for good and all tonight. *"Don't worry,"* her mother had told her. *"Whatever the obstacles, your destined love will be yours.*" But Mama had never loved a man like Tarquin.

Her shadow had grown long across the floor—the sun was almost set. It was time to begin. She took a piece of charcoal and began to draw a pattern on the floor, a knot of complicated curves woven and locked into a circle, a serpent swallowing its tail. At first the work went slowly as she consulted the drawing in her book before each careful line. But as the figure began to take shape, her hand seemed to move of its own accord, faster and faster as she drew the circle around her. When the last stroke was done, the bit of charcoal that was left dissolved into dust in her hand and blew away on a draft of air from nowhere, and the figure began to glow soft green in the fading light. She held her breath as the serpent began to move, not one serpent but a hundred, all writhing and knotted behind one head, the eyes the scarlet-orange of the harvest moon. "Welcome, spirit," she spoke in the faery tongue, her voice trembling only a moment. "Help me work my will." Outside, the clouds had gathered thick and purple, and rain began to fall in fat, cold drops that blew through the open window. "As you are entwined, entwine me with my love," she sang on, feeling the power steal through her like a fever. "As you are enslaved, enslave my love to me." The wind encircled her like a hundred airy arms, a thousand faery fingers in her hair. She rose to her knees, arms outspread, as voices sang around her, faery and Latin and other tongues she didn't understand in her head, but in her heart, she knew them, knew they echoed her words. She was afraid, terrified of what she was doing, but she had never felt such power. She was the sorceress; all that she desired would be hers. "Tarquin!" she cried out, the final magic word.

*   *   *

Pulling his shirt back over his head Tarquin stepped out of the granary just as the rain began to fall. "We made it, Captain," one of the guardsmen said as the doors were shut behind them, but Tarquin wasn't thinking about the harvest. He looked up at the castle's tallest tower, black against the stormy purple dusk. A strange light glowed in the windows, green and pale.

"Where's Malinda?" he asked a woman who was standing nearby, getting water from the well.

"She . . . I don't know," she answered. He looked strange, almost angry. If she hadn't known him, she would have been afraid. "What's wrong?"

"Nothing." A voice was singing in the wind, Malinda's voice, singing words he didn't understand repeated over and over. "Do you hear that?"

"Hear what?" He was already walking away. "Captain!" A flash of lightning lit the sky as he passed through the center of the courtyard, and everyone began to scatter, scrambling for shelter.

As Tarquin pushed his way into the castle, the singing grew louder, but no one else seemed to hear it. A group of serving women were coming down the stairs, chattering to one another. He couldn't hear them, although he saw their mouths moving and saw them stop and laugh. All he could hear was the singing, a thousand voices now entwined around Malinda's as she called out his name. The women were staring at him now; he saw one of them mouth the word "Captain?" He didn't answer as he moved them aside to continue up the stairs.

The serpent was beginning to fade, burning itself out, and Malinda lit the candles, her heart pounding in her breast.

Someone was climbing the stairs, faster now, almost running, and she turned to face the door. "Be with me," she whispered, but to whom she couldn't tell. "Make me strong." The door crashed open, and Tarquin was there.

"What have you done?" He came in slowly, eyes wary, circling her like a predator stalking his prey. She tried to answer, but no words would come, and he came closer. She turned inside her circle, her breath coming short. Outside, the storm was passing, but inside it had barely begun. She put out a hand, almost touching him, and he struck it away, his handsome face twisted in a snarl. His boot came down on the serpent drawing, smearing the charcoal, and a tremor passed through them both, making her gasp aloud. He looked down, obviously appalled. "What have you done, Malinda?"

He thought of his mother, burning her cats' tails and dancing under the moon, worshiping her demons, but nothing she had ever done could begin to compare to this. He felt as if his blood were turned to fire, devouring him from inside. Just touching her conjurer's drawing with his foot had made him feel faint, strong as he was. What sort of demon had she unleashed? She looked so innocent, with the face of an angel and tender feeling in her eyes. He grabbed her wrist, jerked her toward him, out of her circle of power, but the spell remained unbroken. It was inside him; he was the demon she had conjured.

He touched her cheek, traced the structure of her face, eyelids, nose, and mouth, her breath warm against his palm. She turned her face into his touch, her eyes falling closed, and he felt himself go hard with desire unlike anything he had ever felt before. He bent and kissed her, his hand buried in her hair, bound in golden silk, and she responded, soft and yielding in the circle of his arm.

She felt his kiss burn through her, fire in her blood, frightening and sweet. Before, he had always held back, touched her as if she were a fragile thing he feared to break. Now he seemed to want her broken. His tongue pushed between her teeth, opening her mouth to his, and she felt her knees go weak. She melted against his chest as he bent over her, bending her slowly to the floor. She couldn't breathe, couldn't think, and the words of the spell came back to her . . . *Enslave me as you are enslaved.* His hand was tangled in her hair, pulling, arching her throat, and his mouth moved downward, lapping at her skin.

Her pulse throbbed beneath his mouth, and he drew in the salt taste of sweat in the hollow at the base of her throat. She wore his shirt—part of the spell?—and he tore at the lacings, exposing more sweet flesh. He pressed his cheek to her heartbeat, strong and fast, trying to regain some kind of reason, but it was hopeless. She arched beneath him with innocent wanting, and he kissed her again, devouring her mouth as he tore the shirt away.

She was floating. The whole world was Tarquin, the universe was shaped by his touch. Nothing she had imagined was at all like this. She tried to isolate the sensations, make sense of what she felt—the wet of his mouth as he kissed her, the taste of his tongue, the heat of his hands on her skin as he molded the curve of her hips up to her waist. His hair smelled of wheat and rainwater, but there was more; she couldn't grasp it, couldn't think it through. She nuzzled her face against his cheek, tasted salt on his skin—delicious. He was braced above her, dipping his head to kiss her mouth, deep then shallow, a sweet and gentle touch that made her sigh for more, bite his lip to taste the blood, more sweet salt on her tongue. She ran her hands up his arms, felt hard muscle tensed to hold his weight, and she longed to tear the shirt away, strip him naked as he'd stripped her, but she wasn't strong enough. She moaned aloud in frustration as she clutched at his shoulders, then laced her hands behind his neck. He moved as if to break the kiss, and she pulled herself up to hold him. Smiling against her mouth, he allowed her, curved an arm around her to cradle her above the floor.

She tore at him, desperate with desire, and he held her to him, felt her as the demon in his soul refigured as an angel in his arms. He should care who she was, who she would be tomorrow if they didn't stop, but he could not; he had no will or reason, only desire, the fire her will burned to life. Her bare leg curled around him, petal-soft skin against the sweat-slick muscles of his back as she pulled up the shirt he wore. Could she know what she was doing? She cried out as if in answer, an impatient little shriek, and he lifted his head to look down into her face. She was smiling, her green eyes sparkling with triumph, and rage flashed through him, burned hotter as he kissed her again, heard and felt her laugh into his mouth. He would teach her, show her what she sought, the demon she had called on, mindless, fearless hunger. He grabbed her wrists, still entwined around his neck, and pushed her away, rising to his knees. She sat up to reach for him again, trailed a hand along his arm as he unlaced his shirt, her sweet face avid with want—the spell was on her, too.

"Beautiful," she whispered as she watched him, barely aware she had spoken. "You are so beautiful . . ." She touched his stomach, felt the muscles curve beneath her palm as he pulled the shirt over his head. Her hands followed the shape of him upward as she rose to her knees.

"Mine," she whispered, sculpting his shoulders as if she had made him herself. She looked into his eyes and trembled—he looked so furious, so animal. For one moment she was afraid. Then he was kissing her again, holding her wrists behind her back, and she didn't care if he hated her, as long as he didn't stop. Still pinning her hands in one fist, he slipped a hand between her legs. She screamed, pleasure tearing through her as his fingers slipped inside the tender crease. She tore her mouth free of his kiss, and he laughed, rubbing in a languid circle as she bent her head to his shoulder, lost to all but the sweet torture of his touch.

"Is this what you asked for?" he growled against her cheek, the hand that held her wrists letting go to tangle in her hair. "Did you get your wish?"

"Yes . . . Tarquin . . ." He couldn't bear it; he was dying. He cradled her head against his shoulder, felt her arms twine around him, and he moved his hand from her sex, his wanton maid. She turned her head to kiss him, and he crushed her mouth with his, fumbled with the lacings on his breeches, found her hand there already, trying to help him free. He let her touch him, smiled to feel her gasp— now she would be scared. She moved as if to pull away, and he caught her arms, pushed her down to the floor, one knee between her thighs. She opened her mouth to protest, and he kissed her, closed his eyes as he pushed deep inside her, broke her innocence for good and all.

Tarquin, she thought, a moan against his mouth. *I want to see.* But he wouldn't let her go, let her cry out or hold on, and then he was inside her. Nothing else meant anything but the way it felt. She arched beneath him, shattered and alive. *Hurt,* she thought, *this should hurt,* but it didn't—or not like any pain she had ever felt before. She was lost, dissolving—nothing was within her will, not even her own body. He moved inside her, all the fearful power she had loved from the first moment she had seen him focused in their joining, but he was hers, enfolded, captured, safe. She struggled in his grip, trying to free her wrists to hold him, touch him as he touched her, but he wouldn't let her go. Slowly she began to hear him, broken words above the roaring of her blood . . . *angel* . . . *witch* . . . *beloved.* "Tell me," she ordered, arching up to meet him, their rhythm languid like the heartbeat of a dragon. "Tell me you are mine."

He almost smiled, despair like a blade in his heart, a pain like sweetest hope. "Yours," he answered, her obedient slave. He let go of her wrists to cradle her face in his hands, look into her eyes. "I am yours."

"Yes . . ." Her eyes fell shut again as he felt a shudder pass through her, harbinger of the waves to come. He bent to kiss her cheek, then drove into her harder, made her gasp, a sound between a giggle and a sob. "Love me, Tarquin," she half whispered, half sighed as she turned her face against the floor and a smear of black appeared across her cheek from the conjure she had drawn. "Say you love—"

"Yes." He bent closer for a kiss, and she moaned, her heartbeat pressed to his. "Yes," he murmured, cradling her gently, drunk on her desire. "I love you." He felt her tremble around him, felt the sweet waves of her release begin. He kissed her temple, felt her pulse race faster as he held her close in a demon's tender care. Her head fell back, her lips half parted, panting, and he quickened his rhythm, felt her shudder, barely conscious in his arms.

I'm dying, she thought, her heart pounding too fast. *Help me . . . I can't breathe.* And he was there, all around her and inside, breathing for her with his kiss, and she was safe, safe beyond all fear. Exquisite warmth began to flow inside her, flashes like lightning from the center of her soul as he kept kissing her and pounding, destruction bent on adoration. "Please, Tarquin . . ." He froze, barely an instant. Then shudders like her own coursed through him, and her own began again, the warm, wet rush of his climax pulsing through them both. He cried out, called her name, and she drew him down to her, cradling him close. "I love you," she promised, dizzy-blind with feeling. "It's all right."

She was speaking, foolish, childish words, but all he could hear was her heartbeat as he lay down on her breast, conquered and enslaved, her spell complete. Tomorrow . . . tomorrow wouldn't happen. Stupid thought, but it felt true—here was where the world began and ended, in Malinda's arms. He raised his head to look at her, dozing on the cold, stone floor, utterly trusting, this child-witch innocent. He still could not resist her, still had no will to fight. He touched her side, traced the pattern of the dragon imprinted on her skin as they made love, and she giggled, her eyes still closed, curling like a kitten. Palm flattened, he smeared the pattern away, furious again. "Witchery," he muttered, wiping away more. He would be marked as well. "Black magic."

"No." She opened her eyes to protest, but stopped, the intensity of his look burning through her like a flame. "No such thing," she managed, the words barely out before he was kissing her again. He kissed a path down her throat to her shoulder as she sat up. He cupped her breast in his palm. His hands were huge; she put her hand over his and could barely lace her fingers between his. Her nipple grew hard against his touch, and she leaned forward to press her mouth to his throat, breathe in the way he smelled, bathe in the warmth of having him so close. As soon as she slept, the spell would be broken; the book had said as much. Before, when she had decided to do it, she had thought it wouldn't matter, that once he had made love to her, admitted that he loved her, all her worries would be past. He would be hers, enchanted by magic or not. But now that it was done, she wasn't so sure. He wanted her, could not resist her, but it didn't make him happy. Even at the sweetest moment of release, she had seen pain in his eyes, the same self-loathing rage. She had felt it in his touch—even now she felt it in his kiss on the back of her neck. She wrapped her arms around his back, her tears staining his chest. "I'm sorry."

"No, Malinda." He drew back, turned her face up to his. "You conjured up the demon. You aren't allowed to be sorry." With her sweet face distorted in grief, he kissed her, pushed her back down on the floor. He moved down to suckle her breast, not yet sated on the taste of her skin, still starving for her flesh. He lapped hard at the nipple, gave the lightest, most tender of bites, then moved to the other side. He replaced his mouth with his hand, her softness another miracle he couldn't get enough of.

She called his name, "Tarquin," but he didn't seem to hear. He was nuzzling her stomach and below, breathing her in like an animal scenting his mate or his prey. "Tarquin," she repeated, pleading, as he slipped his tongue inside, hot tremors of desire burning through her like the blush burning her cheeks. His mouth pulled hard on her most tender flesh, and she cried out, a sigh into a scream. He was hurting her, not with pain but pleasure too intense to bear. She tried to pull away, and he raised his head, rolled her onto her stomach, biting kisses down her spine.

She let him pose her like a doll on her hands and knees, made no attempt to resist him. Across her back, the dragon's head was still almost complete, and he smeared it quickly away, bent and licked her skin to erase the smudge, the death-dry taste of charcoal on his tongue commingled with her sweetness. He reached beneath her, curved her up to meet him as he pushed himself inside her. He moved more slowly this time, no less desperate but controlled, his body finding order where his mind and heart found none. He pressed his cheek to hers, tender words he barely thought of rising to his lips. "That's it . . . move with me . . . don't stop."

"No," Malinda answered, "never stop." Her hands found the rag that had been the shirt she wore, and she clutched it in her fists, all her strength consumed by the place where they were joined, exquisite friction between them. She felt the first tremors of his release and willed herself to follow, pleasure ripping through her, and he was with her; he was hers. A sound like a sob escaped him as they collapsed, and she turned in his embrace, kissed his eyelids, tasted salt of tears. He crushed her close, cradled her head on his shoulder as he heaved her up in his arms and carried her to the bed. She kissed him as he lay her down, soft, sweet baby kisses all over his face and neck, and he kissed her back, dragged her down to an embrace.

She wanted to go on, wanted to stay awake, but she was so tired, and the bed felt so warm and soft. She felt his breathing deepen, felt his muscles go heavy and slack. "It's all right," she whispered, promising them both.

13

Malinda awoke to the sound of rain, not quite sure where she was, distant thunder like the last murmured secrets of her dream. She nestled deeper into the pillow, inhaled a tantalizing smell . . . Tarquin. She sat up, the night coming back to her in a rush. But she was alone.

She threw back the dusty blanket, a dozen different aches attacking her body at once, and she blushed, remembering. But it was lovely, too . . . *"Is this what you asked for?"* he had asked her, furious and tender. *"Did you get your wish?"* She supposed she had. It hadn't been what she had imagined, making love. It was far more frightening, much more intense. But that was what had made it so exciting. She leaned back and stretched, savoring her aches and the cool, damp draft from the window, smiling her most kittenish smile. She should be worried for a thousand different reasons—the fact that she'd awakened alone was not a promising sign—but she couldn't make herself feel anything but joy. He loved her. She had won.

She leaned back against the pillows and surveyed the remains of her spell. The drawing was no more than a smear of black. No doubt she was wearing most of it, she and Tarquin . . . She giggled, covering her face with her hands even though no one was there to see. Tarquin's poor shirt was a rag, and the book . . . She frowned. Where was her Falconskeep book?

She got up and scanned the room, refusing to panic. She must have just forgotten she had moved it. The table where she thought she'd left it was empty . . . windowsill . . . mantelpiece . . . chest at the foot of the bed . . . stand beside the bed . . . The book was nowhere to be seen. "He took it." She touched the table as if expecting her hands to find what her eyes could not. "He wouldn't . . . Tarquin!" She ran for the door, grabbing up her gown as she went. She was pulling the gown over her head as she reached the door, and she crashed into it full speed before she realized it was locked. "No . . ." She tried the knob, but it wouldn't turn. She pushed against the door as hard as she could with her shoulder, but it wouldn't budge.

"No!" she screamed, banging on the wood with both fists. "Let me out right now! Tarquin!" No answer. It was no use. This room was three stories above any other room in the castle; no one would hear her, even on the battlements. She ran to the window—sure enough, there were guardsmen at their posts below. "Hello!" she shouted, leaning out into the rain as though it might help to get a foot or so closer. "Hello, help!" But it was pointless—they didn't even look up. "Oh, please!" she yelled more in frustration than hope.

Suddenly she heard a cry in answer. Looking up, she saw a hawk soaring up from the forest, battling the rain to reach her. "Rufus!" she laughed, giddy with relief.

He swooped through the window, flapping water from

his feathers as he settled at the foot of the bed, for all the world a tiny soldier annoyed at being called out in the rain. "I'm sorry," Malinda promised with another laugh. "But I'm so very glad to see you." She took the scroll from his leg, barely glancing at the text—*où est Phillipe?* in Druscilla's neat hand—before she turned it over. "No pen . . ." She knelt down on the floor and ran a fingertip over the charcoal smear. It would work, maybe, if she didn't write much. She thought a moment, then smeared two words: *Look up!*

Tarquin watched the rain pour down outside the solar window, his boots propped on the sill. The Falconskeep book lay on the table beside him, turned face down as if the cover might fly open and a thousand devils fly out. They had sat this way for hours, Tarquin and the book, and Tarquin was beginning to suspect they might stay that way forever. He didn't know what else to do. Malinda was safe, for the moment; he should just go. But what about the damned book? Did he dare leave it? Should he take it with him? Would it work to throw it away?

They had quarreled before, he and the book. He had been with Alista when she found it floating in the well under the Falconskeep tower; he had agreed with Brother Paolo when the monk begged her to put it back and never peek inside again. He had seen Druscilla in her selfish innocence use it to help her lover, Geoffrey d'Anjou, try to bring Brinlaw to ruin, and he had tried and failed to retrieve it before disaster struck. Now Malinda, selfish, beautiful, enchanted Malinda, had used it to seduce him, to call his true self out. Even now, he couldn't stop thinking about the way she had looked in that first moment, an angel with her arms outstretched to welcome her destruction. He closed his eyes, breathing in the damp, desperate to push the image away. He had to make a decision, had to fix this somehow, but he couldn't think of anything but touching Malinda again. Any illusions he had cherished of keeping control of the situation were effectively shattered to bits. Malinda was truly a witch; last night had proved it. Black magic apparently came to her like breathing. He could almost laugh, it was so diabolically perfect—in hell, his mother must be smiling. Tabby had done magic to bring her captor to her bed; Alista's magic had lulled him into believing he was safe. Now Malinda had captured him completely in a charm that would make the others' powers look like nothing at all. But he didn't feel fear; he felt hatred, a pain so familiar it was almost like a friend. A pain that was really love.

He heard voices raised in the hall outside—Malinda's voice. "Where is he? Did he leave?" A softer answer, then the door to the solar smashed open, hinges squealing in shock. "How dare you?" she demanded. "How *dare* you?!"

"How dare I what?" he asked coolly. His mystic captor looked as if she'd been flying around the battlements. Her hair was wet and wild; her gown was barely on; she wasn't even wearing any shoes; her face and hands were smeared with streaks of black dust. She looked like a harridan indeed. But she was no less beautiful, not a salt grain's worth less.

"Lock me in the tower!" Malinda demanded. "How—?"

"I wanted to kill you in your sleep," Tarquin answered, surprised he could sound so calm. He'd thought she was safely out of the way for the moment, that he'd have time to think things through before he had to face her, assuming he ever felt ready to face her again. But here she was.

She even had the gall to be angry with him, as if he had been the one in the wrong. Why was he surprised? "Locking you up seemed more kind."

"Did it, in faith?" she asked, sarcastic but going pale.

"Isn't that what happens to witches?" he asked, watching the pure green fury of her eyes. "How did you get out?"

"Never you mind," Malinda snarled. When she'd seen Rufus and known she could escape, she had felt a little better. But now, seeing Tarquin taking his ease in the solar with her book at his elbow, thinking all the while that she was locked in the tower, she became livid all over again. And now he was calling her a witch? She had expected him to be angry, but this was too much. "Give me that book at once."

"Not a chance," he shot back. "The Queen and her guards are on their way. Do you mean to greet them like that? Your father would be so proud."

"If anyone should be worried about my father, it's you, not me," she shot back. "What exactly were you thinking when you locked me in the tower?"

"I wasn't exactly thinking; I was exactly running for my life." That wasn't exactly true, but maybe it would capture her attention. "What were you thinking when you started drawing dragons and chanting a lot of faery nonsense—"

"Some nonsense," she taunted. "It certainly worked on you."

"Aye, lady, it did," he answered, getting up. She took a step back, and it took all the strength he had not to grab her up and crush her in his arms. "And I ought to strangle you for it." He picked up the book, the very feel of the leather binding making him shudder with revulsion. "And throw this in the nearest fire—"

"Don't you dare!" She made a grab for it, but he caught her arm and held her off. "That is mine!"

"No, it isn't; it's your mother's—"

"It is not!" She grabbed for him instead, and he flung her back as if she were a viper. "She gave it to me," she insisted, rubbing her aching wrist.

What could Alista have been thinking? he marveled. Didn't she know her child at all? But Malinda wasn't lying; she was too furious, too full of righteous indignation. She believed the Falconskeep book and its magic to be her rightful possessions, just like Rufus the hawk. Just like Tarquin himself. "Did she tell you how to use it?" he demanded. "Did she teach you how to conjure demons with it, or did you figure it out for yourself?"

"I didn't conjure any demons," she said, rolling her eyes in disdain.

"What would you call it?" She felt no remorse whatsoever. "Drawing dragons on the floor—"

"And chanting faery nonsense, yes, you already said that," she cut him off. "I worked a spell, yes, a spell I found in the book. So what? If you hadn't been acting like such an idiot—"

"And how is that, pray tell?" he demanded, incredulous.

"Treating me as if I were made of glass, insisting you were just here doing your duty, that you didn't care to touch me—"

"I was trying to protect you!" Not care to touch her? Even now, he couldn't even look at her without wanting to ravish her, his so-called duty be damned. "I didn't realize what a little witch you already were. I thought you were innocent—"

"You thought I was a child," she corrected, contempt dripping from each word. "I'm not—"

"Not technically, not anymore," he agreed with a bitter laugh of his own. "Is that what you wanted to accomplish? Was I just convenient? Was virginity such a burden?" How could he be saying such things to her? She had him so confused, he barely knew what he believed.

"I wanted you to love me," she answered, hating the way she sounded, hating him for making her sound that way, pitiful and desperate. She was neither of those things. He loved her; it wasn't just the spell that had made him want her last night. But he was so angry. He had locked her up and taken her book. Was that so he could get away? Could he really have meant what he said? Could he really think she was a witch?

"And when I said no, that didn't matter," he finished. "What did you think I meant?"

"I knew you didn't mean it," she insisted. "You kissed me—"

"Yes, damn it, yes, I kissed you," he agreed, turning away, not sure what he might do if he didn't, kill her or kiss her again. "And that was wrong. I told you before—"

"Yes, you told me and told me and told me until I wanted to scream, but that doesn't make it right." She followed him to the window, wanted to touch him, but she was afraid what he might do. "Tarquin, how can we be back to this?" she asked more gently. "How can you still be saying it's wrong for us to be together after last night, after you promised—"

"I didn't promise anything," he said stubbornly, staring out at the rain.

"You did!" She caught his arm, trying to make him turn around, but it was like trying to move a mountain. "You said you loved me. You said you were mine."

"I was under a spell, remember?" He steeled himself against her, refusing to be moved by her pleas. She didn't know what she was saying any more than she had known what she was doing last night.

"It doesn't matter," she insisted. "It wasn't just the spell. It was true—I know it's true. I know it, Tarquin; we are destined to be together, just like Mama and Papa. I only worked the spell so I could make you admit it."

"And what has that accomplished?" He turned around to face her. "You worked the spell because I told you no," he said. "When I wouldn't give in to you any other way . . ." *You used your powers to force me,* he meant to say, but he couldn't do it. She knew what he meant; he could see the hurt in her eyes. "A man is not a possession, Malinda," he finished. "You can't just have one because you think you want him."

"A man is not a possession," she echoed, looking away. "But a woman is. You talk about my virginity being a burden . . . Yes, beloved, I suppose it was." She thought of being beneath him, the feel of him inside her, his whispered words of love, and tears rose in her eyes. "As long as I had it, I was still worth having," she went on, cutting off each word with acid, "a possession some man might want. So, yes, I suppose you were convenient. Why shouldn't I be free? Is my virtue not my own? Why shouldn't I give it up as I see fit?"

"Because it isn't yours, not really," he answered.

"Who does it belong to, then, my father?" she asked, appalled but laughing. "Tell my mother as much, I dare you."

"So now you're rid of it," he said, refusing to answer that. "You made your choice. What about mine? I chose not to hurt you, not to let you use me to make such a mistake, and you—"

"I worked a spell so you couldn't help yourself, yes, I know," she admitted. "I took your choice away. But you kept on choosing badly, over and over again, and we were running out of time."

"Do you even hear yourself?" he demanded.

"Yes, and I sound awful," she agreed. "But it's true. Tarquin, listen to me. There's no reason in the world why we can't be together, why we can't be married. My parents love you; they don't give a tinker's damn for a title, and even if they did, you could have a title—"

"Holy Christ," he swore, turning away.

"Or not," she said, putting herself in front of him again. "I don't care. Nothing would make me so happy as to be with you on your ship, seeing all those places you talk about. I love it when you talk about being free, and I want that. I want to be with you—"

"Malinda, just stop it—"

"Why?" she demanded. "Why do I have to stop?"

"Because you haven't got the faintest idea what you're talking about," he answered. She was so beautiful, and she painted such a pretty picture . . . How easy it would be to just believe her, to forget everything and pretend her fantasy was real. But if he did, if he let himself be convinced, how long would it be before the fantasy collapsed, before his true nature tore the pretty picture all to bits? "You think you know—"

"I do," she persisted. "I'm not some delicate little creature who's never been out of her castle, no matter what my parents might think. I'm—"

"You're a witch," he finished for her.

"I'm not!" He was staring at her so strangely. He had called her a witch twice now. He couldn't be serious; he was just trying to hurt her. "You know what I am," she insisted, picking up the book. "You know what this is—"

"Yes, lady, I do know," he answered. "I know better than you do." Suddenly he knew he could still save her, that she didn't really understand, didn't mean to do the things she had done. She wasn't damned. She was lost, spoiled and willful, yes, but not evil. Not like him.

"My mother gave it to me so I could learn," she said. "She wants me to understand—"

"She wants you to conjure demons?" he interrupted.

"Stop saying that; it's stupid," she scoffed. He just wanted to frighten her, to punish her for frightening him—taking away his choice, as he quite rightly expressed it. "I never saw a demon in my life."

"That just proves how little you know," he answered. "For you saw one last night."

She rolled her eyes again. "It was just a dragon, and not even a real one, a little faery spirit—"

"Not the drawing," he cut her off. "Me."

She just stared at him. He wasn't just trying to scare her—he was serious. He really believed it. "Tarquin, you are not a demon."

"Oh yes, I forgot," he nodded. "You would know better than I." He looked away, his flesh crawling with horror, but he had started now; it was out. All he could do was finish. If he truly meant to save her, he had to tell her the truth. "In your vision, you say you saw my mother."

"Yes." She touched his arm, but he didn't look at her.

"You saw her die," he went on. "You didn't see her live. She was a witch—not so gifted as you, but she had her talents. She wasn't smart, but she was crafty, and she knew some of the old ways . . . She was a spoil of war, captured in Scotland, and she wanted revenge. So she called up a demon, worked a spell very much like yours, and she and this spirit made a deal. He gave her the power to enslave the man who had captured her."

"Bruel," Malinda said softly.

"She put a spell on him that he couldn't escape." He looked down at her hand on his arm. "She was pretty then, I guess, but nothing like Nan's mother or any of the noble women he met. Without the magic, he would have tired of her soon enough. But the spell made him want her, made him feel a lust he couldn't control so she could have his son."

"She told you this?" She trembled for him, the pain unbearable in his eyes. What must it be like to believe in such a tale?

"Of course." His smile was bitter, more poison pain. "The demon moved through Bruel, and together they made me. She had her revenge, and the demon had his son." His eyes met hers at last. "Bruel killed her, and I killed Bruel."

"You never," she breathed, unable to believe it.

"Ask Nan," he chuckled. "She was there . . . I pushed him." He had never said this aloud, not even to Alista, not even to Nan. They had stood at the top of the stairs together, hand in hand, watching him fall, watching him gasp for breath, his neck broken but his eyes wide-open. "No one cared," he went on. "I told his men he was drunk, that he just happened to fall, and they believed me. I brought Nan here, and I told your parents the same tale, and they believed it, too."

"Why?" She touched his cheek, fascinated and appalled. "Why did you push him? Did he try to hurt Nan?"

He shook his head, saying no and flinching away from her touch. "He smiled at her. He called her 'pigeon,' and he asked her if she wanted to go to London, if she wanted to visit her uncle." He felt as if he were dying, as if his heart would explode if he spoke another word, but he had to tell it all. "We had just heard your father was back from Crusade, you see. Bruel saw it as a chance to be rid of her, to pass her off on someone else. He would have done it; he would have let her go. But I couldn't." He looked into her eyes, willing her to see him as he was, to see the truth behind his mask. "I loved Nan. She was all I had. I couldn't let him take her away from me, let her go live with someone else and leave me there with him. So I pushed him." He closed his eyes, shutting her out, just for a moment, just to let himself breathe. "Nan didn't understand—she thought I did it for her. She still thinks so; she said as much the day of her wedding. But I didn't do it for her; I did it for me, for the demon. She would have been safe; I'm the one who would have been alone."

Malinda turned away from him, her hands and feet like ice. She didn't know what to think, what she was meant to say. What did he want her to say? "He hurt you," she said. "You were afraid—"

"I killed him, Malinda. It was my mother's curse—"

"Tarquin, no." She turned back to him. "You can't really believe—"

"Why not?" She was so sweet. Even now, she didn't run away; even now, she would let him touch her. He let himself remember for just a moment the way she felt, the sweet release of lying in her arms. But this grace she offered, this peace, it was an illusion, sin disguised as absolution. "What child murders his father, no matter how awful he might be?"

"You are not a demon," she insisted. "You're a person, a man as I am a maid—a woman."

He smiled. This little irony was really worst of all. She was a woman, not a maid. More of his dear work. "I am like you," he agreed. "You're a woman and a faery." He picked up her hand, so fragile, enclosing it for a moment in his fist. "I'm a demon and a man." He put her away from him, the loss of her touch like a dagger in his heart—but he couldn't bear it, not yet. "Let me go, Malinda," he said, his hands on her shoulders belying his desperate words.

"The spell is broken," she promised. "As soon as I slept, I lost my power over you."

"No." He pressed a kiss to her brow, and she trembled, almost tearful. Was she afraid? Of course she was afraid. "Your power can't be lost." He kissed her, and she actually reached for him, could still want him. She was as cursed as he was, cursed with loving him. "I'm sorry," he whispered against her cheek. "I'm so sorry . . ." She moved to kiss him again, and he turned his face away. "Your father will come home soon," he said as he let her go. "He will keep you safe."

"No." She grabbed his arm in both hands as if she could hold him by force. It wasn't fair—again, he wasn't giving her time to understand before he pushed her away. "It doesn't have to be this way. Whatever happened then, you're different now—"

"No, my love, I am not." He touched her cheek, still smeared with the soot of her dragon. She had such power; she could fall so easily. "What I love, I destroy."

"No," she repeated. He didn't answer but pulled free of her and walked away. "Tarquin!" She followed him into the hall. "I'll tell my father you abandoned me," she warned. "What about your duty?"

He almost smiled. "Tell him whatever you like. Tell him what I did. With any luck, he'll hunt me down and kill me."

"Don't even say that." His saddlebags were already packed; he had been ready to go even before she awoke. "Tarquin!" She chased him out into the courtyard, running to try to match his massive steps. "Stop!" His horse was already saddled, waiting for him in the rain. It was pouring; water was rushing over her bare feet up past her ankles, soaking the hem of her gown, slowing her down. "Tarquin!" He swung into the saddle before she could reach him, then rode for the drawbridge at a gallop. "Tarquin!" But he didn't even look back.

14

Malinda lay on her side, staring at the window in her room, barely seeing the rain still pouring down outside. She had to get up; she had to make ready for the Queen. But she couldn't seem to move.

"*Malinda.*"

She blinked, her eyelids heavier than she'd realized. She was half asleep and dreaming. The room was still there, the window and the rain, but someone was calling her name, and it didn't seem strange at all. Someone was watching her, a woman with blond hair like her own. She was standing in front of the window, but her body was nearly transparent; the gray light was shining through. "*Malinda.*"

"Lady Malinda." Hildy was looking in at the door, solid as ever. Malinda looked back at the window, but the vision-woman was gone. "They've been sighted; they're nearly here," the maid said. "Will you come downstairs?"

The royal entourage finally arrived just after dark in the very worst of the storm. "Here, my lady," Farrars said, handing over a packet to Malinda as soon as he had crossed the threshold of the hall. "Letters from your mother, I believe."

Malinda just looked at him for moment, too grateful to speak. Letters from Mama . . . Mama would make it all right. "Thank you," she said, catching him in an impulsive and most inappropriate embrace.

The noble lord seemed startled at first, but he recovered quickly, hugging her back with a laugh. "You're most welcome," he smiled as she let him go, embarrassed.

"Apparently, so are you, my lord," Eleanor said with a tiny smile of her own.

"Forgive me, Majesty," Malinda said, making a tardy curtsey.

"Not at all, my lady," Eleanor said. "Please, rise—that's hardly necessary, surely. Let me have a look at you."

"Yes, Majesty." The Queen had changed a great deal since she had last seen her, so much that Malinda was shocked. She seemed smaller somehow, a tiny woman lost inside her velvet cloak, and her face, though no less beautiful, looked older. "You seem tired, chérie," Eleanor said. "You must get more sleep—such beauty as yours should be cherished."

"Thank you, Majesty." If she hadn't been so tired or so unhappy, she might have been insulted. As it was, she hardly heard. "Would you care to see your rooms? They aren't very grand, I'm afraid."

"I'm sure they are lovely, Malinda, thank you," Eleanor demurred, the very soul of grace. "Some servant can show me the way. Stay here and take your ease." She glanced over at the men. "Will you join me, Farrars? Do you not wish to inspect my quarters? Malinda may have hidden troops in the cupboards to help me make an escape."

"I trust her with all my soul," Farrars answered, giving Malinda a wink.

"Then I will retire in peace," the Queen said, nodding. She took the arm offered by one of the other knights and headed for the stairs.

"I'll see to getting her a tray," a serving woman offered.

"Thank you," Malinda answered gratefully. "Come, my lord." She offered Farrars her hand. "Your knights will be served here in the hall, but our dinner is in the solar."

"Perfection." He followed her into the cozier room, looking around in obvious approval. "You are an excellent hostess, Malinda. Your mother has taught you well."

"I thank you, my lord, but in this case, I cannot take the credit," she said as he settled on a bench. "The servants did most of the work."

"You're too modest," he teased. "And were you not to call me Robert?"

"Robert," she corrected, making herself smile back. He really was quite nice; she should make every effort to be charming in return. It was her function, after all.

He watched her fill a trencher with food. "I wonder that your castellan is not here to greet us as well," he said as she set it before him. "Where is FitzBruel?"

She froze, but only for a moment. "Gone," she answered, keeping her tone even. "As soon as he knew you were coming. He said you were a better man than he to keep the castle safe, so he would not be needed."

His smile faded in an instant. "He abandoned you?" he demanded, his face going pale.

"He never wanted to stay here," she said, trying to sound as dry and judgmental as she should, as if Tarquin were no more to her than another of her father's retainers and not a

very loyal one at that. "He only did it because Papa insisted
there was no one else." Robert still looked horrified, and she
tempered her tone. The last thing she wanted was a noble
lord she barely knew chasing Tarquin down, ostensibly on
her behalf. "I think he thought my brother, Mark, might be
with you, or perhaps my kinsman, Phillipe."

"Mark is with your parents," Farrars answered, his manner softening again. "And a fine knight he is."

"Of course," she smiled, filling her own trencher. "And
Phillipe? Is he well?" He didn't answer for so long, she
looked up. "Robert?" He was scowling again. "What is it?"
What now? Would this horrible day never end? "Is Phillipe
all right?"

"As far as I can tell." He took a long swallow from his
mug, obviously loath to continue. "He's with Richard."

"Richard, Duke of Aquitaine? Prince Richard?" She
couldn't believe it. Phillipe could not be a traitor to the
Crown, to her family and his own. "Robert, how can this be?"

"I don't know either of them well, Richard or your
Phillipe," he answered with a sigh. "But 'tis said they are
particular friends."

"Friends or not, Phillipe is my brother's kinsman—
they've been inseparable all their lives. He can't possibly feel
more for Richard than he does for Mark—" He was smiling
so bitterly, she stopped. "What? What are you thinking?"

"Nothing," he promised, instantly contrite. "Forgive me,
Malinda—it's not for me to tell you such things."

"What things?" she pressed. She came and sat beside
him on the bench. "Robert, if you truly mean to be my
friend—"

"Phillipe is not your brother's kinsman or yours," he
said, turning to face her. "He is Richard's cousin, the bas-

tard son of Henry's bastard brother, Geoffrey d'Anjou."
His eyes were warm with sympathy, his face drawn with
regret. "Surely you've noticed the resemblance, love. He
and Richard could be twins—"

"Robert, that can't be true," she interrupted. "Phillipe is
my mother's brother; she has said as much herself a hundred times."

"To protect her friend, no doubt," Farrars answered
gently. "'Tis said she kept the Lady Druscilla from being
punished for her crimes."

"What crimes?" Malinda protested. "No, this makes no
sense. Druscilla was my grandfather's mistress before she
married."

"Aye, she was," Farrars agreed. "But she also . . . Geoffrey
the Bastard was a well-known seducer; I'm sure she was
merely taken in. He wanted your father's castle." He
paused, obviously uncomfortable. "And your father's wife."

"I've heard this silly gossip before," Malinda scoffed.
"I'm surprised at you, Robert, believing such foolishness."

"I knew Geoffrey," Farrars answered. "I was with him
and Will Brinlaw and the king when he put his plot in
motion. He tried to kill Brinlaw, then used this Druscilla
to gain entry to the castle and spirited your mother
away. That's why your father killed him." He stopped.
"But I should never have said so much. It is not my
place."

"You aren't lying, are you?" She thought of Mark at
Christmas, the awful truth he had warned her against. This
must have been it. But if it was true, nothing was as she
had always thought, not even Mama and Papa.

"No," he admitted, "I am not."

"It hardly seems possible." *Tarquin would know,* she

thought. *He was here then. He must have seen.* Less than a
year ago, they had all been together, believing they were
happy. Nan was finally to be married, and . . . Tarquin was
missing, far away doing God only knew what, and she,
Malinda, hadn't cared one whit. "*Whatever I love, I
destroy,*" he had said in the last moment before he was
gone. "I can scarcely believe I'm not dreaming." She took
Mama's letters from her pocket. "Forgive me, Robert," she
said, opening the seal. If Phillipe was a traitor, Mama
would try to explain. "I have to know what she wrote."

"Of course," he said. She moved closer to the fire's light
to read, sinking down beside the hearth.

Poor Mama was stuck mending not only Papa's torn
shirts but several other knights' as well. This made her
daughter laugh; Mama hated sewing the way a bishop hates
the devil. Willie had lost both his baby teeth in front and
was reportedly keeping the King much amused with his
impressions of the Lord Chamberlain, who was similarly
afflicted due to rot but not nearly so young or so droll. Papa
was faring well enough in battle, no more than bumps and
scrapes. His new horse was said to be a marvel. Then
Phillipe . . . Mama wrote her all about it, admonishing her
not to take her friend's so-called treason too much to heart.
Remember, sweeting, that Richard Aquitaine is Henry's son,
she wrote. *When this war is over, Phillipe will be forgiven; he
will come home. So don't worry or let Lisbet worry either.*

Then she went on to write about Phillipe's father, everything Robert had said, or nearly. *Forgive us, my love, for not
telling you the truth,* she finished. *Or rather, forgive me—your
father would have told you long ago. But I could never see why
you should know. It all seemed so long ago, and you were all just
children. You were so beautiful, all of you, so safe and so well*

loved, I couldn't see how the past could hurt you as long as we
kept it away. But you aren't children any more, and others
won't protect you as we have. Seeing how deeply Mark has been
hurt, hearing it at court in bits and whispers, all viciously
meant, the truth mixed in with lies, I know how dearly I was
wrong. How did my sweet ones become adults so quickly? How
did we get so old? I can only pray we can come home to you soon
and that you will understand. I have no doubt that you will, my
wise young woman. We love you and miss you very much.

Malinda bent her head and cried. She wasn't wise; she
didn't understand. Right now, she barely cared about
Phillipe or the past. Tarquin had left her; she didn't understand him, either. She didn't understand anything; she was
stupid. She wanted her mama and papa, to cry out her
heart in their arms. She didn't want to know all these
secrets, theirs or Tarquin's. She didn't want to be a woman
grown; she wanted to be a child. She pressed her fists
against her face and sobbed as if she had gotten her wish.

"Malinda." Robert knelt beside her on the hearth.
"What is it?"

"I cannot tell." She should try to compose herself, act
her age, be a lady—in truth, she had forgotten he was
there. But she just couldn't make herself stop crying.
"Forgive me, my lord."

"It's Robert, remember?" he scolded, taking her into his
arms. "Don't be silly." He stroked her hair and let her cry.
"Can you truly not tell me what's wrong? Is there no way I
can help?"

"No . . ." He was so kind, and he was older, nearly Papa's
age. She was embarrassed, but so grateful, too. She needed
someone to do this, to take things in hand and comfort
her, even if only for a moment.

"My poor angel," he soothed. "Left here all alone." He pressed a kiss to her temple, chaste and warm, a father's tenderness. "Never mind now, shhh," he murmured as she clung to him more tightly, crying harder. "I won't abandon you, my precious child. You need never be alone again."

Malinda was barely dressed in the morning when a message came from the Queen. "Her Majesty asks that you join her in her rooms for breakfast," the maid said, looking over Malinda's simple gown with a mildly horrified eye. "If that will be quite convenient."

"My, my, how things have changed," Hildy murmured, braiding Malinda's hair.

"Not that much," Malinda scolded, giving her a stern look in the mirror. "Tell Queen Eleanor I will be much honored."

"Thank you, my lady," the maid said, making a curtsey before she went out.

"'My lady,'" Hildy sighed. "Congratulations. It would seem you're a lady-in-waiting at last."

"Yes," Malinda nodded, staring at her own reflection. Could she ever truly have cared so much about something that meant so little now? Impossible—that girl was someone else. "I suppose I am." Her face seemed just the same. Eleanor had said she looked tired, and she did have faint shadows under her eyes. But mostly she looked the same as always. She wouldn't cry again; she wouldn't. He was never coming back. She turned away from the mirror. "I have to go to the Queen."

Walking through the familiar doors a few moments later, she thought for a moment that she must have lost her mind. If she hadn't known she was standing in her parents' bedroom, she never would have guessed it—everything, tapestries, furniture, draperies, rugs, was changed. "Malinda," the Queen said, coming to greet her with a hug. "I'm so glad you have come."

"Thank you, Majesty," Malinda murmured, too shocked by the room to be surprised by the embrace. "Where are my mother's things?"

"You must forgive me, chérie," Eleanor laughed. "'Tis an old woman's foolish fancy. I must have my own little nest." She looked much more like herself this morning, refreshed, though she still wore her dressing gown. "Your mother's belongings have been moved into that empty tower," she continued, sitting back down at the table. "Are you offended?"

"No, of course not." Something about this room was familiar. That was to be expected, of course—she'd been born in this room. But something else, something frightening ... She saw her reflection in a long, silver mirror, and her heart skipped a beat, then her blood ran cold. She wanted to run away. A whippet lay in the middle of the velvet-covered bed; it raised its head to stare at her with liquid, intelligent eyes. "It's just rather a shock," she said, the queer feeling beginning to pass.

"No doubt." A second maid finished setting the table and withdrew. "Come and sit with me." Malinda obeyed, and the Queen studied her closely. "Much better—you must have slept better last night."

"Yes." In truth, she had barely slept at all. Robert had sat with her in the solar until past midnight, then she had lain awake until nearly dawn.

"Good," Eleanor smiled. She paused, buttering a slice of bread, and Malinda waited. "You know, chérie, I remember your being more talkative."

"Forgive me, Majesty," she answered automatically. She still felt strangely trapped, but that was silly, and she was being rude. "I don't know what to say."

"I don't doubt it," Eleanor laughed. "I have fallen into a pitiful state, have I not? Damn Henry's eyes . . . but then, you are still a loyal subject like your father. No doubt such talk offends you."

"Henry is my father's king and mine," Malinda answered. "But I bear him no great love." If the King weren't such a womanizing fiend, she would be with her parents right now. She found it hard to think well of him.

"I'm pleased to hear it," Eleanor said. "More pleased than I can say. Here, eat something. Put the roses back in those pretty cheeks." She sighed. "To have such a face again . . . Tell me how you've been, chérie. I was furious when your father wouldn't let you stay on with me at Christmas." She took a dainty bite of bread. "Though in light of all that's happened, I suppose 'twas for the best."

"Did you know the princes would rebel?" Malinda asked. "Did you suspect?"

"I hoped," the Queen laughed. "Henry had become impossible; he needed shaking up. But no, I didn't know—I don't think they knew themselves. Young Henry just suddenly decided to ride off to Paris instead of following his papa back to England, and the next thing we knew, we were at war. The younger boys were with me when we heard, and I managed to get them away. But when I tried to follow . . ." She stopped with a wry smile. "But no doubt you've heard that tale before."

"Yes," Malinda admitted, smiling back. "Do you miss them—your sons, I mean?"

"Horribly—a sweet child like you can hardly imagine."

She focused her attention on a bowl of berries set between them. "But I hope that you will help me."

"I?" Malinda asked, wary and confused. "I hardly see how I can help."

The Queen smiled. "You have grown up, chérie," she said. "Very much since last we met." She set her knife aside. "Your friend, Phillipe, tells me you have an amazing hawk named Rufus."

"Phillipe told you?" Phillipe had spoken about her with Eleanor? He had told the Queen about Rufus? Had he plotted with her? Had she sent him to Richard?

"He said you and his sister used this hawk to send messages back and forth between this castle and Bruel," Eleanor continued. "Is this true?"

"Well, yes," Malinda admitted. "But—"

"Do you think this hawk could find Phillipe?" Her dark blue eyes sparkled with frightening purpose. "Does it know him well enough?"

"I don't know," Malinda said, getting up. "But even if he could—"

"Malinda, I am desperate," the Queen cut her off. "I must somehow have word of my son—"

"I cannot," Malinda cut her off in turn. "You cannot ask me to take such a risk."

"What risk?" Eleanor scoffed. "Who would suspect a magic hawk? I only want to send word to Richard, to tell him I am well—"

"To tell him where you are." Did this woman think she was an utter fool? But then, why not? Everyone else seemed to believe it; she sometimes even believed it herself, seemed to take great pains to prove it. "Forgive me, Majesty, but this is one favor I will not grant," she finished.

"I will not use my pet against my father and his king, not even to please you."

"A favor you will not grant." The older woman smiled, but the look in her eyes was anything but warm. "My goodness, how grown-up we've become. I'm quite impressed." She looked Malinda up and down. "Who is he? What's his name?"

"Forgive me, Majesty," Malinda repeated, her sudden blush giving her away. "I don't know what you—"

"Your lover, chérie," Eleanor retorted. "The man who has shattered your illusions. Last Christmas, you told me you wanted a suitor. Now you know better, I think."

"You're wrong," Malinda lied. "And Phillipe was wrong to make you think I could help you with a well-trained hawk."

"Not trained, Malinda. Magic." She folded her arms across her chest as if in contemplation of the woman before her. "I wonder what other magic you can do, you and your pretty little mama? Will it save your idiot father when he and Henry finally lose this war?"

Malinda stared back at her coldly. "My father will not lose."

Eleanor shrugged. "Perhaps not," she conceded. "Tell me, chérie. What do you think of Lord Farrars?"

Malinda frowned, confused. "Why do you care?"

"He seems quite taken with you," the Queen said pleasantly, a mockery of her previous attitude. "Did you know that both his sons were murdered on Crusade? The second one was actually a priest until his brother was killed, but his father made him abandon the Church to become a Crusader. He said he could serve God better as a soldier. He hates the infidel that much." She smiled. "Can you imagine how he might react if he heard you were a witch?"

"I am not a witch." Suddenly Malinda knew exactly why her father despised this woman. And to think she had wanted more than anything to serve her . . .

"Did I say you were?" She looked perfectly calm, not a single hair turned as she made her threats without ever once raising her voice.

"He wouldn't believe you," Malinda insisted. Surely Robert felt as Brinlaw did; surely he knew Eleanor couldn't be trusted.

"Don't be so certain, Malinda," the Queen said, seeming to hear her thoughts as clearly as her words. "You'd be astonished to discover what I can make a man believe." She turned back to her breakfast, her manner softening somewhat. "You are very beautiful, chérie, but you are also very new to this game. You are a young enchantress. I am an old one." She motioned to the other chair. "Now stop fretting, please. I won't ask you to send a report about troop movements or the number of men in the garrison. I only want Richard to know I'm all right." She met Malinda's eyes as the younger woman sat. "And, as you say, where I am."

"I'm not certain my hawk can find Phillipe." Eleanor was right—hateful, but right. She couldn't say no. Her mother had explained all too clearly what could happen if she were accused as a witch. And while Robert Farrars was a dear, kind man, or seemed to be, he could hardly be expected to understand her heritage. *"You would be tried and burned before we ever knew,"* her mother's voice echoed in her head. "What if he can't?" she said aloud.

"Then he can't," Eleanor said with a smile that was almost beatific. "All I ask is that you try."

15

After four days dead drunk, Tarquin let himself sober up long enough to figure out where he was. He'd been gone from Brinlaw—how long? A month? Nearly two? He hadn't moved in any definite direction, hadn't let himself stop to think long enough to plot a course. But time was running short. He stumbled out of the inn that could barely be called a hovel into a narrow street more properly called a pig lot. Livestock wandered aimlessly and unmolested in every direction, and a shockingly dirty pack of children were gathered by the village well, watching him approach with wary eyes. "This place," he said, looking up and down the street, squinting in the wintry sun. "Does it have a name?"

They looked at each other for a moment. "St. Anne's Mercy," the biggest boy finally answered. "Excepting the abbey's closed." He snickered. "Was you looking for a nun?" His audience laughed with him, and Tarquin smiled and shook his head. "London's that way, four days," the boy went on, pointing southeast. "Chester that way, two." He pointed to the west.

"Thanks." Tarquin tossed a coin, turned away so he wouldn't have to see them tussle for it in the dirt. At least he had lucked into the right direction. He'd arranged to meet Davyd on the last day of November. By his reckoning, faulty as it was, he should still have a little more than a week. He rubbed his face, his own flesh feeling foreign, still half numbed from drink. He wondered where he'd find another bottle . . .

This was stupid, he knew, this drinking. Presumably, someone with a pretty deep purse was still out there wanting him dead, and he wouldn't be so hard to find. Whoever the man was, he had to know by now his mercenaries had failed on the road from Bruel. It had been almost half a year. He stopped dead, his addled brain astonished. Half a year since he'd gone to Brinlaw with Malinda? He'd never have thought he'd have lasted so long. But once he'd finally fallen, he'd done it royally, make no mistake . . . but then, he had to admit he'd had help. In a single, devilish instant, the image he'd been drinking so hard to escape slipped into his mind and took root . . . Malinda's face scant inches from his own, lips parted for his kiss, eyes burning green with love . . . He shook his head to clear it, and pain like a spike shot through his skull. He had to keep moving . . . he had to find a bottle.

Later he rode along a forest path, his bottle half empty, his horse pointed vaguely south. The world was fading out again, leaving him alone with his dreams. Malinda . . . but something was wrong, different from before. In this dream, he was Malinda, and the walls were closing in, slimy with water and blood. Voices screamed all around him. His throat was raw from screaming—he was choking on the sea, deaf from the screams of the dead. Something stirred the air around him, and he wept, but the walls couldn't hear him. The water rose—no escape.

His eyes snapped open. He blinked in the sunlight, his heart pounding in his chest. He was drunk; he couldn't think clearly. He spurred his horse, startling the animal from his own reverie into a gallop. He had to go back, had to save her—but the rope that appeared out of nowhere caught him in mid-chest and scraped him out of the saddle.

"Watch him!" a brigand shouted, dropping his end of the rope to come closer. "He's tricky, make no mistake."

"Are we sure this is the one?" the other rope holder said warily, holding his sword out before him.

"That's him," the first one said. "'Tis not likely I'd forget him, after what happened to the captain."

Tarquin could barely see them, barely stagger to his feet. He must have hit his head, or else he was drunker than he'd thought. He'd galloped right into the trap . . . He reached for his sword, but it was still strapped to his saddle, galloping full speed south. "London . . . four days that way," he mumbled thickly, drawing his dagger instead.

"Careful," the first one warned. They must have been tracking him, must have followed him to the last town and set traps on the only roads out. But there were only two . . . He tried to make his eyes focus, tried to concentrate.

"Don't kill him," the second one chided—Monsieur Anxious.

"I ain't going to kill nobody," Monsieur Careful answered back. "Just be careful he don't kill you."

Tarquin lunged for Careful, got him by the throat as the brigand's sword cut a gash in his arm. But it was no use . . . The world was going black.

By the time he came to, his hands were bound behind his back, and he was lying facedown on the ground. "I still say one of us should go tell the others we got him," Anxious was saying. "He could die before we get him back if we don't hurry."

"He don't look so good," Careful agreed. They were behind him, ten feet or so away, he thought—impossible to tell without letting them know he was conscious. "Stay here and watch him," Careful decided. "I'll go and find the others."

"Oh no," said Anxious. "I'll go."

"Oh no again," said Careful. "You're not leaving me with him alone."

"He's tied, for sweet love's sake," Anxious argued. "If he should die before we get him back—"

"I know, I know. We'll cast lots, then. Where are the dice?"

So they were still alone, but others were expected. If he waited until they worked out who was going, he might have only one to contend with, but if they took too long, relief might turn up on its own. He still couldn't think clearly, but he had to move. But how? They hadn't tied his ankles; that was something. These were foot soldiers, dumb muscle. Nobody had expected them to be the ones to find him. But he couldn't just walk over and start fighting, not without his hands. Somehow he had to bring them to him, both of them, very close.

"Holy Christ!" he roared, bucking and thrashing around on the ground like a man possessed by demons. "Whoreson bitch, it hurts!" He beat his head against the ground like he meant to drive the demons out by force, real pain making his eyes tear up.

"What's wrong with him?" Anxious demanded.

"Some kind of fit," Careful answered, taking a step closer.

"Sweet bastard, make it stop!" Tarquin screamed, flinging himself over on his back, his heels digging trenches in the dirt.

"So what do we do?" Careful ventured, moving closer still.

"Kill me!" Tarquin ordered, his lips drawn back in a snarl.

"Not likely, friend," Anxious answered, pulling up even with his partner. "Calm yourself, why don't—" Tarquin let out a hideous howl, his eyes rolling back in his eyes. "Jesus!" Anxious swore, appalled.

"We've got to do something," Careful decided as Tarquin's teeth began to chatter as he trembled. "Come help me sit him up."

"The hell you say!" Anxious scoffed. "I'm not touching—"

"Remember clearly how he died, then," Careful advised, catching Tarquin's arm and trying to hold him still. "His lordship will want to know."

"Oh, bloody hell." Anxious came and grabbed his other arm. Both of them were close enough.

He lunged up, his skull crashing into Careful's forehead in a bone-crushing blow that made the brigand reel backward, unconscious. Anxious squawked like a startled goose and tried to fall back to draw his sword, but Tarquin was faster. He hooked his legs around the brigand's calf and threw him to the ground, leaping up to plant both knees in his stomach before he could recover. The sword came up, shaky and random, and Tarquin swept it aside with his shoulder as he rolled back to the ground on his side, the blade slicing into his flesh just deeply enough to bleed. Careful was groaning, coming back around, and he kicked him hard in the head before he caught Anxious's neck between his powerful legs. He twisted hard, a trick he had learned from one of his sailors, and the brigand's eyes bulged out and his mouth opened, gasping for air. Tarquin twisted again, and the neck snapped with a thick pop.

Careful had made it to his knees, sword in hand. Tarquin scrambled back, groping desperately behind him for the dead man's sword, trying to cut his hands free. Careful stood, smiling, his eyes beginning to focus, his movements becoming more steady. Tarquin winced as the blade behind him cut into his wrist and blood poured into his palm. Careful raised his sword. "I thought you weren't supposed to kill me," Tarquin said, meeting his eyes. The brigand blinked, and Tarquin, his hands free, brought the other sword up and plunged it into the brigand's stomach. The man grunted once, uttered a garbled word, then fell to his knees, clutching at the blade.

Tarquin looked around, still dizzy, fighting back the dark. His own horse was nowhere in sight, but the other two were still packed. He took Careful's sword and wiped the blade on his shirt, only staggering a little as he stood. He could still make it to the *Falcon* in time, assuming he didn't die on the way. His wounds were bad, he could tell. But there was something else, something he had dreamed that had made him fall into the trap in the first place ... Malinda was in danger. The dream came back to him in a rush—tortured screams and the thick cold smell of death. Could this vision be real? He'd left Malinda to save her from himself. Could he have abandoned her to something worse? His blood ran cold just to think of it, the black threatening to swallow him again. Wouldn't that be justice? Trying to do right, the demon fumbles into evil once again. But maybe not; maybe this vision was the evil, his own wrongheaded desires trying to trick him into doing more damage. But if it was true, if Malinda was really trapped in that horror . . . He had to be sure. Mounting one horse as he grabbed the reins of the other, he rode away at a gallop.

Malinda was walking back from the stables, stripping out of her riding gloves, when suddenly she felt faint. "My lady?" Sir Harold asked, catching her arm as she stumbled. "Are you all right?"

"What?" The whole world had gone black for a moment. She'd felt the ground coming up to meet her—a path in the woods, thick with loam and leaves. But they were in the courtyard . . . "Yes," she said aloud, making herself smile brightly. "Thank you, Sir Harold. I'm fine."

Later, she stood on the highest tower at Brinlaw. Her mantle was wrapped tightly around her, but still the cutting wind was cold. Her mother had stood here once and almost become a falcon, so despairing she wanted to fly. Malinda wasn't so far gone, but she could understand the sentiment now better than she ever had in her life. The strange faintness she had felt before had never completely gone away, becoming a heavy sense of dread that made her feel sick to her stomach. She searched the clouds, hoping for some sign of Rufus. The hawk had been gone for more than a week, carrying the Queen's latest message. "Come home, Rufus," she called into the wind in faery-speak. "If you can't find him, just come home."

A shout came up from the guardsmen below—a pair of

riders were at the gates under the banner of Bruel. Malinda
strained to see who it was, but it was impossible from this
distance. "It can't be," she breathed, her heart pounding . . .
no. They had dismounted to be questioned; they were both
smaller than the guards. Neither of them could be Tarquin.
But they were from Bruel . . . She turned and ran for the
stairs.

She emerged in the courtyard just as they were being let
inside. "Malinda!" Lisbet shouted, throwing back her
hood.

"Lisbet!" She ran to embrace her friend, then Lisbet's
little brother, Paul, who was standing behind her, then
Lisbet again. "Thank God you've finally come."

Tarquin rode for days without stopping, but he was so lost,
he wasn't sure he wasn't riding in circles. The sensation
was strange to him—he'd always had an unerring sense of
direction, even as a child. But he'd never traveled in quite
this condition before. His head was better, he thought—
he'd had no seizures for real—but the wound he'd made in
his wrist trying to cut his bindings had bled a great deal
before he could risk stopping to bandage it, and he was
afraid infection must have set in, either there or in one of
the other shallow wounds in his arms and chest. He felt
feverish and sick all the time now, and chills wracked his
body at night. But he didn't dare stop, even when he
couldn't quite remember where he was going. Sometimes
he seemed to be riding toward Malinda, following her
voice on the wind. Other times he was trying to escape her,
remembering he had to reach Davyd. But he always knew
he couldn't stop.

The dawn was breaking again, sunlight pink on the thin

crust of new-fallen snow. Snow . . . was he too late? His horse emerged from the trees at a leisurely pace—the reins had gone slack in his hand hours, maybe days ago. The other horse had trotted a little ahead, was already drinking from the river. The river . . . he had wanted to find the river, find a boat to hire, move faster. He remembered that much at least. But where had he meant to go?

A tiny cottage stood just down the bank, a thin wisp of smoke rising from the chimney. They had a dock and a boat—a kind of barge or ferry from what he could see, exactly what he needed . . . But where was he going? Malinda, he was going to Malinda . . . But that was wrong. He should stay away from Malinda; he would only hurt her. But she needed him . . . Every time he closed his eyes, he could hear her screaming his name . . .

A bird of prey screamed in the sky far above him, and he looked up, saw the goshawk circling, hunting rabbits in the first light. He tilted his head back further and lost his perspective, shifting in the saddle. "Rufus!" he yelled, a madman's roar, as he slid from the horse to the ground. He heard the hawk scream in answer as the dawning sky turned black . . .

If it hadn't been for the horses, the boy might never have found him. He was on his way to the boat when he saw them, two fair-looking mounts wandering alone on the bank of the river a quarter of a mile from the dock. He put down his fishing net and walked toward them, whistling softly under his breath. Bryon was no great lover of horses, for all his romantic ideals, and he wasn't quite sure how to stop them from running away. But they didn't seem alarmed, just curious, as he came closer. "Hullo there," he murmured, catching the bridle of the first. "How is it you've come here, then?" Scratching the horse's neck, he caught sight of something shiny in the muddy grass—the glint of polished steel. Moving slowly, he took a step toward it, saw the man lying on the ground with his sword fallen beside him. The other horse was standing over him, nuzzling his shoulder, but he didn't stir, and Bryon shivered. Maybe he was dead. He fell to his knees to creep closer, saw the rise and fall of the man's chest. The fellow had been badly hurt—one sleeve was crusted over from shoulder to wrist with blood, and one closed eye was swollen and black. After a few tense moments of consideration, Bryon poked him gently with a stick, but the man didn't move. "Ma!" the boy yelled, leaping to his feet. "Ma, I've found a knight!"

Snow was falling faster as Alista walked out into the garden of the castle at Falaise, and she pulled up her hood. They had been here only two days; now Henry was ready to move again. But at least this time he was taking them all back to England. "We could go back to Brinlaw for a visit," she had suggested to her husband as soon as they were alone.

"We could, maybe," he had agreed, his eyes so weary she wanted to cry just to see him. "But we can't count on it, sweet. You know I want to—"

"I know you do," she had promised, squeezing his hand. If the past few months were any indication, they couldn't count on anything. But her heart had sunk even so. She needed to go home—her dreams were worse every night. Last night, she had barely slept at all. Her hand strayed to her swelling belly . . . If she had to be pregnant at her age, she oughtn't to be stuck doing Henry's bidding, too.

Her youngest son was playing in the snow, and she smiled in spite of herself. He was spinning like a dervish, as easily contented here as anywhere else in the world. But as she drew closer, his mad rotation slowed, and she caught her breath, a chill passing over her heart. Snowflakes were supposed to be random, but around her son, they were falling in a pattern, spiraling halos of white that encircled him from the top of his head to the tips of his outstretched fingers, piling at his feet in a design like the lacy petals of a flower. *"A daisy, Mama, look!"* a voice crowed in her head, Malinda's voice when she was barely three years old. This was Malinda's trick, the first indication her parents had seen that she was a faery indeed. Alista herself had certainly never done such magic.

"Hello, Mama," Willie said, bringing her out of her thoughts. He sounded as sad and tired as she felt, but he continued to spin. "Do you see?"

"I do," she answered. "When did you learn to do that?"

"Just today." He spun faster for a moment, and the snowflakes followed suit, obscuring his face like a veil until he slowed again. "Grammy taught me just before she left."

"Who?" Alista's mother had died when she was only four, and Will's mother had been long dead when they met. But perhaps some other woman—

"Your mama," he explained. "She visits me sometimes." He suddenly stopped spinning, the pattern collapsing, and his little shoulders slumped as if under the weight of the world. "Now she's gone to Malinda."

He sounded so matter-of-fact, as if this shouldn't surprise her in the least, and she tried to follow suit, not to frighten him. "Willie, your grammy is dead—"

"Sort of," he nodded. "And sort of not. She tried to die

as a falcon, but she couldn't, really . . . It's all very confusing, isn't it?"

"Yes," Alista answered, feeling rather dizzy. She sat down on a nearby bench, and he followed. She had seen the falcon die when her father died, seen it forcibly fall from the air. In her heart, she had known it was her mother's spirit, but . . . She couldn't think about it; she'd go mad.

"Mama, are you all right?" Willie asked, touching her arm and frowning in concern.

"Yes, sweeting, quite all right," she promised.

"Malinda will be fine, she thinks," he said, as if to reassure her. "Or at least . . ." He put a hand on her stomach. "This baby is a girl."

"Willie, how could you—?"

"But I don't want a new girl," he protested, suddenly dissolving into angry grief. "I want Malinda." He fell into her arms, clinging with all his childish might as hot tears stained her throat. "She promised," he insisted. "She promised she would be there when we came home."

"And so she will," Alista soothed, stroking his hair. "You must have just had a nightmare—"

"No, Mama." He drew back to look at her, an accusation in his eyes. "You know I'm telling the truth."

"Yes." She drew him close again, pushed back his hood to kiss his hair. "I'm afraid I do." Her own tears burned her cheeks as images from her own dreams rose up in her mind. "What does your grammy say has happened?"

"She wouldn't say," he answered, sounding less desperate now that she was truly listening. "But it isn't over yet, and she didn't know how it would end. I asked if she would come back and tell me, and she just smiled, but she was sad. I think she may be gone for good."

"It's all right." She looked down at his hand in hers, the short, thick fingers—her father's hand, not Will's. Had she ever noticed that before? "I remember her being very wise. I'm sure she'll know what to do."

"I hope so." He leaned against her shoulder, too big now to take into her lap. When had he gotten so big? "But couldn't we go home?"

"Yes." She kissed him again, her heart aching with love for him and the children she couldn't hold so near. "I think we must tell Papa and Mark we have to."

16

$\mathcal{E}$leanor looked down at the message, all the color draining from her face but for two bright spots of scarlet, one on either cheek. "My son continues to be pleased to hear I am well," she said crisply. "But he thinks it good that I stay here. I am a woman, after all, and here I will be safe."

"I'm sorry, Majesty." In truth, Malinda wasn't sorry in the least. If Richard didn't want his mother with him, he wouldn't lay siege to Brinlaw to rescue her, and Malinda's treachery against her father's king would matter very little. She was worried about Rufus, though. Ever since his return, he had been acting very strangely. He had come to her at once on the tower and let her remove the message, but once that was done, he had taken flight again, screaming as if in alarm. And still he wouldn't rest. It had taken her the better part of an hour to coax him inside, and he had yet to settle on any perch for more than a minute at a time.

"Ungrateful fool," Eleanor snapped, breaking back into her thoughts. "He just doesn't realize . . ." She looked over at Malinda. "There's something else you can do. Some other charm to get me past the guards—"

"No," Malinda cut her off, shaking her head.

"Don't lie; I know there is," the queen insisted. "Some way to make yourself vanish—you did it at Montferrand last Christmas night."

How could she know that? "Why would you think—?"

"I sent someone after you, a minstrel," Eleanor said, warming to her subject as she remembered the details. "He couldn't find you. One moment you were there, he said; the next moment you were gone. Show me how you did it."

"It isn't that simple," Malinda protested.

"Malinda, please!" She sat down, obviously struggling to regain her composure. "I don't want to see you harmed; I don't want to threaten or frighten you. But I have to reach my son. I can't stay locked up here any longer; I'll go mad." She reached out and took the younger woman's hand. "I know you understand, chérie. I knew it the first time we talked. Do you remember?"

"Yes." She had loved the Queen with all her heart. Eleanor had seemed to understand her better than any other soul in all the world, even her own mother. But Alista had been the one who had warned her not to use magic at court, not even a simple vanishing glamour. Mama was the one who had truly understood. Unfortunately, Mama wasn't here to see her prophecy come true.

"You understand what it means to be caged," Eleanor pressed on. "You know how dear a price I would pay to be free."

Something about these words struck at something deep inside Malinda's heart, not so much in sympathy as in something more dark, something having to do with herself more than the Queen. "Yes," she answered again, sinking into a chair.

"Think of what I can offer you, the life I could give you when this stupid war is over and Henry is gone," Eleanor said. "Richard can't marry Alice now, princess or not; she's been Henry's whore too long. I see no reason why he shouldn't marry you. You're beautiful and smart enough to challenge him, and an alliance with your father could help him after Henry is gone."

Malinda just stared at her, struck dumb. A year ago, if someone had told her that today, Eleanor of Aquitaine would make her such an offer, she would have been beside herself with joy. A princess, perhaps even a queen . . . What else could she possibly want? But it was an illusion, all of it, a childish fantasy, and the thought that she could want it made her shudder, made her want to laugh. "And you could do this?" she finally managed. "You would suggest—?"

"I would compel," Eleanor said, her eyes bright with triumph. "And he will love you, ma belle, I swear it. How could he not?"

Something about this made the urge to break up in giggles even harder to resist. "I . . . you would have to let me think on this, Majesty," she said, hoping the catch in her voice made her sound more flattered than amused. In truth, it wasn't funny. She would have to answer this, have to think of what to do, and right now, no solution was apparent. But it was funny, too; it was hilarious. She had already called on the spirit of a dragon to make one man love her, and just see how that had fared. What would she have to do to win the heart of a future king?

A knock came at the door before the Queen could answer. "Forgive the intrusion, Majesty," Lisbet said, making a curtsey. "The King's herald has come with a privy message for you."

"My husband's latest taunts," Eleanor answered with a brittle smile. "Very well, chérie; you may think on what I've said. But pray think quickly."

As soon as she was gone, Malinda collapsed to the floor, bent over double with helpless laughter. "Shall I fetch a priest?" Lisbet asked dryly, raising an eyebrow.

"Aye, at once," Malinda sighed, sobering enough to speak. "Tell him I am dead."

"I will not," Lisbet said, joining her on the rug. She had been at Brinlaw for more than a week, had known nearly all of Malinda's secrets almost as long. "I knew it!" she had said when Malinda confessed her love for Tarquin. "He'll come back, daisy, see if he doesn't. He hasn't any choice." Even after Malinda told her about the seduction spell and Tarquin's fury, she had refused to be dissuaded. "You're meant to be together," she insisted. "You will be."

"I take it the news from Phillipe was not to Her Majesty's liking," she said now.

"No," Malinda agreed, wiping away her tears. "Richard doesn't want her, so she wants me to make her invisible so I can marry him."

Lisbet just looked at her for a moment. "May I have another pass at that, please?"

"Richard wants her to stay here out of the way; he has no intention of rescuing her," Malinda explained more slowly. "But she thinks he's wrong, that he doesn't realize what a help she could be to him. She wants me to make her invisible so she can get past the guards and escape. Somehow, she knows I turned myself invisible at Montferrand last Christmas."

"I *told* you not to do that," Lisbet scolded. "But what is this about your marrying Richard?"

"Eleanor says if I will help her escape, she will make Richard fall in love with me and marry me." Suddenly she didn't find this idea the least bit funny; she wanted to cry instead. "But I don't want to marry Richard."

Lisbet took her hand and squeezed it. "Of course you don't."

"I want to marry Tarquin."

"Of course you do."

"But Tarquin isn't here." She got up and went to the window, gazed out at the gathering dark. She wished she could close her eyes and will this all away, that she knew the words to whisper to make it all disappear. She would turn around, and Eleanor and all her possessions would be gone, and her parents would be home to put everything to rights again. But that wasn't going to happen. Her parents had left her with Tarquin, and she had driven him away, too. Now she couldn't go back, not with all the magic in the world. "Where do you suppose he went?" she sighed. "Where is he, Lisbet?"

"I wish I knew." Her friend came and put an arm around her shoulders. "Maybe we could find him," she suggested. "Eleanor can't leave, but I'll bet we could."

"And go where?" Malinda answered. "It sounds wonderful, but we wouldn't have the first idea how to find him."

"But Rufus would," Lisbet insisted. "If he can find Phillipe, he can certainly find Tarquin."

"Tarquin could be in Africa by now," Malinda pointed out. "Besides, he doesn't want to be found. And even if he were here, there's nothing he could do—"

"I can't believe that," Lisbet scoffed. "He loves you, just as you love him." She chewed her lip for a moment in thought. "You could do a spell," she said, "to find him. Surely there must be something."

"Maybe," Malinda agreed, a new hope beginning to dawn. "It has to be worth a try, doesn't it?"

In the shadows, a tray rattled in hands trembling in shocked delight. Holding her breath, the maid turned and slipped away before either girl even knew she was there.

"One man." Farrars looked again at the scroll before him as if he couldn't quite believe he'd read it aright. "One man— a drunk, alone, with no notion he's being followed; a common mercenary who began from a fixed point at a fixed time well-known to his pursuers, and yet he cannot be found. We know he lives; we know he is no phantom—he's been seen." He dropped the stack of reports, scattering them across the table. The solar was dark but for the fire and a single candle; the castle was quiet, the rest of the household long since asleep. "For one brief moment, he was in our grasp, wounded and alone. We know this because we found our friends after he murdered them— *both* of them—to escape. And yet we cannot find him." He looked up at his servant, his usually pleasant face twisted mad with fury. "One man."

"No, my lord," the old man grinned. His nose, never an object of great beauty, had been smashed pretty well out of existence by Tarquin's fist in Corsica, and his shoulders had healed in a misshapen, twisted hump, but his evil sense of humor remained remarkably intact. "Tarquin FitzBruel is not a man at all. He's a demon."

"I don't care!" He pushed back from the table with such force, his chair crashed over behind him. "Capture him in a holy relic—"

"We can't capture him at all," the old man complained. "If my men could simply kill him, bring you back his head or his heart—both, if you prefer, or something more poetic—"

"No!" Farrars grabbed the front of his shirt and yanked him close enough to smell his stinking breath. "This man—this demon, as you call him—murdered my son— my *only* son. *I* will scourge him; *I* will exorcise him; *I* will cast him out; *I* will bring him back to God, and as God is my witness, demon or not, *I* will see him dead."

"Excuse me, my lord." Nicole had been his spy in Eleanor's chambers for most of her young life, and she moved as quietly as a cat in fleece stockings. Now she smiled sweetly as she saw she had their full attention. "I think perhaps I can help."

Malinda sat on the bed in the highest tower bedroom, her magic book open before her, Rufus dozing on his perch. "Show me my love," she sang softly in the faery tongue, remembering the last night she had spent in this room, entwined in Tarquin's arms. "Tonight I would lie with my love . . ."

"*As would I,*" a voice spoke in the air around her, a woman's voice, gentle and sad. "*But we may not always work our will, even with our best magic.*"

Malinda whipped her head around, saw a figure standing in the shadows, the same woman she had glimpsed in her own room after Tarquin had left her. "I am dreaming," she said, rising from the bed.

"*You will dream,*" the woman said, nodding. "*You cannot stay, Malinda.*" Her eyes were the same green as Malinda's own, her hair the same golden blond, but she seemed older, and her features were more fine.

"Mama," Malinda said, feeling faint as the room turned warm around her. "You have my mother's face."

The woman smiled. *"Nay, sweeting. She has mine."* Malinda took a step closer, and the woman backed away, her body beginning to fade. *"No, my love, not to me,"* she warned. *"Do not come to me."* Her form dissolved completely, but her voice remained, a distant song of faery on the air. *"Falconskeep. You must go to Falconskeep."*

Malinda rushed forward. "I don't understand!" But the woman was gone and the wall behind her as well. Brinlaw had disappeared. She was standing in the common hall of another castle, a great room bustling with strangers. A woman with curly red hair was mending a tiny gown beside the fire, and a small crowd of knights-at-arms in old-fashioned armor were gathered around the table, poring over a scroll, and servants hurried to and fro all around. Suddenly, the vision-woman ran past Malinda close enough to touch, a solid figure now. "My lady!" Malinda called, but the woman, intent on other business, didn't seem to hear, her face drawn with worry. "Wait!" But she disappeared through an archway, and as Malinda tried to follow, the room began to change. Tapestries crumbled and unraveled into tatters on the walls, and dust began to roll across the floor to cover the tables and chairs. "Wait!" she cried again, turning in a circle, but no one seemed to hear. The people were dissolving into dust as well, leaving her alone in a dark and silent ruin. One wall fell away completely with a horrible crash that lasted less than a moment, and she could see the stars glittering in the sky, hear the gentle roar of breakers in the distance—this was a castle by the sea. "Falconskeep," she whispered. "I am at Falconskeep."

Pushing through a door half-hanging on its hinges, she found a spiral stair, damp and slick with moss. Tiny vines grew through a network of cracks in the walls, and pale blue flowers bloomed in beams of moonlight. She touched a blossom, and the petals closed as if to shut her out. But something was calling to her, something she wanted was waiting at the top of the stairs.

The door at the top was still whole, but it was standing ajar, and firelight threw shadows through the crack. She pushed it open and found a cozy room with candles burning in sconces on the walls, and a tiny glow burning on the hearth. Moving inside, she saw a bed, fluffy and inviting with hangings of red and gold, and her heart beat faster. Someone was lying still beneath the blankets. "Tarquin . . ." Tears spilled down her cheeks. "Please, God, let it be true." He was sleeping, golden lashes shadowed on his skin, and she bent and kissed his mouth just as she had at Bruel. But this time when he woke, he reached to kiss her back, drew her closer. "Yes," she mumbled through a sob, tumbling into his arms.

He drew back after a moment, rose up on one elbow to look down on her. "It's all right," he teased with a smile, brushing her tears away. "I think I like this dream."

"So do I," she whispered, hardly daring to breathe. "I would rather die than wake." She ran her hands over his shoulders, found a bandage under his shirt. "But you're hurt."

"It's all right," he promised, sitting up. "It's almost healed." She reached up to kiss him again, and he lifted her into his lap, cradling her close, as if she weighed nothing at all. She nuzzled his throat, breathing in his scent—even his smell seemed real.

"I love you," she said softly as he kissed her hair. "I don't care what you are or what you might have done. I love you."

He laid her back on the bed and kissed her mouth. "I love you." He kissed her eyelids, kissed away her tears, and his hands were on her body, tender caresses, reverent and soft. She buried her hands in his hair, drew his mouth back down to hers for a deeper kiss, and his touch turned more insistent, burning her skin through her shift.

"I need you," she murmured, her lips against his cheek. "I need to feel you . . ." She fumbled with the lacings of his breeches, and he chuckled, kissed her quickly as he reached down to help. She slipped out of her shift as he undressed, then savored the heat of his bare skin as he came back to her arms. She kissed his shoulder just above the bandage, nuzzled his chest, and felt him harden against her—a tender threat against the softness of her thigh.

"Malinda," he murmured, hot breath against her throat. "I can't give you up . . . I can't . . . I thought I could, but I can't . . ."

"I'm yours," she promised, the pain in his voice breaking her heart. "Just yours, forever . . . Please come back to me." She felt him push inside her, and she gasped, her eyes falling closed while her body opened up to take him in. Her arms fell limp at her sides as her hips rose up to meet him, her blood replaced by liquid fire, and suddenly she heard the falcons, crying her name to the wind. "Tarquin . . ." She wrapped her arms around him, and he crushed her closer, reached under her to shift her closer, drive himself deeper inside. She cried out, sobbing triumph in release, and she felt the hot rush of him as well, her own waves cresting higher. She felt him kiss her, tasted his tongue in her mouth, but everything was fading; the dream was dissolving to mist.

"No!" she screamed, trying to hold on, and he was holding her as well, calling out her name, but she was falling. The world had vanished, and she was plummeting down into darkness. The salt-rot smell of rancid meat and ocean flooded her senses. Walls closed in around her in the dark, and she screamed, raw sound tearing at her throat . . .

Tarquin's dream was fading, the tower room at Falconskeep dissolving, Malinda turning to a phantom in his arms. He cried out, calling her name as she disappeared completely, but all he could hear were her screams of pain or terror, close enough at first to have come from his own throat, then distant, out of reach. The tower was above him—he was standing alone on the beach. Dawn was breaking in the east, and falcons circled above, shrieking like gulls in alarm. "Malinda!"

He turned back toward the cliffs and the tower beyond and saw the fabric of the sky being ripped apart, the dawning light rent open by the dark. The screams went on, his true love's voice entangled in the falcons' cries, and he began to run, mindless of his senses. A figure stood alone on the cliffs, a shadow edged in red against the rising sun, and in this dream-turned-nightmare Tarquin hated him as he had never hated any man before. "I will kill you!" he shouted as the demon rage burned through him, but his legs wouldn't carry him forward, the sand melting like mud beneath his feet, sucking him down.

"*Never mind*," a woman sighed as he sank into the void, the voice of a stranger overcome by grief. "*We are already too late.*" He saw a flash of golden hair, a glimpse of wide green eyes, then she was gone as well, another fistful of nothing in his grasp.

"No!" he roared. And then he was awake.

He opened his eyes in the dark, his heart pounding, slick with sweat in spite of the cold winter draft. He was in a cottage, a small, low-ceilinged room that smelled of sweet, dry grass and cooking. Somewhere in the dark, someone else was snoring.

"Hush now. You're still very ill, warrior."

He blinked, unsure of his sight. "Dreaming," he mumbled, his tongue now thick and dry. "I must still be dreaming." A woman sat beside his cot, the woman he had almost seen in the dream but hadn't been able to touch. Golden hair streamed over her shoulders, reaching almost to the floor, and she touched his brow with a hand as white as moonlight. She smiled Alista's smile, gazed down on him with Malinda's eyes, but she was a stranger. Behind her, a fire burned in the tiny fireplace . . . he could see straight through her form.

"You have to sleep again," she told him, her voice like a thought inside his own head. *"You will need all your great strength."* Her smile faded, and tears rose in her eyes. *"You must save Malinda. Bring her home to Falconskeep."*

"How?" He tried to reach for her, but she backed away, her image beginning to fade. Was this another of Malinda's spells, another demon conjured to find him and lure him back into her arms? So be it—he could think of no better place. She needed him; he could feel it. Even now, he could hear her calling out his name. Damned or not, he was hers, and somehow, she was in danger, a peril more evil than he was. He thought again of the figure on the cliff, the man he hadn't known but had hated with all his damned soul. "Tell me how to save her," he demanded, trying to sit up.

"I don't know." The vision was almost gone, fading into firelight. *"But I will come again."* He tried to follow, but he was still too weak with fever to stand. He collapsed back on the cot again as the world went black.

17

Malinda stood at the solar window, arms crossed, shivering in the cold. Snow was falling in the courtyard outside, but her chill came from inside, the memory of her nightmare like ice around her heart. She had been so happy, but then it all went wrong, and both of the visions were real. Tarquin did love her; she had touched him; she knew it. But the other was true as well, a vision of her fate. Even now, safe in her father's castle, she could feel the walls closing in around her, smell the stench of death like a mist that clung to her skin.

She had stood in just this spot with Tarquin not so very long ago. He had called her a witch and himself a demon. "Come back to me, Tarquin," she whispered, her forehead pressed to the freezing window frame. "If you are my demon, come and save me from this hell."

"Malinda?" Robert had come in without her hearing him; now he was close enough to touch her arm. "Malinda, what is wrong?"

"Nothing," she began, turning to him, making her lips form a smile to hide how sorely she was startled. But as his hand made contact, she stopped, swallowing a scream. A terrible feeling of horror flowed through her from his touch, a vision of evil so cold it took her breath away. Powerful emotions wracked her thoughts, shadows from inside his heart that only her faery self could touch. Hate . . . he hated . . . dancing, scaly figures with eyes of bluest fire. He saw them in his dreams; he feared them, feared the devils, felt their icy fingers on his heart, shriveling his soul . . . A man—he wanted a man. *Bring him to me! Vengeance* . . .

"Malinda?" he repeated, his face drawn with concern. For a moment, blue flame danced inside his eyes, and she thought she would have to scream aloud. Then just as quickly, the vision was gone. "Sweeting, answer me, please."

"I'm all right," she promised, her heart still pounding in her breast. She must be losing her mind—Robert Farrars was the sweetest man alive. He could never feel such hatred, could never be so cruel. Her faery self was playing tricks, conjuring new demons from the air. "I didn't sleep well last night," she explained, moving away from him, retreating from his touch to give herself a moment to recover. "I had nightmares."

"Poor child." He watched her sit down with her sewing, his blue eyes warm and fond, the perfect opposite of the flames she'd seen before. "You must tell me what you dreamed. If you hear it aloud, it will likely seem very silly—"

"No," she said quickly, softening her sharpness with a smile. "Forgive me, but I'd rather not remember."

"Of course," he nodded, smiling back. He settled on the floor at her feet, a gesture that belied his years and station.

He had always seemed so nice—'twas the only word that fit. She must have been mistaken. But had her faery senses ever lied to her before? "I hope what I mean to say will comfort you," he was going on. "But perhaps it will frighten you more." He plucked at her skirt as if he were the one who was anxious. "I have given this matter a great deal of thought, and I have come to a decision." He put a hand over hers, stopping her from sewing. "I want you to be my wife."

If he had suddenly lopped off her arm with his sword, she couldn't have been more shocked. "Robert . . . I don't know what to say," she began, utterly at a loss. She would have thought he was joking if he hadn't looked so serious. But how could he possibly want to marry her? She thought again of her vision—was this the peril it was meant to warn her of? No, she was simply distraught; she wasn't herself. This proposal was unexpected, but hardly diabolical.

"You needn't look so frightened," Robert laughed, seeming to echo her thoughts. "I know we are not of an age, but that doesn't mean I could never make you happy." He closed her hand in his. "Do you not wish to be happy?"

Good question, she thought but didn't say. It was true; Robert Farrars was a kind, rich man who would likely dote on her. She would never want for anything, and if she managed to produce him a son or two to replace the ones he'd lost, he would love her even more. Well, maybe not love, but care for her, anyway, and wasn't that what a noble maid was supposed to want? Wasn't that the perfect prospect that was supposed to make her happy? And she had to admit, happiness was not an emotion she could easily attach to Tarquin. He made her elated; he made her furious; he made her laugh and cry and scream and sigh in ecstasy, all in the space of a minute. But she loved him, even when she hated him. She wanted him, even when he cursed her very soul, and she knew he felt the same. She might not be happy with Tarquin, but she would always feel. She almost smiled. With Tarquin, she would never be safe.

"Robert, please don't think I'm not honored," she began, leaning down to him. "I know your worthiness, that you are a noble man."

"Please, I shall swoon," he teased.

"I'm sorry . . ."

"No, Malinda, don't be." He held her hand as he had a dozen times before in these weeks past, and she saw no vision of devils, felt no chill of frozen flame. He was the same dear Robert as always. He had comforted her when she thought she couldn't live; he had never been anything but kind. She wouldn't marry him, but she didn't want to hurt him, either. "I could hardly expect you to think of me as a lover," he was going on. "I'm much too old, much too boring, not nearly handsome enough. My wooing is nothing but pathetic. From the look on your face, I would say you never even noticed it."

"I thought you were my friend." She tightened her grip on his hand, made her mouth form a smile. "I felt very lucky to have you."

"I am your friend, Malinda, and that is all I ever wish to be, really. You're right; I'm no one's idea of a lover, not even my own." He raised her hand to his lips, but his kiss was barely a touch, an almost empty gesture. "I am no more in love with you than you are with me, so you needn't spare my feelings."

"Then why—?"

"Because I need a wife," he said, flat as an anvil, but his smile didn't dim. "You need a husband, someone who will care for you without being turned into an addle-pated fool every time you toss those golden curls."

"I'm glad to hear my charms leave you so cold," she retorted, her smile becoming more real. No hate-twisted villain could behave so naturally.

"On the contrary," he protested. "Your charms suit me quite well. I wish to pass them on to my sons."

"Ah, I see." Just as she suspected, it was a family he wanted, all the things fate had taken away returned. She could hardly blame him for that. In truth, if things had been different, she might have accepted him, might have let him make her the noblewoman the world assumed she was born to be. But she wasn't that woman, nor could she ever be; she was the faery of Falconskeep. "I am flattered, Robert," she answered him at last. "Any maid would be. You must know that."

"And yet you mean to refuse," he said, his smile not quite covering a darker look.

"Not at all." She looked down at their joined hands, her lips curving in a shy half smile that she knew would seem to hide sweet depths. She was a sorceress and an accomplished flirt besides. She could pretend for the moment. "But I can't marry without my father's permission, war or not. You are the most eligible of suitors, but my judgment is not my own. I have to wait for my father."

He touched her chin, turned her face up to his, and his own eyes were serious. "Are you quite certain, Malinda? Will you not tell me yes?"

He looked so sad, not for himself but for her. Bless him; he was such a man, sweet as any lamb but arrogant as a lion. Whichever maid accepted his suit would find herself lucky indeed. "Not yet, Robert," she said, putting his hand away. "I can't."

He smiled. "Then I must respect your wishes," he sighed as he straightened up. "All the more reason to pray this war ends soon."

"Amen." She left him with a curtsey, and the door slammed shut behind her, caught in a sudden draft. She shivered, turning around to face the closed door. She meant to slam many more than this—the door to home, the door to family, the door to everything she had ever known. She had known it when she woke this morning, and now she was even more sure. She couldn't stay at Brinlaw and wait for her nightmares to come true, for Eleanor to bully her into treason or Robert to make her a convenient wife. She thought again of the dream of being buried alive. *"You cannot stay here,"* the woman she had seen had warned. *"You must go to Falconskeep."* She remembered Tarquin's kiss, the tower bedroom by the sea. Somehow she had to escape the darkness and find her lover again; she knew it in her soul. Tarquin was her destiny, the bond that would make her free. "Forgive me, Robert," she murmured, turning away.

In the solar, Farrars sat in a chair by the hearth, his hands like deadly talons gripping the dragon-carved arms. "I tried to save you, dear one," he said softly, staring into the depths of the fire. "Always remember I tried."

Tarquin stood in the tiny clearing in front of the peasant cottage as the sun rose over the trees, his sword gripped tightly in his hands. His legs still felt a little shaky, but for the first time in weeks, his head felt clear. He had a purpose, a plan, born of a supernatural vision, but it was a plan nonetheless. He would surrender to the faeries who haunted his dreams, return to Malinda as she commanded. She was in danger; he would save her. He would take her to Falconskeep, just as the faery ghost had told him he must. And he would not be too late.

He focused on the stark, black shape of a tree across the clearing as he raised the sword above his head, moving slowly as time, feeling every muscle as it lengthened and curved in the motion. Bringing the sword around in an arc, he let his mind go blank until his entire body seemed to be an extension of the stroke, his blood flowing out through the blade. "Learn the motion perfectly in calm," Alista had taught him when he was just a child, the two of them alone at Falconskeep. "Then it is yours when you need it." Later in the east, he had watched the ritual movements of Arab and Asian warriors who had refined this simple principle into an art, rehearsing what seemed like hundreds of different elegant movements that refigured physical combat into a spiritual dance. Tarquin had never aspired to such technique. He might have been strong or even agile enough to master the movements themselves, but his mind and heart would never know the kind of calm that seemed to be required. His killing was passion, not prayer. But he had maintained his own discipline even so, and it had served him well. He could only hope it would help him now.

The sun was full and bright by the time he was done, and he was satisfied. His arms and shoulders ached from so much exercise after being idle so long, but he did not feel faint or sick. Real hunger made his stomach growl— another good sign. Putting his sword back into its sheath, he went back into the cottage.

"You look much better," his nursemaid said. She was a kindly woman, though little given to conversation. In the two weeks he had been in her house, they had passed only a handful of words. But now that he was up and moving, she apparently thought he must be ready to talk. "I think you must be going to live."

"I'm leaving," he answered, sitting down at the table as she brought his breakfast.

She just nodded, not surprised. "My boy said you were fighting ghosts."

Tarquin smiled, looking over at her son, a boy of twelve or so braiding a rope by the fire. "I was."

"He thinks you are a knight." She brought more water and another loaf of bread—another surprising kindness. Indeed, they had treated him very well for a stranger, and he was grateful. They could just as easily have left him to die. The house was by the river, but he hadn't noticed any fishing nets, no fields beyond a kitchen garden, but they seemed comfortable enough. "He wonders if you need a squire."

"I'm not a knight," Tarquin answered brusquely, turning his attention to his food.

"I think you are." The boy stood up, thin as a rail but sturdy, and his blue eyes were sharp with wit. "I think you travel under a curse."

Tarquin couldn't help but smile. "Someone has been telling you fairy tales."

"I could help you and your lady," the boy persisted. "Carry messages, or put villains off your trail, or fight, even." He stopped, blushing but determined. "I could."

"No doubt." He pushed back his chair to look the boy over again. "What makes you think I have a lady?"

The boy blushed harder. Had anyone told him his

name? If they had, he didn't remember. "You called her name in your illness," he answered. "You called it last night, too." He looked away from Tarquin's gaze. "I won't say her name aloud, for 'tis sacred to you, and I know her not."

"We've had troubadours too often in this house," his mother sighed. "When his father lived, he ran a boat on the river, and we had many visitors, travelers too poor for the inns."

"Her name isn't sacred; it's Malinda," Tarquin said, an idea beginning to form. "I'm Tarquin."

"I know," the boy answered, smiling all over his face. "I'm Bryon, in case you forgot."

"Bryon." It must be nearly Christmas, maybe after—no, not so late as that. But still, Davyd would be long gone. But if he was not, he wouldn't be far away. He could meet them at Falconskeep, help him spirit Malinda away from whatever it was that threatened her. He could go to Brinlaw and collect her, then meet Davyd at Falconskeep. "Where is your father's boat, Bryon?"

Alista stood in the bow of the ship, the English coastline growing larger in the distance. Willie stood beside her, her hand clasped tight in his. "Will we be in time, do you think?" she asked him as if he were a man full-grown instead of a little child. Her own visions of her mother and Malinda had continued to be confused, impossible to interpret. But Willie seemed so sure . . .

"I don't know," he answered.

"Don't know what?" his father asked, coming up behind them. Mark was with the captain, consulting him again on what they would likely find on the shore. Richard's troops had taken this beach more than once in the past year; they could be sailing straight into an enemy force. Will put his arms around Alista, pressing her close.

"Don't know if Malinda is all right," Willie answered, reaching for his father's hand.

"Malinda is fine," Will promised. "She will be home when we get there, and she'll tell us we're all very silly."

Alista smiled, leaning her head back against her husband's chest. He didn't believe his own words for a moment, but bless him, he sounded so sure. "May God will it so."

Tarquin stood on the tiny dock and watched Bryon puzzle over the strange Arabic characters of his message. "And he will be able to read this?" the boy asked doubtfully.

"Yes." He looked up at the sky, a prickle of apprehension crawling down his spine. The morning was half wasted; he should have been long gone. "Do you remember what I told you about the ship?"

"A falcon on the sail," Bryon nodded. "A man named Davyd who can read this gibberish."

Tarquin almost smiled, almost wished he were a knight in need of a squire. Perhaps Will would take Bryon on . . . but no. If he did as he intended, he doubted he would have the chance to recommend squires to Will Brinlaw. But what did he intend? If he took Malinda to Falconskeep, did he mean to stay with her there? He pushed the question away. He would make sure she was safe, then he would wrestle with his demon. After the visions he had seen, he couldn't do anything else.

"Master?" The boy tugged at his sleeve.

"Don't do that," Tarquin ordered, pulling away. "Don't call me that."

"Tarquin, then," he said with a shrug. "Your instructions—did I get them right?"

"You have them perfect." He ruffled the boy's hair, trying not to remember how it had felt to have Will touch him so, trying not to think about how the loss of Malinda would hurt him and Alista, too. He couldn't stop to think any more, or he'd lose his mind again, find himself back where he started, drunken and confused, and Malinda . . . He thought again of the end of the dream, the same horrific vision he had seen before on the road, the walls closing in, the stench of the dead left to rot. "I have to go," he muttered, more to himself than the boy.

"How long should I wait?" Bryon asked him, following him to his horse. "For this Davyd, I mean?"

"Don't wait at all," Tarquin said, swinging into the saddle. "If the ship isn't there when you get there, come straight back home to your mother. If he's not there, he'll be long gone."

"Godspeed, Tarquin!" the boy called as the horse wheeled around, his hand on his heart in a gesture from a courtier's romance. "I swear I shall not fail!"

Tarquin just nodded, embarrassed and amused. Giving the boy a final wave, he rode away toward Brinlaw.

Malinda found Lisbet making candles in the drafty second hall, the only room in the castle with a fire big enough for the task that wasn't already full of people. "Eleanor must never sleep, nor her entourage either," she informed Malinda as she came through the arch. "We've used more candles in the past month than we'd normally use in a year."

"We're going to Falconskeep," Malinda answered. "Tonight, as soon as it's safe to slip out."

"All right," Lisbet smiled, the candles quite forgotten. "Just tell me what to do."

From his perch in the gallery above, Eleanor's minstrel, Gaston, watched the lady and her handmaid hurry back out through the arch, a bemused smile on his face. He'd been quite curious about this Malinda ever since the night she'd managed to dodge him and his royal summons. Now she meant to slip away again. Taking up the lute he'd brought to this secluded spot to practice, he went off in search of his queen.

18

ᕕ᠐ᕗ

*M*alinda and Lisbet were packed and ready, waiting only for the midnight bells, when a knock came at the door. "Good evening, Lady Malinda," the minstrel said when she opened the bedroom door. He made a sweeping bow that almost hid his flash of mocking grin. "Her Majesty the Queen wishes to see you."

"At this hour?" Malinda asked, a sinking feeling in her stomach. "I hardly think—"

"But you are dressed, my lady," the minstrel pointed out. "And Her Majesty insists."

"Going somewhere?" Eleanor asked in acid tones as soon as they walked through the door, hardly waiting for the minstrel to retire.

"Forgive me, Majesty," Malinda began. "You have to understand—"

"How dare you?" Eleanor hissed, obviously struggling to keep her voice below a shriek. "How dare you even think to leave me here?"

"Why should she not?" Lisbet demanded, less careful in

her rage. "Why should she care what becomes of you? 'Tis you who have put her in this fix."

"Harlot!" Eleanor gasped.

"Both of you, be quiet," Malinda ordered. "You'll wake the whole castle in a moment." Her mind was racing, searching out her course. She had to go and quickly; that much was already decided. If she refused to help the Queen escape as well, Eleanor would make certain she was caught. So the Queen would have to have her way after all, and worries over treason could go hang. "Do you know where you will go if you escape?" she asked the older woman. "Have you friends to help you, give you horses and protection?"

"All that we could wish," Eleanor answered, the gleam of triumph in her eyes.

"Then I will help you," Malinda said. "But you must do exactly as I say."

Later she stood with hands outstretched, the Falconskeep book laid open on the table. The castle was quiet— "Quiet as the grave," Lisbet whispered as she clasped Malinda's hand. A tiny fire was lit in a bowl on the table, two candles burned in the windowsill, and the hearth was a pile of glowing embers; otherwise the room was dark. Shadows danced across the faces of her companions, Eleanor on her right, Lisbet on her left, and the curling lines of faery text seemed to dance as well, writhing on the page. This spell was one of the oldest in the book, but the writing was as starkly black as if it had been penned that moment—*a cloak which cannot fail.* Far more complicated than an ordinary glamour, it would stay intact no matter what they touched and would work as well for the others as it did for her, a conjure rather than faery. A dragon was painted on the table, twisted around the bowl of flame. "Are we ready?" she asked softly, the sound of her voice strange and hollow in her ears. "Are we sure?"

Lisbet squeezed her hand, a wry little smile on her face belied by the fear in her eyes. "Now or never," she murmured back, stifling a nervous giggle. They had determined that Lisbet would go first, then the Queen, then Malinda herself.

"We trust you, Malinda," Eleanor said more calmly, taking her other hand. "We put ourselves in your hands."

"And in yours, Majesty," Malinda answered with a nod. She closed her eyes and breathed in deeply, filling her lungs with the smoke from the magic fire. In truth, most of it was rubbish—incense and sweet-smelling herbs combined with the necessary components to make a better show. If the Queen wanted sorcery, sorcery she would have. But the illusion helped Malinda as well, gave her a feeling of control. Releasing Eleanor to take Lisbet's other hand, she closed her eyes, letting her mind go blank. She was a vessel; she was mystic; she was faery . . . In this moment, the power was hers. "Breathe in," she told her friend, squeezing her hands for comfort. "Don't be afraid."

"I'm not," Lisbet promised, barely a tremble in her voice.

Malinda smiled, her eyes still gently shut. "Good." A distant rumble of thunder seemed to drift in from the window. Thunder in December? Part of the magic, perhaps. She prayed it wouldn't wake the guard. She whispered a word in faery, and the flames shot up from the bowl in a shower of sparks, more theatrics to impress the Queen, and she let her head fall back. "Say what I say, Lisbet. Repeat the words after me."

"I don't know how to say them," Lisbet protested, her hands going cold.

"It's all right," Malinda promised, suddenly so calm she thought she might drift off to sleep. "Just let them come . . ." She seemed to hear music, flutes sweeter than any ever played in royal courts, and the ancient incantation spilled out of her in song. *"My body is a burden,"* she sang in faery words.

"My body is a burden," Lisbet sang back, barely stumbling over the lilt, singing back each line as it came.

"Melt me into air . . ."
"Leave me myself, but hide me from men's eyes . . ."
"Hide me from my sisters . . ."
"My children's eyes will seek for me in vain . . ."
"I will be as the wind, free to cover all the earth."

"No!" Eleanor suddenly grabbed Malinda's arm as if to hold her fast, and the faery woman opened her eyes, snapped back into solid form. But Lisbet had disappeared. "Holy Christ," the Queen muttered, her fingers clinging tight.

"May He forgive and never be offended," Malinda answered with a catlike smile. "You are an old enchantress, Majesty, but I am a young one."

"Chérie, you are indeed," Eleanor answered as she slowly let her go, her smile nearly as wide. "Shall we continue?"

"Hurry up," Lisbet's voice complained, so unexpected the other women laughed. "I'm freezing, and I think I might be sick."

"Don't, or you'll turn into a toad," Malinda teased. "It's all right, I promise. In an hour, you'll be yourself again." She held out her hand to Eleanor. "So I think we'd better hurry."

"One hour," Eleanor sighed, taking Malinda's hand.

The thunder growled as she closed her eyes again, an echo to her song. *"My body is a burden . . ."*

Suddenly the door burst open with a rush of wind and light. The fire in the bowl leapt up, and Eleanor turned with a shriek of anger to glare at Farrars with half a dozen men behind him. "How dare you?" the Queen demanded as they rushed into the room.

"How dare we, Majesty?" Two of the men laid hold of Malinda and dragged her back from the table, but Farrars was still focused on the Queen. "What manner of daring is this?"

"Take care, Robert," Eleanor warned, a haughty laugh in her voice. "This power may be more insidious than yours."

"Stop it," Malinda demanded, struggling to free herself from the guardsmen's grip. Lightning flashed outside the window, and another crack of thunder shook the castle. "Let me go—"

"What is this?" Farrars looked down at the table, fire and book and dragon curled around all, and he drew back as if the dragon were real, his honest-looking face twisted in horror. "What are you—?"

"Show him, Malinda," Eleanor urged, laughing in earnest. "Turn his men into pigs—"

"I can't—" The storm was raging harder, the lightning seeming to rip through her as it struck, her head snapping back as she screamed. The men who held her dropped her arms and leapt back as if they thought she might burst into flame.

"Hold her!" Farrars ordered, pale as milk with fury.

"If you dare," Eleanor cried, throwing back the drapes as if to call the storm inside.

Malinda thought her skin must be splitting; she felt herself ripping apart. Her vision was layered, room on top of room, moment on top of moment. On the bed, her mother raised an infant into the air, Malinda herself, naked and crowing with joy, and the real Malinda cried out to her, tried to reach past the men who would hold her. "Mama, please!" But the guards were too strong—strangers, none of them a man she knew. Jerked around in their grip, she seemed to be falling, falling forever into the dark, and she screamed, felt icy water rising all around her, sucking her down, a woman's voice crooning comfort but cold, so cold . . .

"Hold her still," Farrars demanded, sweeping the bowl of fire to the floor, stomping out the flames under his boot. "Tell me what you've done, Malinda." He moved closer as one of the men caught her hair in his fist, yanked her head back against his shoulder.

"She is a sorceress," Eleanor said. "She will see you damned—"

"Quiet!" he roared, turning on the older woman. "Or you will pay her price." Eleanor blanched, and Malinda began to laugh . . . Her Majesty, the Queen. She could see her own face in Eleanor's mirror, another vision laid over what was real. She had seen all this before . . . Blanche had seen.

"Answer me, Malinda," Farrars ordered, grabbing her by the throat. "Tell me what you have done." Blue flames danced inside his eyes, and she laughed harder. All the pieces had been there, the truth laid out for her, but she had been too stupid, too arrogant to see. A name came into her mind as if communicated from his angry touch—Tarquin FitzBruel. Tarquin was the man he hated, the man he wanted to kill. Suddenly it all made terrible sense, and her laughter rose another pitch. Somehow they were connected, a perfect triangle of pain, and the power to put it right had been in her hands all along. But she had been too selfish, and now it was too late. "Tell me!" he demanded, his grip tightening for one agonizing moment before he let her go.

"You see, do you not?" she rasped. "You must, for I see you."

His eyes widened, his mouth falling open in shock. "Do you indeed?" He took up the book, looked down at the text he couldn't read. "Demonology . . ."

"Idiot," she retorted. "You wouldn't know a demon—"

"Silence!" He took the book and flung it in the fire.

"No!" She could still see her face in the mirror, but it wasn't hers. Another woman seemed to stand in her place, her mouth agape with horror—the woman from her visions. When she screamed, the other screamed as well, their voices intertwined as the mirror shattered, glass flying in every direction. The window shattered as well, the candles flying, wild light lost in the midst of the lightning. Eleanor was screaming as well, falling to the floor, but Malinda couldn't break free, couldn't save her magic. The book burst into flame as if it had been soaked in pitch, flames leaping and curling out of the hearth, and Malinda lunged for it, her arms nearly torn from their sockets as she tried to tear out of her captors' grip. "*Forgive me,*" she wept in faery-song. "*Give me pardon, sisters—free me to avenge us—*"

Farrars raised his fist and struck Malinda across the brow, knocking her unconscious, silencing her incantation. "Take her," he told the men, shaking to the marrow of his bones.

"Her mother is as powerful as she is," Eleanor warned as the girl was carried out. "Her father is more powerful than you."

"They will never know." He turned a threatening step toward her, the look in his eyes unmistakable. "Will they?"

The Queen laughed, but most of the humor was gone. "Don't you think they'll notice when they come home and she's not here?"

"If they come home." He turned away, watched the guards that were left put out the fire the candles had made in the drapes. "She ran away . . . I did my best to find her." He looked back at the Queen. "You will be my witness."

"I will not—"

"You will be my witness, or Henry will know his wife is using black magic against him," he cut her off. "The priests would love that, don't you think? And Henry . . . with you at the stake, he could marry Alice and make peace with the Pope in a single, righteous stroke. Malinda Brinlaw was only an innocent child, taken in by you. She certainly looked the part." He smiled, enjoying the fear in her eyes. "She might even have been so horrified by what you made her do she took her own life. Let Brinlaw roar for your blood a little as well. All in all, a most satisfying ending to the saga of your life, don't you think?"

Eleanor took a deep breath, took a step back in her mind. Farrars wasn't bluffing; she had schemed with him before. But she had been in worse corners than this one many times; she would come out all right. She might even save Malinda, if she could be clever enough. "So what am I to say, Robert?" She seated herself in the only chair left standing, calm by force of will. "Why did she run away? To escape your marriage proposal?"

"Why not?" he answered. "To be with her traitorous lover—that will play rather well, I think."

"Lover?" Eleanor echoed, feigning shock. "And who might that be, pray?"

"Never you mind," he ordered. "Or perhaps you should know—she made you her confidante. She did admire you so."

"Does admire me," she corrected. "Let's not strangle her just yet."

He only smiled—not a good sign. "The man's name is Tarquin—a nobody, one of Brinlaw's retainers."

"The routier," she nodded, surprised but hiding it. Little Malinda had a more adventurous spirit than even she had known. "And what is your interest—?"

"I think that will do," he cut her off, a deadly light in his eyes that silenced her better than words. "I may not need you at all, but if I do, that will be enough. She didn't want to marry me; she ran away to be with Tarquin. She told you what she intended, and you tried to stop her, but she wouldn't be dissuaded."

"In spite of my great influence." She nodded. There was something he was missing. Someone he hadn't considered. "I could even write a letter to that effect, expressing my regret. Her father hates my soul, but her mother might appreciate the gesture. I'm a mother myself, after all."

"So 'tis rumored." His eyes narrowed, and she made her expression placid, the beautiful mask that might be showing cracks but still gave nothing away. "Write the letter," he ordered. "Then have this mess swept up."

She nodded graciously, and he retired, leaving only one guard. "Tell me, sirrah, do you read and write?" she asked this man, taking out vellum and ink.

"No, Majesty," he said, stone-faced at the door.

"Very well, then," she sighed, dipping her stylus herself.

Lisbet got up from her crouch in the corner, too furious to be afraid. She had tried several times to duck out the door, follow Malinda wherever the bastard might have sent her, but every time she tried, another one of those oafs got in the way. And Eleanor—Malinda had risked her life to help her, and she was going to tell lies—? But wait . . . the Queen was up to something. She crept closer to the table, close enough to see the page where Eleanor was writing. Yes! *Lisbet,* she had written. *Be ready. I will distract him in a moment, and you can escape. Go to Brinlaw; tell him everything. There are jewels and money sewn into my cloak; use them. I will try to find out where he's taken her; I will get word to Phillipe.*

If you're reading this, give me some sign.

Lisbet looked around frantically. What was she supposed to do? A candle had been set on the desk, just beside Eleanor's wrist. Glancing once at the guard to see if he was watching, she knocked the candle over, splashing hot wax on the Queen.

"God's blood!" Eleanor cried, leaping up as flames caught her letter and raced across the desk. The guard ran to her aid, and Lisbet ducked past him, touching the older woman's hand as she passed. Eleanor's head whipped around for a moment, then she went back to the chaos of the moment. "Hurry, before we all go up in ashes," she snapped, covering the sound of the door snapping open and shut.

Lisbet's first thought was to run from the castle as quickly as her feet would carry her, but she made herself slow down. Malinda had said the spell was good for an hour; she should still have several minutes left. Perhaps Malinda was still in the castle somewhere, but where?

Rufus, she thought, turning back and running for the room she and Malinda shared, her soft boots almost soundless on the stones.

The hawk was frantic. Malinda had tethered him to his perch for fear his cries would give them away. "She didn't want to leave you," Lisbet whispered, trying to approach without upsetting him even more. He was trying to fly, beating the air with his wings, and when she reached for him, his talons flashed toward her face as if he saw her plain as day. "Oh, no." She looked back at the mirror, but there was no reflection; she was still invisible. But Rufus was part of the magic as well; maybe such spells didn't work on him. "You have to let me help you," she pleaded. "And shut up, for pity's sake. If we wake the whole castle, we'll never have time to catch up and save her." This seemed to work; he quieted at once. "Now I'm going to let you go . . . I hope." She worked at the leather bindings with trembling fingers—he had tightened the knots fighting to be free. "Oh bollocks . . ." She took out her tiny dagger and slashed the tether, and the hawk sprang free, sweeping over her head so close she felt his feathers brush her hair. He flew to the window, beat his wings against the shutter as if to batter himself to pieces if she didn't let him free. "But I need you," she protested. "You can't just fly away." She put up her arm, trying to coax him back, but it was useless. "All right, if you must." She lifted the latch and pulled the shutter back, and he soared free, circling up into the night. "Find her, then," she whispered, watching as he disappeared. "I'm going to find Tarquin."

19

Malinda felt as though she were drowning, swimming back to the surface for the thousandth time only to sink again. Her head was still sore from the blow from Robert's fist, but surely if that had been enough to make her still unconscious, she would have died by now. No, there was something more. She was drunk and sick as well; she must have been drugged. The world seemed to be rocking back and forth like a careless cradle . . . A carriage—she was in a carriage. She had been in a kind of trance . . . Perhaps she had been dreaming . . . She had been trying to escape, but she had been caught, and the world had split in pieces. Tarquin . . . Farrars hated Tarquin. Had he said as much? He had said so many things—terrible things. He had called her a witch, and he had struck her. But had he said anything about Tarquin? Not at Brinlaw. She had been this way so long, and she could hear them talking, the men who had taken her, talking to each other, talking to Farrars. Farrars was with her. Farrars was taking her away.

Her hands and feet were bound, she realized, and she

was gagged and blind. Something was over her head. She could rock her head a bit and wiggle her fingers, but otherwise she could barely move. Why should she be so bound, as if she were some dangerous . . . oh yes. She *was* dangerous; she had frightened them. The lightning had come, and all the glass had broken. She had seen someone else in the mirror on Eleanor's wall—her mother's wall, for that room belonged to her mother. She had seen her mother, too. She closed her eyes more tightly, trying to push some of the thoughts back so she could sort them out. The woman in the mirror . . . she wasn't real, or wasn't solid. No one else had seen her but Malinda. She was Blanche, Malinda's grandmother—the faery who had turned into a falcon. They had been as one, two halves of the same woman, and together they had shattered the glass. But it hadn't helped. She had been so angry—her book! They had taken her book and thrown it in the fire! Tears she hadn't yet shed for herself slid down her cheeks for the book. Mama had trusted her, and she had lost it, lost herself as well. Mama . . . would anyone ever know what happened? Would Mama ever find her? Tarquin . . . Tarquin was coming after her, he had to be, but how would he know where to look? She didn't even know herself. What did Farrars mean to do to her? She thought of his eyes, the hatred and fear she had seen in him when he knew she could do magic. And Tarquin . . . he hated him. She had known it when he hit her, had felt Tarquin in his rage. He had hurt her as he longed to hurt Tarquin. But Tarquin would hurt him . . . He was coming. He had to be coming; otherwise, she was lost.

Her heart beat faster, and she tried again to move, but it was hopeless. She was tied down to something, something hard under the soft mattress where she lay. Panic raced through her like ice, and she thought she was going to be sick. She had to get away. She tried to cry out, but the gag was too tight, and her mouth was too dry. All that would come out was a muffled, rasping squeak. *Help me,* she thought desperately. *Help me, someone, please.* Tarquin had been with her in the nightmare; he had known she was afraid. She had heard him calling out to her as she fell into the darkness, had known he was trying to save her. *Tarquin!* she screamed inside her mind. *Tarquin, I am here!*

A cry like the sound she longed to make came to her from a distance, the scream of a falcon in flight. Rufus . . . Rufus was with her. A kind of fatal calm settled over her, made her drift back into a faint. At least she wasn't alone.

Lisbet was jostled awake by a rough shake. "We're here, boy," the freeman farmer said, slapping the side of the wagon. "Help me see to the horses."

She got up and climbed over the side, trying to look like someone who did this sort of thing every day of her life, blinking in the failing sun. It was almost night again already; she must have slept for hours. At least she and Malinda had managed to have the foresight to pack some masculine clothes for their ill-fated little adventure. She had found their bundles and Eleanor's cloak, changed her clothes as soon as she could see herself to do it, and transferred the Queen's little treasure trove to a pocket inside her own tunic. Then she had run as far and fast as she could. Just after dawn, this farmer had come along, carrying a load of home-brewed mead to town, and offered her a ride in exchange for her help at the inns. So now all she had to do was hoist kegs that weighed roughly half as much as she did without giving away her sex, figure out what town she was in, and try to find someone who knew something about the whereabouts of Tarquin. Go to Lord Brinlaw, Eleanor had advised, and it was good advice. She could have gone to her own father as well—at least she knew the way. But Malinda had believed that Tarquin was on his way back to Brinlaw Castle. If that was true, he could be closer.

"Climb back up," the farmer scolded, looking at her as if he thought her daft. "Toss one down."

"Oh . . . aye," she answered, trying to lower her voice without sounding utterly ridiculous. Her brother, Paul, was roughly the age she looked as a boy; she should just try to think of him. He had delivered her at Brinlaw more than a week ago; he'd be home at Bruel again by now, home with Mama and Papa. Would she ever see any of them again? She pushed the question out of her mind. "Any of these?" she asked, eyeing the kegs.

"Aye, lad," the farmer said with exaggerated patience. "Any one will do."

"Right." She grabbed hold of the nearest keg, game to try, but it was hopeless. The thing felt as if it were nailed to the one beneath it. She should just give it up, tell the truth—but no. If this good man knew she was a woman traveling alone, he would want to know why, would think she was either a runaway servant or worse. She'd find herself in front of a sheriff before the sun finished setting, and then where would Malinda be? She thought again of her friend falling lifeless to the floor, the look of hatred in Farrars' face as he struck her. "Be ready," she advised, leaning her shoulder to the job. Giving a mighty heave, she sent it rolling down into its maker's arms.

"Thank ye kindly," the farmer laughed. "Now go inside and have yourself a bite."

That sounded like an excellent idea, she suddenly realized, still rather proud of herself. She had been too frantic that morning to eat anything from the bundle of supplies, and the bundle had been too heavy to carry, so she'd just left it like a fool. Food sounded very good indeed.

The inn was packed with men, very few of the sort to which she was accustomed. Keeping her head down and trying not to look at anybody, she made her way to a corner and sat down. "It's all right, puppy," a girl about her own age in a dirty apron said, plopping down a trencher before her. "You'll be all right."

"I hope so," Lisbet answered, digging in with boyish spirit, table manners be damned.

"Slow down, there," the other girl laughed. "Some of that meat might be turned; you want to give it a moment going down."

"I'll risk it," Lisbet said bravely, but her stomach did a flip-flop nonetheless.

"What's your name, dearie?" She leaned across to fill a mug, exposing an alarming expanse of bosom, and Lisbet almost laughed. *Please God,* she prayed, *may I live to tell my papa about this.*

"Paul," she said aloud.

"Well, Paul, what brings you here?" She set the mug down, and Lisbet took a sip—the worst concoction she'd ever tasted in her life, so bad she couldn't help but sputter. "Seeing the world?"

"Looking for someone." She looked around the room at her companions with an inward sigh. Like it or not, this was just the sort of place where Tarquin might have been seen. "Have you seen a man named Tarquin Fitz-Bruel?"

"Who wants to know?" a drunken slur demanded. A bearded monster turned around from a nearby table to glare down at her, and the serving wench made herself scarce. "What is this, an infant?" he went on, standing up to tower over her. "What's the password, boy?"

"I don't . . . What do you mean?" Lisbet stammered, terrified. Should she stand up and try to bluff her way out of this? Should she sit where she was and hope he went away? Should she try to make a run for it? None of her options seemed a sure thing at the moment, but she had to make up her mind.

"If you're looking for FitzBruel, you ought to be one of us," the man said, planting a fist on the table on either side of her, neatly caging her in. "And if you're one of us, you ought to know the password."

"And if you are one of us, you ought to shut your mouth," another voice said, much more calmly but with an accent so thick the words were barely English at all. A giant in a long, black cloak loomed behind the man who threatened her, his hood pulled low to hide his face. For a moment, her heart leapt up—it was Tarquin! But no, this man was as tall, maybe taller, but not so broad at the shoulders, and that accent wasn't a fake. "This boy is my servant. Paul, wait for me outside," he ordered, jerking his head toward the door.

"Who are you, then?" the other man demanded, turning his attention from Lisbet to the other man but not quite moving away.

"The light of the cross," the man said, drawing his sword. "Is that not the password?" Before the other brigand could react, he thrust the sword through his belly, a single, clean stab that snuffed his life out like a candle. "Tell his lordship I saved him some trouble," he said, tossing a handful of coins on the table in front of the other man's companions, his sword still sticky with blood. "Come, Paul." Before Lisbet could stop staring at the dead man and answer, he had grabbed her by the collar and was dragging her toward the door.

Things were bad before, but this was worse. "Let me go," she ordered, trying to wrest herself free, and he let go of her collar to grab her arm instead. "Whatever your quarrel was with that man, I don't know it. I'm grateful—"

"Shut up, girl, and keep walking," he said tersely. "I am a friend."

"I know my friends," she muttered back, the blood racing to her cheeks, her heart pounding harder. They had reached the door. No one looked as if they meant to follow. What would he do to her once he had her outside?

"I'm pleased to hear you know something," he retorted. "My name is Davyd. I am Tarquin's friend."

Davyd . . . Tarquin had mentioned him, the infidel who'd kept his ship while he came home. She looked up and saw his face under the hood, half expecting a demon. He was quite dark, but he was handsome. It was strange; she felt as if she'd seen him before. She almost smiled at him. But was he really Tarquin's friend? "I don't—" He jerked her through the door, pushed her ahead of him into the courtyard. "What was he talking—?"

"Please, be quiet," he ordered, wiping off his sword. "Are you alone?"

"Yes—no—why do you—?"

"That man was not alone, and his friends don't know

me," he said, leaning so close she could smell his breath, sweeter than hers at the moment. "I know their code, so they think I might be one of them, but they aren't sure, and they did know the man I killed. In a moment, they will have put their ruined brains together enough to figure out I might be worth killing." She took a step back, and he straightened up. "So you have a choice," he said with a wry smile. "You can run with me, or you can wait for them."

"Or I can run by myself," she pointed out, taking another step back.

"You can," he agreed, heading for the stables. "But that would not be wise." She chased him into the stable, watched him throw a saddle over his shoulder without bothering to put it on the horse he'd led out of the stall. "Do you have a horse?"

"No," she admitted. "I don't have—"

"Then come on." He grabbed her around the waist and tossed her onto the horse's back. "You can explain who you are on the way." He swung up before her in a single leap as if he'd never heard of stirrups, the heavy saddle still thrown over his shoulder.

"Lisbet," she answered, clinging to his back. Sure enough, the men who'd been with the dead man had come out of the inn, were standing in the courtyard looking stupid and enraged. Davyd clucked to the horse, and she buried her face in his shoulder, silently mouthing a prayer as he rode through them like a pack of dogs. She wasn't any safer, but at least she wasn't alone.

Malinda woke again as she was being lifted from the carriage, strong arms underneath her hoisting her up. She could smell the sea, and her blood froze. Her dream, this was her dream. She struggled, and the arms tightened. "Careful, princess," an unfamiliar voice said, not unkindly. "You don't want to be dropped on these rocks." She went limp again, trying to breathe, trying not to panic. The bag over her head was hot and close, clinging to her face, and she wanted to scream, but she knew all that would come out was a whimper. Farrars could be right beside her; she'd die indeed before she would whimper for him.

Finally the man set her down, upright in a chair but still swaddled and bound. "Food?" a voice suggested.

"No." Farrars' voice, cold as death. "Is she secure?"

"She's going nowhere. Shall I stay?"

"Outside. I'll need you when I'm done."

A long pause, tension in the air. Then, finally, resignation. "As you wish, my lord."

She concentrated, willing herself to stay calm, to think of a way out of this. She was a sorceress. She had brought down lightning to save her beloved; surely she could think of some way to save herself. But she was too frightened, too sick. Nothing like this had ever happened to her; she had never dreamed of such a thing. *I want to wake up,* she thought, the words like a chant in her mind. *Please, just let me wake up from this nightmare.* But she was not asleep.

"He thinks you are truly a princess," Farrars' voice suddenly spoke. "He thinks me capable of anything, apparently." A touch on her shoulder; she flinched away. "But that is all to the good. I haven't your father's way with soldiers; fear is very useful to me." The hand slipped under the sack, caressed the ends of her hair, the skin at the base of her throat. "But you need never have feared me, Malinda. I would have made you happy, just as I promised." Why was he talking if he wouldn't let her speak? "I had no idea," he went on. "Even now, I hesitate to look on your face, for I know it will break my heart."

How could she ever have trusted this monster? All his tenderness, his friendship—it was poison to her now. She couldn't believe she ever thought it was real. "When I saw what you were, I couldn't believe my eyes." He sounded almost tearful! She wanted to kill him, wanted to tear out his heart with her hands.

Suddenly the sack was ripped off, and she could see, and a stench that had been in the background overwhelmed everything else. They were in a ruined room of stone lit with torches, the ceiling broken in large patches to reveal cold starlight above. Hanging in chains on the wall directly before her was a corpse, or what was left of it, a man flayed and split open like a carcass of beef. A tiny sound escaped her, and Farrars touched her hair. "Never fear, my dear one. He cannot hurt you now," he soothed. "Or is it that you grieve?" He squatted beside her, his cheek almost touching her own. "Either way, I thought you should see what became of your Tarquin FitzBruel."

He's lying, she thought, desperate to be sure. *Tarquin is alive, or I would know. He is mine; I saw him.* "In truth, Malinda, I never realized what he meant to you," Farrars was saying. "I never thought you would care, thought he was only my concern. But a little bird tells me that's not so, that you love him. That you want to marry him." He stood up. "As you can see, that won't be possible. Forgive me, dearest, I would have given you the world, but not that." He looked her in the face for the first time, and she shuddered at the hatred in his eyes. "Not witchcraft, and not that." She tried to shout past the gag, to tell him she wasn't a witch, to tell him he was a liar, but he turned his face away. "Stop it . . . I'm not ready to hear you speak. You're not ready." He touched the gag on her mouth, and she fell silent, hoping he would stop. "You think you knew him, Malinda, but you did not. You could not have loved him if you knew, unless your soul is damned indeed. You did not know he killed my son." His fingertips traced the line of her jaw, but his eyes were focused far away. "He was a saint, my son—a priest, or would have been. But when his brother was killed, that was no longer possible. I had no choice; Henry could not be allowed to stay unquestioned on his throne, not after what he had done. My son was dutiful, Malinda. Unlike you, he knew how to do as he was told. He went to the Holy Land, as he was bidden, and beyond, a priest in the armor of a soldier, and he would have triumphed. But he was murdered before his quest was half begun." He grabbed her chin, snapped her head back to look into her eyes. "So for the sake of his innocent soul, his murderer must . . . your Tarquin had to die."

He almost slipped, she thought, a tiny ray of triumph. He almost told me Tarquin still lives, that this monstrosity isn't him. He still wants him dead. He still means to kill him, but he hasn't managed it yet. "And now you," he continued, his tone returning to its deadly calm. "What am I to do with you?" She narrowed her eyes, glaring pure hate, and he smiled. "Would you care to defend yourself?" He took a dagger and cut the leather strap that held the gag in place. She gasped, her mouth so dry and sore she couldn't catch her breath. "So tell me. Why were you practicing witchcraft? What became of your friend Lisbet?"

"I am not a witch," she finally managed to answer. She swallowed hard, willing her thirsty throat to make words, to let her sound brave. "Lisbet . . . is gone. You'll never find her, no more than you'll find Tarquin."

"Tarquin is found," he smiled, a mockery of the smile she'd thought she knew. "Lisbet will be found. It is you who are lost." He took the knife he'd used to cut her gag and laid it in the fire that burned in a nearby brazier. "I want to save you, Malinda, save your soul. I cannot believe this is all your fault. But you have to help me." He touched her cheek with the back of his hand. "Will you confess your fault? Will you let me cleanse your soul?"

"As if you could," she said scornfully. "That power is of Christ—"

"And I will be His agent," he answered.

"Blasphemer—"

He slapped her hard across the face, and her soul seemed to shrink inside her breast. No one had ever struck her before, and now he had done it twice. "You may kill me," she said, swallowing the tremor in her voice. "But I promise you my father will kill you, or my brother, or—"

"Or your dead lover?" he cut her off. "I think not. As for your father, he will count himself fortunate if he escapes the stake himself." He took the knife out of the fire, his leather glove steaming from the heat, and held it in front of her eyes. The handle was a crucifix, a holy and unholy thing, Christ's agony turned to an instrument of mortal death. "This belonged to my son," he said. "He died with it clutched in his hand, trying in vain to defend himself. It was his prized possession." With his free hand, he unlaced the shirt she wore, his touch as delicate as a maid's. "Confess, Malinda. Confess your evil. Let it go—it cannot save you now. But if you renounce it, your soul will go to God."

"God will receive my soul," she answered, fearful but sure. "I have no evil to confess—" He pressed the dagger to her breast, and she screamed, shock as devastating as the pain and the smell of her burning flesh. "Stop it," she said breathlessly as he took the brand away, tears streaming down her cheeks.

"Yes." His own face was pale, his eyes haunted. He lifted the heartstone in his palm, the stone dull, pinkish gray. "Yes, there is no hope." He jerked the chain until it broke.

"Give that back!" she demanded, a whole new fear racing through her.

"Perhaps you will see your error on your own," he said, opening a trapdoor in the floor. "You will have time, I fear."

"What is that?" He went and called the other man back in. "What are you doing?" she demanded, her voice rising in panic. She could hear screaming, cries of agony like an echo in her head, and she struggled in her bonds, kicked out at the man as he tried to pick her up. "Leave me! Let me go!"

"That's the general idea," Farrars said sadly. "Good-bye, Malinda."

He turned away as the other man heaved her over his shoulder and carried her to the trap. She thrashed with all her might, but her hands and feet were still tied; she couldn't grab on, couldn't make a fist or even scratch. She bit him hard on the side of the neck as he shifted her around, but it was no use. "Sorry, princess," he muttered, dropping her into the hole.

"No!" She seemed to fall forever, into the screaming dark.

20

Lisbet awoke to the sound of shouting, men greeting one another in a language she didn't understand. She raised her head, slipping precariously on the back of the horse. For a moment, she wasn't quite sure where she was. "It's all right," Davyd said, catching her arm still entwined around his waist. "We're home."

"What?" She looked past him to the beach where half a dozen men were gathered, all of them smiling, most of them coming toward them. "What is this?" Then she saw the ship. The falcon sail was down, and it was docked some distance away, but she knew it just the same. "That is Tarquin's ship."

"Of course." He slid down and helped her down as well. "Come and sit. We need to talk more about your friend."

"We don't need to talk about her, we need to save her," Lisbet insisted, following him to the camp and ignoring the grins of the crew. "I have to find Tarquin—"

"As I told you last night, so do I," Davyd answered. He motioned her to a cushion by the fire and sank down himself. "Those men are working for a lord who means to kill him. There are dozens of them all over this hideous country, trying to track him down and capture him."

"But why?" One of them brought her a flask of wine and some bread—a breakfast fit for a queen, as far as she was concerned.

"I can't be sure, but I have a theory." He took a bit of bread of his own. "Tarquin accidentally killed a young man in Corsica just before he came back here. The boy was mad, and he attacked him. The young man's servant said Tarquin would hear from the boy's father, that he would hunt him to the ends of the earth." He took a long swallow of wine. "The boy was English, I believe, or maybe French, and he wore the clothes of a penitent priest underneath his armor."

"That does sound mad," Lisbet agreed. "Malinda said that they were attacked on the road on the way back to Brinlaw by men who seemed to be trying to capture Tarquin—"

"Probably the same," he nodded. "The point is, they are looking for Tarquin. We are looking for Tarquin. So why have none of us seen him? Where is he?"

"You're asking me?" she said, smiling in spite of herself.

"I'm asking Allah," he smiled back. "But if you know, please, feel free to say."

"I wish I did." Malinda had been lost for days now; anything could have happened. "But even if we don't find him—"

"If we don't find him, I doubt very much if we will find your friend," he broke in sadly. "Even if we do . . ." He let the thought trail off unfinished.

"She's still alive," she insisted stubbornly. "So what do you suggest, that we just stay here and hope Tarquin turns up?"

"He ain't gonna turn up here," one of the crewmen offered helpfully. "He sent word he was someplace else."

Davyd turned slowly and looked at him. "He did what?"

"Some boy on a river skiff brought a message a day or so ago," the sailor answered. "He said he was with FitzBruel two days before, and that he told him to come here and find you, if he could. He wanted to stay with us, but we sent him packing back to his mama. Shall I fetch the note?"

Davyd glanced at Lisbet as if praying for patience. "Yes," he said with exaggerated care. "Please." The crewman went off in the direction of the ship and returned with a scroll. "Thank you."

"What does he say?" Lisbet demanded, peering over his shoulder. "Good Lord, what sort of gibberish is that?"

"Civilized gibberish," Davyd answered. "It is Arabic." He finished reading. "He says he is going to a place called Falconskeep. He gives the location by a system only he and I know, but he must have written it wrong—he can't mean for us to sail north in the middle of December."

"Falconskeep is north," Lisbet said eagerly. "It's where Malinda's mother was born, near Wales, north and west of here."

"North and west," he repeated. "Impossible."

"Why?" she demanded. "That ship only sails south and east?"

"In the middle of winter, yes," he retorted. "The west coast of your England will be nothing but squalls this time of year."

"But if Tarquin is going to Falconskeep, maybe he's already found Malinda," she said, catching his arm for emphasis. "That would be the perfect place to hide. And besides, what else can we do? Don't you want to find him?"

"Of course I want to find him." He frowned, but he squeezed her hand, too. "I just wish I could find him somewhere else."

Malinda braced herself against the walls with both hands and screamed with every ounce of strength she could find. Her throat was so raw, she tasted blood already, but she couldn't stop, couldn't give up. The oubliette was only wide enough for her to stand, the walls close around her on every side, and the floor was ankle-deep in sea water that rose higher with the tide, icy cold, numbing her to the bone and seeming to cut into her flesh. The first time the water rose, she had panicked, thinking it would cover her head, but it had only reached her waist before it fell again. Now after three high tides, she was almost praying to drown. For worse than the pain, worse than the cold, worse even than the terrible feeling of being trapped without escape were the visions. This trap was old, built in the days of Roman Britannia, and a hundred men had died here just as she was dying, frozen and starving. She was so thirsty she had resorted to wetting her lips and tongue with sea water, but she knew it would get worse. She could feel it in the other deaths around her, closing in more tightly than the walls. Sometimes she screamed in Latin, sometimes Saxon, sometimes English or French. Sometimes she was herself; sometimes she was not. But always she was dying, for that was the moment that remained, the moment when the prisoner finally escaped, his life consumed by the dark.

"Please, help me," she sobbed, her head bent to the wall, bruising her brow on rough stone. "Somebody . . . please!" Her voice rose to another scream, something in her throat letting go with an agonizing snap. They had to be here still, Farrars and his men. Surely they couldn't have left her here alone. She could smell the stench from above, the body that was rotting on the wall . . . Could it really be Tarquin? She had been so sure it wasn't, but now it seemed to make perfect sense. The world was over; she was in hell. "Mama!" she cried, a rasping sob. "I want my mama . . ." She tried to think of Brinlaw, and Mama, and being safe in her arms, but she couldn't make that vision come; it couldn't reach her here in this place surrounded by death. And Tarquin . . . why didn't Tarquin come? "Because he's dead," she whispered, sound crawling over the walls, nasty as the slime. "Everything is dead . . ."

Tarquin let his horse slow to a walk again to save her strength, but only with an effort. All he wanted was to push forward at a gallop. For three days and nights he had ridden without stopping for more than a few minutes at a time, and still every thought in his head, every fiber of his flesh burned to hurry, the supernatural sense of urgency that had come to him in his dream of Falconskeep growing stronger by the moment. But his body was growing tired. Soon he would have to stop and rest, eat a proper meal and sleep. But not yet. He couldn't make himself stop yet. Malinda needed him; she was frightened and in pain.

He let his thoughts drift back to the dream, playing it over in his mind as he had a thousand times already. He had awakened in the tower room at Falconskeep—he remembered it from when he was a child. Malinda had been there. He had opened his eyes to find her standing over him. Even now, frightened and furious as he was, this memory was enough to make his heart skip a beat with joy.

She had asked him to return to her; together they had made love. If the vision had ended there, he might have believed it was only a dream, no more than wishful thinking.

But it didn't end there; indeed, what had followed had almost blotted out the joy of the beginning entirely in his mind. Some force had torn Malinda from his arms. Some evil darker than his own had come between them—the figure on the cliff. Whoever this man was, he had taken Malinda, was threatening her somehow even now. He was the reason she had called out to Tarquin with her magic in the first place, the reason she was calling to him still. If he closed his eyes now, he could still hear her screams. Worst of all, he knew why she was screaming; with his eyes closed, he was there again. Somewhere there was a hole, a deep, dark hole full of nothing but water and death, and inside was Malinda, buried alive. He could see it as clearly with his eyes closed as he saw the trees and road when they were open, feel it as vividly as he felt the wind on his face. Was this a vision of the future or the past? *"Too late,"* the faery ghost had told him. *"We are already too late."* His heart beat faster, rage and panic unlike anything even he had ever felt before burning in his blood. He couldn't be too late—not even God could be so cruel, not even to him. He was a demon, but Malinda was the one in agony. Where was the justice in that? Surely just to love him could not be so great a sin.

For he knew she loved him with all her precious soul. He thought of her seduction spell. *"Say you are mine,"* she had ordered, and he had obeyed. He had punished her for it, abandoned her, denounced her for a witch and run away in hopes of saving her soul, but in that, he was too late. She still loved him. She had seen his secret heart, heard him confess his blackest sin, and still she loved him. And now she was in hell, and he didn't know how to save her. The vision-faery said he was too late . . .

"*Falconskeep*," the faery's voice now whispered in his ear. The darkness of Malinda's hell was fading, but his eyes were still closed. He was dreaming, standing on the beach again at Falconskeep, this time in the light. "*You must find her, Tarquin, bring her here*," the ghost continued, standing by his side. The wind stirred her hair, rippled through her gray-green gown. She turned to him and smiled, but her eyes were sad. "*Here she will be safe.*"

"Find her where?" he demanded. Something was wrong; there was something she wasn't saying. He saw pity in her eyes. "Isn't she at Brinlaw?"

"*No, my love, she is not. But you will find her.*" She was starting to fade away again, and he reached out and grabbed her arm—in this dream world, she was as solid as he. "*Let me go to her, Tarquin. We will wait until you come.*"

"Come where?" The dream was fading; he was waking up. "Tell me!" he roared, the screams of falcons echoing above, his shout making his horse stumble, startled out of a doze of her own. He opened his eyes and found the road again, the solid world of the present, but a single scream continued, a real bird, not a dream. Looking up, he saw the hawk swooping toward him, wings beating barely fast enough to keep the bird in flight. He raised his arm, his heart pounding harder, and Rufus settled on his wrist. His feathers were bedraggled, his talons were crusted with blood, but it was Rufus, no question.

"Where is she?" he asked, stroking the snow-white breast, dizzy with hope and disbelief. "Do you know?" The bird let out a painful shriek as if in answer. "You will show me then," Tarquin soothed. "We will save her. We will not be too late."

Malinda . . . who was Malinda? A voice kept saying that name, but it wasn't real, the voice or the name . . . Nothing was real but the cold and the dark and pain. Pain was real . . . Her throat was pain, and her hands—blood, yes, blood was real, too. Hungry . . . was she still hungry? She licked her bleeding palm, and the pain in her stomach lurched higher . . . Hunger was still there, too. But thirst . . . thirst she never forgot, even for an instant. The freezing water was at her knees again . . . How many tides was this? She had long ago lost count—nearly ten, at least, less than a hundred, she was almost sure. "*Malinda . . .*" She pressed her fists to her ears, trying to shut it out. The other voices were awful, but at least they never called her name. Her name—she was Malinda. She laughed, pleased as a child who has performed some trick for the very first time. She had remembered her name.

"*Malinda . . . listen to me, little bird.*" She opened her eyes as if it would do her good—the darkness hadn't changed. But the woman in the mirror . . . in her mind, she saw her, holding out her hands. "*You must come to me.*"

"I can't," she cried out—slice of agony like swallowing a shard of glass. "I can't get out."

"*You can come in.*" Someone was touching her hair, not snatching at it like the other ghosts, but with a soothing caress. She squeezed her eyes shut, a dry sob rising in her throat. "*It's all right, my darling,*" the voice crooned, and Malinda could hear she was crying, too. "*I won't leave you. Your grammy won't leave you alone.*" She felt a kiss on her brow, and when she turned, she seemed to sink against a slender shoulder, feel an arm around her waist, though the oubliette was too small; no one else could have fit. "Don't leave me," she echoed, clinging tight. She could even smell her gown, dry lavender infused in soft linen. "Don't let me die alone."

"You won't die, my faery . . . you will live." But about this she sounded less sure, as if she were trying to convince herself as much as Malinda. Blanche . . . her name was Blanche. She began to sing, a lullaby Malinda remembered, a faery mother's song, and suddenly the pain seemed to fade, along with the hunger, even her thirst. Singing with her, she seemed to sink into the bed at Falconskeep, the bed where Tarquin had loved her without fury, where she had been safe. She felt the quilts drawn up beneath her chin. *I can come in,* she thought, sinking deeper until she didn't think at all.

21

F rantic with worry after another week of nightmares, Alista had convinced Will they had to ride on at the last sunset, putting them home at Brinlaw in the middle of the night. The garrison was caught by surprise, most of them scrambling over themselves to open the gates and greet their lord. But she saw strangers among them as well, watching with cool, suspicious eyes—Lord Farrars' men, she supposed.

"My lord, thank God you've come," Sir Bruce said, rushing out into the courtyard with his boots unlaced and tunic half undone.

"Where is Tarquin?" Will demanded, helping Alista down from her horse.

Not here, Alista's faery sense whispered, her own voice inside her head. *My daughter is not here.* "Where is Malinda?" she asked the knight aloud.

"Gone," Bruce answered, glancing from Will's face to her own and back.

"Which one?" Mark said. He and Bruce were friends; he trusted him, she could tell.

"Both," Bruce said. "And Lisbet as well. FitzBruel went first, before the Queen arrived, but the others . . ." His voice trailed off. "You had better talk to Farrars."

"Farrars be damned," Alista said, pushing past the knight and heading for the door. "Where is Eleanor?"

The Queen had apparently been awakened by the commotion in the courtyard, for she was out of bed and in a dressing gown, but she obviously wasn't prepared to receive a visitor in her room, particularly one as furious as Alista. "Lady Brinlaw," she began, her eyes wide with shock.

"Where is my daughter?" Alista cut her off. "Where is Malinda?"

"In truth, my lady, I don't know," Eleanor answered, rising to meet her. "Lord Farrars seems to think she ran away of her own free will, such as it was, and took her little friend with her."

"Why?" Alista demanded. "This is her home—why would she run away?"

"She confided to me that she was . . ." Her voice trailed off as she saw Will come in behind his wife, then Mark with Willie in his arms. "That she had feelings for Tarquin FitzBruel," Eleanor finished. "She believed you would object to the match, and I told her if I were you, I certainly would. Then Farrars made her a marriage proposal of his own, and I believe that may—"

"Farrars proposed to Malinda?" Mark interrupted, aghast. "He's old enough to be her father!"

"I believe your sister felt the same," Eleanor said. Alista was still watching her intently, and a faint blush crept over the royal cheeks in spite of their layer of powder. "But she didn't openly refuse him. She simply disappeared." Willie had climbed down from his brother's arms and was staring at the Queen as well, a strange, angry light in his eyes. "She's a very willful girl."

"Yes, Eleanor, she is," Will said, his own anger perfectly plain in his tone and with no attempt at form. "But she isn't stupid. She wouldn't leave her home in the middle of winter with no horse or escort to chase after anyone, no matter what sort of feelings she might have." The very idea seemed to give him pause. He stopped and shook his head. "She wouldn't even know where to find Tarquin."

"Actually, Farrars believes she might have done, Will," Eleanor said, addressing him just as familiarly. "He seems to think Malinda was inadvertently involved in some sort of larger plot, FitzBruel and that other boy, Phillipe, using her to conspire against the Crown, somehow passing messages to Richard. He thinks that's why FitzBruel left here when he did, to escape detection and join Richard—"

"I don't give a damn what Farrars might believe," Alista snapped, her patience at the breaking point. As if Tarquin would care enough about politics to conspire with anyone—as if he or Malinda would ever even think to betray Brinlaw and his king. "I'm asking you, Majesty. What happened to my daughter?"

"Her Majesty doesn't know," a voice interrupted. Turning, they found Robert Farrars standing in the doorway. His eyes were rimmed in red, and he looked sad enough to weep again. "I haven't told her . . . I couldn't bear it." He looked at Will, his pale face going whiter. "I know you will never forgive me, Brinlaw. In your place, I would not."

"What have you done?" Alista demanded, trying to maintain her focus. The room suddenly seemed too warm; she felt dizzy.

"I only wanted to protect her," Farrars answered. "But apparently I drove her away." He was holding something in his hand, and Alista's heart began to pound. "I went after her to stop her, but I was too late," he went on. "By the time I found her . . ." He held out the heartstone.

Alista reached out to take it, forcing her arm to move by will instead of reflex. "Where did you . . . ?" Her voice failed; she had to start again. "Why would she take this off?"

"She did not, my lady," Farrars answered gently. "I took it from her. I knew you would know it as hers. She is dead." He put the pendant in her hand. "I'm so sorry—"

"Stop it!" If he spoke another word, she would murder him herself. Will was looking at her, the look on his face a perfect match to the howl of pain inside her, and she closed her hand around the heartstone to reach for him.

Suddenly a flood of images flashed through her like a lightning strike—this room on fire, a mirror shattered, her mother's book of magic exploding into flames. A terrible, physical pain shot through her chest, molten steel pressed to her flesh, and she screamed. Will was calling her name, reaching out to catch her, but she was still falling, falling forever into black.

Tarquin lay flat on the ground, dry sea grass giving him cover, as did the tree curved like an old man's grasp above his head. Rufus was flying again, circling the ruined villa on the cliff just opposite. Malinda had to be there.

His first instinct had been to ride straight in, sword drawn, but his judgment had managed to control his heart at least enough to watch for an hour first. There were men there, but not many. He had counted four, one of them bent and slow, very old or a cripple. The others were well armed but careless. They weren't expecting anyone. He had seen no sign of Malinda.

Rufus swept down into the tree above him, and though he glared at him as if to ask what was taking so long, he didn't cry out, and the men opposite didn't seem to notice the bird at all. "Big mistake," he muttered, retreating from the edge.

The first one was easy. He waited for the man to wander off to relieve himself and cut his throat mid-piss. The other two young ones were harder. They were playing cards and seemed content to stay in the same spot forever, directly in front of the broken doorway, though he noticed they were either too drunk or too stupid to realize their companion hadn't come back. The old man wandered in and out, fretting and muttering to himself, shaking his head. Tarquin recognized him, the old villain he had let live in Corsica, the one who knew him from his childhood at Bruel. The man who wanted him dead had taken Malinda; he had pretty well known as much. But the coincidence was spooky, nonetheless.

"Someone should go in," the old man suddenly said.

"You go," one of the others answered, glancing up at his friend. "I've heard enough."

"Too much," the other one agreed with an exaggerated shudder. "How long is this supposed to take, anyway?"

"How should I know?" the first one shrugged. "But it's nasty, quick or slow."

"We should check," the old man repeated, shuffling back inside.

Tarquin couldn't wait any longer. Springing out of his hiding place with a roar to wake the dead, he kicked the smaller of the two in the face to knock him off balance, then drove his sword down on the other. The poor fool barely resisted, he was so surprised. The other man managed to parry a stroke or two before Tarquin stabbed him in the chest.

As soon as he stepped through the doorway, he smelled the corpse, the stench as solid and disconcerting as the sudden dark. His eyes adjusted just in time to see the old man turn to flee, and he lunged, grabbing him by the twisted shoulder. "Where is she?" he snarled. The old man sank to his knees, his eyes wild with fright.

"She lives," the old man insisted. "In there—you can still save—" Before he finished, Tarquin had struck him with his sword hilt, killing him or knocking him unconscious, he cared not.

The only room that remained intact was a kind of dungeon. The corpse was there, hanging like a trophy on the wall. But he could see no sign of Malinda. "Malinda!" he shouted, his voice echoing weirdly in the broken halls. "Answer me!" But there was nothing . . . He'd begun to think he'd hit the old man too soon, should have made him show him, when he heard a tiny sound. "Malinda?" It was a voice, but it didn't sound like her. In truth, it didn't sound like any living creature he had ever heard. "Malinda?" His heart beat faster as he searched the room, trying to find the source. "Tell me where you are, sweeting!" he called, but the voice didn't change, didn't stop or grow louder. She was singing, sort of—there was no discernible tune. An iron chest stood in a corner, and the voice seemed to be coming from there—she couldn't possibly be inside something no bigger— But no. It wasn't coming from inside the chest but under it. The dream . . . she really was buried alive.

"Holy Christ." He dropped to his knees to shove the chest aside, the muscles screaming in his arms. Underneath was a trapdoor barely as wide as his shoulders. "It's all right, angel," he promised, his voice rough with angry tears. "I'm coming."

He threw back the door, and her voice grew louder, but it still sounded distant and small. He took a torch and lay down flat on the floor to peer inside. The oubliette was deeper than any he had ever seen. He could barely glimpse a glimmer of golden hair. "Malinda? Do you hear me?" No answer but the song. "Damn it, Malinda, answer me!" He wanted to hear her say his name, wanted her to look up. But nothing changed; she didn't seem to notice him at all.

Something was different, she thought, snuggling deeper in the pillows. Someone else was calling to her, someone she should know. But she was so comfortable . . . If she tried to answer, she would wake up, and all the pain would come back. She would have to go back to . . . that awful place she didn't want to think about. "*Malinda,*" her grandmother said, leaning down to murmur in her ear. "*It's time to wake up, darling.*" No, she thought, I will not.

Tarquin looped the chain around a crumbling column, praying it would hold their weight and the chain was long enough. If the column broke and he fell, they would die together. Wrapping his arm around the chain for support, he lowered himself down the hole, bracing his feet against the wall. Hopefully if he could reach her, she would at least reach up; he didn't think they'd both fit side by side. "Malinda? It's all right . . . it's me." For a moment, the chain snagged, and he thought he'd run out of slack, and for that one moment, he knew what she had known, what it felt like to be trapped in this hole, and his heart pounded painfully in his chest. Voices more despairing than his love's seemed to rise around him, screaming for mercy, for rescue, and the walls seemed to close in. He clung tighter to the chain, heaved himself up a little just to prove he could. He wasn't trapped; he could still climb out. But he couldn't go without Malinda. The chain pulled free of the snag, and he could move downward again.

The singing had become unbearable by the time the back of his heel touched something soft. He was almost on top of her, but she hadn't stopped her song. Her voice was almost gone, more a croak than a voice, but it continued without pause, a chant to conjure up the dead. The words were clearer now, but he didn't understand them. They were faery song. "Reach up to me, Malinda," he ordered. "Let me pull you up." But it was no use. She wouldn't answer—didn't even know he was there.

Stop it, Malinda thought, brushing away her grandmother's tender touch. *I won't go back; you can't make me.*

"*No*," Blanche said sadly, "*I cannot.*"

Careful not to hurt her, Tarquin slid the rest of the way to the bottom, the two of them crushed together close enough for an embrace. "Malinda, listen to me." He found her face, framed it in his hands, and the singing stopped. "Do you feel me?" He felt along her arms—her wrists were bound before her. "Why won't you answer me?" He found her mouth with his, but it was like kissing a corpse. If he hadn't been able to feel her heart beating against his chest, he would have believed she was dead, that the voice he had heard had been no more than a ghost. "I'm sorry, angel," he wept, pressing a kiss to her brow. "I'm so sorry . . . I won't leave you again."

"*Don't leave him, Malinda,*" Blanche was urging. "*Go back while you still can.*"

No, Malinda answered, smiling in her sleep. In the distance, she could hear music . . . The faeries were coming; soon she could go home.

Tarquin lifted her up, held her around the waist with one arm to loop her arms around his neck with the other. She was like a doll, utterly limp in his grasp. Climbing, she would be dead weight. But she was giving him no better choice. "Come on, angel," he muttered, beginning to climb.

The sun was up again, and it was snowing; in one world, it was snowing. Malinda's world had split in two, and she watched them both from a tiny slice of nothing in the middle. In one world was Tarquin—she had remembered his name. He was talking to someone, a man with a horse. He was talking about her. He needed that man's horse because he had to ride faster, and he had to have a place to put her. She frowned. She didn't want her own horse; she wanted to ride with him. That was the only nice thing about that world, the only thing she could stand to feel, his arms around her as they rode the horse. But she couldn't speak to him, couldn't tell him to stop. If she spoke, the other world would be lost, and she would have to live in his, would have to feel everything again. Bad things happened in his world, and he could go away. In the faery world, she would be safe.

She could see it, too, see it as if from a distance, a beautiful place where no one felt pain because no one ever died. There was music there, beautiful music; if she strained, she could hear it drawing closer. Her magic was beautiful there; she would be safe. No one would ever try to hurt her, no matter what, and she would be free. All she had to do was wait until it came closer, just a little longer until the two worlds touched, and she could let go and be free. She could step into that world forever, real forever, and nothing would ever change again. But she couldn't take Tarquin with her. *"He isn't faery, little bird,"* her grandmother agreed, holding her hand at the blank space in between. *"You would have to leave him behind, leave them all behind."*

"Leave Farrars," she said in faery-speak, the silent speech of the mind. "Leave Eleanor. Leave that awful dark."

"Yes," Blanche soothed, stroking her hair. *"Those would be left, too."*

Tarquin turned away from the peasant farmer to find Malinda watching him, or at least she seemed to be. Her green eyes were focused on him so intently, his heart skipped a beat. "Malinda?" He drew closer, reached up and touched her hand, still laid on the horse's neck where he had left it when he got down. But her eyes didn't follow him; she was still staring at the spot where he had been. "It's all right," he promised, speaking more to himself than to her. "Everything will be all right."

Last night when they were far enough away from the ruins that he felt safe to stop, he had looked her over and been horrified by what he saw. Her nails were broken, and her hands and arms were torn and bloodied from the sharp-edged stones. Her dress and slippers were in tatters from the rocks and bones below and the salt water that had risen with the tides. A deep, cross-shaped brand had been burned into her chest just above the swell of one breast— the same mark the boy in Corsica had worn. When he had seen the mark on Malinda, he had screamed, raging at God as much as at the man who had done it, but even then she hadn't spoken, hadn't even looked up. He knew he had hurt her, dressing her wounds, but she had never flinched. The only time she reacted at all was when he gave her water; that was the only time he had felt hope. She had drunk eagerly, as much as he dared pour down her throat, and every time he held the skin to her mouth, she drank again, though as yet she wouldn't eat unless he fed her like a mother bird, pushing soft bits of bread and meat into her mouth with his hand and letting her swallow it whole. Even Rufus seemed concerned; he kept bringing freshly killed rabbits and mice as if to tempt her to eat. "It's over now, Malinda," he had promised her time and again. "You're safe." All night long, he had held her close and murmured in her ear until the words became a kind of chant, a spell of his own to conjure her back, as she had conjured him. "You win, sweet love, I promise—I am yours. Come back to me. I have come, just as you told me to do. I am here and yours. I will not let you go." He was hoarse from saying it, on and on through tears until the sun began to rise and they moved on. Even on the road he had begged her, "Come back to me, my love." But she never seemed to hear.

Now he lifted her hand to his lips, pressed a fervent kiss to her palm. "We have to move faster," he said, making conversation in hopes she might be listening, somewhere deep inside. "We're going someplace safe."

Falconskeep, she thought, shivering in eagerness and fear. *We're going to Falconskeep.*

He felt her shudder, looked up, but her face was the same. "Forgive me, angel," he muttered, tying her hands to the horse's bridle. He hated to do it, but he couldn't risk her falling off, and in this state, she would do nothing to hold herself in the saddle.

No! she moaned inside her mind, pain threatening to tear her trance apart. *Don't tie me, please. Don't leave me.* But she couldn't make herself say it out loud, couldn't risk falling back into the real. *Please, Tarquin, just know . . .*

He swung into the saddle, adjusted the stirrups on the peasant's rough tack to fit his longer legs. Straightening up, he looked over at Malinda. Tears were streaming down her cheeks. "What is it? Oh no . . ." He dropped back to the ground, cut her bonds and dragged her down into his arms. "I'm sorry," he promised, kissing her tear-stained cheek as they sank to the ground. "I'm so sorry . . . I won't do it again." She was still like a doll in his embrace, but the tears stopped, and he imagined he felt her press her face against the hollow of his throat. "You're going to wake up," he said, holding her more tightly. "You're going to come back to me, Malinda. You belong to me."

Hush now, she thought, luxuriating in the warmth of his arms. *Take me home.*

He lifted her back into the saddle, climbed up behind her. The second horse would help; they could switch. They would get there soon enough. "Come on, angel," he said softly. "We're going to Falconskeep."

When Alista opened her eyes again, pale, wintry daylight was falling over her from the window of a bedroom in the tower, and she was lying on her own bed. Will stood at the window looking out, his back to her, and Mark was sitting in front of the fire, his head bent to his hands. Willie was sitting beside her on the bed, the heartstone pendant in his hands. As soon as he saw her move, he grinned. "Papa, look!" He jumped down from the bed with a thump. "She's awake!"

"Alista." Will rushed to her with a look to break her heart. "I'm so sorry—I should have known—"

"Hush, love, hush," she soothed. "It's all right. Malinda is alive." She took the pendant from Willie and held it out to Will. "Look at this. Remember when you thought I was dead, when I was with Geoffrey? The stone looked just the same."

He frowned, but she could see hope in his eyes. "But Farrars said—"

"Farrars is a liar," she insisted. She thought again of her vision, her hand going unconsciously to her chest where she had felt the terrible burn. "Where is he now?"

"Papa sent him away," Mark said, coming to join them. His eyes were too wide and bright. He was still in shock.

"I was furious—I still am," Will explained. "I told him I could damned well guard Eleanor without him. I sent him back to Henry."

"Mama, what did he do to Malinda?" Willie demanded.

"I don't know. Maybe nothing," Alista answered. "Maybe it was just his proposal."

"What makes you think he was lying?" Will asked, touching her cheek.

"Because he said he saw Malinda's body dead, and I know she is alive," she answered, taking his hand. "And the other things he said, too. Tarquin would never hurt Malinda or conspire against Henry—"

"How can you be so certain?" Mark asked.

"No, she's right about that much," Will nodded. "But Malinda could still have been killed if she ran away. He could still have found her—"

"No," Alista insisted, shaking her head. "He made it all up. I just don't know why. Malinda may have left here on her own, and she may be with Tarquin, but there was no conspiracy, and Farrars has not seen her dead. She was afraid of Farrars. There was a quarrel . . ." She tried in vain to make the images come clear in her mind. Her talent had always been like this, giving her just enough truth to drive her mad and trick her into some terrible mistake. "I don't know what happened, Will, but Malinda isn't dead. She's hurt and frightened, but she lives."

"Where is she?" Will asked, obviously ready to leave that very instant to find his child and bring her home. "Where would she have gone?"

"I don't know," Alista began, tears of frustration threatening to overtake her again, then she stopped. Her dreams were coming back to her, soft words in her mother's voice. "Falconskeep," she said. "We will find her at Falconskeep."

"Fine," Will said, getting up. "We haven't unpacked yet. We can leave at once."

"Papa, wait," Mark said, following him. "Mama can't travel anymore, not in her condition, not yet, and besides, what about Eleanor? Someone has to stay here with her, or we are forsworn to the King. Let me go after Malinda."

"You've never been to Falconskeep," Will began.

"You can tell me where it is," Mark insisted. "I can find it. Please, Papa, let me be the one to go." His eyes were pleading harder than his words, and Alista's heart ached for him. He had been through so much in the past few months—Phillipe's betrayal had hurt him more than any of them could guess, she knew. "Please?"

Will looked at her, his own desperate plea in his eyes,

but she shook her head. "All right," he said, resigned. "I will tell you the way."

They reached the beach at Falconskeep at midday, Tarquin's favorite spot in all the world. Rufus took flight from his wrist and mounted high into the sky, a smaller blot of brown among the circling falcons, shrieking greetings as he flew. "He acts as if he has come home," Tarquin said, looking back down at the woman in his arms. Her eyes were closed as if she were sleeping, her lips slightly parted. "We're home."

Gwyneth's cottage in the woods was just where he remembered, but when he knocked, a woman no older than Malinda opened the door. "Bless us, look who has come," she cried, throwing her arms around his neck. "Tarquin, all grown up!"

"Gwyneth?" he guessed, confused. The last time he had seen the faery had been at Malinda's birth, and she had seemed well into her middle years, her red hair streaked with gray, her figure comfortably lush. Now she was slender as a willow, and her hair burned like a sunset, falling loose down her back. But her eyes as she drew back were the same, ancient as earth and dancing with laughter. "How . . . ?"

"I'd grown too old; I had to start over," she laughed. "But who have you brought . . . oh no." Her expression turned grave, her whole manner changing as she went to Malinda, still sitting on the horse, staring into space. "Who did this?" Gwyneth demanded, her voice rough with unshed tears. "My poor sweet girl . . ." She looked back at Tarquin. "Bring her in and tell me everything."

As he related all he knew of his love's ordeal, the faery

attended her hurts, bathing her and dressing her in a fresh white gown, even washing her tangled hair. She wept over her many times, never so hard as when she saw the brand burned into her breast. "They dare," she murmured angrily, the first words she had said since he began. "No wonder you want to leave them." She stroked Malinda's curls. "Never fear, poppet. You have made it just in time."

"What are you talking about?" Tarquin asked, fear like a finger of ice on his heart.

"She has gone between," Gwyneth explained. "Between the faery world and this one. That's why she doesn't speak or seem to hear or see. She has given up her mortal body, abandoned mortal pain."

"She isn't dead—"

"Of course not, naught of the sort." She lifted Malinda's hand and let it hover in the air. "But she isn't here."

Tarquin took the hand and put it back into her lap. "Tell me how to bring her back."

Gwyneth shook her head, her eyes dim with pity. "You cannot," she said gently. "Best to let her go."

"I will not." He drew Malinda close to him, an arm around her shoulders, and she leaned against his chest, biddable as a doll. "Tell me a spell—"

"There is no spell," the faery cut him off. "She is too frightened, too hurt. If she were a mortal only, she would have simply run mad. As it is, at least she has somewhere to go." She watched his face, aching for his pain. He was still the same as he had been as a boy, such a fierce, mortal heart, raging and loving at once. "But you are tired, sweeting," she soothed as she stood up. "Come and sleep. Look, your love is asleep already."

Malinda had indeed closed her eyes again, her head resting in the hollow of his shoulder, her breath warm through his shirt. "I will not let her go," he repeated stubbornly.

"Bring her along, then," Gwyneth said, leading the way into the tiny bedroom. "Time enough to worry when you wake."

22

*f*arrars had stopped at the crossroads a few miles from Brinlaw Castle—a pretty symbol, he thought with a bitter smile. To the south was London, then Southampton, then France—Henry's bidding, in short. To the west was his own English holding, the ruin by the sea—open rebellion at last. Brinlaw had sent him back to Henry as if he had the power to do so, as if he, Brinlaw, the son of a traitor descended from Saxon trash, could command a descendant of the greatest kings of France. If he'd been thinking clearly, he would have taken the castle right then; he had sufficient troops. But he had been so surprised.

Brinlaw turning up at all had been enough to rattle him in his present state. He was tired; he wasn't himself. He hadn't slept well in nearly a week, not since that nasty business with Malinda. The crisis was coming; that was the cause. All his plans, all his sacrifice—it was all about to come to fruition. Henry's reign was in chaos, the few loyal nobles he had left scattered all over the kingdom. Brinlaw turning up with his son at their own castle was proof enough of that. The time to strike was now, and he was ready, all except for one detail. FitzBruel still lived.

"Gone," he muttered under his breath, his captain looking over at him from his own horse with a question in his eyes. "He must be—gone back to the heathens." He looked up and met the man's look with a scowl. He had to focus; he had to rest. He could make a fatal mistake. Chasing FitzBruel so long was a mistake. He could find him later, once Henry and his demon spawn were destroyed for good and all. And Brinlaw, he was now in for his share as well . . .

"My lord." One of his lesser soldiers was standing by his horse with little Nicole, his spy from Eleanor's chambers, behind him, enswathed in a great, black mantle with a hood. "This girl says you will want to speak with her."

"Does she?" The little viper's eyes were fairly twinkling with secrets. "Perhaps she is right." Dismounting, he tossed the reins to the soldier and led the girl aside. "You have something to tell me?"

"Brinlaw does not believe his daughter is dead," she said without preamble. "He does not believe her lover is a spy. He has sent his son to find them at some place called Falconskeep."

His flesh crawled with a sickening kind of rage, but he forced his voice to sound calm. "And where is this place?"

"I know not, but the boy has only just left, headed north and west," she answered. "He shouldn't be hard to catch."

"No." He made himself smile. "You've done well, petite." He handed her a coin. "Now you may give the Queen your full attention—"

"No." She put the coin back into his hand. "I've had my fill of Her Majesty, the Queen. I want to go with you."

More foolishness he did not need. "Don't be ridiculous." He tried to turn away, but she caught him by the arm. "Are you mad?"

"Not likely," she said with a sneer that did nothing for her looks. "Take me with you, or you will see how wise I am. Think you not that Brinlaw would pay handsomely to know what became of his daughter?"

"No doubt," he chuckled, the rage rising higher, making his head begin to buzz. "'Tis too bad you don't know."

"I can guess," she said with a smile.

"Can you?" He brought the dagger up so quickly, he barely knew what he intended until the deed was done. Her eyes widened, her mouth falling open in shock. He stepped back, and she fell forward to the ground, her blood pouring scarlet on the snow. "Now you know," he said, turning away. He didn't need her any longer anyway; the time for listening at Eleanor's curtains had passed. "You, come here," he said to his captain, who was gawking at the dying girl as if she were a unicorn. "You heard what she said about Brinlaw's son?"

"My lord?" The man stood gaping at him for a moment, recovering his wits. "Yes, yes, my lord, I heard."

"Send someone after him, find out where he's gone." He wiped his sticky hand on his mantle, the cause already forgotten. "Gather the rest of our soldiers at the ruins. King Henry's turn has come."

Tarquin sat on the floor beside the bed, one hand gently stroking Malinda's forehead. "Are you really sleeping, angel?" He brushed a golden lock of hair back from her temple, soft and fine as silk. "I don't believe you are." Her eyes were closed, her features placid as an alabaster mask. "You mean to punish me for leaving you." He traced the shape of her mouth with his fingertips, felt the warmth of her breath that proved she was alive. "I meant to keep you safe." She could awake at any moment, eyes flashing emerald fire, call him a fool, demand her will at any cost. He would weep for joy to see it, promise her anything. "I love you." He put a hand behind her head, bent and kissed her mouth. Her lips opened to his tongue just as they did when he fed her, but she didn't kiss him back. His faery witch was gone, leaving a golden-haired doll in her place. "*She isn't here,*" Gwyneth had said. "*Best to let her go.*"

"Never," he swore, fury edged again in tears. He climbed in bed beside her, drew her close against his chest. "I will never let you go."

Malinda felt the bed sink beneath his weight, felt his arms around her, felt his heartbeat under her cheek, slow but still strong as eventually he slept. This was the mortal world as much as the other, love as much as pain. "*Is it worth it?*" her grandmother whispered. "*Will you lose this to be safe?*" But the faeries were so close, almost close enough to touch. She heard the music, heard them calling in the voices of the falcons. *We have love,* they seemed to say, *love that will never die. Come and sing with us.*

"Is it true?" she asked aloud. Blanche was standing in the room now, as solid as she was herself, as solid as Tarquin beside her. "Do the faeries love?"

"*All things in equal measure,*" Blanche answered. "*They choose no special loves, for their time cannot run short.*"

Malinda got up from the bed, passing a hand across her lover's face so he wouldn't feel her leave. Her mortal form was now in her control, but it was like moving a doll. She felt distant, already absent from her body. It was like being invisible, only more so. "Can I truly go to them?"

"*If you wish*," Blanche nodded. "*Tonight the worlds will overlap, and you have faery blood. You can be a falcon, or you can keep your shape, or you can move from one to the other as it pleases you in their world. But your mortal self will die.*"

"And I will be safe." She walked toward the door. "Will I miss this world?" She touched the knob, marveled at the feel of it after so many days of feeling nothing.

"*I don't know,*" Blanche admitted. "*You will have forever. Perhaps you will forget.*"

"I will forget," she echoed, looking back at Tarquin. She loved him so, and others, too, her parents and brothers and Lisbet . . . What had become of Lisbet? But they could leave her. Tarquin could leave her, and she would be alone again in the dark.

She took a step toward the bed, something about the way he slept striking a chord deep in the chaos of her mind. She had seen him so before . . . Suddenly a pain tore through her solid form, pain in the shape of a cross setting her flesh on fire. "No," she said, her human voice rising through real tears in her throat. The world of pain was so close; she could so easily be captured. "Leave me . . . I will not." She closed her mortal eyes and reached for the faery world with her mind, and the mortal pain receded. She was a spirit moving in a doll again. Turning her back on Tarquin, she opened the door and went out, letting the music weave its charm, drawing her closer to the faery world.

Tarquin's eyes snapped open, some small sound . . . Music, he heard music. He felt confused, and he just lay there for a long moment, trying to work it out. Something was wrong, but the music seemed to say no, to urge him back to sleep . . . Malinda! Malinda was gone.

He threw open the bedroom door, found Gwyneth at the cottage door, her back to it as if to stop him going out. "Where is she?" He looked around the room frantically. How far could she have ventured in such a state?

"Let her go, Tarquin, please," Gwyneth begged. "Better she should be a faery than live mortal as she is."

He would not hear this, would not even try to understand. It was wrong, just wrong, and Gwyneth would never understand. She was a faery, like the ones who were waiting on the beach. "Get away," he ordered, grabbing her shoulders to fling her aside if he must.

"Tarquin, no," Gwyneth ordered, catching hold of his arm with surprising strength. "You can't follow her. The worlds are overlapped; 'tis faery on the beach. If you go there, you will be lost."

"I don't care—"

"You are mortal; you can't stay in that world. They will let you in; indeed, 'tis their favorite trick. But when they pass on in the morning, Malinda will go, and you will be left behind." Tears rose in her eyes. "Your mind won't bear it; you will run mad."

"I am already mad," he answered. "Is Malinda there?" The music was familiar—he had heard it before.

"*Come,*" the voices sang. "*All you ever wept for will be found. Peace and joy and love . . . come and dance with your love.*"

"She will go with them," Gwyneth said. "She will be safe."

"I don't want her to be safe," he retorted. "I want her to be with me."

"I cannot save you if you do this," she warned, following him out into the snow. "I cannot go there; I am banished."

"I won't need you." Already the music seemed fainter, already he could be too late. Shaking off her hand, he began to run.

But at the foot of the rocks, he had to stop for a moment, paralyzed with shock. It was real, all of it. His vision had come to life, the vision that had first called him to his love. Fires dotted the beach, true fire and a blue-green glow that floated above the sand, and between the fires, the faeries danced. In the woods, it was late December cold, but here, the air was warm with spring-time, the wind thick with the sweet scent of flowers.

"Life is here," the faeries sang, voice and flute entwined in a single language. *"Bring your life to dance."*

He moved out into the throng, rage throbbing through him like a pulse. Their sweet songs didn't tempt him; nothing could be further from himself than these shining creatures with their childish prattle of love. Looking into their innocent faces, he felt nothing but contempt. Ancient they may have been, but they knew nothing, understood nothing of the world they had left behind. That world was pain as much as pleasure, death as much as life. The love they sang of was nothing, an empty thrill in an endless parade of delights. Real love lived with pain and vanquished it, reached past death to give life. Malinda knew this; she had fought him to teach him as much. She could never live among these faeries; 'twas her soul that would be lost.

"Malinda!" A faery woman touched his arm, just as in his dream, entreated him to dance, but he pushed her away. "Leave me!" She frowned, but only for a moment, drawn back into the dance by another of her kind. Another touched his shoulder as he turned away toward the crashing sea. "Malinda!" He pushed through another line of dancers, glowing bodies giving way to let him pass.

She was standing in the surf, just as he knew she would be, twirling slowly in a dance of her own. She stopped when she saw him, took a step back into the sea. "Come back," he ordered, holding out his hand. She was still herself, still in her mortal form. He could see the bruise fading on her cheek, her broken, bloodied nails as she held up a hand to ward him off. Tabby's hands had looked that way after her brawls with Bruel, nails broken trying to claw him to ribbons. "*Let her go, demon,*" Tabby's voice seemed to urge inside his head, part of the faery song. "*Must you see her die? Haven't you hurt her enough? Must you destroy her yourself?*"

"No," Malinda said, her brows drawn in a tiny frown. "Liar . . . leave him alone." A wave broke white around her ankles, making her stagger, but she didn't fall. "She lies," she said, so softly he could barely hear, but her eyes met his, saw him at last.

Malinda saw her mortal beloved standing in the faery world, a shadow in the light. He felt no joy in the music, felt no warmth from the fires. He hated them; he felt pain. He should never have come to this place. He should let her go. She held up a hand to warn him away . . . but she was wrong. He wasn't shadow; he was light. The darkness was outside him, a woman's shape that curled and clung around him like a dragon and a shroud, whispering evil in his heart, refusing to let him go. "*Let her go,*" the darkness sang, claws around his throat. "*Must you see her die?*" She meant Malinda—she was using Malinda to hurt him. "*Haven't you hurt her enough. Must you destroy her yourself?*"

"No," she said aloud, finding mortal voice, risking another slip. "Liar . . . leave him alone." Something cold and wet dragged at her feet, something from the mortal world trying to drag her back to where she could be hurt. She had to turn away or pain would find her. Already she could feel it, the cross beginning to tingle on her breast. But she couldn't leave Tarquin where he was, in the clutches of this shadow. "She lies," she told him, willing him to break free.

"Malinda . . ." Tarquin's heart beat faster, desperate tears in his eyes. Crying as well, she retreated further as he took another step. "Malinda, please," he begged, desperate with frustrated love.

The shadow still surrounded him, Malinda saw; she wouldn't let him go. "Come with me," Malinda said, almost a whisper. The pain was growing stronger, the music of the faeries beginning to fade. She looked back toward the beach, desperate with fear—she had to go to them. "Come and take me home."

"I can't." He reached out to her, wanted to simply grab her, but what would she do if he did? The falcons screamed above them. She could still escape, leave him holding empty air and dust. "You have to stay with me." Words seemed to echo in the falcons' cries, words in faery from her spell. "As you are entwined, entwine me with my love," he spoke in the faery tongue, drawing closer, the words strangely natural in his mouth. "As you are enslaved, enslave my love to me."

Malinda saw the shadow draw into herself with a hiss of rage or pain, saw her lover coming closer in the light. The words he spoke had power of their own, warmth and joy like faery song and fire. His hand closed over hers, and she felt him, solid and warm, not from a distance as she had for so many days, but with her indeed, touching her body and soul.

Tarquin saw her gasp as he touched her, fleeting pain in her eyes, but she didn't pull away. "Be with me, Malinda," he said in simple English, cradling her cheek in his palm.

"Yes," she whispered, gazing up into his eyes. *I have come for you,* they seemed to say, just as he had told her in the woods the very first time they had met. He bent and kissed her mouth, and she melted into his kiss. "Yes . . ." The shadow was around them both, but the music engulfed them as well, a mix of darkness and light. The pain was strong now, as real as Tarquin's kiss, but she could bear it, sheltered in his arms.

He felt her arms entwine around his neck as he lifted her out of the surf, her hands in his hair as he carried her back to the beach. She felt him, kissed him back; she was alive. "Don't leave me," she ordered as his kiss moved to her cheek. "Don't you dare."

"Never," he promised, looking down into her eyes. "Never again." He kissed away her tears, felt her tremble as he pressed her close. "I promise, angel . . . I promise."

"Then I will not leave you." The faery folk were drawing closer. She could see them over his shoulder, hungry interest gleaming in their eyes. They wanted Tarquin, not as his mother's demon shadow wanted him in hate or as she herself wanted him in love, but something in between. His purely mortal soul was a novelty to them, something different in a world that was always the same. They wanted it as a toy. "The tower," she said, wrapping her arms more tightly around him. "Take me to the tower."

"Are you sure?"

"I love you, Tarquin." She touched his cheek and made him look into her eyes. "Make love to me in the tower."

"I love you." He carried her over the rocks, the faeries forgotten, their music nothing more than memory in his mind as the falcons swooped and cried in triumph overhead. The castle was in ruins, but the tower was intact, tiny blue flowers blooming in the cracks between the stones in spite of the winter cold. Malinda reached out to touch these as they passed, and Tarquin shivered, trembling to remember the power he carried in his arms. "Magic," he said softly, a cold shadow touching his heart.

"Yes, my love," she promised, drawing his mouth down to hers as they crossed the threshold of the uppermost room. He lowered her to the bed, and she almost swooned, faint with sweet relief. This was real in every world; finally she was here.

"My love," he echoed, climbing over her. He kissed her throat and downward, tasted the sea on her skin. Everything he ever loved was here, cradled in his arms. His mouth moved to her breast, heaven-soft beneath his cheek, sweet nipple going hard against his tongue.

"Tarquin," she sighed, tangling her hand in his hair. He tore her gown open to reach her skin, and she caught her breath, the cross-shaped burn coming alive with pain as it touched the air. He kissed her there as well, barely a touch, and she felt his tears on her skin. "Shhh . . . it's all right."

"I'm so sorry," he wept, hiding his face in the curve of her throat.

"It's not your fault," she promised. "You didn't do it."

"I left you—"

"You came back." She tugged at his hair until he raised

his head. "You came back," she repeated, framing his face in her hands.

He smiled like sunlight breaking through the dark, making her heart leap up. "As if I had a choice," he answered, bending to kiss her again.

He felt her mouth open to him, felt her hands caress his shoulders, one leg entwined around him as if to hold him close. She was here; she was his. He could not give her up. "Mine," she whispered as he broke the kiss. She kissed his cheek and jaw and throat as his hand slid up her leg. "Love me . . . come inside."

"Yes . . ." She smiled as his tongue teased her ear, sighed as his hands slipped hot beneath her skirt, molding the curve of her hips. She wanted to touch him everywhere, to ravish him with her mouth, but it was too perfect to melt into his kisses, to let him ravish her instead. "Malinda," he murmured, warm breath against her cheek. He spoke her name like a prayer. He pushed inside her, and she cried. *Yours,* she thought, *I am yours.*

Your slave, he thought, *I am yours.* This was the snare that would hold him, this Malinda-witch who held him now. This was the home he had never thought to find. He raised her up beneath him, drove in deeper as he fell with her back to the bed.

She screamed his name, a falcon's cry, arms aching as she clung with all her might. Release tore through her, but still she wanted him; she could never have enough. This was freedom, this rapture, this love. With him inside her, she was free. His mouth caught hers, feeding on her cries, and she pushed her tongue inside him, wrapped her legs around him, too, desperate to be one.

He reached under her to draw her up to him again, shift

her closer as she gasped aloud, her climax rising higher. He could feel it, his flesh and hers combined, commingled as their souls to be saved or damned as one. "Malinda," he cried, spilling inside her, all separation lost.

"Yes," she murmured, "my love." He sank against her shoulder, and she twined her arms around him, savoring his weight. Music faded from the air as the draft from the window turned cold—the faery world was lost. "I don't care," she whispered, smiling as she drifted into sleep.

23

Ⲥⲙⲱ

*M*ark stood on the beach, deciding what to do next. Something had happened here, and recently. Great, black smears of ash stained the sand at regular intervals, some of them still smoking as the tide slipped slowly away. But now there was no one in sight.

He looked back at the cliffs above him and the ruined castle beyond. His father had said it was a wreck twenty years ago, and from what he could see, its condition had not improved. But there was something strange about it, almost inviting. Birds circled above the central tower—falcons, of course. Watching them, a kind of peace settled over his heart, a calm he had not felt since he'd come home and found Malinda gone. Home . . . this place felt like home.

"Brinlaw!" A pretty girl with curly red hair was coming toward him, clamoring over the rocks. "Bless us, is it Brinlaw?"

"One of them," he smiled, the warmth in his heart extending to her as well. "I'm Mark, Will Brinlaw's son."

"Mark," she repeated, meeting him at the edge of the

sand. "You look just the way your father did the first time he came here."

"As if you could remember," he teased. He was smiling, and she smiled back, but suddenly he felt a chill. She looked young, as young as he, but suddenly he saw her eyes were old. Something about her reminded him of his mother, but not in a comfortable way. And Malinda. "Malinda," he said aloud. "I'm looking for my sister, Malinda." Her smile faded, and a spark of pity flashed for a moment in her eyes. "She's a noble lady, and she's taller than you, with blond hair. She might be with a man—a brigand."

"Tarquin," the girl said sadly. "I know him, Mark, and your sister . . . I have seen her."

"Who are you?" He grabbed her by the shoulders. "Where is Malinda?" She started to speak, but he stopped her, then let her go to walk away. Two figures were walking hand in hand down the path from the castle, a man built like a mountain and a woman with long blond hair. "Malinda!" he shouted, racing toward her.

For a moment, Malinda thought she must be seeing visions again, figures conjured from her heart. Then she heard her brother's shout, saw him recognize her, and her paralysis broke. Giving Tarquin's hand a squeeze, she let him go and raced down the path, mindless of her slippers. "Mark!" she shrieked, throwing herself into his arms.

"Where have you been?" he demanded, crushing her close. "You frightened everyone to death!"

"I know, I know." She returned his hug in kind, refusing to feel the pain it caused her still-fragile frame. "Me most of all. But I'm all right now, I promise."

"Yes," Gwyneth agreed, staring at her wide-eyed but

smiling nonetheless. "And you as well." The faery turned and took hold of Tarquin's hand, shaking it as if she were not quite sure he was real. "How did you escape?"

"I didn't," Tarquin answered, meeting Malinda's eyes and winking. "I am faery-touched."

"Malinda, look at you," Mark scolded, accusing Tarquin of all manner of crimes with his eyes. Indeed, his sister did present quite a picture, wrapped in a blanket over her tattered shift with nothing on her feet but sopping slippers. No doubt the bruise on her cheek had not escaped notice, either.

"Mark, I'm all right," she promised, letting go of her brother to take her lover's hand again. "Tarquin didn't do it."

"Good," he retorted, apparently still unconvinced. "But still, I want you inside."

"Amen to that," Tarquin said, scooping her off her feet and turning toward the path that led to the forest.

"Oh no," Gwyneth said, stepping in front of him. "Not to the cottage, you. This lady must go to her tower."

The faery kept the conversation moving briskly as they went inside, explaining who she was to Mark and building up the fire as Malinda changed into some of Gwyneth's clothes. But once the porridge was started and the lady was dressed, Mark would keep silent no more. "You look much better," he told his sister with a scowl just like his father's. "But how did you end up in such a state? Malinda, Farrars had the heartstone. He told us you were dead. How did he get the heartstone?"

"He took it from me," Malinda said, the bread she'd been chewing turning to sand in her mouth. She had been starving a moment before; now the very idea of swallowing was almost more than she could bear. "He accused me of being a witch." Somehow the bread went down and the words came out, cold and flat and calm. But how could she speak of these things? She looked at Tarquin, the shock and fury in his eyes, and suddenly she thought perhaps she could. "He hit me and burned me and left me buried in a hole to die."

"Holy Christ," Mark breathed, going so pale he looked faint.

"Farrars?" Tarquin stood up, the rage in his eyes so terrible now she could hardly bear to see it—rage against himself, she realized with a sinking in her heart.

"Robert Farrars, yes." She went to him, touched him, refusing to be afraid. "He hates you. He says you killed his son. He told me he had killed you. He showed me a dead man with no face, with all his skin pulled off. He told me that was you." She could see how much her words hurt him, but she couldn't seem to stop. She was hurt; she was afraid. She needed him to see her fear and drive it back, to tell her again that the nightmare was over, that finally they were awake. "He said that you were gone. He said you would never come."

"But I thought you ran away," Mark said, confused and horrified. "Were you not with Tarquin?"

"No." Tarquin's mask had fallen over his face, the expression that was no expression that shut out all the world, closing him in with his pain. "I left her." He turned his back on her, shutting her out even more. "I left her with Farrars."

"Malinda, where is Lisbet?" Mark said. "Did Farrars take her as well?"

"No, I don't think so," Malinda said, distracted from her

love for a moment by the question. Lisbet—what had become of Lisbet? How could she have forgotten to think of her sooner? "He didn't see her. I had made her invisible. We were trying to run away, Lisbet and Eleanor and I. I had worked the spell on Lisbet, and the Queen was next—"

"Queen Eleanor was there?" Mark demanded, aghast. "She saw? I can't believe this! Papa will see her burned, I swear it."

"And what will that accomplish?" Malinda snapped. "She couldn't fight Farrars any better than I could."

"She could have told us the truth," Mark insisted. "Papa would have—"

"Papa loathes her, and she knows it," Malinda answered, but she stopped before she finished. Tarquin was walking away.

"She lied, Malinda," Mark insisted, again talking to her as to a silly girl. "She told Papa you ran away to be with Tarquin."

"Tarquin!" she called after him, Mark all but forgotten. He had left the room, was walking down the stairs without looking back. "Tarquin, wait!"

"Let him go, poppet," Gwyneth advised, catching her. "Let him work it out for himself."

"No," Malinda said, pushing her away. In her mind, she saw the shadow the faery world had shown her, the evil spirit crouched around her lover like a dragon. She didn't want to see it. She wanted to nurse her own hurts, to be comforted and loved, to have her fears all kissed away. But she didn't have a choice. "He's had thirty years to work it out already," she said, grabbing up Mark's mantle and hurrying out after her love.

She found him on the beach near where they had stood

the night before when he had pulled her back into the world. The tide had receded, turning the gray strip of beach into a cold, white desert. Tarquin's eyes were turned to the horizon where the waves retreated, and he barely looked up as she approached. "I want a miracle," she said, stopping at his side. She wanted to touch him, but she didn't. She couldn't bear it if he pulled away. "I want to tell you that none of this is your fault, and I want you to believe me."

He almost smiled, but it was more like a grimace. "I wish I could."

"Do you?" Not for the first time, she wanted to hit him, hard, with both fists. But she was too tired, and besides, it wouldn't help. Blows wouldn't cure him any better than kisses; she needed stronger magic. "You had no way of knowing what Robert would do. You didn't know him any better than I did—not as well, in fact."

"But Malinda, don't you see?" The mask that had hidden his feelings was gone, she saw as he turned to face her. She should count herself lucky for that much, though it was hard to feel grateful, seeing such pain in the face of her dearest love. "I did kill his son. I didn't mean to . . ." He looked away again, obviously fighting for control. "I never mean it."

"I know," she said, her anger all but forgotten, her heart aching for him.

"But I don't have any choice." Tears choked him. Shadows he had refused to see all morning closed in around him. He had awakened so happy—Malinda was alive! She had come back to him; they were safe, for the moment, anyway. But now he thought again of his dream of this beach, the one that had first brought Blanche to warn him. He looked back at the cliff, real now and solid, remembering the dark figure he had seen there, edged in red and laughing as darkness swallowed the sky. He had stood in Tarquin's way, kept him from the tower, from Malinda, screaming for him in pain. "It isn't in my nature," he went on. "Everything I touch turns to evil, whether I will it or not."

"Your mother's curse," Malinda said softly, putting her hand in his.

"I knew it," he said, the words coming out in a rush. "I tried to go away, to leave you all alone, your parents and Nan, and you, too, the little girl who was you, your father's precious child. I thought I could keep you all safe if I just stayed away, kept myself with people I could never love who deserved whatever harm I brought them. But I couldn't. You wouldn't let me. You—" He broke off, looking away.

"I?" Malinda pressed. "What did I do?"

"You called to me," he answered, still not meeting her eyes. "In Africa a year ago, I was on my ship. I took a potion." He tried to remember why he had taken it, what madness had possessed him. Destiny. He almost smiled to think of it. He'd been looking for his destiny. "I had a vision of this place, just as it was last night, faery folk and all. I saw you." He touched her cheek, seeing for a moment not the woman he had come to know and love but the fatal beauty from his vision, the irresistible unknown that touched his heart and turned his will to nothing. His sin and his salvation. "I loved you without knowing how or why, and I couldn't resist that love. I had to come back."

"Tarquin," Malinda sighed as he turned away again. "Tarquin, don't you see?" She moved in front of him again.

"Your vision was like mine, just the same as when I saw you as a child in that horrible place at Bruel. You saw me when I would need you most, when only you could save me. You knew I was yours even before you knew my name. You loved me, you saw my need, and you saved me. If you hadn't come back, if you had stayed away in Africa, I would have died in that oubliette. If you hadn't loved me with all your soul just as I love you, you couldn't have stopped me last night, and I would be dead to this world."

"If I had stayed in Africa, you never would have been in danger," he answered stubbornly. "You said it yourself; Farrars hates me. He hurt you to hurt me, because I killed his son—"

"He hates me for myself, for not being what he thought I was," she cut him off. "He wanted me to marry him, to be his dutiful wife, the mother to the sons he would have to replace the ones he lost. He thought I was an innocent maid, which to him means a brainless fool. But I'm not, nor would I wish to be. I'm a sorceress, a faery—a witch in Robert's eyes, an unnatural thing to be destroyed." She looked up into his eyes. "Do you believe he's right?"

He looked as if she had struck him. "Of course not! How can you say such a thing?"

"I didn't say it—you did." She touched him to soften her words, both palms laid on his chest, but she didn't stop. "You called me a witch, and you were right."

"No—"

"Did I not seduce you with magic?" she asked. "Not just once, not just to bring you to bed, but before. You said it yourself just now. You meant to stay away from England; you were content. But somehow I called to you; somehow my magic drew you back to this place, to me, whether you willed it or not. Once you were here, and you knew who I was, you tried to protect me, but I wouldn't let you, remember? I did everything in my feminine power to make you want me, and when that didn't work—"

"It did work," he muttered.

"I bewitched you indeed, driving you away, when all you wanted was to keep me safe. Is that not so?"

"Yes, but—"

"If I had not worked that spell on you, you would have stayed at Brinlaw," she finished.

"I would have kept you safe." He touched her face, marveling again to see her, so beautiful even now—a princess in disguise, furious and loving and alive. He thought of the creature she had been just one day before, the lifeless doll whose eyes showed only fear, and his heart clenched like a fist. He drew her close and wrapped her in his arms. "You are not a witch," he murmured, closing his eyes to lose himself in the smell of her hair.

"And you are not a demon." She was clinging to him with all her might, and her heart was pounding; he could feel it against his own chest. Suddenly he realized she wasn't really angry; she was still afraid. "The demon isn't you," she went on, words broken apart with tears. "But I can't convince you. She won't let you go."

"Malinda, what are you talking about?" he asked, confused. He drew back to see her face. "Who do you mean?"

"Last night when you were reaching out to me, calling me back, I saw this curse that plagues you so, this demon that you say is you." She touched his cheek. "I saw a shadow all around you, the shadow of a dragon." He stared at her, aghast, but he couldn't speak. He wanted to tell her she was wrong, that what she described was not possible, but he was not a fool. He had been on the beach; he had seen the world of faery. He saw the light now haunting her eyes, and he knew she spoke the truth. "You told me once about the spell your mother used to bewitch Bruel. You said it was like mine, a dragon spell. Do you remember?"

"Yes."

"It was your mother's spirit I saw, beloved—her evil, her demon, not yours." Cold wind swirled suddenly around them, snatching at her hair. "It comes from outside you, from her, not inside you," she insisted.

"Malinda . . ." Tears were streaming down her cheeks— more pain he had caused.

"But you won't believe me; you can't." She turned away from him, toward the cliffs and the tower beyond. "She has made certain of that." He put his hands on her shoulders from behind, pressed a kiss to her cheek, desperate to comfort her, to banish the pain he heard in her voice. "I fear her, Tarquin," she said, so softly he barely heard. She turned her face to his kiss, reached back to clasp his hand. "Far more than I fear Robert Farrars." The wind had picked up indeed, and swollen clouds hung in the sky, thick and dark with rain that would surely turn to ice. "All he can do is kill me. She will take you away."

"No." He turned her around, framed her face in his hands. "No, love, she will not—"

"It's already happening, just like before. I can feel it. As soon as you heard that Farrars is the man who hurt me, you began to blame yourself. You forgot how you saved me. All you could think was that you had put me in danger. You forgot to love me; you were too busy feeling guilty."

He smiled his grim little smile. "I could never forget to love you."

"Yea, love, you have loved me all along," she agreed, angry again. "But you left me all the same, not because of me but because of you, or so you said, because you are cursed. How long will it take for this curse to tear you away from me again, to pull you back into the dark? She will whisper lies I cannot hear, come into your heart where I can't see. She'll make you believe it again, that you can't help but destroy me if you stay—you already believe it. She'll say I could be happy if only you left me alone, that only by losing you will I ever be safe."

He had heard enough. "It doesn't matter," he cut her off, grabbing her by the arms. "I don't care if you're happy; I don't care if you're safe." He kissed her fervently, her lips and more, half a dozen kisses all over her beautiful face. "If I did, I would have let you go, let the faeries have you. They wanted to take you from me, and Gwyneth said to let you go . . ." He kissed her; words weren't enough.

Her beloved was kissing her again, and Malinda melted against him, sweet relief making her weak. She had won; somehow, she had won her love at last. "I saw you," she told him as she kissed him back, remembering the night before. "I wanted to stay with you, but I was so afraid." She pressed her cheek against his heart. "I'm so sorry I was afraid."

"Hush now," he soothed, a tender rumble as he held her close. The first curtain of sleet swept over them from the surf, and she shivered, curling closer still. "Don't be afraid, sweet faery." He stroked her hair, the cold nothing to the burning in his heart. "I won't give you up, demon or not."

There they were, the words she needed, but someone else was speaking as well, making her look up. "Malinda!" a voice called on the wind—Mark's voice, impatient and annoyed. Drawing back from Tarquin to look up at the cliffs, she saw him, holding his hands cupped before his mouth to make himself heard. "Come inside right now!" he shouted, or words to that effect—with the storm and the surf, she could hardly be sure.

"He's right," Tarquin said, smiling. "We should go before we freeze."

"Wait." She took his hand in both of hers. She had to know for sure. "Mark will want to go home to Brinlaw."

"Yes." If Mark was back in England, Will and Alista would likely be as well. What would Brinlaw say to him when they met? He shuddered even to imagine.

"And Farrars lives," Malinda went on. "Anything could still happen." She was trembling again, her fear colder than the storm in spite of all his comfort. Only one promise could put it to rest. "But whatever comes, I can stand it, so long as we're together." She looked up, met his eyes with hers. "Can you promise me? Promise that no matter what, we will be together? That even if we die . . ." She let the words trail off.

"I won't leave you." He touched her chin, her cheek, learning her face in this moment, letting the sight of her burn into his soul. Until death do us part . . . it wasn't nearly long enough. "I won't let you leave me."

"You swear it?" she whispered.

He kissed her softly on the lips. "I swear."

Standing on the cliff, Mark watched them in despair, his sister and her love. "I warned you, Papa," he sighed as he turned away.

The first streaks of dawning light were glowing over the watchtowers as Will Brinlaw came into his courtyard, headed for the stables. By the time his horse was saddled, the sun would be up. But for now, he would have quiet.

The heavy door screamed in protest as he pushed it open, the hinges wet and frozen, but he still could have sworn he heard a thump from inside. "Hello?" he called, frowning. At this hour, even the grooms should still be abed. He heard a scurrying scrabble, too large for a rat. "Who's there?"

He rounded the corner, a lantern held before him. Another, smaller light was hanging from a rail near the tack racks. Coming closer, he saw a saddle had been taken from its stand and dropped on the floor—the thud he had heard. But he saw no sign of a man. Frowning, he picked up the saddle with his left hand while he drew his sword with his right. Strange matters were afoot at Brinlaw lately, only the worst of which was Malinda's disappearance. Another girl had been found dead at a crossroads less than a mile from the castle, one of Eleanor's serving maids. Now someone was stealing saddles—or horses, more likely—in the middle of the night. "Who's there?" he said again, turning slowly in a circle.

Then he saw the bundle.

He recognized the wrappings at once—an old mantle of his own that his youngest son had commandeered for play. It had been the sail of a warship the last time he had seen it, tied to a broomstick and propped over a washtub in the solar. But now it was strapped up in a surprisingly neat supply pack with one of Alista's old scarves and Willie's best belt. "Willie," he said, putting down his sword. The pile of straw behind him rustled again. "William Brinlaw." He got a muffled sneeze for answer with a slightly less muffled oath to follow. He turned toward the sound.

"Come on, come out," he ordered, trying not to sound amused.

The haystack shuddered and slid over as a head of dark, curly hair emerged from underneath. "Hullo, Papa," Willie mumbled, standing up.

"Hullo," Will answered, trying to think what to say next. *Let's go see your mother,* sprang immediately to mind. But Alista was worried enough already without the prospect of another runaway. "Where are you going?" he asked the boy instead.

For a moment, Willie didn't answer, a mutinous light that was his mother all over coming into his eyes. His little jaw was set; his little feet were planted—he was Alista reborn, or her father, more like. Old Mark of Brinlaw and Falconskeep had once been the bane of Will's existence, and his grandson looked just like him. "To Falconskeep," the boy said at last. "I'm going to save Malinda."

Will sat down on a stool to be closer to his son's level and give himself a moment to think. In truth, he had been thinking the same thing, coming out to ride before the sun was up. But Eleanor was still in residence at Brinlaw; he couldn't just leave her unattended. And Alista was halfway through her pregnancy; could she make such a ride? "Your brother, Mark, has already gone to Falconskeep," he pointed out, meeting Willie's eyes.

"But he won't be enough, nor Tarquin either," Willie insisted, suddenly rushing forward to his father. "I've seen it, Papa. I've seen it."

"I know," Will mumbled, hugging him close, though in truth he didn't know at all, didn't understand. "It's all right." Alista's dreams were haunted, too, with falcons and the tower and images she either couldn't or wouldn't describe and he could never understand. This magic was hers alone, hers and Malinda's, a feminine mystery he had always accepted but never dared examine too closely. Alista could manage it all quite well without him. Malinda had been her project; the boys were his. She would keep Malinda from turning the castle upside down, and he would turn their sons into noble knights. As for Falconskeep, it was half a country away, and its legend was over and done. When Alista had killed Geoffrey d'Anjou and he himself had saved her from transforming into a falcon, they had left that tower behind forever, never to return, and its magic was something for the women alone.

But Malinda was lost; Alista's dreams called her back to the tower. And his baby son, his namesake, was being torn apart by magic alongside his beautiful mother. "It's all right," he repeated, holding his little one close. "You can't go to Falconskeep alone—"

"But, Papa, I have to—"

"But we can go together."

Farrars stared down at the bodies of his three retainers, rage like a fever burning through him. The first two had obviously been murdered, but the old man had killed himself, stabbed himself in the heart with his own dagger. No doubt he preferred death to facing his master. "The first of the troops are assembled here and ready, my lord," his captain said, joining him on the rise. "The rest should be here by sunset. We only await your command."

"Keep waiting." He went inside the ruin, followed the stench into the fetid dungeon. He had to see; he had to be certain. Whoever had killed his men—but he knew, didn't he? He knew who had done it. But the killer had been too late. The witch would surely have been dead. But he had to see; he had to be certain. Everything seemed to be crumbling in his hands, but once he saw, he would know he was still right. He would see the hand of God; God was on his side.

The corpse he'd left hanging on the wall had been cut down, and a blanket had been thrown over what little was left of it. An annoying gesture, but nothing really—the demon had felt pity toward his own. He turned away and forgot it. But on the other side of the room, he saw a more troubling sight. The chest over the oubliette had been moved, and the trapdoor was thrown back. "No," he muttered, sweat breaking out on his brow as he drew closer. "She could not . . . could not escape." He dropped his torch into the trap, watched the flame as it fell. Nothing . . . Malinda was not there.

"Away . . ." His voice was not his own. Imps of blue fire danced before his eyes, and the ground felt soft beneath his feet. The Christ walked on the waters . . . a witch could not be drowned. "Somehow she flew away . . ."

"My lord?" The voice was unfamiliar. His captain would know better than to speak to him at such a moment. He turned with a snarl and found a boy, the spy who'd gone after Brinlaw's son. He was staring at his master with eyes like a calf's, wide and stupid, and Farrars' hand went to his dagger. "My lord, please," he stammered. "I bring news— good news!"

"What is it?" He grabbed hold of the boy, snatched him up by his shirt. "Tell me, what?"

"I have found them," the boy stammered, a tiny smile of triumph breaking through his fear. "I have found FitzBruel."

24

*T*he storm raged for days until the cliffs around the Falconskeep tower were thick with blue-white ice that glowed in the light of the moon. Tarquin sat on the wide window ledge of the highest room, gazing out and barely feeling the cold. The others were sleeping, Mark curled up before the fire, Malinda and Gwyneth sharing the bed. He smiled to remember the young knight's face the first night they'd spent here when Malinda had announced her intention to sleep with Tarquin instead.

"Over my bleeding corpse," Mark had said, giving his sister's lover a look that left no doubt he was in earnest. Malinda had wanted to argue, but Tarquin had relented at once—the poor boy was having to choke down quite enough ugly truth without seeing his sister dishonored before his very eyes. He had wanted to set off for Brinlaw at once, storm or not, and Tarquin had been inclined to agree. But in this, Malinda had won.

"No one knows we're here except Mama and Papa and Willie," she had pointed out. "Robert knows nothing of this place—no one does outside our own family. And I'm tired." Her tone had been perfectly ordinary when she said it—the same old Malinda determined to have her way. But in her eyes, Tarquin had seen something more, a shadow that gave him pause. She might seem well enough—she might even insist that she was—but not so long ago she had been on the point of death.

"We can at least wait out the storm," he had decided, and Mark had quickly agreed. No doubt he knew his sister, too.

Turning now toward the cozy room, his eyes strayed again to a deep brown stain on the flagstone floor, still visible in the firelight. Geoffrey d'Anjou's blood.

"What is it?" Malinda said softly, breaking into his thoughts. She got up from the bed and crept barefoot to join him. "FitzBruel is smiling? The world must be coming to an end." She kissed his mouth, settling into his arms.

"No." He pressed a kiss to her brow. "The world has just begun." He lifted her onto the ledge, and she leaned back against him with a sigh. "Why are you awake?" he asked, brushing her hair back as she rested her head on his shoulder.

"I was thinking about Mama. I should send her a message by Rufus," she answered. "She and Papa are frantic, Mark said." The goshawk was still keeping close to his mistress, closer than ever since the night she had almost turned true faery. Tarquin doubted he could be convinced to leave her now, even for so worthy a quest.

"You'll soon be home yourself," he said, cuddling her. "All of us will."

"Yes," she agreed, holding his hand. "They'll want us to be married, you know."

"I know." In truth, he had thought of this a lot over the

past few days; it was the thought that had kept him awake tonight. It almost seemed redundant, having a wedding after all they'd already been through and done. They were joined more surely than any priest could make them; they had promised each other as much. *"Even if we die,"* his love had said, the memory of her words making him shiver even now. As a child, he had craved a mother's love, the warm glow of Alista's smile as she bent down to kiss him good night. But now, all he could ever want was here, the sorceress Malinda. "My sweetest witch," he murmured, the words lost in her hair. She turned her head to kiss him, looked into his eyes. "Will you marry me?"

Her smile was like the moonlight, too beautiful to be real. "Yes," she whispered, touching his face as he kissed her. "Of course I will." He kissed her again, and she turned in his arms to face him, caught his lower lip between her teeth. "I will."

Mark's snore broke through the silence, a broken trumpet, and she giggled, burying her face in Tarquin's neck to muffle the sound, and he had to bite the inside of his cheek to keep from laughing himself. "Your brother," he murmured as she turned around again.

"Yes." She laced her fingers with his, their hands entwined in her lap. "Talk to me, then." She snuggled back against him. "Tell me about Alexandria."

"All right," he said, kissing her cheek. He would talk to her all night.

He awoke at dawn to the smell of smoke. "Fire," Malinda said, already awake.

"Where?" Mark demanded, rushing to the window. "Holy Christ . . ."

The tower had been set aflame. Brush had been piled all around the walls and soaked with pitch, from the look of it. "Get back," Tarquin ordered, pulling Malinda away from the window and blocking Mark's way. At this height, they should be out of an arrow's range, but he wasn't taking any chances.

"How many?" Mark asked, putting on his sword.

"An army," Tarquin answered grimly. Troops filled the courtyard below, mostly foot soldiers but with a sprinkling of mounted horsemen—an excellent siege force, he would have to say. Another group of mounted men waited at the edge of the tree line, one better armed and armored than the others. "And I've only seen him once, but I believe that man is Lord Farrars."

Malinda gasped, and Gwyneth ran to her side as if to steady her. "Impossible," Mark said, going pale. He pushed past Tarquin to look out the window himself. "No . . . how could he have found us?" He looked back at Malinda, his brown eyes wild with horror. "God's truth, I told no one I was coming here, I swear it."

"It's all right," Tarquin said, clamping a hand down on his shoulder. The last thing he needed was a hysterical knight.

"What do we do?" Malinda asked, willing herself to stay calm. *He can't hurt me,* she chanted inside her head. *There's nothing he can do to hurt me now.*

"This tower is stone; it won't burn," Mark told her, obviously trying to sound encouraging.

"No," Tarquin agreed. "They mean to smoke us out."

"They can't if we're not here," Gwyneth said, taking Malinda's hand.

"It's a bit late for that," Mark pointed out with a bitter laugh.

"The well, Tarquin," the faery interrupted. "We can go down the well."

"No, thank you," he muttered, loading a crossbow and tossing it to Mark. "Malinda, get dressed."

"Yes, but what does she mean?" Malinda said, tugging on her gown. "Gwyneth, how can we go down the well? Wouldn't we drown?"

"Naught of the sort," Gwyneth said, helping her. "There's a passageway a few feet down that leads to the caves under the castle. You'd be safe from the smoke, and those villains would never know where to find you."

Farrars would wait, Tarquin thought but didn't say, looking out the window again. From this distance, his lordship's expression was impossible to read, but waves of hatred seemed to rise off him like heat. He had killed again and again in pursuit of his prey. Now that he had run it to ground, he would never give it up. He had tortured Malinda and left her to die a death that was a hell of its own just to punish her for disappointing him.

No, Tarquin wouldn't hide.

"A passage down a well?" Malinda asked, trying not to let her voice tremble. "To caves under the ground?" The very idea made her shudder, visions of Farrars' oubliette threatening to reduce her to a quivering mass of fear good for nothing but wringing her hands. But if this was the only escape, she would take it. So long as Tarquin was with her, she could make herself do anything.

"It will be all right," Tarquin told her now. "Come on, and stay together."

The air in the stairwell was so thick with smoke, they could barely see, much less breathe. Malinda put a hand on the wall—the tiny blue flowers the Lady Blanche's magic had called up were black and dead, their vines shriveled dry in the heat. "Grand-mère, are you here?" she whispered, despair touching her heart. Tarquin took her other hand and held it fast, and she smiled. They would be all right.

She heard him swear from the smoky dark, felt a jerk on her arm. "Tarquin?" she said, alarmed.

"I tripped." He bent down to pick up something from the stairs—a sword, the blade so bright it glittered even through the smoke. "Over your father's sword."

"What is that doing here?" Mark demanded. He tried to move past Malinda to see and nearly fell over the side of the narrow stairway.

"As if it matters," Gwyneth scolded, catching him just in time.

"Brinlaw left it the last time he was here," Tarquin explained, sheathing his own sword to hold up the falcon blade. It felt good in his hand, familiar somehow. Just holding it, he felt calmer, better able to do what he must. "The well-spirit tried to drown him on these stairs, and he dropped it."

"A lovely story," Mark muttered. "Where is this spirit now, Gwynnie? What's to keep her from drowning us?"

"You're safe with Malinda," Gwyneth promised.

At the bottom of the stairs, the smoke began to clear, as if the well had a bubble of clean air all around it. "This is better," Malinda said, letting go of Tarquin's hand to peer down the shaft. In one way, she did feel better. Something about this room was familiar, and a sense of warm well-being seemed to rise from the mouth of the well, quite the opposite of what she had expected. Somehow, it wasn't like the oubliette at all. But something was wrong, something she couldn't see. Shadows flickered in the torchlight—a clawed hand seemed to reach around the wall. But when she turned, she saw only Tarquin. "This won't be so bad."

"No," he lied, making himself smile at his beloved, ignoring the cold sweat breaking out on his brow. The first time he had seen this well, the spirit inside had called to him as his mother. He had reached for her, and she had grabbed him and tried to drag him down to his death. Alista had pulled him back kicking and screaming to be let go. The second time, he had been with Will and Raynard, and the water had come exploding out like a fountain from hell. He had sworn to leave the thing alone, and he had no intention of breaking that vow. But Malinda couldn't know it. "It will be fine."

"Here, poppet, take this," Gwyneth said, unlooping a rope from the wall. "She will let you come in and find the passage. She'll even help you if you ask. You can take this with you as a way to guide the rest of us."

"Malinda is not going first," Mark protested.

"And why not?" Malinda smiled. "Don't you trust me?" She took the rope and tied it around her waist, mischief glinting in her eyes. For the first time since Tarquin had found her, she looked like the Malinda of old, and a fist clenched tight around his heart. "I'll tie off the rope once I get inside, assuming there's a place to do it."

"Be careful," Tarquin ordered, checking her knot.

"Careful? Me? You can't be serious." She touched his cheek. "You, too. Be careful, I mean."

"I will." He kissed her but not too deeply, careful not to make the kiss seem too significant, not to let it feel as though he thought it might be their last.

"Good luck, poppet," Gwyneth said.

Malinda sat on the edge of the well and swung her legs over. Taking care not to look at Tarquin, she took a deep breath and let herself drop into the water.

At first, the shock of the cold was too much to bear; she couldn't think. But in a moment or so, it passed, and she felt strangely buoyant, almost as if someone or something were trying to hold her up. *"Sister,"* a feminine voice said softly, coming from all around her. *"You are safe."* She sounded relieved, as if she had worried long.

"Actually, I'm not," Malinda answered with her mind. *"There's a man who wants to kill me. I'm trying to run away."*

"Then come."

Her hands found an opening in the smooth stone wall, a tiny wooden door wedged shut. She pushed it hard with all her strength and it gave way, sweeping her inside.

Tarquin could have sworn he heard voices coming from the water, Malinda's and another, but no one else seemed to notice, so he decided to keep his peace. Suddenly he felt a tug on the rope, one hard, and two shorter. "She made it," he said, turning back to Gwyneth. "Just use the rope as a guide. We don't know how well she ties knots."

"I'll be careful," Gwyneth promised, holding out her hands to be lowered into the well.

"You next," Mark said when she had tugged the rope to let them know she had made it. "Malinda won't feel easy until you're there."

"I'm not going." Muffled voices could be heard from the passageway above them, men calling to each other through the smoke. "Now come, you have to hurry," Tarquin finished, motioning the boy toward the well.

"Are you mad?" Mark demanded. "There's an army out there! You can't—"

"You're right; I can't," Tarquin cut him off. "Farrars wants me dead, Mark. That's why he's here, to kill me."

"And you mean to give him what he wants." Grim understanding dawned in the young knight's eyes, a wisdom too old for his face.

"Not if I can kill him first," Tarquin answered with a bitter smile. "But lacking that, I can at least save Malinda." He caught Mark's arm. "Farrars won't give me up, but he may not know Malinda lives."

"And if you are dead, he will stop looking for her," Mark finished. "He will go away."

"And Malinda will be safe," he nodded, the words like ashes in his mouth. "You can take her home." She would hate him for this, would curse his name through this world and the next. But he had to try.

"Let me go with you," Mark insisted. "Two would surely be better than one—"

"You have to stay with Malinda," he said. "You have to keep her from coming after me. Now hurry—they're probably worried already."

Mark didn't look happy, but he nodded. "You've given me the harder task," he muttered. "She's going to kill me, you know." Tarquin nodded, and they shared a smile. "Good luck, Cuz," Mark said, clasping his arm before disappearing into the well.

Tarquin waited until he knew he was gone, then leaned down into the shaft. He remembered a lever, just outside his reach as a child—yes, there it was. He pulled it, and the water receded, sucking back down from the mouth. "*Soon,*" a voice seemed to call from the depths, his mother's voice. "*Soon, my love, we will be as one.*"

"Not if I can help it," he muttered, straightening up. He

lifted the falcon sword as footsteps began to clatter down the stairs. "Not if I can win."

Malinda stood in a circular chamber of shining, silver-black stone, walls and ceiling and floor all smooth and glittering as beaded glass. Words in the faery tongue were carved in every surface, almost impossible to read by sight amidst the dancing light . . . Why was there light at all? The door from the well led to a pool that rose from the center of the chamber, shallow at the edges. She stood now in the shallows. But from its center came an eerie glow, white light shining as from impossible depths, illuminating this magical hall. "Sister," Malinda murmured, holding out a hand to the light.

"Are you warm enough, my lady?" Gwyneth asked, straightening up and wringing water from her skirt. "These caverns can be cold to human folk."

"I'm fine." Tarquin would be here soon; he would keep her warm. She touched the wall, felt the runes beneath her fingertips, sharp as if they'd just been cut. The rock was the same as the heartstone, or so it appeared. It would be hard as diamonds. "Who made this place, Gwyneth?" she asked, a shiver running through her. "Who carved these words?"

"The spirit made her chamber in the rocks, just as she made all these caverns," Gwyneth answered. "As for the carvings, some say she made them as well. But some say not, that they were made by the women of the tower in ancient times as a record of their magic."

"So they are spells?"

"Spells and stories, or so your grandmother said." The faery's voice was sad. "She used to study them and put them in her book."

"The book I lost." Mark was coming through the door,

and she turned to meet him. "You might have taken off your armor," she teased him as he struggled to his feet.

"I might," he muttered, slamming the door shut behind him.

"Mark, wait," she protested. "Tarquin—"

"Tarquin isn't coming," he answered, his expression grim. "He went to face Farrars." Sympathy flashed in his eyes. "It was his choice, Malinda."

"No!" She grabbed at him to push him out of the way, her fingers scrabbling for purchase on his water-slick chain mail shirt. "He doesn't get to choose. Let me pass—"

"No, Malinda." He tried to catch her by the arms to hold her fast. "Stop it. Let him go—"

"No!" She tore free, pounding at him, shoving at him with all her strength and weight, but he wouldn't budge. "Mark, please—"

"I can't, love." He caught her in an embrace, fighting to hold her still. "You know I can't." She went limp against him, and he relaxed his hold, hugging her as she cried. "You'll be safe," he soothed. "He wants you to be safe."

"Poor poppet," Gwyneth sighed, stroking her hair.

No, Malinda thought, fury knotted inside her. *I will not be what you want.* Mustering all the strength her body could hold, she threw Mark off and backed away. "He can't choose that for me," she said, backing toward the opening that led to the caverns beyond.

"My lady, be careful," Gwyneth warned, but her eyes said she understood.

"Take care of my brother," she answered. "Keep him safe." Before Mark could react, she turned and ran into the caverns as fast as her legs would carry her.

"Malinda, no!" Mark shouted, running to the passage.

"Where do these caves lead?" he demanded, turning on Gwyneth.

"All over," the faery answered. "You would be lost in half a moment, never to be found." She put a hand on his shoulder. "But the faery will find her way."

Lisbet stood at the point of the *Falcon's* bow, desperately searching the coastline for some sign of Falconskeep Castle. The ice storm had blown them badly off course, and Davyd's charts didn't show this shore in any detail. "Look there," he said, putting his hands on her shoulders to turn her the right way.

"Smoke," she answered, drawing in her breath. "Something is on fire."

"Big enough to be a village," the first mate surmised, scratching at his grizzled chin. "Them Irish still raiding this far in?"

"I don't think so," Davyd said mildly. A large flock of land birds was circling above the cliffs just around the next peninsula near the pillar of smoke. Was this the castle they sought?

Suddenly one of the birds, smaller than the others, broke formation and turned toward the ship, bearing down with obvious purpose. "Rufus!" Lisbet shrieked as the creature swooped down to the deck, scattering sailors in every direction. "It's Rufus!" She put out her arm, and the goshawk settled on her wrist. "Is she here, Rufus?" she crooned, stroking his soft-feathered breast. "Is Malinda found?"

"If she is, she needs help," Davyd said. The ship was rounding the point, and the castle could be seen, its tower pouring smoke. The beach was crowded with troops under banners showing a black cross on a field of gold. "The light of the cross."

"Oh no," Lisbet moaned as Rufus took flight again. "Not Farrars."

"The one who's after the captain?" the first mate asked. "Are them his troops, then?" He grinned. "Ye'd better pray for him, milady." He glanced back at the other sailors who were already scrambling to put the launches in the water. "He's about to have a problem."

Tarquin fought his way up the stairs, flinging another soldier howling over the side. Here he had the advantage—the stairs were only wide enough for one man at a time, and he knew the way, could move with confidence in spite of the smoke. But once he reached the hall and the troops there realized he wasn't one of them, he was besieged on every side, the falcon sword flashing like lightning through the dark, its blade glowing bright. He fought them not as separate men but rather a single monster with a hundred arms, cutting through a chaos of death, blind with fire and fury. The hall was no more than a circle of flames, the broken walls all blazing. As he drove a path toward the archway, he could tell they still meant to take him alive. He could hear them shouting to one another, snatches of words caught over the clash of swords and his own voice, roaring murder. But he would not be captured. He would reach Farrars or die. A blade sliced across his shoulder, cutting to the bone, and he screamed, but he didn't stop fighting, didn't even slow down. He was the demon; pain was life.

Suddenly, the world opened up—he was in the courtyard. The flames were gone, but the troops were denser here, better organized. The ruined gate of the old castle wall gaped before him like a toothless maw, and the stones under his boots were slick with ice. A knight in chain mail armor bore down on him from his left, his wounded side, and he swung toward him, both hands solid on the sword hilt, bashing the flat of the blade against the man's head hard enough to send his pointed little helmet flying. "Farrars!" he roared, snapping the blade back to cleave the man's head from his shoulders. "Coward! Where are you?"

Malinda emerged from the caves into chaos. The beach was crowded with soldiers, Farrars' troops fighting other, rougher men who were pouring out of boats they were dragging from the surf. "Tarquin!" she yelled, confused, as a pair of combatants rolled past her feet, a knight in armor set upon by a cackling brigand with a dagger in each hand. "What is happening?" She turned toward the ocean, saw the ship anchored beyond the breakers, its falcon sail loose and flapping in the wind. Tarquin's ship—these were Tarquin's men! A miracle! She put her hands to her face and laughed, tears streaming down her cheeks.

"Hello, Malinda." A hand clamped down on her arm, and cold steel slid against her throat, cutting off her scream. "Where did you come from?" She couldn't turn around, but there was no mistaking the voice or the touch. "Clever girl," Farrars said softly, almost pleasantly, against her ear, though she could feel him trembling. "However did you escape?"

"Let me go," she ordered, going still as death.

"Don't be ridiculous," he scoffed. "Where is your demon love?" She didn't answer, and he pressed the blade more tightly against her skin. She felt a sting of pain sharp enough to make her eyes water, felt a thin stream of blood against her throat. "Don't make me kill you."

"You did already," she said coldly. "Remember?"

Another roar swept over the battleground as trumpets sounded from the cliffs above. She tried to turn her head to look, but he was holding her too tightly. "Come, my dearest," he snarled, dragging her back toward the cliffs.

Alista felt sick, watching the battle from the relative safety of the cliff opposite the tower. Will's troops were riding into a fully pitched battle, Farrars' troops against a mob of brigands she could only assume fought for Tarquin. The tower was burning, a sight that snatched her back into the worst moment of her childhood. Her mother was dead . . . Malinda would die. They were too late.

"*Hush now, little bird,*" a woman's voice spoke beside her. A translucent form rose up beside her, a figure made of morning mist with a veil of golden hair. "*All may yet be well.*"

"Mama?" She was afraid to speak above a whisper, barely dared to breathe. She had seen her so often in her dreams, but now she was awake.

"*Come,*" Blanche said, taking her hand, her touch warm as life in spite of the chill light that shone through her. "*There may be much to be done.*"

Tarquin was still standing, had even managed to move forward a few steps closer to the gate. But he was fading. He was wounded badly, not just his shoulder but his chest and leg, and his leather armor was soaked with blood. But Farrars was coming. He could feel it. The men he fought were holding him at bay rather than trying to finish him off, forming a wary circle around him as if he were a bear or a wild boar. His first real hunt had been at Brinlaw . . . Will had given him a boar spear of his own . . . A soldier took a step forward, and he rushed him, buried the falcon sword in his chest up to the hilt, pinning him to the ground. But when Tarquin started to back away, to stand, the man twisted, and his dagger stabbed into Tarquin's stomach, piercing him through.

"Sweet Christ," Tarquin muttered, rising only to stumble back, falling to his knees. He had stabbed the boy just this way, by accident as he fell. The madman who was Farrars' son. He tried to get to his feet again, but his legs were like water; his body was suddenly stone, too heavy for them to bear. He grabbed the falcon sword and pulled, felt it come free of the corpse, and he almost fell again, almost sprawled on his face.

"Tarquin!" Malinda's voice, cut off in mid-shout. He looked up, appalled, and saw her, captured in Farrars' arms.

"No," he groaned, the world going black at the edges. His love was supposed to be safe.

"I will let her go," Farrars said. He looked so ordinary, Tarquin thought, except for his eyes. His eyes were made of flame. "Die, demon, and she lives."

"No," Malinda said. She wasn't crying; she wasn't afraid. In truth, she was almost smiling. "He cannot make me live." A terrible, beautiful calm was settling over her. She knew just what to do. "You promised me, my love," she said in the faery tongue, knowing that in this moment, her love would understand. "Even if we die . . ."

Tarquin smiled in surrender, flexing his fist on the sword, answering her in kind. "I am your slave."

"Stop it," Farrars ordered, his fear plain in his voice. "Die, demon, and she will be free."

"I am free," Malinda said as she closed her eyes, feeling the change begin. Above her, the falcons screamed, calling out her name. It would only take a moment.

"Come back to me," Tarquin ordered, his witch's eyes locked to hers. *I came for you,* he said once, the truest words she'd ever heard.

"I am your slave," she promised. She let her head fall back, and her body kept falling, the falcon flying free.

"No!" Farrars flung the lifeless shell away, screaming like a woman. "Witch!" he shrieked as the falcon swept over his head, her wings beating his face, her cries deafening. "Kill it!" He struck wildly with the knife, but she avoided him easily, swooping in circles all around him.

Tarquin made it to his feet, the sight of his true love's eyes staring lifeless at the sky giving him new strength. The falcon swept past him, over his shoulder, and he struck, burying the sword in Farrars' heart. "No!" he heard a woman scream, a voice he knew and loved, but it didn't matter. Nothing mattered now. He fell forward, driving Farrars to the ground with his weight. He twisted the sword, leaving nothing to chance, then rolled away, the world swimming and spinning beneath him. Death was so close he could taste it in the air; to surrender would be easy. But he still had one task to complete. He let the sword fall from his hand and made himself sit up.

The falcon had come to rest on the ground beside him, and he reached out to her, a beautiful thing with feathers like spun gold. She cried out, a scream of fury, and he seemed to hear her human voice. *You promised . . . remember your promise.* He took her in his hands, cradled her against his chest as he crawled to where her human body lay. *Even if we die . . .*

He touched her mouth, pain tearing through him far deeper than his wounds. The woman from before was speaking, coming closer . . . Somehow Alista was there. He looked up and saw her running toward him, saw the faery ghost beside her, the Lady Blanche. But nothing could stop him now. He had promised. He picked up the dagger that had stabbed him, still sticky with his blood. He touched Malinda's hair, closed her staring eyes, sobbing like a child—a demon child who could kill. "I don't want to," he said, almost a whisper. "Tell me to stop." But her eyes were closed; her breath was gone. The falcon flew to his shoulder, nudged at his ear.

"Tarquin, no!" Alista screamed, gasping for breath. She had run so far; she was so tired; she couldn't stop him. He grabbed the bird and drove the dagger through her breast, his own cry as terrible as her scream. The falcon didn't struggle, didn't fight, only folded her wings, cradled in his arms. "No," Alista wept, sinking to her knees as the man fell to the ground.

"*Wait,*" Blanche whispered, fading away to mist.

"Wait," Malinda mumbled, opening her eyes. Tiny pricks of pain raced through her as the life flowed back into her veins. She was alive. She could move. "Tarquin . . ." Her beloved lay beside her, soaked in blood, and she bent over him, shaking with fear. "Tarquin, stay with me."

He was dreaming; this could not be real. Nothing he destroyed could live; he could not find such grace. But she was there, his angel, weeping real tears, and he still felt pain. This could be neither heaven nor hell. "Malinda . . ."

"Stay with me," she ordered. She kissed his mouth,

tasted blood. "Stay with me." His eyes fell closed. "Tarquin!"

"It's all right," her mother promised, standing over them. Malinda looked up, barely able to credit her senses.

"Mama!" She hugged Alista tight, almost knocking her over to reach her. "Mama, help me, please."

"I will, sweet daughter," Alista promised. "It will be all right."

25

CRIMD

The battle raged on into the afternoon, but Brinlaw's troops had turned the tide. With their leader slain, the treacherous knights who had conspired with Farrars lost what little heart they had left and surrendered to Will, and their routiers were soon rounded up and disarmed. Davyd had a bit of trouble convincing Tarquin's sailors that the knights should not be stripped of their possessions or at least held for ransom, but with Brinlaw's help, he managed at last. Mark was found miraculously unhurt, having emerged from the tower only a few minutes after Tarquin and having fought his way to the beach to make the necessary introductions between his father's men and the sailors. Once the danger was past, Davyd had sent a launch back to the ship for Lisbet, who took one look at Mark, burst into tears, and fell into his arms.

But Malinda saw none of this. She, her mother, and the faery, Gwyneth, were in Gwyneth's cottage with Tarquin, trying to conjure a cure. The wounds in his leg and shoulder were bad but easily stitched, and a simple charm stopped their bleeding. But the puncture in his stomach required stronger magic.

"You can do it, Malinda," Alista said, her hands laid over her daughter's on Tarquin's stomach, pressing into the bleeding wound. "Say the words again."

"What if I'm saying them wrong?" Malinda asked, fear sapping away her strength. "I lost the book. What if you don't remember the spell properly?"

"I do remember," Alista promised. "Believe me, I could never forget."

"Then it's me," Malinda insisted. "My magic isn't strong enough. What if I've used it all up?" She had never felt such doubt before, such remorse. She could feel it throbbing through her like a pulse. She had cut her palm just the way Mama had told her, bled into Tarquin's wound as she sang the healing spell. But as soon as it was done, she had felt herself weaken, as if it were she who had been hurt. And Tarquin hadn't gotten any better. "He's going to die," she said now, her words slurring as if she were drunk. "It's my fault. It isn't going to work."

"It is working, sweeting," Alista promised. When she had worked this spell to save her husband, she had felt herself in the desert, all the guilt he still carried from his time on Crusade mixed with the terrible grief and rage that still haunted him from the deaths of his father and sister. All the pain of his secret heart—the strain of it had almost killed her. How much worse it must be for Malinda. Compared to Tarquin, Will had known a life of perfect peace. But Malinda was strong, even stronger than she knew. "You can do it."

"I can't." Terrible images rose in her mind, a monster breathing fire in the dark. "I want Blanche to come. I need my grammy to help me."

"She can't," Willie said, standing at the foot of the bed. He had come in long ago, unnoticed by everyone but Gwyneth, who had greeted him with only a smile. "She's gone." Malinda and his mother turned to look at him as one. "When Tarquin killed you as the falcon, she took your place," he explained as if this were the most natural thing in the world. "He set her free as well."

"Wonderful," Malinda muttered, barely bothering to wonder how her baby brother could know such a thing. "She is free, I am free, but Tarquin is going to die."

"Malinda?" Willie ventured, coming around the bed. His sister was so pale, her eyes so wild, he was frightened. *How did it feel to fly?* he longed to ask her, but he didn't dare. "I will help you," he said instead. "Tell me how to help."

"Teach me how to slay a dragon," she answered dully, her eyes turned back to the man on the bed. "Or please, just go away."

"Go on, now, lordling," Gwyneth urged. "Leave your sister in peace."

"It's all right, Willie," Mama promised, barely giving him a smile.

How to slay a dragon, he thought, going back outside. *You need a special sword.* He suddenly remembered something and tore off for the castle.

The fires were out, and a detail of the lowest-ranking soldiers was clearing away the bodies from the courtyard. "Your father isn't here, little captain," one of them said with a friendly smile that showed his missing teeth. "I think he's on the beach."

"Thank you," Willie answered. "I have to get something for my sister." The falcon sword still lay where he had seen it when they'd carried Tarquin away, thrown into a pile of weapons taken from the dead. Glancing around quickly to make sure no one was watching, he grabbed the hilt and ducked into the castle, dragging it behind him.

The tower stairs were treacherous, and the sword was heavy. But the further down he went, the lighter it seemed, until by the time he reached the bottom he could hold it up almost like a man. "I hold this blade in trust," he sang in the strange language of his dreams, the words rising to his lips without a thought. "I would wield it for my blood." White light shone up from the mouth of the moss-covered well, and he drew closer. "Give my falcon power," he sang, dipping the bloody blade into the water. A filigree of crimson bled into the shining white. "Renew it with your light." A tremor raced up his arm into his body, but he wasn't afraid. This was his right; this power was given in love. "Thank you," he said in simple English, lifting the blade from the water and running for the stairs.

Lisbet was in the front room of the cottage when he returned, standing near a tall stranger with long, black hair. "There you are, monster," she said, covering her worry with a laugh. "What are you doing with a sword?"

"I have . . . to give it . . . to Tarquin," Willie answered, badly winded from his run.

"Tarquin doesn't need a sword, darling," she said, trying to pull him back from the bedroom door.

"Leave him be, Lis-ah," the stranger said, watching Willie with queer, black eyes. "Who knows what Tarquin may need?"

Mama had moved to a chair near the fire, but Malinda was still where he had left her, her hands still pressed to

Tarquin's stomach. "He needs this," Willie said, dragging the sword to her. "To slay the dragon."

She just stared at him for a moment, aghast. But he seemed so hopeful, so sure. "All right." She took the sword in one hand while holding her other hand in place, loath to break the contact even if it wasn't doing any good. She laid the blade beside her beloved and curled his hand around the hilt. He looked even worse this way, a corpse laid out with his weapon. But somehow, she felt better, as if a candle had been lit in the dark.

Tarquin felt something in his hand, saw a light begin to glow in the dark. He had been wandering for what seemed like hours, blind and freezing, with only a voice to guide him. *"Come,"* Tabby's voice kept saying, a sibilant hiss in his ear. *"Time for my demon to come home."*

Now suddenly blue light burst forth from his hand, and he saw the serpent all around him, coiled and knotted in a pattern he couldn't work out. Its scales were the color of copper, its eyes the same gold as his own. The light came from a sword he held, but he couldn't pick it up. The creature's tail was curled around his arm, too heavy for him to lift, a talon pressed against the pulse at his wrist glistening with poison. *"Welcome,"* the Tabby-dragon hissed, her tongue flickering against his cheek. *"Welcome home, my love."* He tried to answer, but the words caught in his throat; more scaly coils were wound around his chest and neck, holding him silent and still. *"You killed your captor,"* the serpent whispered. *"I saw it. She is dead."*

"No," he answered, choking out the words. "Malinda lives. I can feel her—"

"An illusion," Tabby scoffed, her face human for a

moment but for a serpent's fangs. *"Like that plaything that you carry."*

"What, this?" He strained against the bonds of frozen flesh with all his power, raised the sword at last. The dragon recoiled with a gasp, its face a beast's again. "Do you fear this, Mama?"

"Stolen," she snarled, coils writhing up to his waist, a sea of serpents roiling around his legs. *"It doesn't belong to you."*

"It was a gift." He pulled his other arm free, grasped the hilt of the sword in both hands, and the thing screamed out in terror. This beast was not his mother—his mother was dead and gone. But he was still alive. Malinda held him harder than this creature; she held him by the heart. "A gift given freely, whether I deserve it or not." He raised the sword and struck with all his strength, all the rage he'd ever known poured into a single blow. The serpent screamed and writhed, hot blood that stank of brimstone pouring over Tarquin in a flood.

Then he was falling into blackness . . . No. He was descending a stair, an endless staircase down to nothing, and the further he walked, the smaller he became. The sword in his hand turned soft and warm, a hand, Nan's hand in his. He was ten, and Nan was four. They were walking down the stairs at Bruel, and their father was coming toward them, climbing but stumbling drunk. "Hello, pigeon," he said, watching Nan with his piggy little eyes. "Would you like to go to London?"

"No," she said, recoiling from him, crossing her arms to keep him from taking her hand and trying to hide behind Tarquin.

"Would you like to see your uncle?" Bruel persisted,

leaning down and obviously trying to smile though he only produced a grimace. "Ride in a carriage? Have a pretty new dress?"

"Go away," she ordered.

"You're scaring her," Tarquin said. "Leave her alone."

"Stay out of this," the brute snarled, cuffing him hard enough to knock him down.

"No, you won't!" Nan screeched. "You no hit my brother no more!" She flung herself against Bruel with all her baby weight, and suddenly he was falling. He was overbalanced, bent over to talk to her, and he was drunk, and her one little shove was enough to send him over. He tried to catch himself, to straighten up, but this did more harm than good, made him fall backwards when he might have just broken his nose. He tumbled the full length of the stairs, his neck breaking with a snap the moment he hit bottom.

"We have to hurry, Tarquin," Nan said, slipping her hand back in his. "We have to run away." He didn't answer, couldn't speak, and he was growing taller, growing back into a man. "Tarquin? Tarquin?"

"Tarquin?" Malinda was bending over him, close enough for a kiss. "Tarquin, please wake up."

"I am awake." He opened his eyes, saw her gazing down at him with tears shining on her cheeks. "I love you," he said, drawing her down to his kiss.

"I love you," she answered, crying harder but feeling only joy. "You broke your promise. You left me."

"No, sweet angel, I didn't." He touched her cheek, blinded with tears of his own. "Nor will I ever again."

Watching them for only another moment, Alista finally slipped out. Will was waiting in the front room with the others, leaning on the mantel, still wearing his mud-spattered armor. He turned as she came out, and she smiled. "Tarquin is awake," she said, going to his arms. "They both will live."

"Thank God." He squeezed her tightly, and she felt a tear against her cheek that wasn't her own. But when he finally let her go, his eyes were angry and dry. "Because I am going to kill them."

"Will," she began, trying not to laugh. "You can't."

"But not until the morning," he finished, pulling her close.

By morning, Tarquin felt almost himself again. The wound in his stomach had healed completely. "Magic," Malinda teased, washing away the last sign of blood. "Witchcraft of the blackest sort."

"You don't scare me," he retorted. "I've seen the worst you can do."

Suddenly they heard voices raised outside the door. "Will, don't," Alista was pleading. "They need rest. They're exhausted."

"As well they might be," he thundered, throwing open the bedroom door.

"Hello, Papa," Malinda said, getting up. Her first instinct was to run and hug him—she hadn't realized just how much she had missed him until now. But the fury in his eyes was rather daunting. "Papa, I can explain—"

"I doubt it," he cut her off with a scowl. "What would you say?"

"I . . . I don't know," she was forced to admit. In truth, she had done everything he and Mama had ever forbidden her to do and made up a few new sins they'd never thought of, resulting in every dire consequence they had ever predicted and more they could never have imagined. "I . . . I'm sorry, Papa."

"No, she isn't," Tarquin said, sitting up to face the man who by all rights ought to have him drawn and quartered. "She may think she is, but she's not. She doesn't know how to be."

"Tarquin!" Malinda cried, appalled. Mama was actually smiling!

"And what about you?" Will demanded.

"I've been sorry all my life," Tarquin answered. "But none of this is my fault."

"Don't you dare," Malinda ordered, giving him a look to freeze his blood.

"Leaving aside the fact that I told you I'd make a mess of it if you made me castellan, I tried my best to do exactly what you asked," her love went on relentlessly, merriment dancing in his eyes. "I tried to protect Malinda from everything and everyone, including herself, in spite of the fact that she did all in her power to make me miserable."

"Malinda!" Alista scolded.

"Then just when I thought I'd brought her to heel, she put a spell on me to seduce me," he continued.

Malinda took one look at her father's face and turned pale to her toes. "Tarquin FitzBruel, if you don't shut up this instant—"

"So I left Brinlaw to keep myself from dishonoring her more," he cut her off. "And for that I am sorry." He took Malinda's hand. "I left her alone, just as I promised I would not, even though I loved her—love her with all my soul. I was a coward, and she was hurt because of it." His eyes met hers. "But it wasn't all my fault, was it, love? Didn't you tell me as much?"

"Yes," she grumbled, squeezing his hand nonetheless. "But you picked a fine time to tell me you agree."

"Gwyneth told us what Farrars did," Will said, his expression softening as he touched his daughter's cheek. "But it sounds to me as if there's plenty of blame to go around."

"Yes, it does, and I think I know the perfect punishment," Alista said with a smile. "We must make them marry each other."

"Misery in equal measure," Will said, almost smiling. "That sounds fair."

"Yes." Malinda turned and kissed her intended, wanton as the wind in spite of who was watching. "That sounds quite fair indeed."

Epilogue

~~~~~

$\mathcal{M}$alinda FitzBruel sat at the stern of her husband's ship reading a letter from home, the lighthouse of Alexandria rising white in the distance. *Henry and his sons made peace in September,* her mother wrote. *So everyone who used to be a traitor is now made a faithful subject of the Crown again, the one exception being the Queen. Your father says Eleanor will never know freedom again while her husband lives, and I am inclined to believe him.*

"Poor Eleanor," Malinda sighed.

"Bollocks, whatever it is," Tarquin muttered, stripping out of his clothes for a swim. They were anchored in a secluded cove well outside the city harbor, but he was shameless nonetheless, and she was shocked at him. Raising an eyebrow as he shucked off his breeches, she tried very hard not to smile. "Care to join me?" he asked with a lecherous grin.

"No, thank you," she said airily, turning the page of her letter. "I will decline to be naked before your crew today."

"Alas, men, I tried," he said with mock regret as he climbed up on the rail.

Giving the first mate a wink, she pretended to read, watching all the while as he dove into the water. "Lovely, lovely," she murmured, returning to reading indeed.

Phillipe has been given a castle of his own in Aquitaine, Alista went on. *His great friendship with Prince Richard continues, and that duchy remains in Richard's hands. Druscilla is very proud of him.*

Your father has been gifted with the lands of Robert Farrars, both here in England and in France. The English ruin has been taken down to bare earth, and I doubt he will build any other structure there. None of our blood could ever live in such a place as that, knowing what was done to you there.

"What's the matter?" Tarquin asked, climbing the ladder. "You look pale."

"It's nothing," she promised. He flopped down on the deck beside her without making the slightest effort to cover himself. "Tarquin, really."

"Read your letter," he ordered, caressing her bare foot.

But the French estate may make a fine inheritance for Master Willie someday or a dowry for your little sister, Mary, she read. *She continues to be well, and her blue eyes have turned brown. It seems I may have a daughter who looks like me after all. We shall have to make her very sweet and accomplished to mask any defects in her appearance.*

"What's funny?" Tarquin asked, watching her smile.

"Nothing." He held her foot between his hands, massaging the delicate arch. "Stop that," she ordered, the dreamy look in her eyes putting her words to lie.

"I will not." He traced a finger up the curve of her calf. "It's not as though I'm your slave."

"Oh yes, it is," she demurred with a smile as she put the

letter aside. "It is exactly like that." He climbed to his knees, putting his face nearly level with hers, and she draped her arms around his neck. "And don't you ever forget it."

"As if I could." He kissed her, holding all the good of the world in his embrace. "As if I ever could."